Other Fiction by Arthur C. Clarke

Across the Sea of Stars*
Against the Fall of Night
Childhood's End
The City and the Stars
The Collected Stories*
Cradle (with Gentry Lee)
The Deep Range
Dolphin Island
Earthlight
Expedition to Earth
A Fall of Moondust
The Fountains of Paradise
From the Oceans, from the
    Stars*
The Garden of Rama (with
    Gentry Lee)
The Ghost from the Grand
    Banks
Glide Path
The Hammer of God
Imperial Earth
Islands in the Sky
The Lions of Comarre
The Lost Worlds of 2001
A Meeting with Medusa*
More than One Universe*
The Nine Billion Names of
    God*

The Other Side of the Sky
Prelude to Mars*
Prelude to Space
Rama II (with Gentry Lee)
Rama Revealed (with
    Gentry Lee)
Reach for Tomorrow
Rendezvous with Rama
Richter 10 (with Mike
    McQuay)
The Sands of Mars
The Sentinel*
The Songs of Distant Earth
Tales from Planet Earth*
Tales from the White Hart
Tales of Ten Worlds
The Trigger (with Michael P.
    Kube-McDowell)
The Wind from the Sun
2001: A Space Odyssey
2010: Odyssey Two
2061: Odyssey Three
3001: The Final Odyssey

*collections

Other Fiction by Stephen Baxter

Anti-Ice
Flux
Moonseed
Raft
Ring
Silverhair
Time

Timelike Infinity
The Time Ships
Titan
Traces
Vacuum Diagrams
Voyage
Space
Longtusk

THE LIGHT OF OTHER DAYS

Arthur C. Clarke
and Stephen Baxter

TOR®

A TOM DOHERTY ASSOCIATES BOOK
NEW YORK

This is a work of fiction. All the characters and events portrayed in this book are either products of the author's imagination or are used fictitiously.

THE LIGHT OF OTHER DAYS

Copyright © 2000 by Arthur C. Clarke and Stephen Baxter

Edited by Jane Johnson and Patrick Nielsen Hayden

A Tor Book
Published by Tom Doherty Associates, LLC
175 Fifth Avenue
New York, NY 10010

www.tor.com

Tor® is a registered trademark of Tom Doherty Associates, LLC.

ISBN: 0-812-57640-3

First edition: March 2000
First mass market edition: January 2001

Printed in the United States of America

0 9 8 7 6 5 4 3 2 1

To Bob Shaw

Is it not possible—I often wonder—that things we have felt with great intensity have an experience independent of our minds; are in fact still in existence? And if so, will it not be possible, in time, that some device will be invented by which we can tap them? . . . Instead of remembering here a scene and there a sound, I shall fit a plug into the wall; and listen in to the past . . .

—VIRGINIA WOOLF (1882–1941)

Prologue

Bobby could see the Earth, complete and serene, within its cage of silver light.

Fingers of green and blue pushed into the new deserts of Asia and the North American Midwest. Artificial reefs glimmered in the Caribbean, pale blue against the deeper ocean. Great wispy machines labored over the poles to repair the atmosphere. The air was clear as glass, for now mankind drew its energy from the core of Earth itself.

And Bobby knew that if he chose, with a mere effort of will, he could look back into time.

He could watch cities bloom on Earth's patient surface, to dwindle and vanish like rusty dew. He could see species shrivel and devolve like leaves curling into their buds. He could watch the slow dance of the continents as Earth gathered its primordial heat back into its iron heart. The present was a glimmering, expanding bubble of life and awareness, with the past locked within, trapped unmoving like an insect in amber.

For a long time, on this rich, growing Earth, embedded in knowledge, an enhanced humankind had been at peace: a peace unimaginable when he was born.

And all of this had derived from the ambition of one man—a venal, flawed man, a man who had never even understood where his dreams would lead.

How remarkable, he thought.

Bobby looked into his past, and into his heart.

ONE

THE GOLDFISH BOWL

We ... know how cruel the truth often is, and we wonder whether delusion is not more consoling.

—Henri Poincaré (1854–1912)

1

THE CASIMIR ENGINE

A little after dawn, Vitaly Keldysh climbed stiffly into his car, engaged the SmartDrive, and let the car sweep him away from the run-down hotel.

The streets of Leninsk were empty, the road surface cracked, many windows boarded up. He remembered how this place had been at its peak, in the 1970s perhaps: a bustling science city with a population of tens of thousands, with schools, cinemas, a swimming pool, a sports stadium, cafés, restaurants and hotels, even its own TV station.

Still, as he passed the main gateway to the north of the city, there was the old blue sign with its white pointing arrow: TO BAIKONUR, still proclaiming that ancient deceptive name. And still, here at the empty heart of Asia, Russian engineers built spaceships and fired them into the sky.

But, he reflected sadly, not for much longer.

The sun rose at last, and banished the stars: all but one, he saw, the brightest of all. It moved with a leisurely but unnatural speed across the southern sky. It was the ruin of the International Space Station: never completed, abandoned in 2010 after the crash of an aging Space Shuttle. But still the Station drifted around the Earth, an unwelcome guest at a party long over.

The landscape beyond the city was barren. He passed a camel standing patiently at the side of the road, a wizened woman beside it dressed in rags. It was a scene he might have encountered any time in the last thousand years, he thought, as if all the great changes, political and technical and social, that had swept across this land had been for nothing. Which was, perhaps, the reality.

But in the gathering sunlight of this spring dawn, the steppe was green and littered with bright yellow flowers. He wound down his window and tried to detect the meadow fragrance he remembered so well; but his nose, ruined by a lifetime of tobacco, let him down. He felt a stab of sadness, as he always did at this time of year. The grass and flowers would soon be gone: the steppe spring was brief, as tragically brief as life itself.

He reached the range.

It was a place of steel towers pointing to the sky, of enormous concrete mounds. The cosmodrome—far vaster than its western competitors—covered thousands of square kilometers of this empty land. Much of it was abandoned now, of course, and the great gantries were rusting slowly in the dry air, or else had been pulled down for scrap—with or without the consent of the authorities.

But this morning there was much activity around one pad. He could see technicians in their protective suits and orange hats scurrying around the great gantry, like faithful at the feet of some immense god.

A voice floated across the steppe from a speaker tower. *Gotovnosty dyesyat minut.* Ten minutes and counting.

The walk from the car to the viewing stand, short as it was, tired him greatly. He tried to ignore the hammering of his recalcitrant heart, the prickling of sweat over his neck and brow, his gasping breathlessness, the stiff pain that plagued his arm and neck.

As he took his place those already here greeted him. There were the corpulent, complacent men and women who, in this new Russia, moved seamlessly between legitimate authority and murky underworld; and there were young technicians, like all of the new generations rat-faced with the hunger that had plagued his country since the fall of the Soviet Union.

He accepted their greetings, but was happy to sink into isolated anonymity. The men and women of this hard future cared nothing for him and his memories of a better past.

And nor did they care much for what was about to happen here. All their gossip was of events far away: of Hiram Patterson and his wormholes, his promise to make the Earth itself as transparent as glass.

It was very obvious to Vitaly that he was the oldest person here. The last survivor of the old days, perhaps. That thought gave him a certain sour pleasure.

It was, in fact, almost exactly seventy years since the launch of the first *Molniya*—"lightning"—in 1965. It might have been seventy days, so vivid were the events in Vitaly's mind, when the young army of scientists, rocket engineers, technicians, laborers, cooks, carpenters and masons had come to this unpromising steppe and—living in huts and tents, alternately baking and freezing, armed with little but their dedication and Korolev's genius—had built and launched mankind's first spaceships.

The design of the *Molniya* satellites had been utterly ingenious. Korolev's great boosters were incapable of launching a satellite to geosynchronous orbit, that high radius where the station would hover above a fixed point on Earth's surface. So Korolev launched his satellites on elliptical eight-hour trajectories. With such orbits, carefully chosen, three *Molniya*s could provide coverage for most of the Soviet Union. For decades the U.S.S.R. and then Russia had maintained constellations of *Molniya*s in their eccentric orbits, providing the great, sprawling country with essential social and economic unity.

Vitaly regarded the *Molniya* comsats as Korolev's greatest achievement, outshining even the Designer's accomplishments in launching robots and humans into space, touching Mars and Venus, even—so nearly—beating the Americans to the Moon.

But now, perhaps, the need for those marvelous birds was dying at last.

The great launch tower rolled back, and the last power umbilicals fell away, writhing slowly like fat black snakes. The slim form of the booster itself was revealed, a needle shape with the baroque fluting typical of Korolev's antique, marvelous, utterly reliable designs. Although the sun was now high in the sky, the rocket was bathed in brilliant artificial light, wreathed in vapor breathed by the mass of cryogenic fuels in its tanks.

Tri. Dva. Odin. Zashiganiye!

Ignition . . .

As Kate Manzoni approached the OurWorld campus, she wondered if she had contrived to be a little more than fashionably just-late-enough for this spectacular event, so brightly was the Washington State sky painted by Hiram Patterson's light show.

Small planes crisscrossed the sky, maintaining a layer of (no doubt environmentally friendly) dust on which the lasers painted virtual images of a turning Earth. Every few seconds the globe turned transparent, to reveal the familiar OurWorld corporate logo embedded in its core. It was all utterly tacky, of course, and it only served to obscure the real beauty of the tall, clear night sky.

She opaqued the car's roof, and found afterimages drifting across her vision.

A drone hovered outside the car. It was another Earth globe, slowly spinning, and when it spoke its voice was smooth, utterly synthetic, devoid of emotion. "This way, Ms. Manzoni."

"Just a moment." She whispered, "Search Engine. Mirror."

An image of herself crystallized in the middle of her field of vision, disconcertingly overlaying the spinning drone. She checked her dress front and back, turned on the programmable tattoos that adorned her shoulders, and tucked stray wisps of hair back where they should be. The self-image, synthesized from feeds from the car's cameras and relayed to her retinal implants, was a little grainy and prone to break up into blocky pixels if she moved too quickly, but that was a limitation of her old-fashioned sense-organ implant technology she was prepared to accept. Better she suffer a little fuzziness than let some cack-handed CNS-augment surgeon open up *her* skull.

When she was ready she dismissed the image and clambered out of the car, as gracefully as she could manage in her ludicrously tight and impractical dress.

OurWorld's campus turned out to be a carpet of neat grass quadrangles separating three-story office buildings, fat, top-heavy boxes of blue glass held up by skinny little beams of reinforced concrete. It was ugly and quaint, 1990s corporate chic. The bottom story of each building was an open car lot, in one of which her car had parked itself.

She joined a river of people that flowed into the campus cafeteria, drones bobbing over their heads.

The cafeteria was a showpiece, a spectacular multi-level glass cylinder built around a chunk of bona fide graffiti-laden Berlin Wall. There was, bizarrely, a stream running right through the middle of the hall, with little stone bridges spanning it. Tonight perhaps a thousand guests milled across the glassy floor, groups of them coalescing and dispersing, a cloud of conversation bubbling around them.

Heads turned toward her, some in recognition, and some—male and female alike—with frankly lustful calculation.

She picked out face after face, repeated shocks of recognition startling her. There were presidents, dictators, royalty, powers in industry and finance, and the usual scattering of celebrities from movies and music and the other arts. She didn't spot President Juarez herself, but several of her cabinet were here. Hiram had gathered quite a crowd for his latest spectacle, she conceded.

Of course she knew she wasn't here herself solely for her glittering journalistic talent or conversational skills, but for her own combination of beauty and the minor celebrity that had followed her exposure of the Wormwood discovery. But that was an angle she'd been happy to exploit herself ever since her big break.

Drones floated overhead, bearing canapés and drinks. She accepted a cocktail. Some of the drones carried images from one or another of Hiram's channels. The images were mostly ignored in the excitement, even the most spectacular—here was one, for example, bearing the image of a space rocket on the point of being launched, evidently from some dusty steppe in Asia— but she couldn't deny that the cumulative effect of all this technology was impressive, as if reinforcing Hiram's famous boast that OurWorld's mission was to inform a planet.

She gravitated toward one of the larger knots of people nearby, trying to see who, or what, was the center of attention. She made out a slim young man with dark hair, a walrus mustache and round glasses, wearing a rather absurd pantomime-soldier uniform of bright lime green with scarlet piping. He seemed to be holding a brass musical instrument, perhaps a euphonium. She recognized him, of course, and as soon as she did so she lost interest. Just a virtual. She began to survey the crowd around him, observing their childlike fascination with this simulacrum of a long-dead, saintly celebrity.

One older man was regarding her a little too closely. His eyes were odd, an unnaturally pale gray. She wondered if he had possession of the new breed of retinal implants that were rumored—by operating at millimeter wavelengths, at which textiles were transparent, and with a little subtle image enhancement—to enable the wearer to see through clothes. He took a tentative step toward her, and orthotic aids, his invisible walking machine, whirred stiffly.

Kate turned away.

". . . He's only a virtual, I'm afraid. Our young ser-
geant over there, that is. Like his three companions, who
are likewise scattered around the room. Even my father's
grasp doesn't yet extend to resurrecting the dead. But of
course you knew that."

The voice in her ear had made her jump. She turned,
and found herself looking into the face of a young man:
perhaps twenty-five, jet-black hair, a proud Roman nose,
a chin with a cleft to die for. His mixed ancestry told in
the pale brown of his skin, the heavy black brows over
startling, cloudy blue eyes. But his gaze roamed, rest-
lessly, even in these first few seconds of meeting her, as
if he had trouble maintaining eye contact.

He said, "You're staring at me."

She came out fighting. "Well, you startled me. Anyhow I know who you are." This was Bobby Patterson,
Hiram's only son and heir—and a notorious sexual predator. She wondered how many other unaccompanied
women this man had targeted tonight.

"And I know *you*, Ms. Manzoni. Or can I call you
Kate?"

"You may as well. I call your father Hiram, as everyone does, though I've never met him."

"Do you want to? I could arrange it."

"I'm sure you could."

He studied her a little more closely now, evidently
enjoying the gentle verbal duel. "You know, I could
have guessed you were a journalist—a writer, anyhow.
The way you were watching the people reacting to the
virtual, rather than the virtual itself . . . I saw your pieces
on the Wormwood, of course. You made quite a splash."

"Not as much as the real thing will when it hits the
Pacific on May 27, 2534 A.D."

He smiled, and his teeth were like rows of pearls.
"You intrigue me, Kate Manzoni," he said. "You're ac-
cessing the Search Engine right now, aren't you? You're
asking it about me."

"No." She was annoyed by the suggestion. "I'm a journalist. I don't need a memory crutch."

"I do, evidently. I remembered your face, your story, but not your name. Are you offended?"

She bristled. "Why should I be? As a matter of fact—"

"As a matter of fact, I smell a little sexual chemistry in the air. Am I right?"

There was a heavy arm around her shoulder, a powerful scent of cheap cologne. It was Hiram Patterson himself: one of the most famous people on the planet.

Bobby grinned and, gently, pushed his father's arm away. "Dad, you're embarrassing me again."

"Oh, bugger that. Life's too short, isn't it?" Hiram's accent bore strong traces of his origins, the long, nasal vowels of Norfolk, England. He was very like his son, but darker, bald with a fringe of wiry black hair around his head; his eyes were intense blue over that prominent family nose, and he grinned easily, showing teeth stained by nicotine. He looked energetic, younger than his late sixties. "Ms. Manzoni, I'm a great admirer of your work. And may I say you look terrific."

"Which is why I'm here, no doubt."

He laughed, pleased. "Well, that too. But I did want to be sure there was one intelligent person in among the air-head politicos and pretty-pretties who crowd out these events. Somebody who would be able to record this moment of history."

"I'm flattered."

"No, you're not," Hiram said bluntly. "You're being ironic. You've heard the buzz about what I'm going to say tonight. You probably even generated some of it yourself. You think I'm a megalomaniac nutcase—"

"I don't think I'd say that. What I see is a man with a new gadget. Hiram, do you really believe a gadget can change the world?"

"But gadgets do, you know! Once it was the wheel, agriculture, ironmaking—inventions that took thousands of years to spread around the planet. But now it takes a generation or less. Think about the car, the television. When I was a kid computers were giant walk-in wardrobes served by a priesthood with punch cards. Now we all spend half our lives plugged into SoftScreens. And *my* gadget is going to top them all. . . . Well. You'll have to decide for yourself." He studied Kate. "Enjoy tonight. If this young waster hasn't invited you already, come to dinner, and we'll show you more, as much as you want to see. I mean it. Talk to one of the drones. Now, do excuse me. . . ." Hiram squeezed her shoulders briefly, then began to make his way through the crowd, smiling and waving and glad-handing as he went.

Kate took a deep breath. "I feel as if a bomb just went off."

Bobby laughed. "He does have that effect. By the way—"

"What?"

"I was going to ask you anyhow before the old fool jumped in. Come have dinner. And maybe we can have a little fun, get to know each other better . . ."

As his patter continued, she tuned him out and focused on what she knew about Hiram Patterson and OurWorld.

Hiram Patterson—born Hirdamani Patel—had dragged himself out of impoverished origins in the fen country of eastern England, a land which had now disappeared beneath the encroaching North Sea. He had made his first fortune by using Japanese cloning technologies to manufacture ingredients for traditional medicines once made from the bodies of tigers—whiskers, paws, claws, even bones—and exporting them to Chinese communities around the world. That had gained him notoriety: brickbats for using advanced technology to serve such primitive needs, praise for reducing the pressure on the remaining populations of tigers in India, China, Russia, and Indonesia. (Not that there were any tigers left now anyhow.)

After that Hiram had diversified. He had developed the world's first successful SoftScreen, a flexible image system based on polymer pixels capable of emitting multicolored light. With the success of the SoftScreen Hiram began to grow seriously rich. Soon his corporation, OurWorld, had become a powerhouse in advanced technologies, broadcasting, news, sport and entertainment.

But Britain was declining. As part of unified Europe—deprived of tools of macroeconomic policy like control of exchange and interest rates, and yet unsheltered by the imperfectly integrated greater economy—the British government was unable to arrest a sharp economic collapse. At last, in 2010, social unrest and climate collapse forced Britain out of the European Union, and the United Kingdom fell apart, Scotland going its own separate way. Through all this Hiram had struggled to maintain OurWorld's fortunes.

Then, in 2019, England, with Wales, ceded Northern Ireland to Eire, packed off the Royals to Australia—where they were still welcome—and had become the fifty-second state of the United States of America. With the benefit of labor mobility, interregional financial transfers and other protective features of the truly unified American economy, England thrived.

But it had to thrive without Hiram.

As a U.S. citizen, Hiram had quickly taken the opportunity to relocate to the outskirts of Seattle, Washington, and had delighted in establishing a new corporate headquarters here, at what used to be the Microsoft campus. Hiram liked to boast that he would become the Bill Gates of the twenty-first century. And indeed his corporate and personal power had, in the richer soil of the American economy, grown exponentially.

Still, Kate knew, he was only one of a number of powerful players in a crowded and competitive market. She was here tonight because—so went the buzz, and as he had just hinted—Hiram was to reveal something new, something that would change all that.

Bobby Patterson, by contrast, had grown up enveloped by Hiram's power.

Educated at Eton, Cambridge and Harvard, he had taken various positions within his father's companies, and enjoyed the spectacular life of an international playboy and the world's most eligible bachelor. As far as Kate knew he had never once demonstrated any spark of initiative of his own, nor any desire to escape his father's embrace—better yet, to supplant him.

Kate gazed at his perfect face. This is a bird who is happy with his gilded cage, she thought. A spoilt rich kid.

But she felt herself flush under his gaze, and despised her biology.

She hadn't spoken for some seconds; Bobby was still waiting for her to respond to his dinner invitation.

"I'll think about it, Bobby."

He seemed puzzled—as if he'd never received such a hesitant response before. "Is there a problem? If you want I can—"

"Ladies and gentlemen."

Every head turned; Kate was relieved.

Hiram had mounted a stage at one end of the cafeteria. Behind him, a giant SoftScreen showed a blown-up image of his head and shoulders. He was smiling over them all, like some beneficent god, and drones drifted around his head bearing jewel-like images of the multiple OurWorld channels. "May I say, first of all, thank you all for coming to witness this moment of history, and for your patience. Now the show is about to begin."

The dandy-like virtual in the lime green soldier suit materialized on the stage beside Hiram, his granny glasses glinting in the lights. He was joined by three others, in pink, blue and scarlet, each carrying a musical instrument—an oboe, a trumpet, a piccolo. There was scattered applause. The four took an easy bow, and stepped lightly to an area at the back of the stage where a drum kit and three electric guitars were waiting for them.

Hiram said easily, "This imagery is being broadcast to us, here in Seattle, from a station near Brisbane, Australia—bounced off various comsats, with a time delay of a few seconds. I don't mind telling you these boys have made a mountain of money in the last couple of years—their new song 'Let Me Love You' was number one around the world for four weeks over Christmas, and all the profit from that went to charity."

"*New song*," Kate murmured cynically.

Bobby leaned closer. "You don't like the V-Fabs?"

"Oh, come on," she said. "The originals broke up sixty-five years ago. Two of them died before I was born. Their guitars and drums are so clunky and old-fashioned compared to the new airware bands, where the music emerges from the performers' dance . . . and anyhow all these *new* songs are just expert-system extrapolated garbage."

"All part of our—what do you call it in your polemics?—our cultural decay," he said gently.

"Hell, yes," she said, but before his easy grace she felt a little embarrassed by her sourness.

Hiram was still talking. ". . . not just a stunt. I was born in 1967, during the Summer of Love. Of course some say the sixties were a cultural revolution that led nowhere. Perhaps that's true—directly. But it, and its music of love and hope, played a great part in shaping me, and others of my generation."

Bobby caught Kate's eye. He mimed vomiting with a splayed hand, and she had to cover her mouth to keep from laughing.

". . . And at the height of that summer, on 25 June 1967, a global television show was mounted to demonstrate the power of the nascent communications network." Behind Hiram the V-Fab drummer counted out a beat, and the group started playing, a dirgelike parody of the *Marseillaise* that gave way to finely sung three-part harmony. "This was Britain's contribution," Hiram called over the music. "A song about love, sung to two hundred million people around the world. That show was called *Our World*. Yes, that's right. That's where I got the name from. I know it's a little corny. But as soon as I saw the tapes of that event, at ten years old, I knew what I wanted to do with my life."

Corny, yes, thought Kate, but undeniably effective; the audience was gazing spellbound at Hiram's giant image as the music of a summer seven decades gone reverberated around the cafeteria.

"And now," said Hiram with a showman's flourish, "I believe I have achieved my life's goal. I'd suggest holding on to something—even someone else's hand. . . ."

The floor turned transparent.

Suddenly suspended over empty space, Kate felt herself stagger, her eyes deceived despite the solidity of the floor beneath her feet. There was a gale of nervous laughter, a few screams, the gentle tinkle of dropped glass.

Kate was surprised to find she had grabbed on to Bobby's arm. She could feel a knot of muscle there. He had covered her hand with his, apparently without calculation.

She let her hand stay where it was. For now.

She seemed to be hovering over a starry sky, as if this cafeteria had been transported into space. But these "stars," arrayed against a black sky, were gathered and harnessed into a cubical lattice, linked by a subtle tracery of multicolored light. Looking into the lattice, the images receding with distance, Kate felt as if she were staring down an infinitely long tunnel.

With the music still playing around him—so artfully, subtly different from the original recording—Hiram said, "You aren't looking up into the sky, into space.

Instead you are looking *down*, into the deepest structure of matter.

"This is a crystal of diamond. The white points you see are carbon atoms. The links are the valence forces that join them. I want to emphasize that what you are going to see, though enhanced, is not a simulation. With modern technology—scanning tunneling microscopes, for instance—we can build up images of matter even at this most fundamental of levels. *Everything you see is real.* Now—come further."

Holographic images rose to fill the room, as if the cafeteria and all its occupants were sinking into the lattice, and shrinking the while. Carbon atoms swelled over Kate's head like pale gray balloons; there were tantalizing hints of structure in their interior. And all around her space sparkled. Points of light winked into existence, only to be snuffed out immediately. It was quite extraordinarily beautiful, like swimming through a firefly cloud.

"You're looking at space," said Hiram. " 'Empty' space. This is the stuff that fills the universe. But now we are seeing space at a resolution far finer than the limits of the human eye, a level at which individual electrons are visible—and at this level, quantum effects become important. 'Empty' space is actually *full*, full of fluctuating energy fields. And these fields manifest themselves as particles: photons, electron-positron pairs, quarks . . . They flash into a brief existence, bankrolled by borrowed mass-energy, then disappear as the law of conservation of energy reasserts itself. We humans see space and energy and matter from far above, like an astronaut flying over an ocean. We are too high to see the waves, the flecks of foam they carry. But they are there.

"And we haven't reached the end of our journey yet. Hang on to your drinks, folks."

The scale exploded again. Kate found herself flying into the glassy onion-shell interior of one of the carbon atoms. There was a hard, shining lump at its very center, a cluster of misshapen spheres. Was it the nucleus?—and were those inner spheres protons and neutrons?

As the nucleus flew at her she heard people cry out. Still clutching Bobby's arm, she tried not to flinch as she hurtled into one of the nucleons.

And then . . .

There was no shape here. No form, no definite light, no color beyond a blood-red crimson. And yet there was motion, a slow, insidious, endless writhing, punctuated by bubbles which rose and burst. It was like the slow boiling of some foul, thick liquid.

Hiram said, "We've reached what the physicists call the Planck level. We are *twenty* order of magnitudes deeper than the virtual-particle level we saw earlier. And at this level, we can't even be sure about the structure of space itself: topology and geometry break down, and space and time become untangled."

At this most fundamental of levels, there was no sequence to time, no order to space. The unification of spacetime was ripped apart by the forces of quantum gravity, and space became a seething probabilistic froth, laced by wormholes.

"Yes, wormholes," Hiram said. "What we're seeing here are the mouths of wormholes, spontaneously forming, threaded with electric fields. Space is what keeps everything from being in the same place. Right? But at this level space is grainy, and we can't trust it to do its job anymore. And so a wormhole mouth can connect any point, in this small region of spacetime, to any other point—*anywhere:* downtown Seattle, or Brisbane, Australia, or a planet of Alpha Centauri. It's as if spacetime bridges are spontaneously popping into and out of existence." His huge face smiled down at them, reassuring. *I don't understand this any more than you do,* the image said. *Trust me.* "My technical people will be on hand later to give you background briefings in as much depth as you can handle.

"What's more important is what we intend to do with

all this. Simply put, we are going to reach into this quantum foam and pluck out the wormhole we want: a wormhole connecting our laboratory, here in Seattle, with an identical facility in Brisbane, Australia. And when we have it stabilized, that wormhole will form a link down which we can send signals—*beating light itself.*

"And this, ladies and gentlemen, is the basis of a new communications revolution. No more expensive satellites sandblasted by micrometeorites and orbit-decaying out of the sky; no more frustrating time delay; no more horrific charges—the world, our world, will be truly linked at last."

As the virtuals kept playing there was a hubbub of conversation, even heckling questions. "Impossible!" "Wormholes are unstable. Everyone knows that." "Infalling radiation makes wormholes collapse immediately." "You can't possibly—"

Hiram's giant face loomed over the seething quantum foam. He snapped his fingers. The quantum foam disappeared, to be replaced by a single artifact, hanging in the darkness below their feet.

There was a soft sigh.

Kate saw a gathering of glowing light points—atoms? The lights made up a geodesic sphere, closed over itself, slowly turning. And within, she saw, there was another sphere, turning in the opposite sense—and within that another sphere, and another, down to the limits of vision. It was like some piece of clockwork, an orrery of atoms. But the whole structure pulsed with a pale blue light, and she sensed a gathering of great energies.

It was, she admitted, truly beautiful.

Hiram said, "This is called a Casimir engine. It is perhaps the most exquisitely constructed machine ever built by man, a machine over which we have labored for years—and yet it is less than a few hundred atomic diameters wide.

"You can see the shells are constructed of atoms—in fact carbon atoms; the structure is related to the natural stable structures called 'buckyballs,' carbon-60. You make the shells by zapping graphite with laser beams. We've loaded the engine with electric charge using cages called Penning traps—electromagnetic fields. The structure is held together by powerful magnetic fields. The various shells are maintained, at their closest, just a few electrons' diameters apart. And in those finest of gaps, a miracle happens. . . ."

Kate, tiring of Hiram's wordy boasting, quickly consulted the Search Engine. She learned that the "Casimir effect" was related to the virtual particles she had seen sparkling into and out of existence. In the narrow gap between the atomic shells, because of resonance effects, only certain types of particles would be permitted to exist. And so those gaps were emptier than "empty" space, and therefore less energetic.

This negative-energy effect could give rise, among other things, to antigravity.

The structure's various levels were starting to spin more rapidly. Small clocks appeared around the engine's image, counting patiently down from ten to nine, eight, seven. The sense of energy gathering was palpable.

"The concentration of energy in the Casimir gaps is increasing," Hiram said. "We're going to inject Casimir-effect negative energy into the wormholes of the quantum foam. The antigravity effects will stabilize and enlarge the wormholes.

"We calculate that the probability of finding a wormhole connecting Seattle to Brisbane, to acceptable accuracy, is one in ten million. So it will take us some ten million attempts to locate the wormhole we want. But this is atomic machinery and it works bloody fast; even a hundred million attempts should take less than a second. . . . And the beauty of it is, down at the quantum level, links to any place we want *already exist*: all we have to do is find them."

The virtuals' music was swelling to its concluding chorus. Kate stared as the Frankenstein machine beneath her feet spun madly, glowing palpably with energy.

And the clocks finished their count.

There was a dazzling flash. Some people cried out.

When Kate could see again, the atomic machine, still spinning, was no longer alone. A silvery bead, perfectly spherical, hovered alongside it. A wormhole mouth?

And the music had changed. The V-Fabs had reached the chantlike chorus of their song. But the music was distorted by a much coarser chanting that preceded the high-quality sound by a few seconds.

Aside from the music, the room was utterly silent.

Hiram gasped, as if he had been holding his breath. "That's it," he said. "The new signal you hear is the same performance, but now piped here through the wormhole—*with no significant time delay.* We did it. Tonight, for the first time in history, humanity is sending a signal through a stable wormhole—"

Bobby leaned to Kate and said wryly, "The first time, apart from all the test runs."

"Really?"

"Of course. You don't think he was going to leave this to chance, did you? My father is a showman. But you can't begrudge the man his moment of glory."

The giant display showed Hiram was grinning. "Ladies and gentlemen—never forget what you've seen tonight. This is the start of the true communications revolution."

The applause started slowly, scattered, but rapidly rising to a thunderous climax.

Kate found it impossible not to join in. I wonder where this will lead, she thought. Surely the possibilities of this new technology—based, after all, on the manipulation of space and time themselves—would not prove limited to simple data transfer. She sensed that nothing would be the same, ever again.

Kate's eye was caught by a splinter of light, dazzling, somewhere over her head. One of the drones was carrying an image of the rocket ship she'd noticed before. It was climbing into its patch of blue-gray central Asian sky, utterly silently. It looked strangely old-fashioned, an image drifting up from the past rather than the future.

Nobody else was watching it, and it held little interest for her. She turned away.

Green-red flame billowed into curving channels of steel and concrete. The light pulsed across the steppe toward Vitaly. It was bright, dazzlingly so, and it banished the dim floods that still lit up the booster stack, even the brilliance of the steppe sun. And, even before the ship had left the ground, the roar reached him, a thunder that shook his chest.

Ignoring the mounting pain in his arm and shoulder, the numbness of his hands and feet, Vitaly stood, opened his cracked lips and added his voice to that divine bellow. He always had been a sentimental old fool at such moments.

But there was much agitation around him. The people here, the rat-hungry, ill-trained technicians and the fat, corrupt managers alike, were turning away from the launch. They were huddling around radio sets and palmtop televisions, jewel-like SoftScreens showing baffling images from America. Vitaly did not know the details, and did not care to know; but it was clear enough that Hiram Patterson had succeeded in his promise, or threat.

Even as it lifted from the ground, his beautiful bird, this last *Molniya*, was already obsolete.

Vitaly stood straight, determined to watch it as long as he could, until that point of light at the tip of the great smoke pillar melted into space.

. . . But now the pain in his arm and chest reached a climax, as if some bony hand was clutching there. He gasped. Still he tried to stay on his feet. But now there was a new light, rising all around him, even brighter than the rocket light that bathed the Kazakhstan steppe; and he could stand no longer.

2

THE MIND'SEYE

As Kate was driven into the grounds, it struck her as a typical Seattle setting: green hills that lapped right down to the ocean, framed under a gray, lowering autumn sky.

But Hiram's mansion—a giant geodesic dome, all windows—looked as if it had just landed on the hillside, one of the ugliest, most gaudy buildings Kate had ever seen.

On arrival she handed her coat to a drone. Her identity was scanned—not just a reading of her implants but also, probably, pattern-matching to identify her face, even a nonintrusive DNA sequencing, all done in seconds. Then she was ushered inside by Hiram's robot servants.

Hiram was working. She wasn't surprised. The six months since the launch of his wormhole DataPipe technology had been his busiest, and OurWorld's most successful, ever, according to the analysts. But he'd be back in time for dinner, said the drone.

So she was taken to Bobby.

The room was large, the temperature neutral, the walls as smooth and featureless as an eggshell. The light was low, the sound anechoic, deadened. The only furniture was a number of reclined black-leather couches. Beside each of the couches was a small table with a water spigot and a stand for intravenous feeds.

And here was Bobby Patterson, presumably one of the richest, most powerful young men on the planet, lying alone on a couch in the dark, eyes open but unfocused, limbs limp. There was a metal band around his temples.

She sat on a couch beside Bobby and studied him. She could see that he was breathing, slowly, and the intravenous feed he'd fitted to a socket in his arm was gently supplying his neglected body.

He was dressed in loose black shirt and shorts. His body, revealed where the loose clothing lay against his skin, was a slab of muscle. But that didn't tell much about his lifestyle; such body sculpting could now be achieved easily through hormone treatments and electrical stimulation. He could even do that while he was lying here, she thought, like a coma victim lying in a hospital bed.

There was a trace of drool at the corner of his parted lips. She wiped the drool away with a forefinger, and gently pushed the mouth closed.

"Thank you."

She turned, startled. Bobby—another Bobby, identically dressed to the first—was standing beside her, grinning. Irritated, she threw a punch at his stomach. Her fist, of course, passed straight through him. He didn't flinch.

"You can see me, then," he said.

"I see you."

"You have retinal and cochlear implants. Yes? This room is designed to produce virtuals compatible with all recent generations of CNS-augment technology. Of course, to me you're sitting on the back of a mean-looking phytosaur."

"A what?"

"A Triassic crocodile. Which is beginning to notice you're there. Welcome, Ms. Manzoni."

"Kate."

"Yes. I'm glad you took up my, our, dinner invitation.

Although I didn't expect it would take you six months to respond."

She shrugged. "*Hiram Gets Even Richer* really isn't much of a story."

"Umm. Which implies you've now heard something new." Of course he was right; Kate said nothing. "Or," he went on, "perhaps you finally succumbed to my charming smile."

"Perhaps I would if your mouth wasn't laced with drool."

Bobby looked down at his own unconscious form. "Vanity? We should care how we look even when we're exploring a virtual world?" He frowned. "Of course, if you're right, it's something for my marketing people to think about."

"*Your* marketing people?"

"Sure." He "picked up" a metal headband from a couch near him; a virtual copy of the object separated from the real thing, which remained on the couch. "This is the Mind'sEye. OurWorld's newest VR technology. Do you want to try it?"

"Not really."

He studied her. "You're hardly a VR virgin, Kate. Your sensory implants—"

"—are pretty much the minimum required to get around in the modern world. Have you ever *tried* getting through SeaTac Airport without VR capabilities?"

He laughed. "Actually I'm generally escorted through. I suppose you think it's all part of a giant corporate conspiracy."

"Of course it is. The technological invasion of our homes and cars and workplaces long ago reached saturation point. Now they are coming for our bodies."

"How angry you are." He held up the headband. It was an oddly recursive moment, she thought absently, a virtual copy of Bobby holding a virtual copy of a virtual generator. "But this is different. Try it. Take a trip with me."

She hesitated—but then, feeling she was being churlish, she agreed; she was a guest here after all. But she turned down his offer of an intravenous feed. "We'll just take a look around and come back out before our bodies fall apart. Agreed?"

"Agreed," he said. "Pick a couch. Just fit the headset over your temples, like this." Carefully he raised the virtual set over his head. His face, intent, was undeniably beautiful, she thought; he looked like Christ with the crown of thorns.

She lay down on a couch nearby and lifted a Mind'sEye headband onto her own head. It had warmth and elasticity, and when she pulled it down past her hair it seemed to nestle into place.

Her scalp, under the band, prickled. "Ouch."

Bobby was sitting on his couch. "Infusers. Don't worry about it. Most of the input is via transcranial magnetic stimulation. When we've rebooted you won't feel a thing. . . ." As he settled she could see his two bodies, of flesh and pixels, briefly overlaid.

The room went dark. For a heartbeat, two, she could see, hear nothing. Her sense of her body faded away, as if her brain were being scooped out of her skull.

With an intangible thud she felt herself fall once more into her body. But now she was standing.

In some kind of mud.

Light and heat burst over her, blue, green, brown. She was on a riverbank, up to her ankles in thick black gumbo.

The sky was a washed-out blue. She was at the edge of a forest, a lush riot of ferns, pines and giant conifers, whose thick dark foliage blocked out much of the light. The heat and humidity were stifling; she could feel sweat soak through her shirt and trousers, plastering her fringe to her forehead. The nearby river was broad, languid, brown with mud.

She climbed a little deeper into the forest, seeking firmer ground. The vegetation was very thick; leaves and shoots slapped at her face and arms. There were insects everywhere, including giant blue dragonflies, and the jungle was alive with noise: chirping, growling, cawing.

The sense of reality was startling, the authenticity far beyond any VR she'd experienced before.

"Impressive, isn't it?" Bobby was standing beside her. He was wearing khaki shorts and shirt and a broad hat, safari style; there was an old-fashioned–looking rifle slung from his shoulder.

"Where are we? I mean—"

"*When* are we? This is Arizona: the Late Triassic, some two hundred million years ago. More like Africa, yes? This period gave us the Painted Desert strata. We have giant horsetails, ferns, cycads, club mosses . . . But this is a drab world in some ways. The evolution of the flowers is still far in the future. Makes you think, doesn't it?"

She propped her foot on a log and tried to scrape the gumbo off her legs with her hands. The heat was deeply uncomfortable, and her growing thirst was sharp. Her bare arm was covered by a myriad sweat globules which glimmered authentically, so hot they felt as if they were about to boil.

Bobby pointed upward. "Look."

It was a bird, flapping inelegantly between the branches of a tree . . . No, it was too big and ungainly for a bird. Besides, it lacked feathers. Perhaps it was some kind of flying reptile. It moved with a purple, leathery rustle, and Kate shuddered.

"Admit it," he said. "You're impressed."

She moved her arms and legs around, bent this way and that. "My body sense is strong. I can feel my limbs, sense up and down if I tilt. But I assume I'm still lying in my couch, drooling like you were."

"Yes. The proprioception features of the Mind'sEye are very striking. You aren't even sweating. Well, probably not; sometimes there's a little leakage. This is fourth-generation VR technology, counting forward from crude Glasses-and-Gloves, then sense-organ implants—like yours—and cortical implants, which allowed a direct interface between external systems and the human central nervous system—"

"Barbaric," she snapped.

"Perhaps," he said gently. "Which brings me to the Mind'sEye. The headbands produce magnetic fields which can stimulate precise areas of the brain. All without the need for physical intervention.

"But it isn't just the redundancy of implants that's exciting," he said smoothly. "It's the precision and scope of the simulation we can achieve. Right now, for example, a fish-eye map of the scene is being painted directly onto your visual cortex. We stimulate the amygdala and the insula in the temporal lobe to give you a sense of smell. That's essential for the authenticity of the experience. Scents seem to go straight to the brain's limbic system, the seat of the emotions. That's why scents are always so evocative, you know? We even deliver mild jolts of pain by lighting up the anterior cingulate cortex—the center, not of pain itself, but of the conscious awareness of pain. Actually we do a lot of work with the limbic system, to ensure everything you see packs an emotional punch.

"Then there's proprioception, body sense, which is very complex, involving sensory inputs from the skin, muscles and tendons, visual and motion information from the brain, balance data from the inner ear. It took a lot of brain mapping to get that right. But now we can make you fall, fly, turn somersaults, all without leaving your couch . . . and we can make you see wonders, like this."

"You know this stuff well. You're proud of it, aren't you?"

"Of course I am. It's my development." He blinked, and she became aware that it was the first time he'd looked directly at her for some minutes; even here in this mocked-up Triassic jungle, he made her feel vaguely uneasy—even though she was, on some level, undoubtedly attracted to him.

"Bobby—in what sense is this *yours*? Did you initiate it? Did you fund it?"

"I'm my father's son. It's his corporation I'm working within. But I oversee the Mind'sEye research. I field-test the products."

"Field-test? You mean you come down here and play hunt-the-dinosaur?"

"I wouldn't call it playing," he said mildly. "Let me show you." He stood, briskly, and pushed on deeper into the jungle.

She struggled to follow. She had no machete, and the branches and thorns were soon cutting through her thin clothes and into her flesh. It stung, but not *too* much— of course not. It wasn't real, just some damn adventure game. She plunged after Bobby, fuming inwardly about decadent technology and excess wealth.

They reached the edge of a clearing, an area of fallen, charred trees within which small green shoots were struggling to emerge. Perhaps this had been cleared by lightning.

Bobby held out an arm, keeping her back at the edge of the forest. "Look."

An animal was grubbing with snout and paws among the dead, charred wood fragments. It must have been two meters long, with a wolflike head and protruding canine teeth. Despite its lupine appearance, it was grunting like a pig.

"A cynodont," whispered Bobby. "A protomammal."

"Our ancestor?"

"No. The true mammals have already branched off. The cynodonts are an evolutionary dead end. . . . Shit."

Now there was a loud crashing from the undergrowth on the far side of the clearing. It was a *Jurassic Park* dinosaur, at least two meters tall; it came bounding out of the forest on massive hind legs, huge jaws agape, scales glittering.

The cynodont seemed to freeze, eyes fixed on the predator.

The dino leapt on the back of the cynodont, which was flattened under the weight of its assailant. The two of them rolled, crushing the young trees growing here, the cynodont squealing.

She shrank back into the jungle, clutching Bobby's arm. She felt the shaking of the ground, the power of the encounter. Impressive, she conceded.

The carnosaur finished up on top. Holding down its prey with the weight of its body, it bent to the proto-mammal's neck and, with a single snap, bit through it. The cynodont was still struggling, but white bones showed in its ripped-open neck, and blood gushed. And when the carnosaur burst the stomach of its prey, there was a stink of rotten meat that almost made Kate retch. . . .

Almost, but not quite. Of course not. Just as, if she looked closely, there was a smooth fakeness to the spurting blood of the protomammal, a glistening brightness to the dino's scales. Every VR was like this: gaudy but limited, even the stench and noise modeled for user comfort, all of it as harmless—and therefore as meaningless—as a theme-park ride.

"I think that's a dilophosaur," murmured Bobby. "Fantastic. That's why I love this period. It's a kind of junction of life. Everything overlaps here, the old with the new, our ancestors and the first dinosaurs . . ."

"Yes," said Kate, recovering. "But it isn't *real*."

He tapped his skull. "It's like all fiction. You have to suspend your disbelief."

"But it's just some magnetic field tickling my lower brain. This isn't even the genuine Triassic, for God's sake, just some academic's bad guesswork—with a little color thrown in for the virtual tourist."

He was smiling at her. "You're always so angry. Your point is?"

She stared at his empty blue eyes. Up to now he had set the agenda. If you want to get any further, she told herself, if you want to get any closer to what you came for, you'll have to challenge him. "Bobby, right now you're lying in a darkened room. None of this counts."

"You sound as if you're sorry for me." He seemed curious.

"Your whole life seems to be like this. For all your talk of VR projects and corporate responsibilities, you don't have any *real* control over anything, do you? The world you live in is as unreal as any virtual simulation. Think about it: you were actually alone, before I showed up."

He pondered that. "Perhaps. But you did show up." He shouldered his rifle. "Come on. Time for dinner with Dad." He cocked an eyebrow. "Maybe you'll stick around even when you've got whatever it is you want out of us."

"Bobby—"

But he had already lifted his hands to his headband.

Dinner was difficult.

The three of them sat beneath the domed apex of Hiram's mansion. Stars and a gaunt crescent Moon showed between gaps in the racing clouds. The sky could not have been more spectacular—but it struck her that thanks to Hiram's wormhole DataPipes, the sky was soon going to get a lot more dull, as the last of the low-orbit comsats were allowed to fall back into the atmosphere.

The food was finely prepared, as she'd expected, and served by silent drone robots. But the courses were fairly plain seafood dishes of the type she could have enjoyed in any of a dozen restaurants in Seattle, the wine a straightforward Californian Chardonnay. There wasn't a

trace here of Hiram's own complex origins, no original-
ity or expression of personality of any kind.

And meanwhile, Hiram's focus on her was intense and
unrelenting. He peppered her with questions and supple-
mentaries about her background, her family, her career;
over and again she found herself saying more than she
should.

His hostility, under a veneer of politeness, was unmistakable. *He knows what I'm up to,* she realized.

Bobby sat quietly, eating little. Though his disconcerting habit of avoiding eye contact lingered, he seemed
more aware of her than before. She sensed attraction—
that wasn't so difficult to read—but also a certain fascination. Maybe she'd somehow punctured that complacent, slick hide of his, as she'd hoped to. Or, more likely,
she conceded, he was simply puzzled by his own reac-
tions to her.

Or maybe this was all just fantasy on her part, and
she ought to keep from meddling in other people's
heads, a habit she so strongly condemned in others.

"I don't get it," Hiram was saying now. "How can it
have taken until 2033 to find the Wormwood, an object
four hundred kilometers across? I know it's out beyond
Uranus, but still—"

"It's extremely dark and slow moving," said Kate. "It
is apparently a comet, but much bigger than any comet
known. We don't know where it came from; perhaps
there is a cloud of such objects out there, somewhere
beyond Neptune.

"And nobody was especially looking that way anyhow. Even Spaceguard concentrates on near-Earth space,
the objects which are likely to hit us in the near future.
The Wormwood was found by a network of sky-gazing
amateurs."

"Umm," said Hiram. "And now it's on its way here."

"Yes. In five hundred years."

Bobby waved a strong, manicured hand. "But that's
so far ahead. There must be contingency plans."

"*What* contingency plans? Bobby, the Wormwood is a giant. We don't know any way to push the damn thing away, even in principle. And when that rock falls, there will be nowhere to hide."

" 'We' don't know any way?" Bobby said dryly.

"I mean the astronomers—"

"The way you were talking I'd almost imagined you discovered it yourself." He was needling her, responding to her earlier probing. "It's so easy to mix up one's own achievement with that of the people one relies on, isn't it?"

Hiram was cackling. "I can tell you kids are getting on just fine. If you care enough to argue . . . And you, of course, Ms. Manzoni, think the people have a right to know that the world is going to end in five hundred years?"

"Don't you?"

Bobby said, "And you've no concern for the consequences—the suicides, the leap in abortion rates, the abandonment of various environment-conservation projects?"

"I brought the bad news," she said tensely. "I didn't bring the Wormwood. Look, if we aren't informed, we can't act, for better or ill; we can't take responsibility for ourselves—in whatever time we have left. Not that our options are promising. Probably the best we can do is send a handful of people off to somewhere safer, the Moon or Mars or an asteroid. Even that isn't guaranteed to save the species, unless we can establish a breeding population. And," she said heavily, "those who do escape will no doubt be those who govern us, and their offspring, unless we shake off our electronic anaesthesia."

Hiram pushed his chair back and roared with laughter. "Electronic anaesthesia. How true that is. As long as I'm selling the anaesthetics, of course." He looked at her directly. "I like you, Ms. Manzoni."

Liar. "Thank you—"

"Why are you here?"

There was a long silence. "You invited me."

"Six months and seven days ago. Why now? Are you working for my rivals?"

"No." She bristled at that. "I'm a freelance."

He nodded. "Nevertheless there is something you want here. A story, of course. The Wormwood is already receding into your past, and you need fresh triumphs, a new scoop. That's what people like you live on. Don't you, Ms. Manzoni? But what can it be? Nothing personal, surely. There is little about me that is not in the public record."

She said carefully, "Oh, I dare say there are a few items." She took a breath. "The truth is I heard you have a new project. A new wormhole application, far beyond the simple DataPipes which—"

"You came here grubbing for facts," said Hiram.

"Come on, Hiram. The whole world is getting wired up with your wormholes. If I could scoop the rest—"

"But you know nothing."

She bridled. *I'll show you what I know.* "You were born Hirdamani Patel. Before you were born your father's family was forced to flee Uganda. Ethnic cleansing, right?"

Hiram glared. "This is public knowledge. In Uganda my father was a bank manager. In Norfolk he drove buses, as nobody would recognize his qualifications—"

"You weren't happy in England," Kate bulldozed on. "You found yourself unable to overcome barriers of race and class. So you left for America. You dumped your given name, adopted an anglicized version. You have become known as something of a role model for Asians in America. And yet you cut yourself off from your ethnic origins. Each of your wives has been a WASP."

Bobby looked startled. "*Wives*? Dad—"

"Family is everything to you," Kate said evenly, compelling their attention. "You're trying to establish a dynasty, it seems, through Bobby here. Perhaps it's because you abandoned your own family, your own father, back in England."

"Ah." Hiram clapped his hands, forcing a smile. "I wondered how long it would be before Papa Sigmund joined us at the table. So that is your story. Hiram Patterson is building OurWorld because he is guilty about his father!"

Bobby was frowning. "Kate, *what* new project are you talking about?"

Was it possible Bobby really didn't know? She held Hiram's gaze, relishing her sudden power. "Significant enough for him to summon your brother back from France."

"*Brother . . .*"

"Significant enough for him to take on Billybob Meeks as an investment partner. Meeks, the founder of RevelationLand. Have you heard of that, Bobby? The latest mind-sapping, money-drinking perversion of religion to afflict America's wretched population of the gullible—"

"This is irrelevant," Hiram snapped. "Yes, I'm working with Meeks. I'll work with anybody. If people want to buy my VR gear so they can see Jesus and His tap-dancing Apostles, I'll sell it to them. Who am I to judge? We aren't all as sanctimonious as you, Ms. Manzoni. We don't all have that luxury."

But Bobby was staring at Hiram. "My *brother?*"

Kate was startled, and ran the conversation through her head again. "Bobby . . . You didn't know *any* of this, did you? Not just about the project, but Hiram's other wife, his other child—" She looked at Hiram, shocked. "How could anybody keep a secret like that?"

Hiram's mouth pursed, and his glare at Kate was full of loathing. "A *half*-brother, Bobby. Just a half-brother."

Kate said clinically, "His name is David." She pronounced it the French way: *Dah-veed.* "His mother was French. He's thirty-two—seven years older than you, Bobby. He's a physicist. He's doing well; he's been described as the Hawking of his generation. Oh, and he's Catholic. Devout, apparently." ＼

Bobby seemed—not angry—even more baffled. He said to Hiram, "Why didn't you tell me?"

Hiram said, "You didn't need to know."

"And the new project, whatever it is? Why didn't you tell me about that?"

Hiram stood up. "Your company has been charming, Ms. Manzoni. The drones will show you out."

She stood. "You can't stop me printing what I know."

"Print what you please. You don't have anything important." And, she knew, he was right.

She walked to the door, her euphoria dissipating quickly. *I blew it,* she told herself. *I meant to ingratiate myself with Hiram. Instead I had to have my fun, and make him into an enemy.*

She looked back. Bobby was still seated. He was looking at her, those strange church-window eyes open wide. *I'll see you again,* she thought. *Maybe this wasn't over yet.*

The door began to close. Her last glimpse was of Hiram covering his son's hand with his own, tenderly.

3

THE WORMWORKS

Hiram was waiting for David Curzon in the arrivals hall at SeaTac.

Hiram was simply overwhelming. He immediately grabbed David's shoulders and pulled him close. David could smell powerful cologne, synth-tobacco, a lingering trace of spices. Hiram was nearing seventy, but didn't show it, no doubt thanks to antiaging treatments and subtle cosmetic sculpting. He was tall and dark—where David, taking after his mother, was more stocky, blond, leaning to plump.

And here was that voice David hadn't heard since he was five years old, the face—blue eyes, strong nose—that had loomed over him like a giant Moon. "My boy. It's been too long. Come on. We've got a hell of a lot to catch up on. . . ."

David had spent most of the flight from England composing himself for this encounter. You are thirty-two years old, he told himself. You have a tenured position at Oxford. Your papers, and your popular book on the exotic mathematics of quantum physics, have been extremely well received. This man may be your father. But he abandoned you, and has no hold over you.

You are an adult now. You have your faith. You have nothing to fear.

But Hiram, as he surely intended, had broken through all David's defenses in the first five seconds of their encounter. David, bewildered, allowed himself to be led away.

Hiram took his son straight to his research facility—the Wormworks, as he called it—out to the north of Seattle itself. The drive, in a SmartDrive Rolls, was fast and scary. Controlled by positioning satellites and intelligent in-car software, the vehicles flowed along the freeways at more than 150 kilometers an hour, mere centimeters between their bumpers; it was all much more aggressive than David was used to in Europe.

But the city, what he saw of it, struck him as quite European, a place of fine, well-preserved houses with expansive views of hills and sea, the more modern developments integrated reasonably gracefully with the overall feel of the place. The downtown area seemed to be bustling, as the Christmas buying season descended once more.

He remembered little of the place but childhood fragments: the small boat Hiram used to run out of the Sound, trips above the snow line in winter. He'd been back to America many times before, of course; theoretical physics was an international discipline. But he'd never returned to Seattle—not since the day his mother had so memorably bundled him up and stormed out of Hiram's home.

Hiram talked continually, peppering his son with questions.

"So you feel settled in England?"

"Well, you know about the climate problems. But even icebound, Oxford is a fine place to live. Especially since they abolished private cars inside the ring road, and—"

"Those stuck-up British toffs don't pick on you for that French accent?"

"Father, I am French. That's my identity."

"But not your citizenship." Hiram slapped his son's

thigh. "You're an American. Don't forget that." He glanced at David more warily. "And are you still practicing?"

David smiled. "You mean, am I still a Catholic? Yes, Father."

Hiram grunted. "That bloody mother of yours. Biggest mistake I ever made was shackling myself to her without taking account of her religion. And now she's passed the God virus on to you."

David felt his nostrils flare. "Your language is offensive."

". . . Yes. I'm sorry. So, England is a good place to be a Catholic nowadays?"

"Since they disestablished the Church, England has acquired one of the healthiest Catholic communities in the world."

Hiram grunted. "You don't often hear the words 'healthy' and 'Catholic' in the same sentence. . . We're here."

They had reached a broad parking lot. The car pulled over. David climbed out after his father. They were close to the ocean here, and David was immediately immersed in chill, salt-laden air.

The lot fringed a large open building, crudely constructed of concrete and corrugated metal, like an aircraft hangar. There was a giant corrugated door at one end, partly open, and robot trucks were hauling cartons into the building from a stack outside.

Hiram led his son to a small, human-sized door cut in one wall; it was dwarfed by the scale of the structure. "Welcome to the center of the universe." Hiram looked abashed, suddenly. "Look, I dragged you out here without thinking. I know you're just off your flight. If you need a break, a shower—"

Hiram seemed full of genuine concern for his welfare, and David couldn't resist a smile. "Maybe coffee, a little later. Show me your new toy."

The space within was cold, cavernous. As they walked

across the dusty concrete floor their footsteps echoed. The roof was ribbed, and strip lights dangled everywhere, filling the vast volume with a cold, pervasive gray light. There was a sense of hush, of calm; David was reminded more of a cathedral than a technological facility.

At the center of the building a stack of equipment towered above the handful of technicians working here. David was a theoretician, not an experimentalist, but he recognized the paraphernalia of a high-energy experimental rig. There were subatomic-particle detectors—arrays of crystal blocks stacked high and deep—and boxes of control electronics piled up like white bricks, dwarfed by the detector array itself, but each itself the size of a mobile home.

The technicians weren't typical of a high-energy physics establishment, however. On average they seemed quite old—perhaps around sixty, given how hard it was to estimate ages these days.

He raised this with Hiram.

"Yeah. OurWorld makes a policy of hiring older workers anyhow. They're conscientious, generally as smart as they ever were thanks to the brain chemicals they give us now, and grateful for a job. And in this case, most of the people here are victims of the SSC cancellation."

"The SSC—the Superconducting Super Collider?" A multibillion-dollar particle-accelerator project that would have been built under a cornfield in Texas, had it not been canned by Congress in the 1990s.

Hiram said, "A whole generation of American particle physicists was hit by that decision. They survived; they found jobs in industry and Wall Street and so forth. Most of them never got over their disappointment, however—"

"But the SSC would have been a mistake. The linear-accelerator technology that came along a few years later was far more effective, and cheaper. And besides most fundamental results in particle physics since 2010 or so have come from studies of high-energy cosmological events."

"It doesn't matter. Not to these people. The SSC might have been a mistake. But it would have been *their* mistake. When I traced these guys and offered them a chance to come work in cutting-edge high-energy physics again they jumped at the chance." He eyed his son. "You know, you're a smart boy, David—"

"I'm not a boy."

"You had the kind of education I could never even have dreamed of. But there's a lot I could teach you even so. Like how to handle people." He waved a hand at the technicians. "Look at these guys. They're working for a promise: for dreams of their youth, aspiration, self-fulfillment. If you can find some way to tap into *that,* you can get people to work like pit ponies, and for pennies."

David followed him, frowning.

They reached a guardrail, and one gray-haired technician—with a curt, somewhat awed nod at Hiram—handed them hard hats. David fitted his gingerly to his head.

David leaned over the rail. He could smell machine oil, insulation, cleaning solvents. From here he could see that the detector array actually extended some distance below the ground surface. At the center of the pit was a tight knot of machinery, dark and unfamiliar. A puff of vapor, like wispy steam, billowed from the core of the machinery: cryogenics, perhaps. There was a whirr, somewhere above. David looked up to see a beam crane in action, a long steel beam that extended over the detector array, with a grabbing arm at the end.

Hiram murmured, "Most of this stuff is just detectors of one kind or another, so we can figure out what is going on—particularly when something goes wrong." He pointed at the knot of machinery at the core of the array. "*That* is the business end. A cluster of superconducting magnets."

"Hence the cryogenics."

"Yes. We make our big electromagnetic fields in there, the fields we use to build our buckyball Casimir engines." There was pride in his voice—justifiable, thought David. "This was the very site where we opened up that first wormhole, back in the spring. I'm getting a plaque put up, you know, one of those historic markers. Call me immodest. Now we're using this place to push the technology further, as far and as fast as we can."

David turned to Hiram. "Why have you brought me out here?"

". . . Just the question I was going to ask."

The third voice, utterly unexpected, clearly startled Hiram.

A figure stepped out of the shadows of the detector stack, and came to stand beside Hiram. For a moment David's heart pumped, for it might have been Hiram's twin—or his premature ghost. But at second glance David could detect differences: the second man was considerably younger, less bulky, perhaps a little taller, and his hair was still thick and glossy black.

But those ice blue eyes, so unusual given an Asian descent, were undoubtedly Hiram's.

"I know you," David said.

"From tabloid TV?"

David forced a smile. "You're Bobby."

"And you must be David, the half-brother I didn't know I had, until I had to learn it from a journalist." Bobby was clearly angry, but his self-control was icy.

David realized he had landed in the middle of a complicated family row—worse, it was *his* family.

Hiram looked from one to the other of his sons. He sighed. "David, maybe it's time I bought you that coffee."

*   *   *

The coffee was among the worst David had ever tasted. But the technician who served the three of them hovered at the table until David took his first sip. This is Seattle, David reminded himself; here, quality coffee has been a fetish among the social classes who man installations like this for a generation. He forced a smile. "Marvelous," he said.

The tech went away beaming.

The facility's cafeteria was tucked into the corner of the "countinghouse," the computing center where data from the various experiments run here were analyzed. The counting house itself, characteristic of Hiram's cost-conscious operations, was minimal, just a temporary office module with a plastic tile floor, fluorescent ceiling panels, wood-effect plastic workstation partitions. It was jammed with computer terminals, SoftScreens, oscilloscopes and other electronic equipment. Cables and light-fiber ducts snaked everywhere, bundles of them taped to the walls and floor and ceiling. There was a complex smell of electrical-equipment ozone, of stale coffee and sweat.

The cafeteria itself had turned out to be a dismal shack with plastic tables and vending machines, all maintained by a battered drone robot. Hiram and his two sons sat around a table, arms folded, avoiding each other's eyes.

Hiram dug into a pocket and produced a handkerchief-sized SoftScreen, smoothed it flat. He said, "I'll get to the point. On. Replay. Cairo."

David watched the 'Screen. He saw, through a succession of brief scenes, some kind of medical emergency unfolding in sun-drenched Cairo, Egypt: stretcher-bearers carrying bodies from buildings, a hospital crowded with corpses and despairing relatives and harassed medical staff, mothers clutching the inert bodies of infants, screaming.

"Dear God."

"God seems to have been looking the other way," Hiram said grimly. "This happened this morning. Another water war. One of Egypt's neighbors dumped a toxin in the Nile. First estimates are two thousand dead, ten thousand ill, many more deaths expected.

"Now." He tapped the little 'Screen. "Look at the picture quality. Some of these images are from handheld cams, some from drones. All taken within *ten minutes* of the first reported outbreak by a local news agency. And here's the problem." Hiram touched the corner of the image with his fingernail. It bore a logo: ENO, the Earth News Online network, one of Hiram's bitterest rivals in the news-gathering field. Hiram said, "We tried to strike a deal with the local agency, but ENO scooped us." He looked at his sons. "This happens all the time. In fact, the bigger I get, the more sharp little critters like ENO snap at my heels.

"I keep camera crews and stringers all around the world, at considerable expense. I have local agents on every street corner across the planet. But we can't be everywhere. And if we aren't there it can take hours, days even to get a crew in place. In the twenty-four-hour news business, believe me, being a minute late is fatal."

David frowned. "I don't understand. You're talking about competitive advantage? People are dying here, right in front of your eyes."

"People die all the time," said Hiram harshly. "People die in wars over resources, like in Cairo here, or over fine religious or ethnic differences, or because some bloody typhoon or flood or drought hits them as the climate goes crazy, or they just plain die. I can't change that. If I don't show it, somebody else will. I'm not here to argue morality. What I'm concerned about is the future of my business. And right now I'm losing out. And that's why I need you. Both of you."

Bobby said bluntly, "First tell us about our mothers."

David held his breath.

Hiram gulped his coffee. He said slowly, "All right. But there really isn't much to tell. Eve—David's mother—was my first wife."

"And your first fortune," David said dryly.

Hiram shrugged. "We used Eve's inheritance as seed-corn money to start the business. It's important that you understand, David. I never ripped off your mother. In the early days we were partners. We had a kind of long-range business plan. I remember we wrote it out on the back of a menu at our wedding reception. . . . We hit every bloody one of those targets, and more. We multiplied your mother's fortune tenfold. And we had you."

"But you had an affair, and your marriage broke up," David said.

Hiram eyed David. "How judgmental you are. Just like your mother."

"Just tell us, Dad," Bobby pressed.

Hiram nodded. "Yes, I had an affair. With your mother, Bobby. Heather, she was called. I never meant it to be this way. . . . David, my relationship with Eve had been failing for a long time. That damn religion of hers."

"So you threw her out."

"She tried to throw *me* out. I wanted us to come to a settlement, to be civilized about it. In the end she ran out on me—taking you with her."

David leaned forward. "But you cut her out of your business interests. A business you had built on *her* money."

Hiram shrugged. "I told you I wanted a settlement. She wanted it *all*. We couldn't compromise." His eyes hardened. "I wasn't about to give up everything I'd built up. Not on the whim of some religion-crazed nut. Even if she was my wife, your mother. When she lost her all-or-nothing suit, she went to France with you, and disappeared off the face of the Earth. Or tried to." He smiled. "It wasn't hard to track you down." Hiram reached for his arm, but David pulled back. "David, you never knew it, but I've been there for you. I found ways to, umm, help you out, without your mother knowing. I wouldn't go so far as to say you owe everything you have to me, but—"

David felt anger blaze. "What makes you think I wanted your help?"

Bobby said, "Where's your mother now?"

David tried to calm down. "She died. Cancer. It could have been easier for her. We couldn't afford—"

"She wouldn't let me help her," Hiram said. "Even at the end she pushed me away."

David said, "What do you expect? You took everything she had from her."

Hiram shook his head. "She took something more important from me. *You.*"

"And so," Bobby said coldly, "you focused your ambition on me."

Hiram shrugged. "What can I say? Bobby, I gave you everything—everything I'd have given both of you. I prepared you as best I could."

"*Prepared*?" David laughed, bemused. "What kind of word is that?"

Hiram thumped the table. "If Joe Kennedy can do it, why not Hiram Patterson? Don't you see, boys? There's no limit to what we can achieve, if we work together. . . ."

"You are talking about politics?" David eyed Bobby's sleek, puzzled face. "Is that what you intend for Bobby? Perhaps the Presidency itself?" He laughed. "You are exactly as I imagined you, Father."

"And how's that?"

"Arrogant. Manipulative."

Hiram was growing angry. "And you are just as I expected. As pompous and pious as your mother."

Bobby was staring at his father, bemused.

David stood. "Perhaps we have said enough."

Hiram's anger dissipated immediately. "No. Wait. I'm sorry. You're right. I didn't drag you all the way over here to fight with you. Sit down and hear me out. Please."

David remained on his feet. "What do you want of me?"

Hiram sat back and studied him. "I want you to build a bigger wormhole for me."

"How much bigger?"

Hiram took a breath. "Big enough to look through."

There was a long silence.

David sat down, shaking his head. "That's—"

"Impossible? I know. But let me tell you anyhow." Hiram got up and walked around the cluttered cafeteria, gesturing as he talked, animated, excited. "Suppose I could immediately open up a wormhole from my newsroom in Seattle direct to this story event in Cairo—and suppose that wormhole was wide enough to transmit pictures from the event. I could feed images from anywhere in the world straight into the network, with virtually no delay. Right? Think about it. I could fire my stringers and remote crews, reducing my costs to a fraction. I could even set up some kind of automated search facility, continually keeping watch through short-lived wormholes, waiting for the next story to break, wherever and whenever. There's really no limit."

Bobby smiled weakly. "Dad, they'd never scoop you again."

"Bloody right." Hiram turned to David. "*That's* the dream. Now tell me why it's impossible."

David frowned. "It's hard to know where to start. Right now you can establish metastable DataPipes between two fixed points. That's a considerable achievement in itself. But you need a massive piece of machinery at each end to anchor each wormhole mouth. Correct? Now you want to open up a stable wormhole mouth at the remote end, at your news story's location, *without* the benefit of any kind of anchor."

"Correct."

"Well, that's the first thing that's impossible, as I'm sure your technical people have been telling you."

"So they have. What else?"

"You want to use these wormholes to transmit visible-light photons. Now, quantum-foam wormholes come in at the Planck-Wheeler length, which is ten-to-minus-thirty-five meters. You've managed to expand them up through twenty orders of magnitude to make them big enough to pass gamma-ray photons. Very high frequency, very short wavelength."

"Yeah. We use the gamma rays to carry digitized data streams, which—"

"But the wavelength of your gamma rays is around a *million* times smaller than visible-light wavelengths. The mouths of your second-generation wormholes would have to be around a micron across at least." David eyed his father. "I take it you've had your engineers trying to achieve exactly that. And it doesn't work."

Hiram sighed. "We've actually managed to pump in enough Casimir energy to rip open wormholes that wide. But you get some kind of feedback effect which causes the damn things to collapse."

David nodded. "They call it Wheeler instability. Wormholes aren't naturally stable. A wormhole mouth's gravity pulls in photons, accelerates them to high energy, and that energized radiation bombards the throat and causes it to pinch off. It's the effect you have to counter with Casimir-effect negative energy, to keep open even the smallest wormholes."

Hiram walked to the window of the little cafeteria. Beyond, David could see the hulking form of the detector complex at the heart of the facility. "I have some good minds here. But these people are experimentalists. All they can do is trap and measure what happens when it all goes wrong. What we need is to beef up the theory, to go beyond the state of the art. Which is where you come in." He turned. "David, I want you to take a sabbatical from Oxford and come work with me on this." Hiram put his arm around David's shoulders; his flesh was strong and warm, its pressure overpowering. "Think of how this could turn out. Maybe you'll pick up the

Nobel Prize in Physics, while simultaneously I'll eat up ENO and those other yapping dogs who run at my heels. Father and son together. *Sons.* What do you think?"

David was aware of Bobby's eyes on him. "I guess—"

Hiram clapped his hands together. "I knew you'd say yes."

"I haven't, yet."

"Okay, okay. But you will. I sense it. You know, it's just terrific when long-term plans pay off."

David felt cold. "*What* long-term plans?"

Talking fast and eagerly, Hiram said, "If you were going to work in physics, I was keen for you to stay in Europe. I researched the field. You majored in mathematics—correct? Then you took your doctorate in a department of applied math and theoretical physics."

"At Cambridge, yes. Hawking's department—"

"That's a typical European route. As a result you're well versed in up-to-date math. It's a difference of culture. Americans have led the world in practical physics, but they use math that dates back to World War Two. So if you're looking for a *theoretical* breakthrough, don't ask anyone trained in America."

"And here I am," said David coldly. "With my convenient European education."

Bobby said slowly, "Dad, are you telling us you *arranged* things so that David got a European physics education, just on the off chance that he'd be useful to you? And all without his knowledge?"

Hiram stood straight. "Not just useful to me. More useful to himself. More useful to the world. More liable to achieve success." He looked from one to the other of his sons, and placed his hands on their heads, as if blessing them. "Everything I've done has been in your best interest. Don't you see that yet?"

David looked into Bobby's eyes. Bobby's gaze slid away, his expression unreadable.

4

WORMWOOD

Extracted from Wormwood: When Mountains Melt, *by Katherine Manzoni, published by Shiva Press, New York, 2033; also available as Internet floater dataset:*

. . . We face great challenges as a species if we are to survive the next few centuries.

It has become clear that the effects of climate change will be much worse than imagined a few decades ago: indeed, predictions of those effects from, say, the 1980s now look foolishly optimistic.

We know now that the rapid warming of the last couple of centuries has caused a series of meta-stable natural systems around the planet to flip to new states. From beneath the thawing permafrost of Siberia, billions of tonnes of methane and other greenhouse gases are already being released. Warming ocean waters are destabilizing more huge methane reservoirs around the continental shelves. Northern Europe is entering a period of extreme cold because of the shutdown of the Gulf Stream. New atmospheric modes—permanent storms— seem to be emerging over the oceans and the great landmasses. The death of the tropical forests is dumping vast amounts of carbon dioxide into the atmosphere. The slow melting of the West Antarctic ice sheet seems to be releasing pressure on an ar-chipelago of sunken islands beneath, and volcanic activity is likely, which will in turn lead to a cata-strophic additional melting of the sheet. The rise in sea levels is now forecast to be much higher than was imagined a few decades ago.

And so on.

All of these changes are interlinked. It may be that the spell of climatic stability which the Earth has enjoyed for thousands of years—a stability which allowed human civilization to emerge in the first place—is now coming to an end, perhaps because of our own actions. The worst case is that we are heading for some irreversible climatic breakdown, for example a runaway greenhouse, which would kill us all.

But all these problems pale in comparison to what will befall us if the body now known as the Wormwood should impact the Earth—although it is a chill coincidence that the Russian for "Wormwood" is *"Chernobyl"* . . .

Much of the speculation about the Wormwood and its likely consequence has been sadly misinformed— indeed, complacent. Let me reiterate some basic facts here.

Fact: the Wormwood is *not* an asteroid.

The astronomers think the Wormwood might once have been a moon of Neptune or Uranus, or perhaps it was locked in a stable point in Neptune's orbit, and was then perturbed somehow. But perturbed it was, and now it is on a five-hundred-year collision course with Earth.

Fact: the Wormwood's impact will *not* be comparable to the Chicxulub impact which caused the extinction of the dinosaurs.

That impact was sufficient to cause mass death, and to alter—drastically, and for all time—the course of evolution of life on Earth. But it was caused by an impactor some ten kilometers across. The Wormwood is *forty times* as large, and its mass is therefore some *sixty thousand times* as great.

Fact: the Wormwood will *not* simply cause a mass extinction event, like Chicxulub.

It will be much worse than that.

The heat pulse will sterilize the land to a depth of fifty meters. Life might survive, but only by being buried deep in caves. We know no way, even in principle, by which a human community could ride out the impact. It may be that viable populations could be established on other worlds: in orbit, on Mars or the Moon. But even in five centuries only a small fraction of the world's current population could be sheltered off-world.

Thus, Earth cannot be evacuated. When the Wormwood arrives, almost everybody will die.

Fact: the Wormwood *cannot* be deflected with foreseeable technology.

It is possible we could turn aside small bodies—a few kilometers across, typical of the population of near-Earth asteroids—with such means as emplaced nuclear charges or thermonuclear rockets. The challenge of deflecting the Wormwood is many orders of magnitude greater. Thought experiments on moving such bodies have proposed, for example, using a series of gravitational assists—not available in this case—or using advanced technology such as nanotech von Neumann machines to dismantle and disperse the body. But such technologies are far beyond our current capabilities.

Two years after I exposed the conspiracy to conceal from the general public the existence of the Wormwood, attention is already moving on—and we have yet to start work on the great project of our survival.

Indeed, the Wormwood itself is already having advance effects. It is a cruel irony that just as, for the first time in our history, we were beginning to manage our future responsibly and jointly, the prospect of Wormwood Day seems to render such efforts meaningless. Already we've seen the abandonment of various voluntary waste-emission guidelines, the closure of nature reserves, an upgraded search for sources of nonrenewable fuels, an extinction pulse among endangered species. If the house is to be demolished tomorrow anyhow, people seem to feel, we may as well burn the furniture today.

None of our problems are insoluble—*not even the Wormwood*. But it seems clear that to prevail we humans will have to act with a smartness and selflessness that has so far eluded us during our long and tangled history.

Still, my hope centers on humanity and ingenuity. It is significant, I believe, that the Wormwood was discovered—not by the professionals, who weren't looking that way—but by a network of amateur sky watchers, who set up robot telescopes in their backyards, and used shareware routines to scan optical detector images for changing glimmers of light, and refused to accept the cloak of secrecy our government tried to lay over them. It is in groups like this—earnest, intelligent, cooperative, stubborn, refusing to submit to impulses toward suicide or hedonism or selfishness, seeking new solutions to challenge the complacency of the professionals—that our best and brightest hope of surviving the future may lie. . . .

5

VIRTUAL HEAVEN

Bobby was late arriving at RevelationLand. Kate was still waiting in the car lot for him as the swarms of aging adherents started pressing through the gates of Billybob Meeks' giant cathedral of concrete and glass.

This "cathedral" had once been a football stadium; they were forced to sit near the back of one of the stands, their view impeded by pillars. Sellers of hot dogs, peanuts, soft drinks and recreational drugs were working the crowd, and muzak played over the PA. "Jerusalem," she recognized: based on Blake's great poem about the legendary visit of Christ to Britain, now the anthem of the new post–United Kingdom England.

The entire floor of the stadium was mirrored, making it a floor of blue sky littered with fat December clouds. At the center there was a gigantic throne, covered in stones glimmering green and blue—probably impure quartz, she thought. Water sprayed through the air, and arc lamps created a rainbow which arched spectacularly. More lamps hovered in the air before the throne, held aloft by drone robots, and smaller thrones circled bearing elders, old men and women dressed in white with golden crowns on their skinny heads.

And there were beasts the size of tipper trucks prowling around the field. They were grotesque, every part of their bodies covered with blinking eyes. One of them opened giant wings and flew, eagle-like, a few meters.

The beasts roared at the crowd, their calls amplified

by a booming PA. The crowd got to its feet and cheered, as if celebrating a touchdown.

Bobby was oddly nervous. He was wearing a tight-fitting one-piece suit of bright scarlet, with a color-morphing kerchief draped around his neck. He was a gorgeous twenty-first-century dandy, she thought, as out of place in the drab, elderly multitude around him as a diamond in a child's seashore pebble collection.

She touched his hand. "Are you okay?"

"I didn't realize they'd all be so *old*."

He was right, of course. The gathering congregation was a powerful illustration of the silvering of America. Many of the crowd, in fact, had cognitive-enhancer studs clearly visible at the backs of their necks, there to combat the onset of age-related diseases like Alzheimer's by stimulating the production of neurotransmitters and cell adhesion molecules.

"Go to any church in the country and you'll see the same thing, Bobby. Sadly, people are attracted to religion when they approach death. And now there are more old people—and with the Wormwood coming we all feel the brush of that dark shadow, perhaps. Billybob is just surfing a demographic wave. Anyhow, these people won't bite."

"Maybe not. But they *smell*. Can't you tell?"

She laughed. " 'One should never put on one's best trousers to go out to battle for freedom and truth.' "

"Huh?"

"Henrik Ibsen."

Now a man stood up on the big central throne. He was short, fat and his face shone with sweat. His amplified voice boomed out: "Welcome to RevelationLand! Do you know why you're here?" His finger stabbed. "Do you? Do *you*? Listen to me now: *On the Lord's day I was in the spirit, and I heard behind me a loud voice like a trumpet, which said: 'Write on a scroll what you see . . .' "* And he held up a glittering scroll.

Kate leaned toward Bobby. "Meet Billybob Meeks.

Prepossessing, isn't he? Clap along. Protective coloration."

"What's going on, Kate?"

"Evidently you've never read the Book of Revelation. The Bible's deranged punch line." She pointed. "Seven hovering lamps. Twenty-four thrones around the big one. Revelation is riddled with magic numbers—three, seven, twelve. And its description of the end of things is very literal. Although at least Billybob uses the traditional versions, not the modern editions which have been rewritten to show how the Wormwood date of 2534 was there in the text all along. . . ." She sighed. "The astronomers who discovered the Wormwood didn't do anybody any favors by calling it that. Chapter Eight, verse ten: *The third angel sounded his trumpet, and a great star, blazing like a torch, fell from the sky on a third of the rivers and on the springs of water—the name of the star is Wormwood . . .*"

"I don't understand why you invited me here today. In fact I don't know how you got a message through to me. After my father threw you out—"

"Hiram isn't yet omnipotent, Bobby," she said. "Not even over *you*. And as to why—look up."

A drone robot hovered over their heads, labeled with a stark, simple word: GRAINS. It dipped into the crowd, in response to the summons of members of the congregation.

Bobby said, "Grains? The mind accelerator?"

"Yes. Billybob's specialty. Do you know Blake? *To see a World in a Grain of Sand, / And a Heaven in a Wild Flower, / Hold Infinity in the palm of your hand, / And Eternity in an hour . . .* The pitch is that if you take Grains your perception of time will speed up. Subjectively, you'll be able to think more thoughts, have more experiences, in the same external time. A longer life— available exclusively from Billybob Meeks."

Bobby nodded. "But what's wrong with that?"

"Bobby, look around. Old people are frightened of

death. That makes them vulnerable to this kind of scam."

"What scam? Isn't it true that Grains actually works?"

"After a fashion. The brain's internal clock actually runs more slowly for older people. And that's the mechanism Billybob is screwing around with."

"And the problem is—"

"The side effects. What Grains does is to stimulate the production of dopamine, the brain's main chemical messenger. Trying to make an old man's brain run as fast as a child's."

"Which is a bad thing," he said uncertainly. "Right?"

She frowned, baffled by the question; not for the first time she had the feeling that there was something missing about Bobby. "Of course it's a bad thing. It is malevolent brain-tinkering. Bobby, dopamine is involved in a lot of fundamental brain functions. If dopamine levels are too low you can suffer tremors, an inability to start voluntary movement—Parkinson's disease, for instance— all the way to catatonia. Too *much* dopamine and you can suffer from agitation, obsessive-compulsive disorders, uncontrolled speech and movement, addictiveness, euphoria. Billybob's congregation—I should say his victims—aren't going to achieve Eternity in their last hour. Billybob is cynically burning out their brains.

"Some of the doctors are putting two and two together. But nobody has been able to prove anything. What I really need is evidence from his own labs that Billybob knows exactly what he is doing. Along with proof of his other scams."

"Such as?"

"Such as embezzling millions of bucks from insurance companies by selling them phony lists of church members. Such as pocketing a large donation from the Anti-Defamation League. He's still hustling, even though he's come a long way from banknote-baptisms." She glanced at Bobby. "Never heard of that? You palm a bill during a baptism. That way the blessing of God gets diverted to the money rather than the kiddie. Then you send the note out into circulation, and it's supposed to return to you with interest . . . and to make especially sure it works, of course, you hand the money over to your preacher. Word is Billybob picked up that endearing habit in Colombia, where he was working as a drug runner."

Bobby looked shocked. "You don't have any proof of that."

"Not yet," she said grimly. "But I'll get it."

"How?"

"That's what I want to talk to you about. . . ."

He looked mildly stunned.

She said, "Sorry. I'm lecturing you, aren't I?"

"A little."

"I do that when I'm angry."

"Kate, you are angry a lot. . . ."

"I feel entitled. I've been on this guy's trail for months."

A drone robot floated over their heads, bearing sets of virtual Glasses-and-Gloves. "These Glasses-and-Gloves have been devised by RevelationLand Inc., in conjunction with OurWorld Corporation, for the full experience of RevelationLand. Your credit card or personal account will be billed automatically per online minute. These Glasses-and-Gloves . . ."

Kate reached up and snagged two sets. "Show time."

Bobby shook his head. "I have implants. I don't need—"

"Billybob has his own special way of disabling rival technologies." She lifted the Glasses to her head. "Are you ready?"

"I guess—"

She felt a moist sensation around her eye sockets, as the Glasses extruded membranes to make a light-tight junction with her flesh; it felt like cold wet mouths sucking at her face.

She was instantly suspended in darkness and silence.

Now Bobby materialized beside her, floating in space,

holding her hand. His Glasses-and-Gloves were, of course, invisible.

And soon her vision cleared further. People were hovering all around them, off as far as she could see, like a cloud of dust motes. They were all dressed in white robes and holding big, gaudy palm leaves—even Bobby and herself, she found. And they were shining in the light that streamed from the object that hung before them.

It was a cube: huge, perfect, shining sun-bright, utterly dwarfing the flock of hovering people.

"Wow," Bobby said again.

"Revelation Chapter Twenty-one," she murmured. "Welcome to the New Jerusalem." She tried to throw away her palm leaf, but another simply appeared in her hand. "Just remember," she said, "the only real thing here is the steady flow of money out of your pockets and into Billybob's."

Together, they fell toward the light.

The wall before her was punctured by windows and a line of three arched doorways. She could see a light within, shining even more brightly than the exterior of the building. Scaled against the building's dimensions, the walls looked as thin as paper.

And still they fell toward the cube, until it loomed before them, gigantic, like some immense ocean liner.

Bobby said, "How big *is* this thing?"

She murmured, "Saint John tells us it is a cube twelve thousand stadia to each side."

"And twelve thousand stadia is—"

"About two thousand kilometers. Bobby, this city of God is the size of a small moon. It's going to take a *long* time to fall in. And we'll be charged for every second, of course."

"In that case I wish I'd had a hot dog. You know, my father mentions you a lot."

"He's angry at me."

"Hiram is, umm, mercurial. I think on some level he found you stimulating."

"I suppose I should be flattered."

"He liked the phrase you used. *Electronic anaesthesia.* I have to admit I didn't fully understand."

She frowned at him, as together they drifted toward the pale gray light. "You really have led a sheltered life, haven't you, Bobby?"

"Most of what you call 'brain-tinkering' is beneficial, surely. Like Alzheimer studs." He eyed her. "Maybe I'm not as out of it as you think I am. A couple of years ago I opened a hospital wing endowed by OurWorld. They were helping obsessive-compulsive sufferers by cutting out a destructive feedback loop between two areas of the brain—"

"The caudate nucleus and the amygdala." She smiled. "Remarkable how we've all become experts in brain anatomy. I'm not saying it's all harmful. But there is a compulsion to tinker. Addictions are nullified by changes to the brain's reward circuitry. People prone to rage are pacified by having parts of their amygdala— essential to emotion—burned out. Workaholics, gamblers, even people habitually in debt are 'diagnosed' and 'cured.' Even aggression has been linked to a disorder of the cortex."

"What's so terrible about all of that?"

"These quacks, these reprogramming doctors, don't understand the machine they are tinkering with. It's like trying to figure out the functions of a piece of software by burning out the chips of the computer it's running on. There are *always* side effects. Why do you think it was so easy for Billybob to find a football stadium to take over? Because organized spectator sport has been declining since 2015: the players no longer fought hard enough."

He smiled. "That doesn't seem too serious."

"Then consider this. The quality and quantity of original scientific research has been plummeting for two decades. By 'curing' fringe autistics, the doctors have removed the capacity of our brightest people to apply themselves to tough disciplines. And the area of the brain linked to depression, the subgenual cortex, is also associated with creativity—the perception of meaning. Most critics agree that the arts have gone into a reverse. Why do you think your father's virtual rock bands are so popular, seventy years after the originals were at their peak?"

"But what's the alternative? If not for reprogramming, the world would be a violent and savage place."

She squeezed his hand. "It may not be evident to you in your gilded cage, but the world out there still is violent and savage. What we *need* is a machine that will let us see the other guy's point of view. If we can't achieve that, than all the reprogramming in the world is futile."

He said wryly, "You really are an angry person, aren't you?"

"Angry? At charlatans like Billybob? At latter-day phrenologists and lobotomizers and Nazi doctors who are screwing with our heads, maybe even threatening the future of the species, while the world comes to pieces around us? Of course I'm angry. Aren't you?"

He returned her gaze, puzzled. "I guess I have to think about it. . . . Hey. We're accelerating."

The Holy City loomed before her. The wall was like a great upended plain, with the doors shining rectangular craters before her.

The swarms of people were plunging in separating streams toward the great arched doors, as if being drawn into maelstroms. Bobby and Kate swooped toward the central door. Kate felt an exhilarating headlong rush as the door arch opened wide before her—but there was no genuine sense of motion here. If she thought about it, she could still feel her body, sitting quietly in its stiff-backed stadium seat.

But still, it was some ride.

In a heartbeat they had flown through the doorway, a glowing tunnel of gray-white light, and they were skimming over a surface of shining gold.

Kate glanced around, seeking walls that must be hundreds of kilometers away. But there was unexpected artistry here. The air was misty—there were even clouds above her, scattered thinly, reflecting the shining golden floor—and she couldn't see beyond a few kilometers of the golden plain.

... And then she looked up, and saw the shining walls of the city rising *out* of the layer of atmosphere that clung to the floor. The plains and straight line edges merged into a distant square, unexpectedly clear, far above the air.

It was a ceiling over the atmosphere.

"Wow," she said. "It's the box the Moon came in."

Bobby's hand around hers was warm and soft. "Admit it. You're impressed."

"Billybob is still a crook."

"But an artful crook."

Now gravity was taking hold. The people around them were descending like so many human snowflakes; and Kate fell with them. She could see a river, bright blue, that cut across the golden plain beneath. Its banks were lined with dense green forest. There were people *everywhere*, she realized, scattered over the riverbank and the clear areas beyond and near the buildings. And thousands more were falling out of the sky all around her. Surely there were more here than could have been present in the sports stadium; no doubt many of them were virtual projections.

Details seemed to crystallize as she fell: trees and people and even dapples of light on the water of the river. At last the tallest trees were stretching up around her.

With a blur of motion she settled easily to the ground. When she looked into the sky she saw a blizzard of people in their snow-white robes, falling easily, without apparent fear.

There was gold *everywhere*: underfoot, on the walls of the nearest buildings. She studied the faces nearest her. They seemed excited, happy, anticipating. But the gold filled the air with a yellow light that made the people look as if they were suffering from some mineral deficiency. And no doubt those happy-clappy expressions were virtual fakes painted on bemused faces.

Bobby walked over to a tree. She noticed that his bare feet disappeared a centimeter or two into the grass surface. Bobby said, "The trees have got more than one kind of fruit. Look. Apples, oranges, limes—"

"*On each side of the river stood the tree of life, bearing twelve crops of fruit, yielding its fruit every month. And the leaves of the tree are for the healing of the nations . . .*"

"I'm impressed by the attention to detail."

"Don't be." She bent down to touch the ground. She could feel no grass blades, no dew, no earth, only a slick plastic smoothness. "Billybob is a showman," she said. "But he's a cheap showman." She straightened up. "This isn't even a true religion. Billybob has marketeers and business analysts working for him, not nuns. He is preaching a gospel of prosperity, that it's okay to be greedy and grasping. Talk to your brother about it. This is a commodity fetishism, directly descended from Billybob's banknote-baptism scam."

"You sound as if you care about religion."

"Believe me, I don't," she said vehemently. "The human race could get along fine without it. But my beef is with Billybob and his kind. I brought you here to show you how powerful he is, Bobby. We need to stop him."

"So how am I supposed to help?"

She stepped a little closer to him. "I know what your father is trying to build. An extension of his DataPipe technology. *A remote viewer.*"

He said nothing.

"I don't expect you to confirm or deny that. And I'm *not* going to tell you how I know about it. What I want you to think about is what we could achieve with such a technology."

He frowned. "Instant access to news stories, wherever they break—"

She waved that away. "*Much* more than that. Think about it. If you could open up a wormhole to *anywhere*, then there would be no more barriers. No walls. You could see anybody, at any time. And crooks like Billybob would have nowhere to hide."

His frown deepened. "You're talking about spying?"

She laughed. "Oh, come on, Bobby—each of us is under surveillance the whole time anyhow. You've been a celebrity since the age of twenty-one; you must know how it feels to be *watched*."

"It's not the same."

She took his arm. "If Billybob has nothing to hide, he's nothing to fear," she said. "Look at it that way."

"Sometimes you sound like my father," he said neutrally.

She fell silent, disquieted.

They walked forward with the throng. Now they were nearing a great throne, with seven dancing globes and twenty-four smaller attendant thrones, a scaled-up version of the real-world display Billybob had mounted out in the stadium.

And before the great central throne stood Billybob Meeks.

But this wasn't the fat, sweating man she had seen out on the sports field. This Billybob was taller, younger, thinner, far better looking, like a young Charlton Heston. Although he must have been at least a kilometer from where she stood, he towered over the congregation. And he seemed to be growing.

He leaned down, hands on hips, his voice like shaped thunder. "*The city does not need the sun or the Moon to shine on it, for the glory of God gives it light, and the*

Lamb is its lamp. . . . " Still Billybob grew, his arms like tree trunks, his face a looming disc that was already above the lower clouds. Kate could see people fleeing from beneath his giant feet, like ants.

And Billybob pointed a mighty finger directly at *her*, immense gray eyes glaring, the angry furrows on his brow like Martian channels. "*Nothing impure will ever come in to it, nor will anyone who does what is shameful or deceitful, but only those whose names are written in the Lamb's book of life.* Is *your* name in that book? Is it? Are *you* worthy?"

Kate screamed, suddenly overwhelmed.

And she was picked up by an invisible hand and dragged into the shining air.

There was a sucking sensation at her eyes and ears. Light, noise, the mundane stink of hot dogs flooded over her.

Bobby was kneeling before her. She could see the marks the Glasses had made around his eyes. "He got to you, didn't he?"

"Billybob does have a way of punching his message home," she gasped, still disoriented.

On row after row of the old sports stadium's battered seats, people were rocking and moaning, tears leaking from the black eye seals of the Glasses. In one area paramedics were working on unconscious people—perhaps victims of faints, epilepsy, even heart attacks, Kate speculated; she had had to sign various release forms when applying for their tickets, and she didn't imagine the safety of his parishioners was a high priority for Billybob Meeks.

Curiously she studied Bobby, who seemed unperturbed. "But what about you?"

He shrugged. "I've played more interesting adventure games." He looked up at the muddy December sky. "Kate—I know you're just using me as a way to get to my father. But I like you even so. And maybe tweaking Hiram's nose would be good for my soul. What do you think?"

She held her breath. She said, "I think that's about the most human thing I've ever heard you say."

"Then let's do it."

She forced a smile. She'd got what she wanted.

But the world around her still seemed unreal, compared to the vividness of those final moments inside Billybob's mind.

She had no doubt that—if the rumors about the capability Hiram was constructing were remotely accurate, and if she could get access to it—she would be able to destroy Billybob Meeks. It would be a great scoop, a personal triumph.

But she knew that some part of her, no matter how far down she buried it, would always regret doing so. Some part of her would always long to be allowed to return to that glowing city of gold, with walls that stretched halfway to the Moon, where shining, smiling people were waiting to welcome her.

Billybob had broken through, his shock tactics had gotten even to her. And that, of course, was the whole point. Why Billybob must be stopped.

"Yes," she said. "Let's do it."

6

THE BILLION-DOLLAR PEARL

David, with Hiram and Bobby, sat before a giant
SoftScreen spread across the Wormworks countinghouse wall. The 'Screen image—returned by a fiber-
optic camera that had been snaked into the heart of the
Wormworks' superconducting-magnet nest—was nothing but darkness, marred by an occasional stray pixel, a
prickle of color and light.

A digital counter in a corner display worked its way
down toward zero.

Hiram paced impatiently around the cramped, cluttered countinghouse; David's assistant technicians cowered from him, avoiding his eyes. Hiram snapped, "How
do you know the bloody wormhole is even open?"

David suppressed a smile. "You don't need to whisper." He pointed to the corner display. Beside the countdown clock was a small numerical caption, a sequence
of prime numbers scrolling upward from two to thirty-
one, over and over. "That's the test signal, sent through
the wormhole by the Brisbane crew at the normal
gamma-ray wavelengths. So we know we managed to
find and stabilize a wormhole mouth—*without* a remote
anchor—and the Australians have been able to locate it."
During his three months' work here, David had quickly
discovered a way to use modulations of exotic-matter
pulses to battle the wormholes' inherent instability.
Turning that into practical and repeatable engineering,
of course, had been immensely difficult—but in the end

successful. "Our placement of the remote mouth isn't so precise yet. I'm afraid our Australian colleagues have to chase our wormhole mouths through the dust out there. Chasing fizzers over the gibbers, as they put it. . . . But still, now we can open up a wormhole to *anywhere*. What we don't know yet is whether we're going to be able to expand the holes up to visible-light dimensions."

Bobby was leaning easily against a table, legs crossed, looking fit and relaxed, as if he'd just come off a tennis court—as perhaps he had, mused David. "I think we ought to give David a lot of credit, Dad. After all he has solved half the problem already."

"Yes," Hiram said, "but I don't see anything but gamma rays squirted in by some broken-nosed Aussie. Unless we can find a way to expand these bloody things, we're wasting my money. And I can't stomach all this waiting! Why just one test run a day?"

"Because," said David evenly, "we have to analyze the results from each test, strip down the Casimir gear, reset the control equipment and detectors. We have to understand each failure before we can go ahead toward success." That is, he added silently, before I can extricate myself from this complex family entanglement and return to the comparative calm of Oxford, funding battles, ferocious academic rivalry and all.

Bobby asked, "What exactly is it we're looking for? What will a wormhole mouth look like?"

"I can answer that one," Hiram said, still pacing. "I grew up with enough bad pop-science shows. A wormhole is a shortcut through a fourth dimension. You have to cut a chunk out of our three-dimensional space and join it onto another such chunk, over in Brisbane."

Bobby raised an eyebrow at David.

David said carefully, "It's a little more complicated. But he's more right than wrong. A wormhole mouth is a sphere, floating freely in space. A three-dimensional excision. If we succeed with the expansion, for the first time we'll be able to *see* our wormhole mouth—with a hand lens, anyhow. . . ." The countdown clock was down to a single digit. David said, "Heads up, everybody. Here we go."

The ripples of conversation in the room died away, and everyone turned to the digital clock.

The count reached zero.

And nothing happened.

There were events, of course. The track counter racked up a respectable score, showing heavy and energetic particles passing through the detector array, the debris of an exploded wormhole. The array's pixel elements, each firing individually as a particle passed through them, could later be used to trace the paths of debris fragments in three dimensions—paths which could then be reconstructed and analyzed.

Lots of data, lots of good science. But the big wall SoftScreen remained blank. No signal.

David suppressed a sigh. He opened up the logbook and entered details of the run in his round, neat hand; around him his technicians began equipment diagnostics.

Hiram looked into David's face, at the empty 'Screen, at the technicians. "Is that it? Did it work?"

Bobby touched his father's shoulder. "Even I can tell it didn't, Dad." He pointed to the prime-number test sequence. It had frozen on thirteen. "Unlucky thirteen," murmured Bobby.

"Is he right? David, did you screw up again?"

"This *wasn't* a failure. Just another test. You don't understand science, Father. Now, when we run the analysis and learn from this—"

"Jesus Christ on a bike! I should have left you rotting in bloody Oxford. Call me when you have something." Hiram, shaking his head, stalked from the room.

When he left, the feeling of relief in the room was palpable. The technicians—silver-haired particle physicists all, many of them older than Hiram, some of them with distinguished careers beyond OurWorld—started to file out.

When they'd gone, David sat before a SoftScreen to begin his own follow-up work.

He brought up his favored desktop metaphor. It was like a window into a cluttered study, with books and documents piled in untidy heaps on the floor and shelves and tables, and with complex particle-decay models hanging like mobiles from the ceiling. When he looked around the "room," the point at the focus of his attention expanded, opening out more detail, the rest of the room blurring to a background wash. He could "pick up" documents and models with a fingertip, rummaging until he found what he wanted, exactly where he'd left it last time.

First he had to check for detector pixel faults. He began passing the vertex detector traces into the analog signal bus, and pulled out a blow-up overview of various detector slabs. There were always random failures of pixels when some especially powerful particle hit a detector element. But, though some of the detectors had suffered enough radiation damage to require replacement, there was nothing serious for now.

Humming, immersed in the work, he prepared to move on—

"Your user interface is a mess."

David, startled, turned. Bobby was still here: still leaning, in fact, against his table.

"Sorry," David said. "I didn't mean to turn my back." How odd that he hadn't even noticed his brother's continued presence.

Bobby said now, "Most people use the Search Engine."

"Which is irritatingly slow, prone to misunderstanding and which anyhow masks a Victorian-era hierarchical data-storage system. Filing cabinets. Bobby, I'm too dumb for the Search Engine. I'm just an unevolved ape who likes to use his hands and eyes to find things. This may look a mess, but I know *exactly* where everything is."

"But still, you could study this particle-track stuff a lot better as a virtual. Let me set up a trial of my latest Mind'sEye prototype for you. We can reach more areas of the brain, switch more quickly—"

"And all without the need for trepanning."

Bobby smiled.

"All right," David said. "I'd appreciate that."

Bobby's gaze roamed around the room in that absent, disconcerting way of his. "Is it true? What you told Dad—that this isn't a failure, but just another step?"

"I can understand Hiram's impatience. After all he's paying for all of this."

"And he's working under commercial pressure," Bobby said. "Already some of his competitors are claiming to have DataPipes of comparable quality to Hiram's. It surely won't be long before one of *them* comes up with the idea of a remote viewer—independently, if nobody's leaked it already."

"But commercial pressure is irrelevant," David said testily. "A study like this has to proceed at its own pace. Bobby, I don't know how much you know about physics."

"Assume nothing. Once you have a wormhole, what's so difficult about expanding it?"

"It's not as if we're building a bigger and better car. We're trying to push spacetime into a form it wouldn't naturally adopt. Look—wormholes are intrinsically unstable. You know that to keep them open at all we have to thread them with exotic matter."

"Antigravity."

"Yes. But the tension in the throat of a wormhole is gigantic. We're constantly balancing one huge pressure against another." David balled his fists and pressed them against each other, hard. "As long as they are balanced, fine. But the smallest perturbation and you lose everything." He let one fist slide over the other, breaking the equilibrium he'd established. "And that fundamental instability grows worse with size. What we're attempting is to monitor conditions inside the wormhole, and adjust the pumping of exotic matter-energy to compensate for fluctuations." He pressed his fists against each other again; this time, as he jiggled the left back and forth, he compensated with movements of his right, so his knuckles stayed pressed together.

"I get it," Bobby said. "As if you're threading the wormhole with software."

"Or with a smart worm." David smiled. "Yes. It's *very* processor-intensive. And so far, the instabilities have been too rapid and catastrophic to deal with.

"Look at this." He reached to his desktop and, with the touch of a fingertip, he pulled up a fresh view of a particle cascade. It had a strong purple trunk—the color showing heavy ionization—with clusters of red jets, wide and narrow, some straight, others curved. He tapped a key, and the spray rotated in three dimensions; the software suppressed foreground elements to allow details of the jet's inner structure to become visible. The central spray was surrounded by numbers showing energy, momentum and charge readings. "We're looking at a high-energy, complex event here, Bobby. All this exotic garbage spews out before the wormhole disappears completely." He sighed. "It's like trying to figure out how to fix a car by blowing it up and combing through the debris.

"Bobby, I was honest with Father. Every trial is an exploration of another corner of what we call parameter space, as we try different ways of making our wormhole viewers wide and stable. There are no wasted trials; every time we proceed we learn something. In fact many of my tests are negative—I actually design them to fail. A single test which proves some piece of theory wrong is more valuable than a hundred tests showing that idea *might* be true. Eventually we'll get there . . . or else we'll prove Hiram's dream is impossible, with present-day technology."

"Science demands patience."

David smiled. "Yes. It always has. But for some it is hard to remain patient, in the face of the black meteor which approaches us all."

"The Wormwood? But that's centuries off."

"But scientists are hardly alone in being affected by the knowledge of its existence. There is an impulse to hurry, to gather as much data and formulate new theories, to learn as much as possible in the time that is left—because we no longer are sure there will be anybody to build on our work, as we've always assumed in the past. And so people take shortcuts, the peer review process is under pressure . . ."

Now a red alert light started flashing high on the countinghouse wall, and technicians began to drift back into the room.

Bobby looked at David quizzically. "You're setting up to run again? You told Dad you only ran one trial a day."

David winked. "A little white lie. I find it useful to have a way to get rid of him."

Bobby laughed.

It turned out there was time to fetch coffee before the new run began. They walked together to the cafeteria.

Bobby is lingering, David thought. As if he wants to be involved. He sensed a need here, a need he didn't understand—perhaps even envy. Was that possible?

It was a wickedly delicious thought. Perhaps Bobby Patterson, fabulously rich, this latter-day dandy, envies *me*—his earnest, dronelike brother.

Or perhaps that's just sibling rivalry on my part.

Walking back, he sought to make conversation.

"So. Were you a grad student, Bobby?"

"Sure. But at HBS."

"HBS? Oh. Harvard—"

"Business School. Yes."

"I took some business studies as part of my first degree," David said. He grimaced. "The courses were intended to 'equip us for the modern world.' All those two-by-two matrices, the fads for this theory or that, for one management guru or another . . ."

"Well, business analysis isn't rocket science, as we used to say," Bobby murmured evenly. "But nobody at Harvard was a dummy. I won my place there on merit. And the competition there was ferocious."

"I'm sure it was." David was puzzled by Bobby's flat tone of voice, his lack of fire. He probed gently. "I have the impression you feel—underestimated."

Bobby shrugged. "Perhaps. The VR division of OurWorld is a billion-buck business in its own right. If I fail, Dad's made it clear he's not going to bail me out. But even Kate thinks I'm some kind of placeholder." Bobby grinned. "I'm enjoying trying to convince her otherwise."

David frowned. Kate? . . . Ah, the girl reporter Hiram had tried to exclude from his son's life. Without success, it seemed. Interesting. "Do you want me to keep quiet?"

"What about?"

"Kate. The reporter—"

"There isn't really anything to keep quiet about."

"Perhaps. But Father doesn't approve of her. Have you told him you're still seeing her?"

"No."

And this may be the only thing in your young life, David thought, which Hiram *doesn't* know about. Well, let's keep it that way. David felt pleased to have established this small bond between them.

Now the countdown clock neared its conclusion. Once more the wall-mounted SoftScreen showed an inky darkness, broken only by random pixel flashes, and with the numeric monitor in the corner dully repeating its test list of primes. David watched with amusement as Bobby's lips silently formed the count numbers: *Three. Two. One.*

And then Bobby's mouth hung open in shock, a flickering light playing on his face.

David swiveled his gaze to the SoftScreen.

This time there was an image, a disc of light. It was

a bizarre, dreamy construct of boxes and strip lights and cables, distorted almost beyond recognition, as if seen through some grotesque fish-eye lens.

David found he was holding his breath. As the image stayed stable for two seconds, three, he deliberately sucked in air.

Bobby asked, "What are we seeing?"

"The wormhole mouth. Or rather, the light it's pulling in from its surroundings, *here*, the Wormworks. Look, you can see the electronics stack. But the strong gravity of the mouth is dragging in light from the three-dimensional space all around it. The image is being distorted."

"Like gravitational lensing."

He looked at Bobby in surprise. "Exactly that." He checked the monitors. "We're already passing our previous best. . . ."

Now the distortion of the image became stronger, as the shapes of equipment and light fixtures were smeared to circles surrounding the view's central point. Some of the colors seemed to be Doppler-shifting now, a green support strut starting to look blue, the fluorescents' glare taking on a tinge of violet.

"We're pushing deeper into the wormhole," David whispered. "Don't give up on me now."

The image fragmented further, its elements crumbling and multiplying in a repeating pattern around the disc-shaped image. It was a three-dimensional kaleidoscope, David thought, formed by multiple images of the lab's illumination. He glanced at counter readouts, which told him that much of the energy of the light falling into the wormhole had been shifted to the ultraviolet and beyond, and the energized radiation was pounding the curved walls of this spacetime tunnel.

But the wormhole was holding.

They were far past the point where all previous experiments had collapsed.

Now the disc image began to shrink as the light, falling from three dimensions onto the wormhole mouth, was compressed by the wormhole's throat into a narrowing pipe. The scrambled, shrinking puddle of light reached a peak of distortion.

And then the quality of light changed. The multiple-image structure became simpler, expanding, seeming to unscramble itself, and David began to pick out elements of a new visual field: a smear of blue that might be sky, a pale white that could be an instrument box.

He said: "Call Hiram."

Bobby said, "What are we looking at?"

"Just call Father, Bobby."

Hiram arrived at a run an hour later. "It better be worth it. I broke up an investors' meeting . . ."

David, wordlessly, handed him a slab of lead-glass crystal the size and shape of a pack of cards. Hiram turned the slab over, inspecting it.

The upper surface of the slab was ground into a magnifying lens, and when Hiram looked into it, he saw miniaturized electronics: photomultiplier light detectors for receiving signals, a light-emitting diode capable of emitting flashes for testing, a small power supply, miniature electromagnets. And, at the geometric center of the slab, there was a tiny, perfect sphere, just at the limit of visibility. It looked silvery, reflective, like a pearl; but the quality of light it returned wasn't quite the hard gray of the countinghouse's fluorescents.

Hiram turned to David. "What am I looking at?"

David nodded at the big wall SoftScreen. It showed a round blur of light, blue and brown.

A face came looming into the image: a human face, a man somewhere in his forties, perhaps. The image was heavily distorted—it was exactly as if he had pushed his face into a fish-eye lens—but David could make out a knot of curly black hair, leathery sun-beaten skin, white teeth in a broad smile.

"It's Walter," Hiram said, wondering. "Our Brisbane station head." He moved closer to the SoftScreen. "He's saying something. His lips are moving." He stood there, mouth moving in sympathy. "*I . . . see . . . you.* I see you. My God."

Behind Walter, other Aussie technicians could be seen now, heavily distorted shadows, applauding in silence.

David grinned, and submitted to Hiram's whoops and bear hugs, all the while keeping his eye on the lead-glass slab containing the wormhole mouth, that billion-dollar pearl.

7

THE WORMCAM

It was 3 A.M. At the heart of the deserted Wormworks, in a bubble of SoftScreen light, Kate and Bobby sat side by side. Bobby was working through a simple question-and-answer setup session on the SoftScreen. They were expecting a long night; behind them there was a heap of hastily gathered gear, coffee flasks and blankets and foam mattresses.

... There was a creak. Kate jumped and grabbed Bobby's arm.

Bobby kept working at the program. "Take it easy. Just a little thermal contraction. I told you, I made sure all the surveillance systems have a blind spot right here, right now."

"I'm not doubting it. It's just that I'm not used to creeping around in the dark like this."

"I thought you were the tough reporter."

"Yes. But what I do is generally legal."

"*Generally*?"

"Believe it or not."

"But *this*—" He waved a hand toward the hulking, mysterious machinery out in the dark. "—isn't even surveillance equipment. It's just an experimental high-energy physics rig. There's nothing like it in the world; how can there be any legislation to cover its use?"

"That's specious, Bobby. No judge on the planet would buy that argument."

"Specious or not, I'm telling you to calm down. I'm

trying to concentrate. Mission Control here could be a little more user-friendly. David doesn't even use voice activation. Maybe all physicists are so conservative—or all Catholics."

She studied him as he worked steadily at the program. He looked as alive as she'd ever seen him, for once fully engaged in the moment. And yet he seemed completely unperturbed by any moral doubt. He really was a complex person—or rather, she thought sadly, incomplete.

His finger hovered over a start button on the Soft-Screen. "Ready. Shall I do it?"

"We're recording?"

He tapped the SoftScreen. "Everything that comes through that wormhole will be trapped right here."

". . . Okay."

"Three, two, one." He hit the key.

The 'Screen turned black.

From the greater darkness around her, she heard a deep bass hum as the giant machinery of the Worm-works came on line, huge forces gathering to rip a hole in spacetime. She thought she could smell ozone, feel a prickle of electricity. But maybe that was imagination.

Setting up this operation had been simplicity itself. While Bobby had worked to obtain clandestine access to the Wormworks equipment, Kate had made her way to Billybob's mansion, a gaudy baroque palace set in woodland on the fringe of the Mount Rainier National Park. She'd taken sufficient photographs to construct a crude external map of the site, and had made Global Positioning System readings at various reference points. That—and the information Billybob had boastfully given away to style magazines about the lavish interior layout—had been sufficient for her to construct a detailed internal map of the building, complete with a grid of GPS references.

Now, if all went well, those references would be sufficient to establish a wormhole link between Billybob's inner sanctum and this mocked-up listening post.

. . . The SoftScreen lit up. Kate leaned forward.

The image was heavily distorted, a circular smear of light, orange and brown and yellow, as if she were looking through a silvered tunnel. There was a sense of movement, patches of light coming and going across the image, but she could make out no detail.

"I can't see a damn thing," she said querulously.

Bobby tapped at the SoftScreen. "Patience. Now I have to cut in the deconvolution routines."

"The what?"

"The wormhole mouth isn't a camera lens, remember. It's a little sphere on which light falls from all around, in three dimensions. And that global image is pretty much smeared out by its passage through the wormhole itself. But we can use software routines to unscramble all that. It's kind of interesting. The software is based on programs the astronomers use to factor out atmospheric distortion, twinkling and blurring and refraction, when they study the stars—"

The image abruptly cleared, and Kate gasped.

They saw a massive desk with a globe-lamp hovering above. There were papers and SoftScreens scattered over the desktop. Behind the desk was an empty chair, casually pushed back. On the walls there were performance graphs and bar charts, what looked like accounting statements.

There was luxury here. The wallpaper looked like handmade English stuff, probably the most expensive in the world. And on the floor, casually thrown there, there was a pair of rhino hides, gaping mouths and glassy eyes staring, horns proud even in death.

And there was a simple animated display, a total counting steadily upward. It was labeled CONVERTS: human souls being counted like a fast-food chain's sushiburger sales.

The image was far from perfect. It was dark, grainy, sometimes unstable, given to freezing or breaking up into clouds of pixels. But still—

"I can't believe it," Kate breathed. "It's working. It's as if all the walls in the world just turned to glass. Welcome to the goldfish bowl. . . ."

Bobby worked his SoftScreen, making the reconstructed image pan around. "I thought rhinos were extinct."

"They are now. Billybob was involved in a consortium which bought out the last breeding pair from a private zoo in France. The geneticists had been trying to get hold of the rhinos to store genetic material, maybe eggs and sperm and even zygotes, in the hope of restoring the species in the future. But Billybob got there first. And so he owns the last rhino skins there will ever be. It was good business, if you look at it that way. These skins command unbelievably high prices now."

"But illegal."

"Yes. But nobody is likely to have the guts to pursue a prosecution against someone as powerful as Billybob. After all, come Wormwood Day, all the rhinos will be extinct anyhow; what difference does it make? . . . Can you zoom with this thing?"

"Metaphorically. I can magnify and enhance selectively."

"Can we see those papers on the desk?"

With a fingernail Bobby marked out zoom boxes, and the software's focus progressively moved in on the litter of papers on the desktop. The wormhole mouth seemed to be positioned about a meter from the ground, some two meters from the desk—Kate wondered if it would be visible, a tiny reflective bead hovering in the air—so the papers were foreshortened by perspective. And besides they hadn't been laid out for convenient reading; some of them were lying facedown or were obscured by others. Still, Bobby was able to pick out sections—he inverted the images and corrected for perspective distortion, cleaned them up with intelligent-software enhancement routines—enough for Kate to get a sense of what much of the material was about.

It was mostly routine corporate stuff—chilling evidence of Billybob's industrial-scale mining of gullible Americans—but nothing illegal. She had Bobby scan on, rooting hastily through the scattered material.

And then, at last, she hit pay dirt.

"Hold it," she said. "Enhance. . . . Well, well." It was a report, technical, closely printed, replete with figures, on the adverse effects of dopamine stimulation in elderly subjects. "That's it," she breathed. "The smoking gun." She got up and started to pace the room, unable to contain her restless energy. "What an asshole. Once a drug dealer, always a drug dealer. If we can get an image of Billybob himself reading that, better yet signing it off— Bobby, we need to find him."

Bobby sighed and sat back. "Then ask David. I can swivel and zoom, but right now I don't know how to make this WormCam pan."

" 'WormCam'?" Kate grinned.

"Dad works his marketeers even harder than his engineers. Look, Kate, it's three-thirty in the morning. Let's be patient. I have security lockout here until noon tomorrow. Surely we can catch Billybob in his office before then. If not, we can try again another day."

"Yes." She nodded, tense. "You're right. It's just I'm used to working fast."

He smiled. "Before some other hot journo muscles in on your scoop?"

"It happens."

"Hey." Bobby reached out and cupped her chin in his hands. His dark face was all but invisible in the cavernous gloom of the Wormworks, but his touch was warm, dry, confident. "You don't have to worry. Just think of it. Right now nobody else on the planet, *nobody*, has access to WormCam technology. There's no way Billybob can detect what we're up to, or anyone else can beat you to the punch. What's a few hours?"

Her breathing was shallow, her heart pumping; she seemed to sense him before her in the dark, at a level deeper than sight or scent or even touch, as if some deep core inside her was responding to the warm bulk of his body.

She reached up, covered his hand, and kissed it. "You're right. We have to wait. But I'm burning energy anyhow. So let's do something constructive with it."

He seemed to hesitate, as if trying to puzzle out her meaning.

Well, Kate, she told herself, you aren't like the other girls he's met in his gilded life. Maybe he needs a little help.

She put her free hand around his neck, pulled him toward her, and felt his mouth on hers. Her tongue, hot and inquisitive, pushed into his mouth, and ran along a ridge of perfect lower teeth; his lips responded eagerly.

At first he was tender, even loving. But, as passion built, she became aware of a change in his posture, his manner. As she responded to his unspoken commands she was aware that she was letting him take control, and—even as he brought her to a deep climax with expert ease— she felt he was distracted, lost in the mysteries of his own strange, wounded mind, engaged with the physical act, and not with her.

He knows how to make love, she thought, maybe better than anybody I know. But he doesn't know how to love. What a cliché that was. But it was true. And terribly sad.

And, even as his body closed on hers, her fingers, digging into the hair at the back of his neck, found something round and hard under his covering of hair, about the size of a nickel, metallic and cold.

It was a brain stud.

In the spring-morning silence of the Wormworks, David sat in the glow of his SoftScreen.

He was looking down at the top of his own head, from a height of two or three meters. It wasn't a comfortable sight: he looked overweight, and there was a small bald spot at his crown he hadn't noticed before, a little pink coin in among his uncombed mass of hair.

He raised his hand to find the bald spot.

The image in the 'Screen raised its hand too, like a puppet slaved to his actions. He waved, childishly, and looked up. But of course there was nothing to see, no sign of the tiny rip on spacetime which transmitted these images.

He tapped at the 'Screen, and the viewpoint swiveled, looking straight ahead. Another tap, hesitantly, and it began to move forward, through the Wormworks' dark halls: at first a little jerkily, then more smoothly. Huge machines, looming and rather sinister, floated past him like blocky clouds.

Eventually, he supposed, commercial versions of this wormhole camera would come with more intuitive controls, a joystick perhaps, levers and knobs to swivel the viewpoint this way and that. But this simple configuration of touch controls on his 'Screen was enough to let him control the viewpoint, allowing him to concentrate on the image itself.

And of course, a corner of his mind reminded him, in actuality the viewpoint wasn't moving at all: rather, the Casimir engines were creating and collapsing a series of wormholes, Planck lengths apart, strung out in a line the way he wanted to move. The images returned by successive holes arrived sufficiently closely to give him the illusion of movement.

But none of that was important for now, he told himself sternly. For now he only wanted to play.

With a determined slap at the 'Screen he turned the viewpoint and made it fly straight at the Wormworks' corrugated iron wall. He couldn't help but wince as that barrier flew at him.

There was an instant of darkness.

And then he was through, and immersed suddenly in dazzling sunlight.

He slowed the viewpoint and dropped it to around eye level. He was in the grounds which surrounded the Wormworks: grass, streams, cute little bridges. The sun was low, casting long crisp shadows, and there was a trace of dew that glimmered on the grass.

He let his viewpoint glide forward—at first at walking pace, then a little faster. The grass swept beneath him, and Hiram's replanted trees blurred past, side by side.

The sense of speed was exhilarating.

He still hadn't mastered the controls, and from time to time his viewpoint would plunge clumsily through a tree or a rock: moments of darkness, tinged deep brown or gray. But he was getting the hang of it, and the sense of speed and freedom and clarity was striking. It was like being ten years old again, he thought, senses fresh and sharp, a body so full of energy he was light as a feather.

He came to the plant's drive. He raised the viewpoint through two or three meters, swept down the drive, and found the freeway. He flew higher and skimmed far above the road, gazing down at the streams of gleaming, beetle-like cars below. The traffic flow, still gathering for the rush hour to come, was dense and fast-moving. He could see patterns in the flow, knots of density that gathered and cleared as the invisible web of software controls optimized the stream of SmartDriven cars.

Suddenly impatient, he rose up further, so that the roadway became a gray ribbon snaking over the land, car windscreens sparkling like a string of diamonds.

He could see the city laid out before him now. The suburbs were a neat rectangular grid laid over the hills, mist-blurred to gray. The tall buildings of downtown thrust upward, a compact fist of concrete and glass and steel.

He rose higher still, swooped through a thin layer of cloud to a brighter sunshine beyond, and then turned again to see the ocean's glimmer—stained, far from land, by the ominous dark of yet another incoming storm system. The horizon's curve became apparent, as land and sea folded over on themselves and Earth became a planet.

David suppressed the urge to whoop. He always had wanted to fly like Superman. This, he thought, is going to sell like hot cakes.

A crescent Moon hung, low and gaunt, in the blue sky. David swiveled the viewpoint until his field of view was centered on that sliver of bony light.

Behind him he could hear a commotion, raised voices, running feet. Perhaps it was a security breach, somewhere in the Wormworks. It was none of his concern.

With determination, he drove the viewpoint forward. The morning blue deepened to violet. Already he could see the first stars.

They slept for a while.

When Kate stirred, she felt cold. She raised her wrist and her tattoo lit up. Six in the morning. In his sleep, Bobby had moved away from her, leaving her uncovered. She pulled at the blanket they were sharing, covering her exposed torso.

The Wormworks, windowless, was as dark and cavernous as when they had arrived. She could see that the WormCam image of Billybob's study was still as it had been, the desk and rhino skins and the papers. Everything since they had set up the WormCam link had been recorded. With a flicker of excitement she realized she might already have enough material to nail Meeks for good—

"You're awake."

She turned her head. There was Bobby's face, eyes wide open, resting on a folded-up blanket.

He stroked her cheek with the back of one finger. "I think you've been crying," he said.

That startled her. She resisted the temptation to brush his hand away, to hide her face.

He sighed. "You found the implant. So now you've screwed a wirehead. Isn't that your prejudice? You don't like implants. Maybe you think only criminals and the mentally deficient should undergo brain-function modification—"

"Who put it there?"

"My father. I mean, it was his initiative. When I was a small boy."

"You remember?"

"I was three or four years old. Yes, I remember. And I remember understanding why he was doing it. Not the technical detail, of course, but the fact that he loved me, and wanted the best for me." He smiled, self-deprecating. "I'm not quite as perfect as I look. I was somewhat hyperactive, and also slightly dyslexic. The implant fixed those things."

She reached behind him and explored the profile of his implant. Trying not to make it obvious, she made sure her own wrist tattoo passed over the metal surface. She forced a smile. "You ought to upgrade your hardware."

He shrugged. "It works well enough."

"If you'll let me bring in some microelectronic analysis gear I could run a study of it."

"What would be the point?"

She took a breath. "So we can find out what it does."

"I told you what it does."

"You told me what Hiram told *you*."

He propped himself up on his elbows and stared at her. "What are you implying?"

Yes, what, Kate? Are you just sour because he shows no signs of falling in love with you—as, obviously, you are falling for this complex, flawed man? "You seem to have—gaps. For instance, don't you ever wonder about your mother?"

"No," he said. "Am I supposed to?"

"It's not a question of being *supposed* to, Bobby. It's just what most people *do*—without being prompted."

"And you think this has something to do with my implant?—Look, I trust my father. I know that everything he's done has been for my best interest."

"All right." She leaned over to kiss him. "It's not my business. We won't talk about it again."

At least, she thought with a guilty frisson, not until I get an analysis of the data I already collected from your head stud—without your knowledge, or your permission. She snuggled closer to him, and draped an arm over his chest, protectively. Maybe it's me who has the gaps in her soul, she thought.

With shocking suddenness, torchlight burst over them.

Kate hastily grabbed the blanket to her chest, feeling absurdly exposed and vulnerable. The torchlight in her eyes was dazzling, masking the group of people beyond. There were two, three people. They wore dark uniforms.

And there was Hiram's unmistakable bulk, his hands on his hips, glaring at her.

"You can't hide from me," Hiram said easily. He gestured at the WormCam image. "Shut that bloody thing off."

The image turned to mush as the wormhole link to Billybob's office was shut down.

"Ms. Manzoni, just by breaking in here you've broken a whole hatful of laws. Not to mention attempting to violate the privacy of Billybob Meeks. The police are already on their way. I doubt if I'll be able to get you imprisoned—though I'll have a bloody good try—but I can ensure you'll never work in your field again."

Kate kept up her defiant glower. But she felt her resolve crumble; she knew Hiram had the power to do just that.

Bobby was lying back, relaxed.

She dug an elbow in his ribs. "I don't understand you, Bobby. He's spying on you. Doesn't that bother you?"

Hiram stood over her. "Why should it bother him?"

Through the dazzle she could see sweat gleaming on his bare scalp, his only sign of anger. "I'm his father. What bothers me is *you*, Ms. Manzoni. It's obvious to me you're poisoning my son's mind. Just like—" He stopped himself.

Kate glared back. "Like who, Hiram? His mother?"

But Bobby's hand was on her arm. "Back off, Dad. Kate, he was bound to figure this out sometime. Look, both of you, let's find a win-win solution to this. Isn't that what you always told me, Dad?" He said impulsively, "Don't throw Kate out. Give her a job. Here, at OurWorld."

Hiram and Kate spoke simultaneously.

"Are you *mad*?—"

"Bobby, that's absurd. If you think I'd work for this creep—"

Bobby held his hands up. "Dad, think about it. To exploit the technology you're going to need the best investigative journalists you can find. Right? Even with the WormCam you can't dig out a story without leads."

Hiram snorted. "You're telling me *she* is the best?"

Bobby raised his eyebrows. "She's here, Dad. She found out about the WormCam itself. She even started to use it. And as for you, Kate—"

"Bobby, it will be a cold day in hell—"

"*You know about the WormCam.* Hiram can't let you go with that knowledge. So—don't go. Come work here. You'll have an edge on every other damn reporter on the planet." He looked from one to the other.

Hiram and Kate glared at each other.

Kate said, "I'd insist on finishing my investigation into Billybob Meeks. I don't care what links you have with him, Hiram. The man is a sham, potentially murderous and a drug runner. And—"

Hiram laughed. "You're laying down *conditions*?"

Bobby said, "Dad, please. Just think about it. For me."

Hiram loomed over Kate, his face savage. "Perhaps I have to accept this. But you will not take my son away from me. I hope you understand that." He straightened up, and Kate found herself shivering. "By the way," Hiram said to Bobby, "you were right."

"About what?"

"That I love you. That you should trust me. That everything I have done to you has been for the best."

Kate gasped. "You heard him say that?" But of course he had; Hiram had probably heard everything.

Hiram's eyes were on Bobby. "You do believe me, don't you? Don't you?"

8

SCOOPS

From OurWorld International News Hour, *21 June, 2036:*
Kate Manzoni (to camera):

... The real possibility, revealed exclusively here, of armed conflict between Scotland and England—and therefore, of course, involving the United States as a whole—is the most significant development in what is becoming the central story of our unfolding century: the battle for water.

The figures are stark. Less than one percent of the world's water supply is suitable and accessible for human use. As cities expand, and less land is left available for farming, the demand for water is increasing sharply. In parts of Asia, the Mideast and Africa, the available surface water is already fully used, and groundwater levels have been falling for decades.

Back at the turn of the century ten percent of the world's population did not have enough water to drink. Now that figure has tripled—and it is expected to reach a startling seventy percent by 2050.

We have become used to seeing bloody conflicts over water—for example in China, and over the waters of the Nile, the Euphrates, the Ganges and the Amazon—places where the diminishing resource has to be shared, or where one neighbor is perceived, rightly or wrongly, as having more water than it requires. In this country, there have been calls in Congress for the Administration to put more pressure on the Canadian and Quebecois governments to release more water to the U.S., particularly the desertifying Midwest.

Nevertheless the idea that such conflicts could come to the developed Western world—just to repeat our exclusive revelation, that an armed incursion into Scotland to secure water supplies has been seriously considered by the English state government—comes as a shock. . . .

Angel McKie (v/o): It is night, and nothing is stirring.

This small island, set like a jewel in the Philippine Sea, is only a half kilometer across. And yet, until yesterday, more than a thousand people lived here, crammed into ramshackle dwellings which covered these lowlands as far as the high-tide line of the sea. Even yesterday, children played along the beach you can see here. Now nothing is left. Not even the bodies of the children remain.

Hurricane Antony—the latest to be spun off the apparently permanent El Niño storm which continues to wreak havoc around the Pacific Rim—touched here only briefly, but it was long enough to destroy everything these people had built up over generations.

The sun has yet to rise on this devastation. Not even the rescue crews have arrived yet. These pictures are brought to you exclusively by an Our-World remote news-gathering unit, once again on the scene of breaking news ahead of the rest.

We will return to these scenes when the first aid helicopters arrive—they are due from the mainland any minute now—and in the meantime we can take you to an underwater view of the coral reef here. This was the last remnant of a great community of reefs which lined the Tanon Strait and the southern Negros, most of it long destroyed by dynamite fishing. Now this last survivor, preserved for a generation by devoted experts, has been devastated. . . .

Willoughby Cott (v/o): . . . now we can see that goal again as we ride on Staedler's shoulder with OurWorld's exclusive As-The-Sportsman-Sees-It feature.

You can see the line of defenders ahead of Staedler pushing forward as he approaches, expecting him to make a pass which would leave Cramer offside. But Staedler instead heads away from the wing into deeper midfield, beats one defender, then a second—the goalkeeper doesn't know which threat to counter, Staedler or Cramer—and *here* you can see the gap Staedler spotted, opening up at the near post, and he puts on a burst of acceleration and *shoots!*

And now, thanks to OurWorld's exclusive infield imaging technology, we are riding with the ball as it arcs into that top corner, and the Beijing crowd is ecstatic. . . .

Simon Alcala (v/o): . . . coming up later, we bring you more exclusive behind-the-scenes pictures of Russian Tsarina Irina's visit to a top Johannesburg boutique—and what *was* Madonna's daughter having done to her nose in this exclusive Los Angeles cosmetic-surgery clinic?

OurWorld Paparazzi: we take *you* into the lives of the famous—whether they like it or not!

But first: here's a General Assembly we'd like to see more of! Lunchtime yesterday, UN Secretary-General Halliwell took a break from UNESCO's World Hydrology Initiative conference in Cuba.

Halliwell thought this rooftop garden was secure. And she was right. Well, almost right. The roof is covered by a one-way mirror—it allows in the sun's soothing rays, but keeps out prying eyes. That is, everyone's eyes but ours!

Let's go on down through the roof now—yes, *through* the roof—and there she is, certainly a sight for sore eyes as she enjoys the filtered Caribbean sunlight au naturel. Despite the mirrored roof Halliwell is cautious—you can see here she is covering up as a light plane passes overhead—but she should have known she can't hide from OurWorld!

As you can see Mr. Gravity has been kind to our SecGen; Halliwell is as much a knockout as when she shimmied across the stages of the world all of forty years ago. But the question is—is she still all the original Halliwell, or has she accepted a little help? . . .

9

THE AGENT

When the FBI caught up with Hiram, Kate felt a rush of relief.

She had been happy enough to be scooping the world—but she had been doing that anyhow, with or without WormCams. And she'd become increasingly uncomfortable with the idea that such a powerful technology should be exclusively in the hands of a sleazy megalomaniac capitalist like Hiram Patterson.

As it happened, she was in Hiram's office the day it all came to a head. But it didn't turn out the way she expected.

Kate paced back and forth. She was arguing with Hiram, as usual.

"For God's sake, Hiram. How trivial do you want to get?"

Hiram leaned back in his fake-leather chair and gazed out of the window at downtown Seattle, considering his reply.

Once, Kate knew, this had been the presidential suite of one of the city's better hotels. Though the big picture window remained, Hiram had retained none of the grand trimmings of this room; whatever his faults, Hiram Patterson was not pretentious. The room was now a regular working office, the only furniture the big conference table and its set of upright chairs, a coffee spigot and a water fountain. There was a rumor that Hiram kept a bed here, rolled up in a compartment built into the walls. And yet there was a lack of a human touch, Kate thought. There wasn't even a single image of a family member—his two sons, for instance.

But maybe he doesn't need images, Kate thought sourly. Maybe his sons themselves are trophy enough.

"So," Hiram said slowly, "now you're appointing yourself my bloody conscience, Ms. Manzoni."

"Oh, come on, Hiram. It's not a question of conscience. Look, you have a technological monopoly which is the envy of every other news-gathering organization on the planet. Can't you see how you're wasting it? Gossip about Russian royalty and candid-camera shows and on-the-field shots of soccer games . . . I didn't come into this business to photograph the tits of the UN Secretary-General."

"Those tits, as you put it," he said dryly, "attracted a billion people. My prime concern is beating the competition. And I'm doing that."

"But you're turning yourself into the ultimate papa-razzo. Is that the limit of your vision? You have such—*power*—to do good."

He smiled. " 'Good'? What does good have to do with it? I have to give people what they want, Manzoni. If I don't, some other bastard will. Anyway I don't see what you're complaining about. I ran your piece on England invading Scotland. That was genuine hard-core news."

"But you trivialized it by wrapping it up in tabloid garbage! Just as you trivialize the whole water-war issue. Look, the UN hydrology convention has been a joke—"

"I don't need another lecture on the issues of the day, Manzoni. You know, you're so pompous. But you understand so little. Don't you get it? People don't want to know about *the issues*. Because of you and your damn Wormwood, people understand that *the issues* just don't matter. It doesn't matter how we pump water around the planet, or any of the rest of it, because the Wormwood is going to scrape it all away anyhow. All people want is entertainment. Distraction."

"And that's the limit of your ambition?"

He shrugged. "What else is there to do?"

She snorted her disgust. "You know, your monopoly won't last forever. There's a lot of speculation in the industry and the media about how you're achieving all your scoops. It can't be long before somebody figures it out and repeats your research."

"I have patents—"

"Oh, sure, *that* will protect you. If you keep this up you'll have nothing left to hand on to Bobby."

His eyes narrowed. "Don't you talk about my son. You know, every day I regret bringing you in here, Manzoni. You've brought in some good stories. But you have no sense of balance, no sense at all."

"Balance? Is that what you call it? Using the WormCam for nothing more than celebrity beaver shots?—"

A soft bell tone sounded. Hiram lifted his head to the air. "I said I wasn't to be interrupted."

The Search Engine's inoffensive tones sounded from the air. "I'm afraid I have an override, Mr. Patterson."

"What kind of override?"

"There's a Michael Mavens here to see you. You too, Ms. Manzoni."

"Mavens? I don't know any—"

"He's from the FBI, Mr. Patterson. The Federal Bureau of—"

"I know what the FBI is." Hiram thumped his desk, frustrated. "One bloody thing after another."

At last, Kate thought.

Hiram glared at her. "Just watch what you say to this arsehole."

She frowned. "This government-appointed law-enforcement arsehole from the FBI, you mean? Even you answer to the law, Hiram. I'll say what I think best."

He clenched a fist, seemed ready to say more, then just shook his head. He stalked to his picture window, and the blue light of the sky, filtered through the tinted glass, evoked highlights from his bald pate. "Bloody hell," he said. "Bloody, bloody hell."

Michael Mavens, FBI Special Agent, wore the standard-issue charcoal-gray suit, collarless shirt and shoelace tie. He was blond, whiplash thin, and he looked as if he had played a lot of squash, no doubt at some ultracompetitive FBI academy.

He seemed remarkably young to Kate: no more than mid- to late twenties. And he was nervous, dragging awkwardly at the chair Hiram offered him, fumbling with his briefcase as he opened it and dug out a Soft-Screen.

Kate glanced at Hiram. She saw calculation in his broad, dark face; Hiram had spotted this agent's surprising discomfort too.

After showing them his badge, Mavens said, "I'm glad to find you both here, Mr. Patterson, Ms. Manzoni. I'm investigating an apparent security breach—"

Hiram went on the attack. "What authorization do you have?"

Mavens hesitated. "Mr. Patterson, I'm hoping we can all be a little more constructive than that."

" 'Constructive'?" Hiram snapped. "What kind of answer is that? Are you acting without authorization?" He reached for a telephone icon in his desktop.

Mavens said calmly, "I know your secret."

Hiram's hand hovered over the glowing symbol, then withdrew.

Mavens smiled. "Search Engine. Security cover FBI level three four, authorization Mavens M. K. Confirm please."

After a few seconds, the Search Engine reported back, "Cover in place, Special Agent Mavens."

Mavens nodded. "We can speak openly."

Kate sat down opposite Mavens, intrigued, puzzled, nervous.

Mavens spread his SoftScreen flat on the desktop. It showed a picture of a big white-capped military helicopter. Mavens said, "Do you recognize this?"

Hiram leaned closer. "It's a Sikorsky, I think."

"Actually a VH-3D," said Mavens.

"It's *Marine One*," said Kate. "The President's helicopter."

Mavens eyed her. "That's right. As I'm sure you both know, the President and her husband have spent the last couple of days in Cuba at the UN hydrology conference. They've been using *Marine One* out there. Yesterday, during a short flight, a brief and private conversation took place between President Juarez and English Prime Minister Huxtable." He tapped the 'Screen, and it revealed a blocky schematic of the helicopter's interior. "The Sikorsky is a big bird for such an antique, but it is packed with communication gear. It has only ten seats. Five are taken up by Secret Service agents, a doctor, and military and personal aides to the President."

Hiram seemed intrigued. "I guess one of those aides has the football."

Mavens looked pained. "We don't use a 'football' anymore, Mr. Patterson. On this occasion the other passengers, in addition to President Juarez herself, were Mr. Juarez, the chief of staff, Prime Minister Huxtable and an English security agent.

"All of these people—and the pilots—have the highest possible security clearances, which in the case of the agents and other staff are checked daily. Mr. Huxtable, of course, despite his old-style title, holds an office equivalent to a state governor. *Marine One* itself is swept several times a day. Despite your virtual melodramas about spies and double agents, Mr. Patterson, modern antisurveillance measures are pretty foolproof. And besides, the President and Mr. Huxtable were isolated inside a security curtain even within the Sikorsky. We don't know of any way those various levels of security can be breached." He turned his pale brown eyes on Kate. "And yet, apparently, they were.

"Your news report was accurate, Ms. Manzoni. Juarez and Huxtable did hold a conversation about the possibility of a military solution to England's dispute with Scotland over water supplies.

"But we have testimony from Mr. Huxtable that his speculation about invading Scotland is—was—private and personal. The notion is his, he hadn't committed it to paper or electronic store, or discussed it with anybody—not his Cabinet, not even his partner. His conversation with President Juarez was actually the first time he'd articulated the idea out loud, to gauge the extent of the President's support for such a proposal, if formulated.

"And at the time you broke the story, neither the Prime Minister nor the President had discussed this with anybody else." He glared at Kate. "Ms. Manzoni, you see the situation. *The only possible source for your story is the Juarez-Huxtable conversation itself.*"

Hiram stood beside Kate. "She's not going to reveal her sources to a goon like you."

Mavens rubbed his face and sat back. "I have to tell you, sir, that bugging the Prez is going to land you with a list of federal charges as long as your arm. An interagency team is investigating this matter. And the President is pretty angry herself. OurWorld could be shut down. And you, Ms. Manzoni, will be lucky to evade jail."

"You'll have to prove it first," Hiram blustered. "I can testify that no OurWorld operative has been anywhere near *Marine One*, to plant a bug or to do anything else. This interagency investigation team you run—"

Mavens coughed. "I don't run it. I'm part of it. In fact the Bureau chief himself—"

Hiram's mouth dropped open. "And does he know

you're here? No? Then what *are* you trying to do here, Mavens? Set me up? Or—blackmail? Is that it?"

Mavens looked increasingly uncomfortable, but he sat still.

Kate touched Hiram's arm. "I think we'd better hear him out, Hiram."

Hiram shook her away. He turned to the window, hands caged behind his back, his shoulders working with anger.

Kate leaned toward Mavens. "You said you knew Hiram's secret. What did you mean?"

And Michael Mavens started talking about wormholes.

The map he produced from his briefcase and spread over the table was hand-drawn on unheaded paper. Evidently, Kate thought, Mavens was straying into speculations he hadn't wanted to share with his FBI colleagues, or even commit to the dubious security of a SoftScreen.

He said, "This is a map of the route *Marine One* took yesterday, over the suburbs of Havana. I've marked time points with these crosses. You can see that when the key Juarez-Huxtable onboard conversation took place—it only lasted a couple of minutes—the chopper was *here*."

Hiram frowned, and tapped a hatched box highlighted on the map, right under the Sikorsky's position at the start of the conversation. "And what's this?"

Mavens grinned. "It's yours, Mr. Patterson. That is an OurWorld DataPipe terminal. A wormhole mouth, linking to your central facility here in Seattle. I believe the DataPipe terminal under *Marine One* is the mechanism you used to get your information from the story."

Hiram's eyes narrowed.

Kate listened, but with growing abstraction, as Mavens speculated—a little wildly—about directional microphones and the amplifying effects of the gravitational fields of wormhole mouths. His theory, as it emerged, was that Hiram must be using the fixed DataPipe anchors to perform his bugging.

It was obvious that Mavens had stumbled on some aspects of the truth, but didn't yet have it all.

"Bull," said Hiram evenly. "There are holes in your theory I could fly a 7A7 through."

"Such as," Kate said gently, "OurWorld's ability to get cameras to places where there *is* no DataPipe wormhole terminal. Like those hurricane-struck Philippine islands. Or Secretary-General Halliwell's cleavage."

Hiram glared at Kate warningly. *Shut up.*

Mavens looked confused, but dogged. "Mr. Patterson, I'm no physicist. I haven't yet figured out all the details. But I'm convinced that just as your wormhole technology is your competitive advantage in data transmission, so it must be in your news-gathering operations."

"Oh, come on, Hiram," she said. "He has most of it."

Hiram growled, "Damn it, Manzoni. I told you I wanted plausible deniability at every stage."

Mavens looked inquiringly at Kate.

She said, "He means, cover for the existence of the WormCams."

Mavens smiled. "*WormCams.* I can guess what that means. I knew it."

Kate went on, "But deniability wasn't always possible. And not in this case. You knew it, Hiram, before you approved the story. It was just too good a lead to pass on . . . I think you should tell him what he wants to know."

Hiram glared at her. "Why the hell should I?"

"Because," said Mavens, "I think I can help you."

Mavens stared wide-eyed at David's first wormhole mouth, already a museum piece, the spacetime pearl still embedded in its glass block. "And you don't need anchors. You can plant a WormCam eye *anywhere*, watch *anything.* . . . And you can pick up sound too?"

"Not yet," Hiram said. "But the Search Engine is a pretty good lipreader. And we have human experts to back it up. Now, Special Agent. Tell me how you can help me."

Reluctantly, Mavens set the glass block down on the table. "As Ms. Manzoni deduced, the rest of my team is only a couple of steps behind me. There will probably be a raid on your facilities tomorrow."

Kate frowned. "Then surely you shouldn't be here, tipping us off."

"No, I shouldn't," Mavens said seriously. "Look, Mr. Patterson, Ms. Manzoni, I'll be frank. I'm arrogant enough to believe that on this issue I can see a little more clearly than my superiors, which is why I'm stepping over the mark. Your WormCam technology—even what I was able to deduce about it for myself—is fantastically powerful. And it could do an immense amount of good: bringing criminals to justice, counterespionage, surveillance—"

"If it was in the right hands," Hiram said heavily.

"If it was in the right hands."

"And that means yours. The Bureau's."

"Not just us. But in the public domain, yes. I can't agree with your reporting of the Juarez-Huxtable conversation. But your exposure of the fraudulent science behind the Galveston desalination project, for example, was a masterful piece of journalism. By uncovering that particular scam alone you saved the public purse billions of dollars. I'd like to see responsible news-gathering of that kind continue. But I *am* a servant of the people. And the people—*we*—need the technology too, Mr. Patterson."

"To invade citizens' privacy?" Kate asked.

Mavens shook his head. "Any technology is open to abuse. There would have to be controls. But—you may not believe it, Ms. Manzoni—on the whole we civil servants are pretty clean.

"And we need all the help we can get. These are increasingly difficult times—as you must know, Ms. Manzoni."

"The Wormwood."

"Yes." He frowned, looking troubled. "People seem reluctant to take responsibility for themselves, let alone for others, their community. A rise in crime is being matched by a rise in apathy about it. Presumably this will only grow worse as the years go by, as the Wormwood grows closer."

Hiram seemed intrigued. "But what difference does it make if the Wormwood is going to cream us all anyhow? When I was a kid in England, we grew up believing that when the nuclear war broke out we'd have just four minutes' warning. We used to talk about it. What would you do with *your* four minutes? I'd have got blind drunk and—"

"We have centuries," said Mavens. "Not just minutes. We have a duty to keep society functioning as best we can, as long as possible. What else can we do? And meanwhile—as has been true for decades—this country has more enemies than any nation in the world. National security may have a higher priority over issues of individual rights."

"Tell us what you're proposing," Kate said.

Mavens took a deep breath. "I want to try to set up a deal. Mr. Patterson, this is your technology. You're entitled to profit from it. I'd propose that you'd keep the patents and industry monopoly. But you'd license your technology to the government, to be used in the public interest, under suitably drafted legislation."

Hiram snapped, "You have no authority to offer such a deal."

Mavens shrugged. "Of course not. But this is obviously a sensible compromise, a win-win for all concerned—including the people of this country. I think I could sell it to my immediate superior, and then . . ."

Kate smiled. "You really have risked everything for this, haven't you? It's that important?"

"Yes, ma'am, I believe it is."

Hiram shook his head, wondering. "You bloody kids and your sentimental idealism."

Mavens was watching him. "So what do you say, Mr. Patterson? You want to help me sell this? Or will you wait for the raid tomorrow?"

Kate said, "They'll be grateful, Hiram. In public, anyhow. Maybe *Marine One* will come collect you from the helipad on your lawn so the Prez can pin a medal on your chest. This is a step closer to the center of power."

"For me and my sons," Hiram said.

"Yes."

"And I'd maintain my commercial monopoly?"

"Yes, sir."

Abruptly Hiram grinned. His mood immediately switched as he accepted this defeat and started to revise his plans. "Let's do it, Special Agent." He reached across the table and shook Mavens' hand.

So the secrecy was over; the power the WormCam had granted Hiram would be counterbalanced. Kate felt an immense relief.

But then Hiram turned to Kate, and glared. "This was your foul-up, Manzoni. Your betrayal. I won't forget it."

And Kate—startled, disquieted—knew he meant it.

10

THE GUARDIANS

Extracted from National Intelligence Daily, produced by the Central Intelligence Agency, recipients Top Secret Clearance and Higher, 12 December 2036:

... WormCam technology has proven able to penetrate environments where it is impractical or impossible to send human observers, or even robotic roving cameras. For example, WormCam viewpoints have given scientists a completely safe way to inspect the interior of waste repositories in the Hanford Nuclear Reservation, where for decades plutonium has been spilling into the soil, air and river. WormCams (operated under strict federal-operative supervision) are also being used to inspect deep nuclear waste sites off the coast of Scotland, and to study the cores of the entombed Chernobyl-era reactors which, though long decommissioned, still litter the lands of the old Soviet Union—inspections which have turned up some alarming results (Appendices F-H). ...

... Scientists are seeking approval to use a WormCam to delve without intrusion into a new giant freshwater lake found frozen deep in the Antarctic ice. Ancient, fragile biota have been entombed in such lakes for millions of years. In complete darkness, in water kept liquid by the pressure of hundreds of meters of ice, the trapped species follow their own evolutionary paths, completely distinct from those of surface forms. The scientific arguments appear strong; perhaps this investigation will prove to be truly non-intrusive, and so spare the ancient, fragile life-forms from immediate destruction even as their habitat is breached—as notoriously happened early in the century, when overzealous scientists persuaded international commissions to open up Lake Vostok, the first such frozen world to be discovered. A commission reporting to the President's Science Advisor is considering whether the matter can be progressed, with results being made available for proper scientific peer review, *without* making the WormCam's existence known outside the present restricted circles. . . .

. . . The recent rescue of Australian King Harry and his family from the wreck of their yacht during the Gulf of Carpentaria storms has demonstrated the WormCam's promise to transform the efficacy of emergency services. Search-and-rescue operations at sea, for instance, should no longer require fleets of helicopters sweeping large areas of gray, stormy water at great risk to the crews involved; SAR operatives working in the safety of land-based monitoring centers will be able to pinpoint accident victims in a few minutes, and immediately focus rescue effort—and unavoidable risk—where it is required. . . .

. . . This fundamentalist Christian sect intended to "commemorate" the two thousandth anniversary (as they had calculated it) of Christ's assault on the moneylenders in the Temple by setting off an electromagnetic pulse nuclear warhead in the heart of every major financial district on the planet, including New York, London, Frankfurt and Tokyo. Agency analysts concur with the headline writers that, if successful, the attack would have been an electronic Pearl Harbor. The ensuing financial chaos—with bank transfer networks, stock markets, bond markets, trading systems, credit networks, data communication lines all badly disrupted or destroyed—could, according to analysts, have caused a sufficiently powerful shock to the interdependent global financial systems to trigger a worldwide recession. Largely thanks to the use of WormCam intelligence, that disaster has been avoided. With this one success alone, the deployment of the WormCam in the public interest has saved estimated trillions of dollars and spared untold human misery in poverty, even starvation. . . .

Extracted from "Wormint: The Patterson WormCam as a Tool for Precision Personal Intelligence and Other Applications," by Michael Mavens, FBI; published in Proceedings of Advanced Information Processing and Analysis Steering Group (Intelligence Community), Tyson's Corner, Virginia, 12-14 December, 2036:

WormCams were first introduced on a trial basis to federal agencies under the umbrella of an interagency steering and evaluation group on which I served. The steering group contained representatives from the Food and Drug Administration, the FBI, CIA, the Federal Communications Commission, the Internal Revenue Service and the National Institutes of Health. The power of the technology has quickly become apparent, however, and within six months, before completion of the formal pilot, WormCam capabilities are being rolled out to all the major pillars of our intelligence enterprise, that is the Federal Bureau of Investigation, the Central Intelligence Agency, the Defense Intelligence Agency, the National Security Agency and the National Reconnaissance Office.

What does the WormCam mean for us?

The WormCam—a surveillance technology which can't be tapped or jammed—cuts through the surveillance and encryption arms race we have been waging since, conservatively, the 1940s. Essentially the WormCam bridges directly across space to its subject, and is capable of providing images of unquestionable authenticity—images, for example, which could be reproduced in the courtroom. By comparison no photographic image, however relevant, has been admissible as evidence in a U.S. court of law since 2010, such has been the ease of doctoring such images.

Domestically WormCams have been used for customs and immigration, food and drug testing and inspection, verification of applications to federal positions, and a variety of other purposes. As regards criminal justice, though the drafting of a legal framework regarding privacy rights to cover the WormCam's use in criminal investigations remains pending, FBI and police teams have already been able to score a number of spectacular successes— for example, uncovering the plans of lone anarchist Subiru, F. (incidentally claiming to be a second-generation clone of twentieth-century musician Michael Jackson) to blow up the Washington Monument.

Let me just remark that in 2035 only an estimated one-third of all felonies was reported—and of that third, only a fifth was cleared by arrest and filing of charges. A fifth of a third: that's around seven percent. The balance of the deterrence equation was tipped toward ineffectiveness. Now, though full figures from the trial period are not yet in, we can already say that apprehension rates will be improved by orders of magnitude. Ladies and gentlemen, it may be that we are approaching an age when, for the first time in human history, it can truly be said that crime does not pay. . . .

Now regarding external affairs: in 2035 the gathering and analysis of foreign intelligence cost $75 billion. But much of this intelligence was of little value: our collection systems were electronic suction systems, picking up much chaff along with the wheat. And in an age in which the threats we face—in general emanating from rogue states or terrorist cells—are precision-targeted, it has long been apparent that our intelligence needs to be precision-targeted also. Merely mapping an enemy's military capability, for instance, tells us nothing of his strategic thinking, and still less of his intentions.

But many of our opponents are as sophisticated in technology as we are, and it has proven difficult or impossible to penetrate with conventional electronic means to the heart of their operations. The solution to this has been a renewed reliance on humint—human intelligence, the use of human spies. But these, of course, are difficult to place, notoriously unreliable, and highly vulnerable.

But now we have the WormCam.

A WormCam essentially enables us to locate a remote camera (in technical terms a "viewpoint") *anywhere*, without the need for physical intervention. WormCam intelligence—"wormint," as the insiders are already calling it—is proving so valuable that WormCam posts have been set up to monitor most of the world's political leaders, friendly and otherwise, the leaders of sundry religious and fanatic groups, many of the world's larger corporations, and so on.

WormCam technology is intimate and personal. We can watch an opponent in the most private of acts, if necessary. The potential for exposure of illicit activities, even blackmail if we choose, is obvious. But more important is the picture we are now able to build up of an enemy's intentions. The

WormCam gives us information on an opponent's contacts—for instance weapons suppliers—and we can assess knowledge factors like his religious views, culture, level of education and training, his sources of information, the media outlets he uses.

Ladies and gentlemen, in the past the geography of the physical battlefield was our crucial intelligence target. With the WormCam, the geography of our enemy's mind is opened up. . . .

Before I move on to some specific early successes of the WormCam teams, I want to touch on the future.

The present technology offers us a WormCam which is capable of high-resolution visual-spectrum imaging. Our scientists are working with the OurWorld people to upgrade this technology to allow the capture of nonvisual-spectrum data—particularly infrared, for nighttime working—and sound, by making the WormCam viewpoint sensitive to physical by-products of sound waves, so reducing our present reliance on lipreading. Furthermore, we aim to make the remote viewpoints fully mobile, so we can shadow a target in motion.

WormCam viewpoints are in principle detectable, and federal/OurWorld tiger teams are investigating hypothetical "anticams," ways in which an enemy might detect and perhaps blind a WormCam. This might conceivably be done, for instance, by injecting high-energy particles into a viewpoint, causing the wormhole to implode. But we don't believe that this will be a serious obstacle. Remember, a WormCam placement is not a one-off event, lost on detection. Rather, we can place as many WormCam viewpoints as we like in a given location, whether they are detected or not.

And besides, at present U.S. agencies have a monopoly on this technology. Our opponents know we have achieved a remarkable upgrade in our intelligence-gathering capabilities, but they don't even know how we are doing it. Far from developing capabilities to obstruct a WormCam, they don't yet know what they are looking for.

But, of course, our edge in WormCam technology cannot last forever, nor can the technology remain covert. We must begin to plan for a transformed future in which the WormCam is public knowledge, and our own centers of power and command are as open to our opponents as theirs have become to us. . . .

From OurWorld International News Hour,
28 January, 2037:
Kate Manzoni (to camera):

In an eerie rerun of the Watergate scandal of sixty years ago, White House staff reporting to President Maria Juarez have been publicly accused of burgling the campaign headquarters of the Republican Party, thought to be Juarez's main opponents at the upcoming Presidential election of 2040.

The Republicans have claimed that revelations made by Juarez's people—concerning possible rule-breaking campaign-funding links between the GOP and various high-profile businesspeople—could only be based on information gathered by illegal means, such as a wiretap or a burglary.

The White House in response have challenged the Republicans to produce hard evidence of such an intrusion. Which the GOP has so far failed to do. . . .

11

THE BRAIN STUD

As Kate watched, John Collins flew into Moscow Airport.

At the airport Collins met a younger man. The Search Engine quickly pattern-recognized him as Andrei Popov. Popov, a Russian national, had links to armed insurgency groups operating in all five countries bordering the Aral Sea—Kazakhstan, Uzbekistan, Turkmenistan, Tajikistan and Kyrgyzstan.

Kate was getting closer.

With a growing sense of exhilaration, she flew the WormCam viewpoint alongside Collins and Popov as they traveled across Moscow—by bus, by subway, in cars and by foot, even through a snowstorm. She glimpsed the Kremlin and the old, ugly KGB building, as if this was some virtual tourist adventure.

But the poverty of the place was striking. Despite his choice of profession, Collins was an archetypal American abroad; Kate saw his mounting frustration with mobile phone dropouts, his amazement at seeing subway ticket vendors using abacuses to compute change, his disgust at the filth he encountered in public toilets, his disbelieving impatience when he tried to call up the Search Engine and received no reply.

She felt a profound relief when Collins reached a small suburban Moscow airport and boarded a light plane, and she was able to initiate the system she thought of as the autopilot.

Here in the gloom of the Wormworks, sitting before a SoftScreen, she was flying the viewpoint using a joystick and some intelligent supporting software. Ingenious though the system was, ghosting a person's movements through a foreign city was intense, unforgiving work; a single slip of concentration could unravel hours of labor.

But WormCam tracking technology had advanced to the point where she could hook the remote viewpoint to various electronic signatures—for instance of Collins' aircraft. So now her WormCam viewpoint hovered, all but invisible, in the airplane cabin—still at Collins' shoulder—as the plane lofted into the deepening Russian twilight, tracking her quarry without her intervention.

It ought to get easier. The Wormworks techs were working on ways of having a viewpoint track an individual person without the need for human guidance.... All that for the future.

She pushed back her chair, stood up and stretched. She was more tired than she'd realized; she couldn't remember when she'd last taken a break.

Absently she scanned the continuing WormCam images. Night was falling over central Asia, and through the plane's small windows she could see how the landscape was scarred, swaths of it brown wasteland, still uninhabitable four decades after the fall of the Soviet Union with its ugly contempt for the landscape and its people—

There was a hand on her shoulder, strong thumbs massaging a knot of muscles there. She was startled, but the touch was familiar, and she couldn't help but relax into it.

Bobby kissed the crown of her head. "I knew I'd find you here. Do you know what time it is?"

She glanced at a clock on the SoftScreen. "Late afternoon?"

He laughed. "Yes, Moscow time. But this is Seattle, Washington, western hemisphere, and on this side of the planet it's just after 10 A.M. You worked through the night. Again. I have the feeling you're avoiding me."

She said testily, "Bobby, you don't understand. I'm tracking this guy. It's a twenty-four-hour job. Collins is a CIA operative who seems to be opening up lines of communication between our government and various shadowy insurrectionists in the Aral Sea area. There's something going on out there the Administration doesn't want to tell us about."

"But," Bobby said with mock solemnity, "the WormCam sees all. . . ." He was wearing casual ski-country gear, bright, colorful, thermal-adaptive, very expensive; in the warmth of this corner of the Wormworks, she could see how its artificial pores had opened up, revealing a faint brown sheen of tanned flesh. He leaned toward the SoftScreen, studied the image and her scribbled notes. "How long will Collins' flight take?"

"Hard to say. Hours."

He straightened up. "Then take some time off. Your target is stuck in that plane until it lands, or crashes, and the WormCam can happily track him by itself. And besides he's asleep."

"But he's with Popov. If he wakes up—"

"Then the recording systems will pick up whatever he says and does. Come on. Give yourself a break. And me."

. . . But I don't want to be with you, Bobby, she thought. *Because there are things I'd rather not discuss. And yet . . .*

And yet, she was still drawn to him, despite what she now knew about him.

You're getting too complicated, Kate. Too introverted. A break from this cold, lifeless place will indeed do you good.

Making an effort to smile, she took his hand.

It was a fine, still day, a welcome interval between the storm systems that now habitually battered the Pacific coast.

Cradling beakers of latte, they walked through the garden areas Hiram had built around his Wormworks. There were low earthworks, ponds, bridges over streams, and unfeasibly large and old trees, all of it imported and installed in typical Hiram fashion, thought Kate, at great expense and with little discrimination or taste. But the sky was a clear, brilliant blue, the winter sun actually delivered a little heat to her face, and the two of them were leaving a trail of dark footsteps in the thick silver layer of lingering dew.

They found a bench. It was temperature-smart and had heated itself sufficiently to dry off the dew. They sat down, sipping coffee.

"I still think you've been hiding from me," Bobby said mildly. She saw that his retinal implants had polarized in the sunlight, turning silvery, insectile. "It's the WormCam, isn't it? All the ethical implications you find so disturbing."

With an eagerness that shamed her, she jumped on that lead. "Of course it's disturbing. A technology of such power—"

"But you were there when we came to our agreement with the FBI. An agreement that put the WormCam in the hands of the people."

"Oh, Bobby . . . *The people* don't even know the damn thing exists, let alone that government agencies are using it against them. Look at all the tax defaulters that suddenly got caught, the parents cheating on child support, the Brady Law checks on gun buyers, the serial sex offenders."

"But that's all for the good. Isn't it? What are you saying—that you don't trust the government? This isn't the twentieth century."

She grunted. "Remember what Jefferson said: 'Every government degenerates when trusted to the rulers of the people alone. The people themselves therefore are its only safe depositories.' . . . And what about the Republican burglary? How can *that* be in the people's interest?"

"You can't know for sure that the White House used the WormCam for that."

"How else?" Kate shook her head. "I wanted Hiram to let me dig into that. He threw me off the case immediately. We've made a Faustian bargain, Bobby. Those guys in the Administration and the government agencies aren't necessarily crooks, but they're only human. And by giving them such a powerful and secret weapon—Bobby, I wouldn't trust *myself* with such power. The Republican spying incident is just the start of the Orwellian nightmare we're about to endure.

"And as for Hiram—have you *any* idea how Hiram treats his employees, here at OurWorld? Job applicants go through screening all the way to a DNA sequence. He profiles all his employees by searching credit databases, police records, even federal records. He already had a hundred ways to measure productivity and performance, and check up on his people. Now he has the WormCam, Hiram can keep us under surveillance twenty-four hours a day if he chooses. And there's not a damn thing any of us can do about it. There have been a whole string of court cases that establish that employees don't have constitutional protection against intrusive surveillance by their bosses."

"But he needs all that to keep the people working," Bobby said dryly. "Since you broke the Wormwood, absenteeism has rocketed, and the use of alcohol and other drugs at work, and—"

"This has nothing to do with the Wormwood," she said severely. "This is a question of basic rights. Bobby, don't you get it? *OurWorld is a vision of the future for all of us*—if monsters like Hiram get to keep the WormCam. And *that's* why it's important the technology is disseminated, as far and as fast as possible. Reciprocity: at least we'd be able to watch them watching us. . . ." She searched his insectile, silvery gaze.

He said evenly, "Thanks for the lecture. And is that why you're dumping me?"

She looked away.

"It's nothing to do with the WormCam, is it?" He leaned forward, challenging her. "There's something you don't want to tell me. You've been this way for days. Weeks, even. What is it, Kate? Don't be afraid of hurting me. You won't."

Probably not, she thought. And that, poor, dear Bobby, is the whole trouble.

She turned to face him. "Bobby, the stud. The implant Hiram put in your head when you were a boy—"

"Yes?"

"I found out what it's for. What it's *really* for."

The moment stretched, and she felt the sunlight prickle on her face, laden with UV even so early in the year.

"Tell me," he said quietly.

The Search Engine's specialist routines had explained it all to her succinctly. It was a classic piece of early twenty-first-century neurobiological mind-tinkering.

And it had nothing to do with any dyslexia or hyperactivity, as Hiram had claimed.

First, Hiram had suppressed the neural stimulation of areas in the temporal lobe of Bobby's brain that were related to feelings of spiritual transcendence and mystical presence. And his doctors tinkered with parts of the caudate region, trying to ensure that Bobby did not suffer from symptoms relating to obsessive-compulsive disorder which led some people to a need for excessive security, order, predictability and ritual—a need in some circumstances satisfied by the membership of religious communities.

Hiram had evidently intended to shield Bobby from the religious impulses that had so distracted his brother. Bobby's world was to be mundane, earthy, bereft of the transcendent and the numinous. And he wouldn't even know what he was missing. It was, Kate thought sourly, a Godectomy.

Hiram's implant also tinkered with the elaborate interplay of hormones, neurotransmitters and brain regions which were stimulated when Bobby made love. For example, the implant suppressed the opiate-like hormone oxytocin, produced by the hypothalamus, which flooded the brain during orgasm, producing the warm, floating, bonding feelings that followed such acts.

Thanks to a series of high-profile liaisons—which Hiram had discreetly set up and encouraged and even publicized—Bobby had become something of a sexual athlete, and he derived great physical pleasure from the act itself. But his father had made him incapable of love—and so, Hiram seemed to have planned, free of loyalties to anyone but his father.

There was more. For instance, a link to the deep portion of Bobby's brain called the amygdala may have been an attempt to control his propensity for anger. A mysterious manipulation of Bobby's orbito-frontal cortex might even have been a bid to reduce his free will. And so on.

Hiram had reacted to his disappointment with David by making Bobby a perfect son: that is, perfectly suited to Hiram's goals. But by doing this Hiram had robbed his son of much that made him human.

Until Kate Manzoni found the switch in his head.

She took Bobby back to the small apartment she'd rented in downtown Seattle. There they made love, for the first time in weeks.

Afterward, Bobby lay in her arms, hot, his skin moist under hers where they touched: as close as he could be, yet still remote. It was like trying to love a stranger.

But at least, now, she understood why.

She reached up and touched the back of his head, the hard edges of the implant under his skin. "You're sure you want to do this?"

He hesitated. "What troubles me is that I don't know how I'll be feeling afterwards . . . Will I still be *me*?"

She whispered in his ear. "You'll feel alive. You'll feel *human*."

He held his breath, then said, so quietly she could barely make it out: "Do it."

She turned her head. "Search Engine."

"Yes, Kate."

"Turn it off."

. . . and for Bobby, still warm with the afterglow of orgasm, it was as if the woman in his arms had suddenly turned three-dimensional, solid and whole, had come to life. Everything he could see, feel, smell—the warm ash scent of her hair, the exquisite line of her cheek where the low light caught it, the seamless smoothness of her belly—it was all just as it had been before. But it was as if he had reached through that surface texture into the warmth of Kate herself. He saw her eyes, watchful, full of concern—concern for *him*, he realized with a fresh jolt. He wasn't alone anymore. And, before now, he hadn't even known he had been.

He wanted to immerse himself in her oceanic warmth.

She touched his cheek. He could see that her fingers came away wet.

And now he could feel the great shuddering sobs that racked his body, an uncontrollable storm of weeping. Love and pain coursed through him, exquisite, hot, unbearable.

12

SPACETIME

The inner chaos didn't subside.

He tried to distract himself. He resumed activities he had relished before. But even the most extravagant virtual adventure seemed shallow, obviously artificial, predictable, unengaging.

He seemed to need people, even though he shied away from those close to him—he was a moth fearing the candle flame, he thought, unable to bear the brightness of the emotions involved. So he accepted invitations he wouldn't otherwise have considered, talked to people he had never needed before.

Work helped, with its constant and routine demands for his attention, its relentless logic of meetings and schedules and resource allocation.

And it was a busy time. The new Mind'sEye VR headbands were moving out of the testing labs and approaching production status. His teams of technicians had, suddenly, resolved a last technical glitch: a tendency for the headbands to cause synaesthesia in their users, a muddling of the sensory inputs caused by cross talk between the brain's centers. It was a cause for long celebration. They knew that IBM's renowned Watson research lab had been working on exactly the same problem; whoever cracked the synaesthesia issue first would be the first to reach the market, and would have a clear competitive edge for a long time to come. It now looked as if OurWorld had won that particular race.

So work was absorbing. But he couldn't work twenty-four hours a day, and he couldn't sleep the rest of the time away. And when he was awake, his mind, unleashed for the first time, was rampaging out of control.

As his car's SmartDrove him to the Wormworks, he cowered in fear from the high-speed traffic. An unremarkable tabloid news item—about vicious killings and rapes in the burgeoning Aral Sea water war—moved him to harsh tears. A Puget Sound sunset, glimpsed through a broken layer of fluffy black clouds, filled him with awe simply at being alive.

When he met his father, fear, loathing, love, admiration tore at him—all overlying a deeper, unbreakable bond.

But he could face Hiram. Kate was different. The surging need he felt—to cherish her, possess her, somehow consume her—was completely overwhelming. In her company he became inarticulate, as out of control of his mind as much as his body.

Somehow she knew how he was feeling; and, quietly, she left him alone. He knew she would be there for him when he was ready to face her, and resume their relationship.

But at least with Hiram and Kate he could figure out *why* he felt the way he did, trace a causal relationship, put tentative labels to the violent emotions that rocked him. The worst of all were the mood swings he seemed to suffer without discernible cause.

He would wake up crying without reason. Or, in the middle of a mundane day, he would find himself filled with an indescribable joy, as if everything suddenly made sense.

His life *before* seemed remote, textureless, like a flat, colorless pencil sketch. Now he was immersed in a new world of color and texture and light and feeling, where the simplest things—the curl of an early spring leaf, the glimmer of sunlight on water, the smooth curve of

Kate's cheek—could be suffused by a beauty he had never known existed.

And Bobby—the fragile ego that rode on the surface of this dark inner ocean—would have to learn to live with the new, complex, baffling person he had suddenly become.

That was why he had come to seek out his brother.

He took great comfort from David's stolid, patient presence: this bearlike figure with his bushy blond hair, hunched over his SoftScreens, immersed in his work, satisfied with its logic and internal consistency, scribbling notes with a surprising delicacy. David's personality was as massive and solid as his body; beside him Bobby felt evanescent, a wisp, yet subtly calmed.

One unseasonably cold afternoon they sat cradling coffees, waiting for the results of another routine trial run: a new wormhole plucked out of the quantum foam, extending further than any had before.

"I can understand a theorist wanting to study the limits of the wormhole technology," Bobby said. "Pushing the envelope as far as you can. But we made the big breakthrough already. Surely what's important now is the application."

"Of course," David said mildly. "In fact the application is everything. Hiram has a goal of turning wormhole generation from a high-energy physics stunt, affordable only by governments and large corporations, into something much smaller, easily manufactured, miniaturized."

"Like computers," Bobby said.

"Exactly. It wasn't until miniaturization and the development of the PC that computers were able to saturate the world: finding new applications, creating new markets—transforming our lives, in fact.

"Hiram knows we won't keep our monopoly forever. Sooner or later somebody else is going to come up with an independent WormCam design. Maybe a better one.

And miniaturization and cost reduction are sure to follow."

"And the future for OurWorld," said Bobby, "is surely to be the market leader, all those little wormhole generators."

"That's Hiram's strategy," David said. "He has a vision of the WormCam replacing *every* other data-gathering instrument: cameras, microphones, science sensors, even medical probes. Although I can't say I'm looking forward to a wormhole endoscopy. . . .

"But I told you I studied a little business myself, Bobby. Mass-produced WormCams will be a commodity, and we will be able to compete only on price. But I believe that with our technical lead Hiram can open up much greater opportunities for himself with differentiation: by coming up with applications which *nobody* else in the market can offer. And that's what I'm interested in exploring." He grinned. "At least, that's what I tell Hiram his money is being spent on down here."

Bobby studied him, trying to focus on his brother, on Hiram, the WormCam, trying to understand. "You just want to *know*, don't you? That's the bottom line for you."

David nodded. "I suppose so. Most science is just grunt work. Repetitive slog; endless testing and checking. And because false hypotheses have to be pruned away, much of the work is actually more destructive than constructive. But, occasionally—only a few times, probably, in the luckiest life—there is a moment of transcendence."

"Transcendence?"

"Not everybody will put it like that. But it's how it feels to me."

"And it doesn't matter that there might be nobody to read your papers in five hundred years' time?"

"I'd rather that wasn't true. Perhaps it won't be. But the revelation itself is the thing, Bobby. It always was."

On the 'Screen behind him there was a starburst of pixels, and a low bell-like tone sounded.

David sighed. "But not today, it seems."

Bobby peered over his brother's shoulder at the 'Screen, across which numbers were scrolling. "Another instability? It's like the early days of the wormholes."

David tapped at a keyboard, setting up another trial. "Well, we are being a little more ambitious. Our WormCams can already reach every part of the Earth, crossing distances of a few thousand kilometers. What I'm attempting now is to extract and stabilize wormholes which span significant intervals in Minkowski space-time—in fact, tens of light-minutes."

Bobby held up his hands. "You already lost me. A light-minute is the distance light travels in a minute . . . right?"

"Yes. For example, the planet Saturn is around a billion and a half kilometers away. And that is about eighty light-minutes."

"And we want to see Saturn."

"Of course we do. Wouldn't it be wonderful to have a WormCam that could explore deep space? No more ailing probes, no more missions lasting years . . . But the difficulty is that wormholes spanning such large intervals are extremely rare in the quantum foam's probabilistic froth. And stabilizing them presents challenges an order of magnitude more difficult than before. But it's not impossible."

"Why 'intervals,' not distances?"

"Physicist jargon. Sorry. An interval is like a distance, but in space*time*. Which is space plus time. It's really just Pythagoras' theorem." He took a yellow legal notepad and began to scribble. "Suppose you go downtown and walk a few blocks east, a few blocks north. Then you can figure the distance you traveled like this." He held up the pad:

(distance) squared = (east) squared + (north) squared

"You walked around a right-angled triangle. The square of the hypotenuse is equal to the sum of—"

"I know that much."

"But we physicists think about space *and* time as a single entity, with time as a fourth coordinate, in addition to the three of space." He wrote on his pad once more:

$$\text{(interval) squared} = \text{(time separation) squared} - \text{(space separation) squared}$$

"This is called the metric for a Minkowski spacetime. And—"

"How can you talk about a separation in *time* in the same breath as a separation in *space*? You measure time in minutes, but space in kilometers."

David nodded approvingly. "Good question. You have to use units in which time and space are made equivalent." He studied Bobby, evidently searching for understanding. "Let's just say that if you measure time in minutes, and space in light-minutes, it works out fine."

"But there's something else fishy here. Why is this a minus sign rather than a plus?"

David rubbed his fleshy nose. "A map of spacetime doesn't work quite like a map of downtown Seattle. The metric is designed so that the path of a photon—a particle traveling at the speed of light—is a null interval. The interval is zero, because the space and time terms cancel out."

"This is relativity. Something to do with time dilation, and rulers contracting, and—"

"Yes." David patted Bobby's shoulder. "Exactly that. This metric is invariant under the Lorentz transformation . . . Never mind. The point is, Bobby, this is the kind of equation I have to use when I work in a relativistic universe, and certainly if I'm trying to build a wormhole that reaches out to Saturn and beyond."

Bobby mused over the simple, handwritten equation.

With his own emotional whirlwind still churning around him, he felt a cold logic coursing through him, numbers and equations and images evolving, as if he was suffering from some kind of intellectual synaesthesia. He said slowly, "David, you're telling me that distances in space and time are somehow equivalent. Right? Your wormholes span intervals of spacetime rather than simply distances. And *that* means that if you do succeed in stabilizing a wormhole big enough to reach Saturn, across eighty light-minutes—"

"Yes?"

"Then it could reach across eighty *minutes*. I mean, across time." He stared at David. "Am I being really dumb?"

David sat in silence for long seconds.

"Good God," he said slowly. "I didn't even consider the possibility. I've been configuring the wormhole to span a spacelike interval, without even thinking about it." Feverishly, he began to tap at his SoftScreen. "I can reconfigure it from right here. If I restrict the spacelike interval to a couple of meters, then the rest of the wormhole span is forced to become timelike. . . ."

"What would that mean? David?"

A buzzer rang, painfully loudly, and the Search Engine spoke. "Hiram would like to see you, Bobby."

Bobby glanced at David, flooded with sudden, absurd fear.

David nodded curtly, already absorbed in the new direction of his work. "I'll call you later, Bobby. This could be significant. Very significant."

There was no reason to stay. Bobby walked away into the darkness of the Wormworks.

Hiram paced around his downtown office, visibly angry, fists clenched. Kate was sitting at Hiram's big conference table, looking small, cowed.

Bobby hesitated at the door, for a few breaths physically unable to force himself into the room, so strong were the emotions churning here. But Kate was looking at him—forcing a smile, in fact.

He walked into the room. He reached the security of a seat, on the opposite side of the table from Kate.

Bobby quailed, unable to speak.

Hiram glared at him. "You let me down, you little shit."

Kate snapped, "For Christ's sake, Hiram—"

"You keep out of this." Hiram thumped the tabletop, and a SoftScreen in the plastic surface lit up before Bobby. It started to run fragments of a news story: images of Bobby, a younger Hiram, a girl—pretty, timid-looking, dressed in colorless, drab, outdated fashions—and a picture of the same woman two decades later, intelligent, tired, handsome. The Earth News Online logo was imprinted on each image.

"They found her, Bobby," Hiram said. "Thanks to you. Because you couldn't keep your bloody mouth shut, could you?"

"Found who?"

"Your mother."

Kate was working the SoftScreen before her, scrolling quickly through the information. "*Heather Mays.* Is that her name? She married again. She has a daughter—you have a half-sister, Bobby."

Hiram's voice was a snarl. "Keep out of this, you manipulative bitch. Without you none of this would have happened."

Bobby, striving for control, said, "None of *what*?"

"Your implant would have stayed doing what it was doing. Keeping you steady and happy. Christ, I wish somebody had put a thing like that in my head when I was your age. Would have saved me a hell of a lot of trouble. And you wouldn't have shot off your mouth in front of Dan Schirra."

"Schirra? From ENO?"

"Except he didn't call himself that, when he met you

last week. What did he do, get you drunk and maudlin, blubbing about your evil father, your long-lost mother?"

"I remember," Bobby said. "He calls himself Mervyn. Mervyn Costa. I've known him a long time."

"Of course you have. He's been cultivating you, on behalf of ENO, to get to *me*. You didn't know who he was, but you kept your reserve—*before*, when you had the implant to help you keep a clear head. And now *this*. It's open season on Hiram Patterson. And it's all your bloody fault, Manzoni."

Kate was still scrolling through the news piece and its hyperlinks. "*I* didn't screw and dump this woman two decades ago." She tapped at her SoftScreen, and an area of the table before Hiram lit up. "Schirra has corroborative evidence. Look."

Bobby looked over his father's shoulder. The 'Screen showed Hiram sitting at a table—this table, Bobby realized with a jolt, *this* room—and he was working his way through a mound of papers, amending and signing. The image was grainy, unsteady, but clear enough. Hiram came to a particular document, shook his head as if in disgust, and hastily signed it, turning it facedown on a pile to his right.

After that the image reran in slo-mo, and the viewpoint zoomed in on the document. After some focusing and image enhancement, it was possible to read some of the text.

"You see?" Kate said. "Hiram, they caught you signing an update of the payoff agreement you made with Heather more than twenty years ago."

Hiram looked at Bobby, almost pleading. "It was over long ago. We came to a settlement. I helped her develop her career. She makes documentary features. She's been successful."

"She was a brood mare, Bobby," Kate said coldly. "He's kept up his payments to keep her quiet. And to make sure she never tried to get near to you."

Hiram prowled around the room, hammering at the

walls, glaring at the ceiling. "I have this suite swept three times a day. How did they get those images? Those incompetent arseholes in Building Security have screwed up again."

"Come on, Hiram," Kate said evenly, evidently enjoying herself. "Think about it. There's no way ENO could bug your headquarters. Any more than you could bug theirs."

"But I wouldn't need to bug them," Hiram said slowly. "I have the WormCam . . . *Oh.*"

"Well done." Kate grinned. "You figured it out. *ENO must have a WormCam as well.* It's the only way they could have achieved this scoop. You lost your monopoly, Hiram. And the first thing they did with their WormCam was turn it on you." She threw back her head and laughed out loud.

"My God," Bobby said. "What a disaster."

"Oh, garbage," she snapped. "Come on, Bobby. Pretty soon the whole world will know the WormCam exists; it won't be possible to keep a lid on it any longer. It has to be a good thing if the WormCam is prized out of the hands of this sick duopoly, the federal government and Hiram Patterson, for God's sake."

Hiram said coldly, "If Earth News have WormCam technology, it's obvious who gave it to them."

Kate looked puzzled. "Are you implying that *I*—"

"Who else?"

"I'm a journalist," Kate flared. "I'm no spy. The hell with you, Hiram. It's obvious what happened. ENO just figured out that you must have found a way to adapt your wormholes as remote viewers. With that basic insight they duplicated your researches. It wouldn't be hard; most of the information is in the public domain. Hiram, your hold on the WormCam was always fragile. It only took one person to figure it out independently."

But Hiram didn't seem to be hearing her. "I forgave you, took you in. You took my money. You betrayed my trust. You damaged my son's mind and poisoned him against me."

Kate stood and faced Hiram. "If you really believe that, you're more twisted than I thought you were."

The Search Engine called softly, "Excuse me, Hiram. Michael Mavens is here, asking to see you. Special Agent Mavens of—"

"Tell him to wait."

"I'm afraid that isn't an option, Hiram. And I have a call from David. He says it's urgent."

Bobby looked from one face to the other, frightened, bewildered, as his life came to pieces around him.

Mavens took a seat and opened a briefcase.

Hiram snapped, "What do you want, Mavens? I didn't expect to see you again. I thought the deal we signed was comprehensive."

"I thought so too, Mr. Patterson." Mavens looked genuinely disappointed. "But the problem is, you didn't stick to it. OurWorld as a corporation. One employee specifically. And that's why I'm here. When I heard this case had turned up, I asked if I could become involved. I suppose I have a special interest."

Hiram said heavily, "What case?"

Mavens picked up what looked like a charge sheet from his briefcase. "The bottom line is that a charge of trade-secret misappropriation, under the 1996 Economic Espionage Act, has been brought against OurWorld: by IBM, specifically by the director of their Thomas J. Watson research laboratory. Mr. Patterson, we believe the WormCam has been used to gain illegal access to IBM proprietary research results. Something called a synaesthesia-suppression software suite, associated with virtual-reality technology." He looked up. "Does that make sense?"

Hiram looked at Bobby.

Bobby sat transfixed, overwhelmed by conflicting

emotions, with no real idea how he should react, what he should say.

Kate said, "You have a suspect, don't you, Special Agent?"

The FBI man eyed her steadily, sadly. "I think you already know the answer to that question, Ms. Manzoni."

Kate appeared confused.

Bobby snapped, "You mean Kate? That's ridiculous."

Hiram thumped a fist into a palm. "I knew it. I knew she was trouble. But I didn't think she'd go this far."

Mavens sighed. "I'm afraid there's a very clear evidentiary trail leading to you, Ms. Manzoni."

Kate flared. "If it's there, it was planted."

Mavens said, "You'll be placed under arrest. I hope there won't be any trouble. If you'll sit quietly, the Search Engine will read you your rights."

Kate looked startled as a voice—inaudible to the rest of them—began to sound in her ears.

Hiram was at Bobby's side. "Take it easy, son. We'll get through this shit together. What were you trying to do, Manzoni? Find another way to get to Bobby? Is that what it was all about?" Hiram's face was a grim mask, empty of emotion: there was no trace of anger, pity, relief—or triumph.

And the door was flung open. David stood there, grinning, his bearlike bulk filling the frame; he held a rolled-up SoftScreen in one hand. "I did it," he said. "By God, I did it. . . . What's happening here?"

Mavens said, "Doctor Curzon, it may be better if—"

"It doesn't matter. Whatever you're doing, it doesn't matter. Not compared to *this*." He spread his SoftScreen on the tabletop. "As soon as I got it I came straight here. *Look* at this."

The SoftScreen showed what looked superficially like a rainbow, reduced to black and white and gray, uneven bands of light that arced, distorted, across a black background.

"Of course it's somewhat grainy," David said. "But

still, this picture is equivalent to the quality of images returned by NASA's first flyby probes back in the 1970s."

"That's Saturn," Mavens said, wondering. "The planet Saturn."

"Yes. We're looking at the rings." David grinned. "I established a WormCam viewpoint all of a billion and a half kilometers away. Quite a thing, isn't it? If you look closely you can even see a couple of the moons, here in the plane of the rings."

Hiram laughed out loud and hugged David's bulk. "My God, that's bloody terrific."

"Yes. Yes, it is. But that's not important. Not anymore."

"*Not important*? Are you kidding?"

Feverishly David began to tap at his SoftScreen; the image of Saturn's rings dissolved. "I can reconfigure it from here. It's as easy as that. It was Bobby who gave me the clue. I just hadn't thought out of the box as he did. If I restrict the spacelike interval to a couple of meters, then the rest of the wormhole span becomes timelike. . . ."

Bobby leaned forward to see. The 'Screen now showed an equally grainy image of a much more mundane scene. Bobby recognized it immediately: it was David's work cubicle in the Wormworks. David was sitting there, his back to the viewpoint, and Bobby was standing at his side, looking over his shoulder.

"As easily as that," David said again, his voice small, awed. "Of course we'll have to run repeatable trials, properly timed—"

Hiram said, "That's just the Wormworks. So what?"

"You don't understand. This new wormhole has the same, umm, *length* as the other."

"The one that reached to Saturn."

"Yes. But instead of spanning eighty light-minutes—"

Mavens finished it for him. "I get it. This wormhole spans eighty minutes."

"Yes," David said. "*Eighty minutes into the past*. Look, Father. You're seeing me and Bobby, just before you summoned him away."

Hiram's mouth had dropped open.

Bobby felt as if the world was swimming around him, changing, configuring into some strange, unknowable pattern, as if another chip in his head had been switched off. He looked at Kate, who seemed diminished, terrified, lost in shock.

But Hiram, his troubles dismissed, grasped the implications immediately. He glared into the air. "I wonder how many of them are watching us right now?"

Mavens said, "Who?"

"In the future. Don't you see? If he's right this is a turning point in history, this moment, right here and right now, the invention of this, this *past viewer*. Probably the air around us is fizzing with WormCam viewpoints, sent back by future historians. Biographers. Hagiographers." He lifted up his head and bared his teeth. "Are you watching me? Are you? Do you remember my name? I'm Hiram Patterson! Hah! See what I did, you arse-holes!"

And in the corridors of the future, innumerable watchers met his challenging gaze.

TWO

THE EYES OF GOD

History . . . is indeed little more than a chronicle of the crimes, follies and misfortunes of mankind.

—*Edward Gibbon (1737–1794)*

13

WALLS OF GLASS

Kate was in remand, waiting for her trial. It was taking a while to come to court, as it was a complex case—and Hiram's lawyers had argued, in confidence through the FBI, that her trial should be delayed anyhow while the new past-viewing capabilities of WormCam technology stabilized.

In fact, such had been the wide publicity surrounding Kate's case that the ruling was being taken as a precedent. Even before its past-viewing possibilities were widely understood, the WormCam was expected to have an immediate impact on almost all contested criminal cases. Many major trials had been delayed or paused awaiting new evidence, and in general only minor and uncontested cases were being processed through the courts.

For a long time to come, whatever the outcome of the case, Kate wouldn't be going anywhere.

So Bobby decided to go find his mother.

Heather Mays lived in a place called Thomas City, close to the Utah-Arizona state line. Bobby flew into Cedar City and drove from there. At Thomas, he stopped the car a few blocks short of Heather's home and walked.

A police car silently cruised by, and a beefy male cop peered out at Bobby. The cop's face was a broad, hostile moon, scarred by the pits of multiple basal-cell carcinomas. But his glare softened with recognition. Bobby could read his lips: *Good day, Mr. Patterson.*

As the car moved on, Bobby felt a shiver of self-consciousness. The WormCam had made Hiram the most famous person on the planet, and in the all-seeing public eye, Bobby stood right at his side.

He knew, in fact, that as he approached his mother's home a hundred WormCam viewpoints must hover at his shoulder even now, gazing into his face at this difficult moment, invisible emotional vampires.

He tried not to think about it: the only possible defense against the WormCam. He walked on through the heart of the little town.

Out-of-season April snow was falling on the roofs and gardens of clapboard houses that might have been preserved for a hundred years. He passed a small pond where children were skating, round and round in tight circles, laughing loudly. Even under the pale wintry sun, the children wore sunglasses and silvery, reflective smears of sunblock.

Thomas was a settled, peaceful, anonymous place, one of hundreds like it, he supposed, here in the huge empty heart of America. It was a place that, three months ago, he would have regarded as deadly dull; if he'd ever found himself here he probably would have hightailed it for Vegas as soon as possible. And yet now he found himself wondering how it would have been to grow up here.

As he watched the cop car pass slowly along the street, he noticed a strange flurry of petty law-breaking following in its wake. A man emerging from a sushi-burger store crumpled the paper his food had been wrapped in and dropped it to the floor, right under the cops' noses. At a crossing, an elderly woman jaywalked, glaring challengingly through the cops' windscreen. And so on. The cops watched tolerantly. And as soon as the car had passed, the people, done with thumbing their

noses at the authorities, resumed their apparently lawful
lives.

This was a widespread phenomenon. There had been
a surprisingly wide-ranging, if muted, rebellion against
the new regime of invisible WormCam overseers. The
idea of the authorities having such immense powers of
oversight did not, it seemed, sit well with the instincts
of many Americans, and there had been rises in petty-
crime rates all over the country. Otherwise law-abiding
people seemed suddenly struck by a desire to perform
small illegal acts—littering, jaywalking—as if to prove
they were still free, despite the authorities' assumed
scrutiny. And local cops were learning to be tolerant of
this.

It was just a token, of liberties defended. But Bobby
supposed it was healthy.

He reached the main street. Animated images on tabloid vending machines urged him to download their latest news, for just ten dollars a shot. He eyed the
seductive headlines. There was some serious news, local,
national and international—it seemed that the town was
getting over an outbreak of cholera, related to stress on
the water supply, and was having some trouble assimi-
lating its quota of sea-level-rise relocates from Galveston
Island—but the serious stuff was mostly swamped by
tabloid trivia.

A local member of Congress had been forced out of
office by a WormCam exposure of sexual peccadilloes.
She had been caught pressuring a high-school football
hero, sent to Washington as a reward for his sporting
achievements, into another form of athletics. . . . But the
boy had been over the age of consent; as far as Bobby
was concerned the Representative's main crime, in this
dawning age of the WormCam, was stupidity.

Well, she wasn't the only one. It was said that twenty
percent of members of Congress, and almost a third of
the Senate, had announced they would not be seeking
reelection, or would retire early, or had just resigned

outright. Some commentators estimated that fully half of all America's elected officials might be forced out of office before the WormCam became embedded in the national, and individual, consciousness.

Some said this was a good thing—that people were being frightened into decency. Others pointed out that most humans had moments they would prefer not to share with the rest of mankind. Perhaps in a couple of electoral cycles the only survivors among those in office, or prepared to run for office, would be the pathologically dull with no personal lives to speak of at all.

No doubt the truth, as usual, would be somewhere between the extremes.

There was still some coverage of last week's big story: the attempt by unscrupulous White House aides to discredit a potential opponent of President Juarez at the next election campaign. They had WormCammed him sitting on the john with his trousers down his ankles, picking his nose and extracting fluff from his navel.

But this had rebounded on the voyeurs, and had done no damage to Governor Beauchamp at all. After all, everybody had to use the john; and probably nobody, no matter how obscure, did so now without wondering if there was a WormCam viewpoint looking down (or, worse, *up*) at her.

Even Bobby had taken to using the lavatory in the dark. It wasn't easy, even with the new easy-use touch-textured plumbing that was rapidly becoming common-place. And he sometimes wondered if there was anybody in the developed world who still had sex with the lights on. . . .

He doubted that even the supermarket-tabloid vendors would persist with such paparazzi exposure as the shock value wore off. It was telling that these images, which would have been shockingly revealing just a few months ago, now blared multicolored in the middle of the afternoon from stands in the main street of this Mormon community, unregarded by almost everyone, young and old, children and churchgoers alike.

It seemed to Bobby that the WormCam was forcing the human race to shed a few taboos, to grow up a little.

He walked on.

The Mayses' home was easy to find. Before this otherwise nondescript house, in a nondescript residential street, here in the middle of classic small-town America, he found the decades-old symbol of fame or notoriety: a dozen or so news crews, gathered before the white-painted picket fence that bordered the garden. Instant-access WormCam technology or not, it was going to take a long time before the news-watching public was weaned off the interpretative presence of a reporter interposing herself before some breaking news story.

Bobby's arrival, of course, was a news event in itself. Now the journalists came running toward him, drone cameras bobbing above them like angular, metallic balloons, snapping questions. *Bobby, this way please . . . Bobby . . . Bobby, is it true this is the first time you've seen your mother since you were three years old? . . . Is it true your father doesn't want you here, or was that scene in the OurWorld boardroom just a setup for the WormCams? . . . Bobby . . . Bobby . . .*

Bobby smiled, as evenly as he could manage. The reporters didn't try to follow him as he opened the small gate and walked through the fence. After all, there was no need; no doubt a thousand WormCam viewpoints were trailing him even now.

He knew there was no point asking for respect for his privacy. There was no choice, it seemed, but to endure. But he felt that unseen gaze, like a tangible pressure on the back of his neck.

And the eeriest thought of all was that among this clustering invisible crowd there might be watchers from the unimaginable future, peering back along the tunnels of time to this moment. What if *he himself*, a future Bobby, was among them? . . .

But he must live the rest of his life, despite this assumed scrutiny.

He rapped on the door and waited, with gathering nervousness. No WormCam, he supposed, could watch the way his heart was pumping; but surely the watching millions could see the set of his jaw, the drops of perspiration he could feel on his brow despite the cold.

The door opened.

It had taken some persuading for Bobby to get Hiram to give his blessing to this meeting.

Hiram had been seated alone at his big mahogany-effect desk, before a mound of papers and SoftScreens. He sat hunched over, defensively. He had developed a habit of glancing around, flicking his gaze through the air, searching for WormCam viewpoints like a mouse in fear of a predator.

"I want to see her," Bobby had said. "Heather Mays. My mother. I want to go meet her."

Hiram looked as exhausted and uncertain as at any time Bobby could remember. "It would be a mistake. What good would it do you?"

Bobby hesitated. "I don't know. I don't know how it feels to have a mother."

"She isn't your mother. Not in any real sense. She doesn't know you, and you don't know her."

"I feel as if I do. I see her on every tabloid show . . ."

"Then you know she has a new family. A new life that has nothing to do with you." Hiram eyed him. "And you know about the suicide."

Bobby frowned. "Her husband."

"He committed suicide, because of the media intrusion. All because your girlfriend gave away the WormCam to the sleaziest journalistic reptiles on the planet. She's responsible—"

"Dad."

"Yes, yes, I know. We had this argument already."

Hiram got out of his chair, walked to the window, and massaged the back of his neck. "Christ, I'm tired. Look, Bobby, any time you feel like coming back to work, I could bloody well use some help."

"I don't think I'm ready right now—"

"Everything's gone to hell since the WormCam was released. All the extra security is a pain in the arse. . . ."

Bobby knew that was true. Reaction to the existence of the WormCam, almost all of it hostile, had come from a whole spectrum of protest groups—from venerable campaigners like the Privacy Rights Clearinghouse, all the way to attempted attacks on this corporate HQ, the Wormworks, and even Hiram's home. An awful lot of people, on both sides of the law, felt they had been hurt by the WormCam's relentless exposure of the truth. Many of them seemed to need somebody to blame for their travails—and who better than Hiram?

"We're losing a lot of good people, Bobby. Many of them haven't the guts to stick with me now I've become public enemy number one, the man who destroyed privacy. I can't say I blame them; it's not their fight.

"And even those who've stayed around can't keep their hands off the WormCams. The illicit use has been incredible. And you can guess what for: spying on their neighbors, on their wives, their workmates. We've had endless rows, fistfights and one attempted shooting, as people find out what their friends really think of them, what they do to them behind their backs. . . . And now you can see into the past, it's impossible to hide. It's addictive. And I suppose it's a taster of what we have to expect when the past-view WormCam gets out to the general public. We're going to ship millions of units, that's for sure. But for now it's a pain in the arse; I've had to ban illicit use and lock down the terminals. . . ." He eyed his son. "Look, there's a lot to do. And the world isn't going to wait until your precious soul is healed."

"I thought business is going well—even though we lost the monopoly on the WormCam."

"We're still ahead of the game." Hiram's voice was getting stronger, his phrasing more fluent, Bobby noticed; he was speaking to the invisible audience he assumed was watching him, even now. "Now we can disclose the existence of the WormCam, there is a whole host of new applications we can roll out. Videophones, for instance: a direct-line wormhole pair between sender and receiver; we can see a top-end market opening up immediately, with mass-market models to follow. Of course that will have an impact on the DataPipe business, but there will still be a need for tracking and identification technology . . . but that's not where my problems lie. Bobby, we have an AGM next week. I have to face my shareholders."

"They aren't going to give you a rough ride. The financials are superb."

"It's not that." He glanced around the room warily. "How can I put this? Before the WormCam, business was a closed game. Nobody knew my cards—my competitors, my employees, even my investors and shareholders if I wanted it that way. And that gave me a lot of leverage, for bluff, counterbluff—"

"*Lying?*"

"Never that," Hiram said firmly, as Bobby knew he had to. "It's a question of posture. I could minimize my weaknesses, advertise my strengths, surprise the competition with a new strategy, whatever. But now the rules have changed. Now the game is more like chess—and I cut my teeth playing poker. Now—for a price—any shareholder or competitor, or regulator come to that, can check up on any aspect of my operation. They can see all my cards, even before I play them. And it's not a comfortable feeling."

"You can do the same to your competitors," Bobby said. "I've read plenty of articles which say that the new open-book management will be a good thing. If you're open to inspection, even by your employees, you're accountable. And it's more likely valid criticism is going to reach you, and you'll make fewer mistakes. . . ."

The economists argued that openness brought many benefits to business. Without any one party holding a monopoly of information there was a better chance of closing a given deal: with information on true costs available to everybody, only a reasonable level of profit-taking was acceptable. Better information flows led to more perfect competition; monopolies and cartels and other manipulators of the market were finding it impossible to sustain their activities. With open and accountable cash flows, criminals and terrorists weren't able to squirrel away unrecorded cash. And so on.

"Jesus," Hiram growled. "When I hear guff like that, I wish I sold management textbooks. I'd be making a killing right now." He waved his hand at the downtown buildings beyond the window. "But out there it's no business-school discussion group.

"It's like what happened to the copyright laws with the advent of the Internet. You remember that? . . . No, you're too young. The Global Information Infrastructure—the thing that was supposed to replace the Berne copyright convention—collapsed back in the nought-noughts. Suddenly the Internet was awash with unedited garbage. Every damn publishing house was forced out of business, and all the authors went back to being computer programmers, all because suddenly somebody was giving away for free the stuff they used to sell to earn a crust.

"Now we're going through the same thing all over again. You have a powerful technology which is leading to an information revolution, a new openness. But that conflicts with the interests of the people who originated or added value to that information in the first place. I can only make a profit on what OurWorld creates, and that largely derives from ownership of ideas. But laws of intellectual ownership are soon going to become unenforceable."

"Dad, it's the same for everybody."

Hiram snorted. "Maybe. But not everybody is going to prosper. There are revolutions and power struggles going on in every boardroom in this city. I know—I've watched most of them. Just as *they* have watched mine. What I'm telling you is that I'm in a whole new world here. And I need you with me."

"Dad, I have to get my head straight."

"Forget Heather. I'm trying to warn you that you'll get hurt."

Bobby shook his head. "If you were me, wouldn't you want to meet her? Wouldn't you be curious?"

"No," he said bluntly. "I never went back to Uganda to find my father's family. I never regretted it. Not once. What good would it have done? I had my own life to build. The past is the past; it doesn't do any bloody good to examine it too closely." He looked into the air, challengingly. "And all you leeches who are working on more exposés of Hiram Patterson can write that down too."

Bobby stood up. "Well, if it hurts too much, I can just turn the switch you put in my head, can't I?"

Hiram looked mournful. "Just don't forget where your true family is, son."

A girl stood at the door: slim, no taller than his shoulder, dressed in a harsh electric blue shift with a glaring Pink Lincoln design. She scowled at Bobby.

"I know who you are," he said. "You're Mary." Heather's daughter by her second marriage. Another half-sibling he'd only just found out about. She looked younger than her fifteen years. Her hair was cut brutally short, and a soft-tattoo morphed on her cheek. She was pretty, with high cheekbones and warm eyes; but her face was pursed into a frown that looked habitual.

He forced a smile. "Your mother is—"

"Expecting you. I know." She looked past him at the clutch of reporters. "You'd better come in."

He wondered if he should say something about her father, express sympathy. But he couldn't find the words, and her face was hard and blank, and the moment passed.

He stepped past her into the house. He was in a narrow hallway cluttered with winter shoes and coats; he glimpsed a warm-looking kitchen, a lounge with big SoftScreens draped over the walls, what looked like a home study.

Mary poked his arm. "Watch this." She stepped forward, faced the reporters and lifted her shift up over her head. She was wearing panties, but her small breasts were bare. She pulled the shift down, and slammed shut the door. He could see spots of color on her cheeks. Anger, embarrassment?

"Why did you do that?"

"They look at me the whole time anyway." And she turned on her heel and ran upstairs, her shoes clattering on bare wooden boards, leaving him stranded in the hallway.

". . . Sorry about that. She isn't adjusting too well."

And here, at last, was Heather, walking slowly up the hallway to him.

She was smaller than he had expected. She looked slim, even wiry, if a little round-shouldered. Her face might once have shared Mary's elfin look—but now those cheekbones were prominent under sun-aged skin, and her brown eyes, sunk deep in pools of wrinkles, were tired. Her hair, streaked with gray, was pulled back into a tight bob.

She was looking up at him, quizzically. "Are you okay?"

Bobby, for a few heartbeats, didn't trust himself to speak. ". . . Yes. I'm just not sure what to call you."

She smiled. "How about 'Heather'? This is complicated enough already."

And, without warning, she stepped forward and wrapped her arms around his chest.

He had tried to rehearse for this moment, tried to imagine how he would handle the storm of emotion he had expected. But now the moment was here, what he felt was—

Empty.

And all the while he was aware, achingly aware, of a million eyes on him, on every gesture and expression he made.

She pulled away from him. "I haven't seen you since you were five years old, and it has to be like this. Well, I think we've put on enough of a show."

She led him into the room he had tentatively identified as a study. On a worktable there was a giant SoftScreen of the finely grained type employed by artists and graphic designers. The walls were covered with lists, images of people, places, scraps of yellow paper covered with spidery, incomprehensible writing. There were scripts and reference books open on every surface, including the floor. Heather, brusquely, picked a mass of papers up off a swivel chair and dumped it on the floor. He accepted the implicit invitation by sitting down.

She smiled at him. "When you were a little boy you liked tea."

"I did?"

"You'd drink nothing else. Not even soda. So—you'd like some?"

He made to refuse. But she had probably bought some specially. And this is your mother, asshole. "Sure," he said. "Thanks."

She went to the kitchen, returned with a steaming mug of what proved to be jasmine tea. She leaned close to give it to him. "You can't fool me," she whispered. "But thanks for indulging me."

Awkward silence; he sipped his tea.

He indicated the big SoftScreen, the nest of paper. "You're a filmmaker. Right?"

She sighed. "I used to be. Documentaries. I regard myself as an investigative journalist." She smiled. "I won awards. You should be proud. Not that anybody cares about that side of my life anymore, compared to the fact that I once slept with the great Hiram Patterson."

He said, "You're still working? Even though—"

"Even though my life has turned to shit? I'm trying to. What else should I do? I don't want to be defined by Hiram. Not that it's easy. Everything has changed so fast."

"The WormCam?"

"What else? . . . Nobody wants thought-through pieces anymore. And drama has been completely wiped out. We're all fascinated by this new power we have to watch each other. So there's no work in anything but docu-soaps: following real people going through their real lives—with their consent and approval, of course. Ironic considering my own position, don't you think? Look." She brought up an image on the SoftScreen, a smiling young woman in uniform. "Anna Petersen. Fresh out of the Navy college at Annapolis."

He smiled. "Anna from Annapolis?"

"You can see why she was chosen. We have rotating teams to track Anna twenty-four hours a day. We'll follow her career through her first postings, her triumphs and disasters, her loves and losses. The word is she's to be sent with the task force to the Aral Sea water-war flashpoints, so we're expecting some good material. Of course the Navy *knows* we're tracking Anna." She looked up into the empty air. "Don't you, guys? So maybe it isn't a surprise she got an assignment like that, and no doubt we'll be getting plenty of mom-friendly, feel-good wartime footage."

"You're cynical."

"Well, I hope not. But it isn't easy. The WormCam is making a mess of my career. Oh, for now there is a demand for interpretation—analysts, editors, commentators. But even that is going to disappear when the great unwashed masses out there can point their own WormCams at whoever they want."

"You think that's going to happen?"

She snorted. "Oh, of course it is. We've been here before, with personal computers. It's just a question of how fast. Driven by competitive pressure and social forces, the WormCams are going to get cheaper and more powerful and more widely available, until everybody has one."

And perhaps—Bobby thought uneasily, thinking of David's time-viewing experiments—more powerful than you know.

". . . Tell me about you and Hiram."

She smiled, looking tired. "Are you sure you want that? Here, on planet Candid Camera?"

"Please."

"What did Hiram say to you about me?"

Slowly, stumbling occasionally, he repeated Hiram's account.

She nodded. "Then that's what happened." And she held his gaze, for long seconds. "Listen to me. I'm more than an appendage of Hiram, some sort of annex to your life. And so is Mary. We're people, Bobby. Did you know I lost a child, Mary, a little brother?"

". . . No. Hiram didn't tell me."

"I'm sure he didn't. Because it had nothing to do with him. Thank God nobody can watch *that*."

Not yet, Bobby thought darkly.

". . . I want you to understand this, Bobby." She looked into the air. "I want everyone to understand. My life is being destroyed, piece by piece, by being *watched*. When I lost my boy, I hid. I locked the doors, closed the curtains, even hid under the bed. At least there were *moments* when I could be private. Not now. Now, it's as if every wall of my house has been turned into a one-way mirror. Can you imagine how that *feels?*"

"I think so," he said gently.

"In a few days the attention focus is going to move on, to burn somebody else. But I'll never know when some obsessive, somewhere in the world, will be peering into my bedroom, still curious even years from now. And even if the WormCam disappeared tomorrow, it could never bring Desmond back.

"Look, it's been bad enough for me. But at least I know this is all because of something *I* did, long ago. My husband and daughter had nothing to do with it. And yet they've been subject to the same pitiless stare. And Desmond—"

"I'm sorry."

She dropped her gaze. Her tea cup was trembling, with a delicate china rattle, in its saucer. "I'm sorry too. I didn't agree to see you to make you feel bad."

"Don't worry. I felt bad already. And I brought the audience. I've been selfish."

She smiled, with an effort. "They were here anyway." She waved her hand through the air around her head. "I sometimes imagine I can disperse the watchers, like flapping away insects. But I don't suppose it does any good. I'm glad you came, whatever the circumstances. . . . Would you like some more tea?"

. . . She had brown eyes.

It was only as he endured the long drive back to Cedar City that that simple point struck him.

He called, "Search Engine. Basic genetics. Dominant and recessive genes. For example, blue eyes are recessive, brown dominant. So if a father has blue eyes and a mother brown, the children should have—"

"Brown eyes? It's not quite as simple as that, Bobby. If the mother's chromosomes carry a blue-eyes gene, then some of the children will have blue eyes too."

"Blue-blue from the father; blue-brown from the mother. Four combinations—"

"Yes. So one in four of the children will be blue-eyed."

". . . Umm." I have blue eyes, he thought. Heather has brown.

The Search Engine was smart enough to interpolate his real question. "I don't have information on Heather's genetic ancestry, Bobby. If you like I can find out—"

"Never mind. Thank you."

He settled back in his seat. No doubt it was a stupid question. Heather must have blue eyes in her family background.

No doubt.

The car sped through the huge, gathering night.

14

LIGHT YEARS

Hiram stalked around David's small room, silhouetted by picture-window Seattle nighttime skyline. He picked up a paper at random, a faded photocopy, and read its title. " 'Lorentzian Wormholes from the Gravitationally Squeezed Vacuum.' More brain-busting theory?"

David sat on his sofa, irritated and disturbed by his father's unannounced visit. He understood Hiram's need for company, to burn off his adrenaline, to escape the intensely scrutinized goldfish bowl his life had become. He just wished it didn't have to be in his space.

"Hiram, do you want a drink? A coffee, or—"

"A glass of wine would be fine. *Not* French."

David went to the refrigerator. "I keep a Chardonnay. A few of the Californian vineyards are almost acceptable." He brought the glasses back to the sofa.

"So," Hiram said. "Lorentzian wormholes?"

David leaned back in the sofa and scratched his head. "To tell the truth, we're nearing a dead end. Casimir technology seems to have inherent limitations. The balance of the capacitor's two superconducting plates, a balance between the Casimir forces and electrical repulsion, is unstable and easily lost. And the electric charges we have to carry are so large there are frequent violent discharges to the surroundings. Three people have been killed in WormCam operations already, Hiram. As you know from the insurance suits. The next generation of

WormCam is going to require something more robust. And if we had *that* we could build much smaller, cheaper WormCam facilities, and propagate the technology a lot further."

"And is there a way?"

"Well, perhaps. Casimir injectors are a rather clunky, nineteenth-century way of making negative energy. But it turns out that such regions can occur naturally. If space is sufficiently strongly distorted, quantum vacuum and other fluctuations can be amplified until . . . Well. This is a subtle quantum effect. It's called a *squeezed vacuum*. The trouble is, the best theory we have says you need a quantum black hole to give you a strong enough gravity field. And so—"

"And so, you're looking for a better theory." Hiram riffled through the papers, stared at David's handwritten notes, the equations linked by looping arrows. He glared around the room. "And not a SoftScreen in sight. Do you get out much? Ever? Or do you SmartDrive to and from work, your head in some dusty paper or other? From the moment you got here you had your Franco-American head stuck up your broad and welcoming backside, and that's where it has remained."

David bristled. "Is that a problem for you, Hiram?"

"You know how much I rely on your work. But I can't help feel that you're missing the point here."

"The point? The point about what?"

"The WormCam. What's really significant about the 'Cam is what it's doing out there." He gestured at the window.

"Seattle?"

Hiram laughed. "Everywhere. And this is before the past-viewing stuff really starts to make an impact." He seemed to come to a decision. He put his glass down. "Listen. Come take a trip with me tomorrow."

"Where?"

"The Boeing plant." He gave David a card; it bore a SmartDrive bar code. "Ten o'clock?"

"All right. But—"

Hiram stood up. "I regard myself as responsible for completing your education, son. I'll show you what a difference the WormCam is making."

Bobby brought Mary, his half-sister, to Kate's abandoned cubicle in the Wormworks.

Mary walked around the desk, touching the blank SoftScreen lying there, the surrounding acoustic partitions. It was all clinically neat, spotless, blank. "This is it?"

"Her personal stuff has been cleared away. The cops took some items, work stuff. The rest we parceled up for her family. And since then the forensics people have been crawling all over."

"It's like a skull the scavengers have licked clean."

He grimaced. "Nice image."

"I'm right, aren't I?"

"Yes. But . . ."

But, he thought, there was still some ineffable Kateness about this anonymous desk, this chair, as if in the months she had spent here she had somehow impressed herself on this dull piece of spacetime. He wondered how long this feeling would take to fade away.

Mary was staring at him. "This is upsetting you, isn't it?"

"You're perceptive. And frank to a fault."

She grinned, showing diamonds—presumably fake—studding her front teeth. "I'm fifteen years old. That's my job. Is it true WormCams can look into the past?"

"Where did you hear that?"

"Well, is it?"

". . . Yes."

"Show her to me."

"Who?"

"Kate Manzoni. I never met her. Show her to me. You have WormCams here, don't you?"

"Of course. This is the Wormworks."

"Everyone knows you can see the past with a WormCam. And you do know how to work them. Or are you scared? Like you were scared of coming here—"

"Up, if I may say so, yours. Come on."

Irritated now, he led her to the cage elevator which would take them to David's workstation a couple of levels below.

David wasn't here today. The supervising tech welcomed Bobby and offered him help. Bobby made sure the rig was online, and declined further assistance. He sat at the swivel chair before David's desk and began to set up the run, his fingers fumbling with the unfamiliar manual keys glowing in the SoftScreen.

Mary had pulled up a stool beside him. "That interface is disgusting. This David must be some kind of retro freak."

"You ought to be more respectful. He's my half-brother."

She snorted. "Why should I be respectful, just because old man Hiram couldn't keep from emptying his sack? Anyhow, what does David do all day?"

"David is working on a new generation of Worm-Cams. It's something called squeezed-vacuum technology. Here." He picked out a couple of references from David's desk and showed them to her; she flicked through the close-printed pages of equations. "The dream is that soon we'll be able to open up wormholes without needing a factory full of superconducting magnets. Much cheaper and smaller—"

"But they will still be in the hands of the government and the big corporations. Right?"

The big SoftScreen fixed to the partition in front of them lit up with a fizz of pixels. He could hear the whine of the generators powering the big, clumsy Casimir injectors in the pit below, smell the sharp ozone tang of powerful electric fields; as the machinery gathered its huge energies, he felt, as always, a surge of excitement, anticipation.

And Mary was, to Bobby's relief, silenced, at least temporarily.

The static snowstorm cleared, and an image—a little blocky, but immediately recognizable—filled up the SoftScreen.

They were looking down over Kate's cubicle, a couple of floors above them here at the Wormworks. But what they saw now was no cleaned-out husk. Now, the cubicle was lived-in. A SoftScreen was slewed at an angle across the desk, and data scrolled across it, unremarked, while a frame in one corner bore what looked like a news broadcast, a talking head with miniature graphics. There were more signs of work in progress: a cut-off soda can adapted as a pencil holder, pens and pencils scattered over the desk with big yellow legal pads, a couple of hard-copy newspapers folded over and propped up.

But what was more revealing—and heartbreaking— was the kipple, the personal stuff and litter that defined this as Kate's space and no other: the steaming coffee in a therm-aware cup, scrunched-up food wrappers, a prop-up calendar, an ugly, angular 1990s-style digital clock, a souvenir portrait—Bobby and Kate against the exotic background of RevelationLand—tacked ironically to one partition.

The chair was pushed back from the desk, and was still rotating, slowly. We missed her by seconds, he thought.

Mary was staring intently at the image, mouth open, fascinated by this window into the past—as everybody was, the first time. "We were just there. It's so different. It's incredible."

. . . And now Kate walked from offstage into the image, as Bobby had known she would. She was wearing a simple, practical smock, and a lick of hair was draped over her forehead, catching her eyes. She was frowning, concentrating, her fingers on the keyboard even before she had sat down.

He found it hard to speak. "I know."

The Boeing VR facility turned out to be a chamber fitted with row upon row of open steel cages—perhaps a hundred of them, David speculated. Beyond glass walls, white-coated engineers moved among brightly lit banks of computer equipment.

The cages were gimbaled to move in three dimensions, and each of them contained a skeletal suit of rubber and steel, fitted with sensors and manipulators. David was strapped tightly into one of these, and he had to fight feelings of claustrophobia as his limbs were pinned in place. He waved away the genital attachment—which was absurdly huge, like a vacuum flask. "I don't think I'll be needing *that* on this trip. . . ."

A female tech held a helmet up before his head. It was a hollowed-out mass of electronics. Before it descended, he looked for Hiram. His father was in a cage at the other end of a row a few ranks ahead of him.

"You seem a long way away."

Hiram raised a gloved hand, flexed his fingers. "It won't make a difference once we're immersed." His voice echoed in the cavernous hall. "What do you think of the facility? Pretty impressive, huh?" He winked.

David thought of the Mind'sEye, Bobby's simple headband apparatus—a few hundred grams of metal which, by interfacing directly to the central nervous system, could replace all this total-touch-enclosure Boeing gadgetry. Once more, it seemed, Hiram had a winner.

He let the tech drop the helmet over his head, and he was suspended in darkness . . .

. . . which cleared slowly, murkily. He saw Hiram's face hovering before him. It was illuminated by a soft red light.

"First impressions," Hiram snapped. He stepped back, revealing a landscape.

David glanced around. Water, a sloping gravelly ground, a red sky. When he moved his head too rapidly the image crumbled, winking into pixels, and he could feel the helmet's heavy movement.

The horizon curved, quite sharply, as if he were viewing it from some great altitude. And on that horizon there were low, eroded, hills, whose shoulders reflected in the water.

The air seemed thin, and he felt cold.

He said, "First impressions? A beach at sunset. . . . But that's no sun I ever saw."

The "sun" was a ball of red light, fading to a yellow-orange at its center. It was sitting on the sharp, mist-free horizon, and was flattened to a lens shape, presumably by refraction. But it was immense: much bigger than the sun of Earth, a red-glowing dome covering perhaps a tenth of the sky. Perhaps it was a giant, he mused, a bloated, aging star.

The sky was deeper than a sunset sky, too: intense crimson overhead, scarlet around that hulking sun, black beyond. But even around the sun the stars shone—in fact, he realized, he could make out glimmering stars *through* the diffuse limb of the sun itself.

Just to the right of the sun was a compact constellation that was hauntingly familiar: that W shape was surely Cassiopeia, one of the most easily recognizable star figures—but there was an extra star to the left of the pattern, turning the constellation into a crude zigzag.

He took a step forward. The gravel crunched convincingly, and he could feel sharp stones beneath his feet—though he wondered if the pressure points on his soles matched what he saw on the ground.

He walked the few paces to the water's edge. Ice glinted on the rocks, and there were miniature floes extending out into the water a meter or so. The water was flat, almost still, heaving with a soft, languid slow motion. He bent and inspected a pebble. It was hard, black, heavily worn. Basalt? Underneath there was a glint of a crystalline deposit—salt, perhaps. Some bright star behind him brought out yellow-white highlights on the stone, even casting a shadow.

He straightened up and hurled the rock out over the water. It flew long but slow—low gravity?—eventually hitting the water with a feeble splash; fat ripples spread in languid circles around the impact point.

Hiram was standing beside him. He was wearing a simple engineer's jumpsuit with the Boeing roundel on the back. "Figured out where you are yet?"

"It's a scene from a science-fiction novel I once read. An end-of-the-world vision."

"No," Hiram said. "Not science fiction. Not a game. This is real . . . at least the scenery is."

"A WormCam view?"

"Yeah. With a lot of VR enhancement and interpolation, so that the scene responds convincingly if you try to interact with it—for instance when you picked up that stone."

"I take it we're not in the Solar System anymore. Could I breathe the air?"

"No. It's mostly carbon dioxide." Hiram pointed to the rounded hills. "There's still some volcanism here."

"But this is a small planet. I can see the way the horizon bends. And the gravity is low: that stone I threw . . . So why hasn't this small planet lost all its internal heat, like the Moon?—Ah. The star." He pointed to the glowing hull on the horizon. "We must be close enough for the tides to keep the core of this little world molten. Like Io, orbiting Jupiter. In fact, that must mean the star isn't the giant I thought it was. It's a dwarf. And we're close to it—close enough for liquid water to persist. If that lake or sea over there *is* water."

"Oh, yes. Though I wouldn't recommend drinking it. Yes, we're on a small planet orbiting a red dwarf star. The 'year' here is only about nine of our days."

"Is there life?"

"The scientists studying this place have found none, nor any relics from the past. A shame." Hiram bent and picked up another basalt pebble. It cast two shadows on his palm, one, gray and diffuse, from the fat red star ahead of them, and another, fainter but sharper, from the light source behind them.

. . . What light source?

David turned. There was a double star in the sky: brighter than any star or planet seen from Earth, yet still reduced to pinpricks of light by distance. The points of light hurt his eyes, and he lifted his hand to shield his face. "It's beautiful," he said.

He turned again, and looked up at the constellation he had tentatively identified as Cassiopeia, that bright additional star tagged onto its end. "I know where we are. The bright stars behind us are the Alpha Centauri binary pair: the nearest bright stars to our sun, some four light years away—"

"About four point three, I'm told."

"And so *this* must be a planet of Proxima Centauri, the nearest star of all. Somebody has run a WormCam as far as Proxima Centauri. *Across four light years*. It's incredible."

"Well done. I told you, you're out of touch. *This* is the cutting edge of WormCam technology. This *power*. Of course the constellations aren't changed much; four light years is small change on the interstellar scale. But that bright intruder up in Cassiopeia is Sol. Our sun."

David stared at the sun: just a point of pale yellow light, bright, but not exceptionally so—and yet that spark of light was the source of all life on Earth. And the sun, the Earth and all the planets, and every place any human had ever visited, might have been eclipsed by a grain of sand.

*   *   *

"She's pretty," Mary said.

Bobby didn't reply.

"It really is a window into the past."

"It's not so magical," Bobby said. "Every time you watch a movie you're looking into the past."

"Come on," she whispered. "All you can see is what some camera operator or editor chooses to show you. And mostly, even on a news show, the people you're watching *know* the camera is there. Now, with *this*, you can look at anybody, any time, anywhere, whether a camera is present or not. You've watched this scene before, haven't you?"

"I've had to."

"Why?"

"Because this is when she's supposed to have committed her crime."

"Stealing virtual-reality secrets from IBM? She doesn't look like she's committing any crime to me."

That annoyed him. "What do you expect her to do, put on a black mask? . . . Sorry."

"It's okay. I know this is difficult. Why would she do it? I know she was working for Hiram, but she didn't exactly love him . . . Oh. She loved *you*."

He looked away. "The FBI case is that she wanted to get some credit in Hiram's eyes. Then Hiram might accept her relationship with me. That was her motive, says the FBI. So, this. At some point she was going to tell him what she had done."

"And you don't believe it?"

"Mary, you don't know Kate. That just isn't her agenda." He smiled. "Believe me, if she wants me she'll just take me, whatever Hiram feels. But there is evidence against her. The techs have crawled all over the equipment she used. They restored deleted files which showed that data about IBM test runs had been present in the memory she used."

Mary gestured at the 'Screen. "*But we can look into the past*. Who cares about computer traces? Has anybody actually *seen* her open up a big fat file with an IBM logo?"

"No. But that doesn't prove anything. Not in the eyes of the prosecution, anyway. Kate knew about the WormCam. Perhaps she even guessed that it would eventually have past-viewing capabilities, and she could be monitored retrospectively. So she covered herself."

Mary snorted again. "She'd have to be a devious genius to pull off something like that."

"You haven't met Kate," he repeated dryly.

"And anyhow, all this is circumstantial. . . . Is that the right word?"

"Yes. If not for the WormCam she'd be out of there by now. But she hasn't even come to trial yet. The Supreme Court is working on a new legal framework governing admissibility of WormCam evidence, and meanwhile a lot of cases—including Kate's—have been put on hold."

With an impulsive stab he cleared the 'Screen.

"Doesn't this trouble you?" Mary asked now. "The way they are using the WormCams?"

" '*They*'?"

"Big corporations watching each other. The FBI, watching us all. I believe Kate is innocent. But *somebody* here surely spied on IBM—with a WormCam." With the certainty of youth, she said, "Either everybody should have WormCams, or nobody should."

He said, "Maybe you're right. But it isn't going to happen."

"But the stuff you showed me, the next generation, the squeezed-vacuum approach—"

"You'll have to find somebody else to argue with."

They sat in silence for a time.

Then she said, "If *I* had a time viewer, I'd use it all the time. But I wouldn't use it to look at shitty stuff over and over. I'd look at nice stuff. Why don't you look back a bit further, to some time when you were happy with her?"

Somehow that hadn't occurred to him, and he recoiled.

She said, "Well, why not?"

"Because it's gone. In the past. What's the point of looking back?"

"If the present is shitty and the future is worse, the past is all you've got."

He frowned. Her face, so like her mother's, was pale, composed, her frank blue eyes steady. "You're missing your father."

"Of course I'm missing him," she said, with a spark of anger. "Maybe it's different on whatever planet you come from." Now her look softened. "I *would* like to see him. Just for a while."

I shouldn't have brought her here, he thought.

"Maybe later," he said gently. "Come on. The weather's fine. Let's go to the Sound. Have you ever been sailing? . . ."

It took him long minutes of persuasion to make her come away.

. . . And later, after a call from David, he learned that some of the references and handwritten notes on squeezed-vacuum wormholes had gone missing from David's workstation.

"Actually it was Disney," Hiram said, matter-of-fact, standing there in Proxima light. "In partnership with Boeing they've installed a giant WormCam facility in the old Vehicle Assembly Building at Cape Canaveral. Once they assembled Moon rockets there. Now, they send spy cameras to the stars. Quite something, isn't it? Of course they mostly rent out their virtual facility to the scientists; but the Boeing management let the staff play here during their lunch breaks. Already they're peering at every bloody planet and moon in the Solar System, without leaving the air-conditioned warmth of their labs.

"And Disney is cashing in. The Moon and Mars seem likely to turn into theme parks for virtual WormCam travelers. I'm told the Apollo and Viking sites are particularly popular, though the old Soviet Lunokhods are a competing attraction."

And, David thought, no doubt OurWorld has a piece of the action.

Hiram smiled. "You're very quiet, David."

David explored his emotions: wonder, he supposed, but laced with dismay. He picked up a handful of rocks, let them fall; their slow low-G bounce wasn't quite authentic. "*This is real.* I must have read a hundred fictional dramas, a thousand speculative studies, about missions to Proxima. And now here we are. It is the dream of a million years to stand here and see this. It's probably a dream rich enough finally to kill off spaceflight. Pity. But that's all this is: a dream. We're still in that chilly hangar on the outskirts of Seattle. By showing us the *destination*, without requiring of us the enervating *journey*, the WormCam will turn us into a planet of couch potatoes."

"You don't think you're being a little excitable?"

"No, I do not. Hiram, before the WormCam, we deduced the existence of this planet of Proxima from minute displacements of the star's trajectory. We calculated what its surface conditions must be like; we pored over spectroscopic analyses of its smudged light to see if we could deduce what it was made of; we strove to build new generations of telescopes which would give us some map of its surface. We even dreamed of building ships which might come here. Now we have the WormCam, and we don't need to deduce anymore, to strive, to *think*."

"Isn't that a good thing?"

"No!" David snapped. "It is like a child turning to the answers at the back of an exercise book. The point, you see, is not the answers themselves, but the mental development we enjoy through striving for those answers.

The WormCam is going to overwhelm a whole range of sciences—planetology, geology, astronomy. For generations to come our scientists will merely count and classify, like an eighteenth-century butterfly collector. Science will become taxonomy."

Hiram said slyly, "You forgot history."

"History?"

"*You* were the one who found out that a WormCam that can reach across four light-years could just as easily reach four years into the past. Our grasp in time is puny compared to space; but it will surely develop. And then all hell's going to break loose.

"Think about it. Right now we can reach back days, weeks, months. We can spy on our wives, watch ourselves on the john, the coppers can track and watch criminals in the act. Facing your own past self is hard enough. But this is nothing, personal trivia. When we can reach back years, you're talking about opening up history. And what a can of worms *that* is going to be.

"Some people out there are preparing the ground already. You must have heard of the 12,000 Days. A Jesuit project, on the orders of the Vatican: to complete a comprehensive firsthand history of the development of the Church—all the way back to Christ Himself." Hiram grimaced. "Much of *that* won't make pretty viewing. But the Pope is smart. Better the Church should do this first than somebody else. Even so, it's going to make Christianity fall apart like a sandcastle. And the other religions will follow."

"Are you sure?"

"Hell, yes." Hiram's eyes gleamed in red light. "Didn't Bobby expose RevelationLand as a fraud dreamed up by a criminal?"

Actually, David thought, though Bobby helped, that was Kate Manzoni's triumph. "Hiram, Christ was no Billybob Meeks."

"Are you sure? Do you think you could bear to find out? Could your Church bear it?"

. . . Perhaps not, David thought. But we must fervently hope so.

Hiram had been right to drag him out of his monkish academic cell, he realized, to see all this. It was wrong of him to hide away, to work on the WormCam with no sense of its wider implications. He made a resolution to immerse himself in the 'Cam's application as well as its theory.

Hiram looked up at the hull of the sun. "I think it's getting colder. Sometimes it snows here. Come on." He began to work the invisible abort buttons on his helmet.

David peered up at the splinter of light that was distant Sol, and imagined his soul returning home, flying from this desolate beach up to that primal warmth.

15

CONFABULATION

Bobby found the interview room, in the bowels of this aging courthouse, deeply depressing. The dingy walls looked as if they hadn't been painted since the turn of the century, and even then only in government-issue pale green.

And it was in this room that Kate's privacy was to be flayed, piece by piece.

Kate and her attorney—an unsmiling, overweight woman—sat on hard plastic chairs behind a scuffed wooden table, on which sat an array of recording devices. Bobby himself was perched on a hard bench at the back of the room, there at Kate's request, the only witness to this strange tableau.

Clive Manning, the psychologist appointed by the court to Kate's case, was standing at the front of the room, tapping at a SoftScreen fixed to the wall. WormCam images, dimly lit and suffering a little fish-eye distortion, flickered as Manning sought his starting point. At last he found the place he wanted. It was a frozen image of Kate with a man. They were standing in a cluttered living room, evidently in the middle of a heated row, screaming at each other.

Manning—tall, thin, bald, fiftyish—took off his wire spectacles and tapped the frame against his teeth, a mannerism Bobby was already finding gratingly irritating, the spectacles themselves an antiquated affectation. "What is human memory?" Manning asked. He gazed at the air as he spoke, as if lecturing an invisible audience—as perhaps he was. "It certainly is not a passive recording mechanism, like a digital disc or a tape. It is more like a storytelling machine. Sensory information is broken down into shards of perception, which are broken down again to be stored as memory fragments. And at night, as the body rests, these fragments are brought out from storage, reassembled and replayed. Each run-through etches them deeper into the brain's neural structure.

"And each time a memory is rehearsed or recalled it is elaborated. We may add a little, lose a little, tinker with the logic, fill in sections that have faded, perhaps even conflate disparate events.

"In extreme cases, we refer to this as confabulation. The brain creates and re-creates the past, producing, in the end, a version of events that may bear little resemblance to what actually occurred. To first order, I believe it's true to say that everything I remember is false." Bobby thought a note of awe entered Manning's voice.

"This frightens you," Kate said, wondering.

"I'd be a fool not to be frightened. We're all complex, flawed creatures, Kate, stumbling around in the dark. Perhaps our minds, little transient bubbles of consciousness adrift in this overwhelmingly hostile universe, need an inflated sense of their own importance, of the logic of the universe, in order to summon up the will to survive. But now the WormCam, without pity, will never again let us evade the truth." He was silent for a moment, then smiled at her. "Perhaps we will all be driven mad by truth. Or perhaps, stripped of illusion at last, we will all become sane, and I will be out of a job. What do you think?"

Kate, wearing a drab black one-piece, sat with her hands tucked between her thighs, her shoulders hunched. "I think you should get on with your show-and-tell."

Manning sighed and replaced his glasses. He tapped

the 'Screen's corner, and the fragment of Kate's vanished life began to play itself out.

On-screen Kate hurled something at the guy. He ducked; it splashed against the wall.

"What was that? A peach?"

"As I recall," Kate said, "it was a kumquat. A little overripe."

"Good choice," Manning murmured. "You need to work on your aim, however."

. . . asshole. You're still seeing her, aren't you?

What's it to do with you?

It's got everything to do with me, you piece of shit. Why you think I'm going to put up with this I don't know. . . .

The man on the 'Screen was called Kingsley, Bobby had learned. He and Kate had been lovers for several years, and had lived with each other for three—up to this point, the moment at which Kate had finally thrown him out.

Watching was difficult for Bobby. He felt he was participating in voyeurism of this younger, different woman who hadn't at the time even known he existed, events of which she'd told him nothing. And, like most WormCam-recorded slices of life, it was hard to follow, the conversation illogical, meandering and repetitive, the words designed to express their users' emotions rather than to progress the encounter in any rational way.

A century and more of scripted TV and cinema had been poor training for the reality of the WormCam. But this real-life drama was typical of life: messy, unstructured, confusing, the participants groping like people in a darkened room toward an understanding of what was happening to them, how they were feeling.

The action shifted from the living room to a catastrophically untidy bedroom. Now Kingsley was cramming clothes into a leather bag, and Kate was grabbing more of his stuff and throwing it out of the room. All the time they maintained a screaming dialogue.

At last, Kingsley stormed out of the apartment. Kate slammed the door shut behind him. She stood rigid for a moment, staring at the closed door, before burying her face in her hands.

Manning reached over and tapped the 'Screen. The image froze on a close-up of Kate's face, hidden by her hands, tears visibly leaking between her fingers, her hair a tangle around her forehead, the whole surrounded by a faint fish-eye–distortion halo.

Manning said, "I believe this incident is the key to your story, Kate. The story of your life, of who you are."

The real Kate, bleak and subdued, stared at her younger self woodenly. "I was framed," she said evenly. "Over the IBM espionage. It was subtle, beyond the reach even of the WormCam. But it's nevertheless true. And that's what we should be focusing on. Not this barroom psychoanalysis."

Manning drew back. "That's as may be. But evidentiary issues are beyond my competence. The judge has asked me to come up with a framework for your state of mind at the time of the crime itself. Motive and intent: a deeper truth than even the WormCam can offer us. And," he said with a trace of steel, "let's remind ourselves that you don't have any choice but to cooperate."

"But that doesn't alter my opinion," she said.

"What opinion?"

"That, like every shrink I've ever met, you are one inhuman asshole." The attorney touched Kate's arm, but Kate shook her off.

Manning's eyes glittered, hard behind his spectacles; Bobby realized Manning was going to enjoy exerting power over this willful woman.

Manning turned to his SoftScreen and ran through the brief breakup scene again. "Let me recall what you told me about this period in your life. You'd been living with Kingsley Roman for some three years when you decided to try for a baby. You suffered a late miscarriage."

"I'm sure you enjoyed watching that," Kate said bleakly.

"Please," Manning said, pained. "You seem to have decided, with Kingsley, that you would try again."

"We never decided that. We didn't discuss it in that way."

Manning blinked owlishly at a notepad. "But you did. February 24, 2032, is the clearest example. I can show you if you like." He looked up at her over his glasses. "Don't be alarmed if your memory differs from the WormCam record. It's common. In fact, I'd go so far as to say it's normal. Confabulation, remember. Shall I go on?

"Despite your stated decision, you don't conceive. In fact you return to the regular use of contraceptives, so that conception is impossible anyhow. Six months after the miscarriage, Kingsley begins his affair with a colleague at his place of work. A woman called Jodie Morris. And a few months after that, he is careless enough to let you find out about it." He studied her again. "Do you remember what you told me about that?"

Kate said reluctantly, "I told you the truth. I think Kingsley decided, on some level, that the baby was my fault. And so he started looking around. And besides, after the miscarriage, work was starting to take off for me. The Wormwood . . . I think Kingsley was jealous."

"And so he started to seek the attention he craved from somebody else."

"Something like that. When I found out, I threw him out."

"He claims he left."

"Then he's a lying asshole."

"But we just saw the incident," Manning said gently. "I didn't see any evidence of clear decision-making, of unilateral action by either of you."

"It doesn't matter what the WormCam shows. I know what is true."

Manning nodded. "I'm not denying that you're telling us the truth as you see it, Kate." He smiled at her, owlish, looming. "You aren't lying. *That* isn't the problem at all. Don't you see?"

Kate gazed at her caged hands.

They took a break. Bobby wasn't allowed to be with her.

Kate's treatment was one of many experiments being run as the politicians, legal experts, pressure groups and concerned citizens worked feverishly to find a way to accommodate the WormCam's eerie historical reach— still not widely known to the public—into something resembling the existing due process of the law, and, even more challenging, into natural justice.

In essence it had suddenly become radically easier to establish physical truth.

The conduct of court cases seemed likely to be transformed radically. Trials would surely become much less adversarial, fairer, much less dependent on the demeanor of a suspect in court or the quality of her representatives. When the WormCam was available at federal, state and county levels, some commentators were anticipating savings of billions of dollars annually: there would be shorter trials, more plea bargains, more civil settlements.

And major trials in future would perhaps focus on what remained beyond the bare facts: motive and intent—hence the assignment of a psychologist like Manning to Kate's case.

Meanwhile, as WormCam-armed law enforcers went to diligent work over unresolved cases, a huge logjam of new cases was heading for the courts. Some Congressmen had proposed that to maximize the clear-up rate a general amnesty should be declared for crimes of lesser severity committed up to the last full calendar year before the WormCam's invention—an amnesty, that is, in return for waiving of Fifth Amendment protection in the relevant case. In fact, evidence gathering was made so much more powerful, thanks to the WormCam, that Fifth Amendment rights had become moot anyhow. But this was proving highly contentious. Most Americans did not appear to feel comfortable with losing Fifth protection.

Challenges to privacy were even more contentious—made so by the fact that even now there was no accepted definition of privacy rights, even within America.

Privacy was not mentioned in the Constitution. The Fourth Amendment to the Bill of Rights spoke of a right against intrusion by the state—but it left a great deal of room for maneuver by those in authority who wished to investigate citizens, and besides offered citizens virtually no protection against other bodies, such as corporations or the press or even other citizens. From a welter of scattershot laws at state and federal levels, as well as a mass of cases in common law to provide precedent, a certain common acceptance of the meaning of privacy had slowly emerged: for instance a right to be "let alone," to be free from unreasonable interference from outside forces.

But all of this was challenged by the WormCam.

Legal safeguards surrounding WormCam use were being promoted, by law-enforcement and investigation agencies like the FBI and the police, as a compensating balance to the loss of privacy and other rights. For example WormCam records intended for legal purposes would have to be collected in controlled circumstances—probably by trained observers, and notarized formally. That wasn't likely to prove a problem, as any WormCam observation could always be repeated as many times as required simply by setting up a new wormhole link to the incident in question.

There were even suggestions that people should be prepared to submit to a form of "documented life." This would effectively grant the authorities legal access to any incident in an individual's past without the need for formal procedures in advance—and it would also be a strong shield against false accusation and identity theft.

But despite protests from campaigners against the erosion of rights, everybody seemed to accept that as far as its use in criminal investigation and prosecution was concerned, the WormCam was here to stay; it was simply too powerful to ignore.

Some philosophers argued that this was no bad thing. After all, humans had evolved to live in small groups in which everybody knew everybody else, and strangers were rarely encountered; it was only recently, in evolutionary terms, that people had been forced to live in larger communities like cities, crammed together with friends and strangers alike. The WormCam was bringing a return to older ways of living, of thinking about other people and interacting with them.

But that was little comfort for those who feared that their perceived need for curtilage—a defined space within which they could achieve solitude, anonymity, reserve and intimacy with loved ones—might no longer be met.

And now, as the WormCam's history-view facilities deepened, even the past was no refuge.

Many people had been hurt, in one way or another, by the revelation of the truth. Many of them blamed not the truth, or themselves, but the WormCam, and those who had inflicted it on the world.

Hiram himself remained the most obvious target.

At first, Bobby suspected, he had almost enjoyed his notoriety. Any celebrity was good for business. But the hail of threats and assassination and sabotage attempts had worn him down. There were even libel actions, as people claimed Hiram must somehow be fabricating what the WormCam was showing about themselves, their loved ones, their enemies, or their heroes.

Hiram had taken to living in the light. His West Coast mansion was drenched in light from floods powered by multiple generators. He even slept in brilliant illumination. No security system was foolproof, but at least Hiram could ensure that anybody who got through would be visible to the WormCams of the future.

So Hiram lived, skewered by pitiless light, alone, scrutinized, loathed.

The gruesome procedure resumed.

Manning consulted his notebook. "Let me set out some of the facts: incontrovertible historical truths, all properly observed and notarized. First, Kingsley's affair with Ms. Morris wasn't his first in his time with you. He had a short, apparently unsatisfactory fling with another woman beginning a month after he met you. And another six months later—"

"No."

"In all, he seems to have had six consummated relationships with other women *before* you challenged him over Jodie." He smiled. "If it's any consolation he's also cheated on other partners, before and since. He seems to be something of a serial adulterer."

"This is ridiculous. I'd have known."

"But you're also human. I can show you incidents where evidence of Kingsley's unfaithfulness was clearly available to you, yet you turned aside, rationalizing it away without even being aware of what you were doing. Confabulation—"

She said coldly, "I've told you how it was. Kingsley started to cheat on me because the miscarriage screwed up our relationship."

"Ah, the miscarriage: the great causal event in your life. But I'm afraid it wasn't like that at all. Kingsley's behavior patterns were well established long before he met you, and were barely altered by the miscarriage incident. You've also said that you believe the miscarriage gave you a spur to working harder at developing your own career."

"Yes. That's obvious."

"This is a little more difficult to establish, but again I can demonstrate to you that the upward trajectory of your career began some months *before* the miscarriage. Again, you were doing it anyhow; the miscarriage didn't really change anything." He studied her. "Kate, you've constructed a kind of story around the miscarriage. You've wanted to believe that it was significant beyond itself. The miscarriage was a horrible trial for you to endure. But it actually changed very little. . . . I sense you don't believe me."

She said nothing.

Manning steepled his fingers and put them to his chin. "I think you've been both right and wrong about yourself. I think that the miscarriage you suffered did change your life. But not in the rather superficial way you think it did. It didn't make you work harder, or cause cracks in your relationship with Kingsley. But the loss of your child did wound you deeply. And I think you're now driven by a fear that it might happen again."

"A fear?"

"Please believe I'm not judging you. I'm merely trying to explain. Your compensatory activity is your work. Perhaps this deeper fear has driven you to greater achievement, greater success. But you've also become obsessive. It has only been your work that has distracted you from what you see as a terrible darkness at the center of your being. And so you're driven to ever greater lengths—"

"Right. And *that's* why I used Hiram's wormholes to spy on his competitors." She shook her head. "How much do they pay you for this stuff, Doctor?"

Manning paced slowly before his SoftScreen. "Kate, you're one of the first human beings to endure this— umm, this *truth shock*—but you won't be the last. We are all going to have to learn to live without the comforting lies we whisper to ourselves in the darkness of our minds—"

"I'm capable of forming relationships: even long-lasting, stable ones. How does that square with your portrait of me as a shock trauma victim?"

Manning frowned, as if puzzled by the question. "You mean Mr. Patterson? But there's no contradiction there." He walked over to Bobby and, with a murmured apology, studied him. "In many ways, Bobby Patterson is one of the most childlike adults I have ever encountered. He is therefore an exact fit for the, umm, the child-shaped hole at the center of your personality." He turned to Kate. "You see?"

She stared at him, her color high.

16

THE WATER WAR

Heather sat at her home SoftScreen. She entered fresh search parameters. COUNTRY: Uzbekistan. TOWN: Nukus . . .

She wasn't surprised to see an attractive turquoise blockout appear before her. Nukus was, after all, a war zone.

But that wouldn't stop Heather for long. She had found reason in her time to find ways past censoring software before. And having access to a WormCam of her own was a powerful motivation.

Smiling, she went to work.

When—after much public pressure—the first enterprising companies started offering WormCam access to private citizens via the Internet, Heather Mays was quick to subscribe.

She could even work from home. From a straightforward menu she selected a location to view. This could be anywhere in the world, specified by geographical coordinates or postal address as precisely as she could narrow it down. The mediating software would convert her request to latitude-longitude coordinates, and would offer her further options. The idea was to narrow her selection down until she had reached a specification of a room-sized volume, somewhere on or near the surface of the Earth, where a wormhole mouth would be established.

There was also a randomizing feature if she had no preference: for instance, if she wanted to view some remote picture-postcard coral atoll, but didn't care which. She could even—at additional cost—select intermediate views, so for example she could view a street and select a house to "call at."

When she'd made her choice, a wormhole would be opened up between the supplier's central server location and the site of her choice. Images from the WormCam would then be sent direct to her home terminal. She could even guide the viewpoint, within a limited volume.

The WormCam's commercial interface made it feel like a toy, and every image was indelibly marked by intrusive OurWorld logos and ads. But Heather knew that intrinsically the WormCam was *much* more powerful than it appeared, in this first public incarnation.

When she'd first mastered the system, she was inordinately pleased, and called Mary to come see. "Look," she said, pointing. The 'Cam image was of a nondescript house, in evening summer sunlight; the image frame was plastered with annoying ad logos. "That's the house where I was born, in Boise, Idaho. In that very room, in fact."

Mary shrugged. "Are you going to give me a turn?"

"Sure. In fact I got it for you, in part. Your homework assignments—"

"Yeah, yeah."

"Listen, this isn't a toy—" Abruptly the 'Screen filled up with a soothing-color blockout.

Mary frowned. "What's wrong? . . . Oh. I get it. It comes with a nanny filter. So we're still only seeing what *they* will allow us to see."

The idea was that the WormCams couldn't be used voyeuristically, to spy on people in their homes or other private places, or to breach corporate confidentiality, or to view government buildings, military establishments, police stations and other sensitive places. The nanny software was also supposed to monitor patterns of usage and, in case of morbid or excessive behavior, to break the service and offer counseling, either by expert system or a human agent.

And, for now, only the remote-viewing facilities of the WormCam had been made available. Past-viewing was considered, by a whole slew of experts, to be *much* too dangerous to be put in the hands of the public—in fact, it was argued, it would be dangerous even to make the existence of the past-viewer facility widely known.

But, of course, all this cotton-wool wrapping would only be as effective as the ingenuity of the human designers behind it. And already, fueled by Internet rumor and industry leaks and speculation, clamor was rising for much wider public access to the WormCam's full power: to the past-viewers themselves.

Heather sensed that this new technology was by its very nature going to be difficult to contain. . . .

But that wasn't something she was about to share with her fifteen-year-old daughter.

Heather cleared down the wormhole and prepared to start a new search. "I need to work. Go. You can play later. One hour only."

With a look of contempt, Mary walked out, and Heather returned her attention to Uzbekistan.

Anna Petersen, USN—heroine of a 24-by-7 WormCam docu-soap—had been heavily involved in the U.S.-led UN intervention in the water war raging in the Aral Sea area. A precision war was being fought by the Allies against the principal aggressor, Uzbekistan: an aggression which had threatened Western interests in oil and sulphur deposits and various mineral production sites, including a major copper source. Bright and technical, Anna had mostly worked on command, control and communications operations.

WormCam technology was changing the nature of warfare, as it had much else. WormCams had already largely replaced the complex of surveillance technology—satellites, monitoring aircraft and land-based stations—which had governed battlefields for decades. If there had been eyes capable of seeing, every major target in Uzbekistan would have sparkled with evanescent wormhole mouths. Precision-guided bombs, cruise missiles and other weapons, many of them no larger than birds, had rained down on Uzbek air-defense centers, military command and control facilities, on bunkers concealing troops and tanks, on hydroelectric plants and natural gas pipelines, and on targets in the cities, such as Samarkand, Andizhan, Namangan and the capital Tashkent.

The precision was unprecedented—and, for the first time in such operations, success could be verified.

Of course, for now, the Allied troops had the upper hand in WormCam deployment. But future wars would have to be fought under the assumption that both sides had perfect and up-to-date information on the strategy, resources and deployment of the other. Heather supposed it was too much to hope that such a change in the nature of war might lead to its cessation altogether. But at least it was giving the warriors pause for thought, and might lead to less meaningless waste.

Anyhow this war—Anna's war, the cold battle of information and technology—was the war which the American public had witnessed, partly thanks to the WormCam viewpoint Heather herself had operated, flying alongside Petersen's shapely shoulder as she moved from one clinical, bloodless scenario to another.

But there had been rumors—mostly circulating in the corners of the Internet that still remained uncontrolled— of another, more primitive war proceeding on the ground, as troops went in to secure the gains made by the air strikes.

Then a report had been released by an English news

channel of a prison camp in the field, where UN captives, including Americans, were being held by the Uzbeks. There were also rumors that female prisoners, including Allied troops, had been taken to rape camps and forced brothels, deeper in the countryside.

Revealing all of this clearly served the purposes of the governments behind the anti-Uzbek alliance. The Juarez Administration's spin doctors weren't above highlighting the distressing idea of wholesome Anna from Iowa in the hands of swarthy Uzbek molesters.

To Heather this was evidence of a dirty, ground-level conflict far removed from the clean video game in which Anna Petersen had colluded. Heather's hackles had risen at the idea that she might be playing a part in some vast propaganda machine. But when she sought permission from her employer, Earth News Online, to seek out the truth of the war, she was refused; access to the corporate WormCam facility would be withdrawn if she attempted it.

While she was in the Hiram's-ex-wife spotlight she had to keep her head down.

But then the glaring focus public attention moved on from the Mayses—and she was able to afford her own WormCam access. She quit from ENO, took a new bill-paying job on a WormCam biography of Abraham Lincoln, and went to work.

It took her a couple of days to find what she was looking for.

She followed Uzbek prisoners being loaded onto an open UN truck and driven away through the rain. They passed through the town of Nukus, controlled by Allied troops, and on into the country beyond.

Here, she found, the Allied troops had established a prison camp of their own.

It was an abandoned iron-mining complex. The prisoners were held in metal cages, stacked up in an ore loader, just a meter high. The prisoners were unable to straighten their legs or backs. They were held without sanitation, adequate food, exercise or access to the Red Cross or its Muslim equivalent Merhamet. Filth dripped from cages above through the grates to those below.

She estimated there must be at least a thousand men here. They were given only a cup of weak soup a day. Hepatitis was epidemic, and other diseases were spreading.

Every other day, prisoners were selected, apparently at random, and taken out for beatings. Three or four soldiers would surround each prisoner, and would beat him with iron bars, wooden two-by-fours, truncheons. After a time the beating would stop. Any prisoner who could walk would be thrown back for further treatment, and the beating continued. They would be carried back to their cages by other prisoners.

That was the general pattern. There were some particular incidents, inflicted on the prisoners almost in a spirit of experimentation by the guards: a prisoner was not allowed to defecate; a prisoner was forced to eat sand; another was forced to swallow his own feces.

Six people died while Heather monitored the camp. The deaths were as a result of the beatings, exposure or disease. Occasionally a prisoner would be shot, for example when attempting to escape or fight back. One prisoner was actually released, apparently to take the news of the determination of these blue-helmeted troops to his comrades.

Heather noticed that the guards were careful to use only captured weaponry, as if they were determined to leave no unambiguous trace of their activities. Evidently, she thought, the power of the WormCam had not yet impinged on the imaginations of these soldiers; they weren't yet used to the idea that they could be watched, any place, any time, even retrospectively from the future.

It was almost impossible to watch these bloody deeds,

which would have been invisible, to the public anyhow, only a few months before.

This would be dynamite up the ass of President Juarez, who in Heather's opinion had already proven herself to be the worst sleazebag to pollute the White House since the turn of the century (which was saying something)—and not to mention, as the first female President, a major embarrassment to half the population.

And maybe—Heather allowed herself to hope—the mass consciousness would stir once more when people saw war as it truly was, in all its bloody glory, as they had briefly glimpsed it when Vietnam had become the first television war, and before the commanders had reestablished control over media coverage.

She even cradled hopes that the approach of the Wormwood would change the way people felt about each other. If everything was to end just a handful of generations away, what did ancient enmities matter? And was the purpose of the remaining time, the remaining days of human existence, to inflict pain and suffering on others?

There would still be just wars, surely. But it would no longer be possible to dehumanize and demonize an opponent—not when anybody could tap a SoftScreen and see for themselves the citizens of whichever nation was considered the enemy—and there could be no more warmongering lies, about the capability, intent and resolve of an opponent. If the culture of secrecy was finally broken, no government would get away with acts like this, ever again.

Or maybe she was just being an idealist.

She pressed on, determined, motivated. But no matter how hard she tried to be objective she found these scenes unbearably harrowing: the sight of naked, wretched men, writhing in agony at the feet of blue-helmet soldiers with clean, hard American faces.

*   *   *

She took a break. She slept a while, bathed, then prepared herself a meal (breakfast, at three in the afternoon).

She knew she wasn't the only citizen putting the new facilities to use like this.

All around the country, she'd heard, truth squads were forming up, using WormCam and Internet. Some of the squads were no more than neighborhood watch schemes. But one organization, called Copwatch, was disseminating instructions on how to shadow police at work in order to provide a "fair witness" to a cop's every activity. Already, it was said, this new accountability was having a marked effect on the quality of policing; thuggish and corrupt officers—thankfully rare anyhow—were being exposed almost immediately.

Consumer groups had suddenly gained power, and were daily exposing scams and con artists. In most states, detailed breakdowns of campaign finance information were being posted, in some cases for the first time. There was a lot of focus on the Pentagon's more obscure activities and its dark budget. And so on.

Heather relished the idea of concerned private citizens, armed with WormCam and suspicion, clustering around the corrupt and criminal like white blood cells. In her mind there was a simple causal chain lying behind fundamental liberties: increased openness ensured accountability, which in turn maintained freedom. And now a technological miracle—or accident—seemed to be delivering the most profound tool for open disclosure imaginable into the hands of private citizens.

Jefferson and Franklin would probably have loved it—even if it would have meant the sacrifice of their own privacy. . . .

There was noise in her study. A muffled giggling.

Heather, barefoot, crept to the half-open door. Mary and a friend were sitting at Heather's desk. "Look at that jerk," Mary was saying. "His hand keeps slipping off the end."

Heather recognized the friend. Sasha, from the class

above Mary's at high school, was known among the local parents' mafia as a Bad Influence. The air was thick with the smoke from a spliff—presumably one of Heather's own store.

The WormCam image was of a teenage boy. Heather recognized him, too, as one of the boys from school—Jack? Jacques? He was in his bedroom. His pants were around his ankles, and before a SoftScreen, with more enthusiasm than competence, he was masturbating.

She said quietly, "Congratulations. So you hacked your way through the nanny."

Both Mary and Sasha jumped, startled. Sasha waved futilely at the cloud of marijuana smoke.

Mary turned back to the 'Screen. "Why not? *You* did."

"I did it for a valid reason."

"So it's all right for you but not for me. You're such a hypocrite, Mom."

Sasha stood up. "I'm out of here."

"Yes, you are," Heather snapped after her retreating back. "Mary, is this *you*? Spying on your neighbors like some sleazy voyeur?"

"What else is there to do? Admit it, Mom. You're getting a little moist yourself—"

"Get out of here."

Mary's laugh turned to a theatric sneer, and she walked out.

Heather, shaken, sat before the 'Screen and studied the boy. The SoftScreen he was staring at showed another WormCam view. There was a girl in the image, naked, also masturbating, but smiling, mouthing words at the boy.

Heather wondered how many more watchers this couple had. Maybe they hadn't thought of that. A WormCam couldn't be tapped, but it was difficult to remember that the WormCam meant global access for *everybody*—anybody could be watching these kids at play.

She was prepared to bet that in these first months,

ninety-nine percent of WormCam use would be for this kind of crude voyeurism. Maybe it was like the sudden accessibility of porn made possible by the Internet at home, without the need to enter some sleazy store. Everybody always wanted to be a voyeur anyhow—so the argument went—and now we can do it without risk of being caught.

At least that was how it *felt;* the truth was that anybody could be watching the watchers too. Just as anybody could have watched Mary and Sasha, two cute teenage girls getting pleasurably horny. And maybe there was even a community who might derive some pleasure from watching *her*, a dry-as-a stick middle-aged woman gazing analytically at this foolish stuff.

Maybe, some of the commentators said, it was the chance of voyeurism that was driving the early sales of this home WormCam access, and even its technological development—just as porn providers had pushed the early development of Internet facilities. Heather would have liked to believe her fellow humans were a little deeper than that. But maybe, once again, she was just being an idealist.

And after all, not all the voyeurism was for titillation. Every day there were news lines about people who had, for one reason or another, spied on those close to them, and discovered secrets and betrayals and creeping foulness, causing a rush of divorces, domestic violence, suicides, minor wars between friends, spouses, siblings, children and their parents: a lot of crap to be worked out of a lot of relationships, she supposed, before everybody grew up a little and got used to the idea of glass-wall openness.

She noticed that the boy had a spectacular *Cassini* spaceprobe image of Saturn's rings on his bedroom wall. Of course he was ignoring it; he was much more interested in his dick. Heather remembered how her own mother—God, nearly fifty years back—would tell her of the kind of future *she* had grown up with, in more expansive, optimistic years. By the year 2025, her mother used to say, nuclear-powered spacecraft would be plying between the colonized planets, bearing water and precious minerals mined from asteroids. Perhaps the first interstellar probe would already have been launched. And so on.

Perhaps teenagers in *that* world might have been distracted from each others' body parts—at least some of the time!—by the spectacle of the explorers in Mars's Valles Marineris, or Mercury's great Caloris basin, or the shifting ice fields of Europa.

But, she thought, in *our* world we're still stuck here on Earth, and even the future seems to end in a black hurtling wall of rock, and all *we* want to do is spy on each other.

She shut down the wormhole link and added new security protocols to her terminal. It wouldn't keep Mary out forever, but it would slow her down a little.

That done—exhausted, depressed—she returned to work.

17

THE DEBUNK MACHINE

David and Heather sat before a flickering SoftScreen, their faces illuminated by the harsh sunlight of a day long gone.

... He was a private, a soldier of the first Maryland Infantry. He was one of a line which stretched into the distance, muskets raised. A drumbeat was audible, steady and ominous.

They hadn't yet learned his name.

His face was begrimed, smeared by sweat, his uniform filthy, rain-stained and heavily patched. He was becoming visibly more nervous as he approached the front.

Smoke covered the lines in the distance. But already David and Heather could hear the crackle of small arms, the booming of cannon.

Their soldier passed a field hospital now, tents set up at the center of a muddy field. There were rows of unmoving bodies, uncovered, lying outside the nearest tent, and—somehow more horrific—a pile of severed arms and legs, some still bearing scraps of cloth. Two men were feeding the limbs into a brazier. The cries of the wounded within the tents were scratchy, remote, agonizing.

The soldier dug into his jacket and produced a pack of playing cards, battered and bound up with string, and a photograph.

David, working the WormCam controls, froze the image, and zoomed in on the little photograph, much thumbed, its image a crude black-and-white graininess. "It's a woman," he said slowly. "And that looks like a donkey. And . . . Oh."

Heather was smiling. "He's afraid. He thinks he might not live through the day. He doesn't want that stuff sent home with his personal effects."

David resumed the sequence. The soldier dropped his possessions into the mud and ground them in with his heel.

Heather said, "Listen. What's he singing?"

David adjusted the volume and frequency filters. The private's accent was remarkably broad, but the words were recognizable: . . . *Into the ward of the clean white-washed halls / Where the dead slept and the dying lay / Wounded by bayonets, sabers and balls / Somebody's darling was borne one day . . .*

A mounted officer came by behind the line, his black, sweating horse visibly nervous. *Close up. Dress, there. . . . Close up.* His accent was stiff, alien to David's ear—

There was an explosion, flying earth. The bodies of soldiers seemed simply to burst, into large, bloody fragments.

David recoiled. It had been a shell. Suddenly, startlingly quickly, war was here.

The noise level rose abruptly: there was cheering, swearing, a rattle of rifle-muskets and pistols. The private raised his musket, fired rapidly, and dug another cartridge from his belt. He bit into it, exposing the powder and ball, and particles of black powder clung to his lips.

Heather murmured, "They say the powder tasted like pepper."

Another shell landed near the wheel of an artillery piece. A horse close to the gun seemed to explode, bloody scraps flying. A man walking alongside fell, and he looked down in apparent surprise at the stump which now terminated his leg.

All around the private now there was horror: smoke,

fire, mutilated bodies, many men littered on the ground, writhing. But he seemed to be growing more calm. He continued to advance.

David said, "I don't understand. He's in the middle of a mass slaughter. Wouldn't it be rational to retreat, to hide?"

Heather said, "He may not even understand what the war is about. Soldiers often don't. Right now, he's responsible for himself; his destiny is in his own hands. Perhaps he feels relief that the moment has come. And he has his reputation, esteem from his buddies."

"It's a form of madness," David said.

"Of course it is. . . ."

They didn't hear the musket ball coming.

It passed through one eye socket and out the back of the private's head, taking a palm-sized chunk of skull with it. David could see matter within, red and gray.

The private stood there a few seconds more, still bearing his weapon, but his body was shaking, his legs convulsing. Then he fell in a heap.

Another soldier dropped his musket and got to his knees beside him. He lifted the private's head, gently, and seemed to be trying to tuck his brain back into his shattered skull—

David tapped his control. The SoftScreen went blank. He ripped his headphones from his ears.

For a moment he sat still, letting the images and sounds of the gruesome Civil War battlefield fade from his head, to be replaced by the composed scientific calm of the Wormworks, the subdued murmur of the researchers.

In rows of similar cubicles all around them, people toiled at dim WormCam images: tapping at SoftScreens, listening to the mutter of ancient voices in headphones, making notes on yellow legal pads. Most had gained admittance by submitting research proposals which were screened by a committee David had established, and then selected by lottery. Others had been brought in as guests of Hiram's, like Heather and her daughter. They were journalists, researchers, academics seeking to resolve historical disputes and special-interest types—including a few conspiracy theorists—with points to prove.

Somewhere, somebody was softly whistling a nursery rhyme. The melody made an odd counterpoint to the horrors still rattling around David's head—but he knew the significance immediately. One of the more enthusiastic researchers here had been determined to uncover the simple tune said to have formed the basis of Edward Elgar's 1899 *Enigma Variations*. Many candidates had been proposed, from Negro spirituals and forgotten music-hall hits to "Twinkle Twinkle Little Star." Now, though, it sounded as if the researcher had uncovered the truth, and David let his mind supply the words to the gentle melody: *Mary Had a Little Lamb . . .*

The researchers had been drawn here because Our-World was still far ahead of the competition in the power of its WormCam technology. The depth of the past accessible to modern scrutiny was increasing all the time; some researchers had already reached as far back as three centuries. But for now—for better or worse—the use of the powerful past-viewer WormCams remained tightly controlled, offered only in facilities like this, where its users were screened and prioritized and monitored, their results edited carefully and given interpretative glosses before public release.

But David knew that no matter how far back he looked, whatever he witnessed, however the images were analyzed and discussed, the fifteen minutes of the War Between the States he had just endured would stay with him forever.

Heather touched his arm. "You don't have a very strong stomach, do you? We've only scratched the surface of this war—barely begun to study the past."

"But it is a vast, banal butchery."

"Of course. Isn't it always? In fact the Civil War was

one of the first truly modern wars. More than six hundred thousand dead, nearly half a million wounded, in a country whose population was only thirty million. It's as if, today, we lost five million. It was a peculiarly American triumph for such a young country to stage such a vast conflict."

"But it was just." Heather was working on the Civil War period as part of her research for the first WormCam-compiled TrueBio of Abraham Lincoln, funded by an historical association. "Will that be your conclusion? After all the war led to the eradication of slavery in the United States."

"But that wasn't what the war was about. We're about to lose our romantic illusions about it—to confront the truth that the braver historians have faced all along. The war was a clash of economic interests, North against South. The slaves were an economic asset worth billions of dollars. And it was a bloody affair, erupting out of a class-ridden, unequal society. Troops from Gettysburg were sent to New York to put down antidraft riots. Lincoln jailed around thirty thousand political prisoners, without trial—"

David whistled. "You think Lincoln's reputation can survive our seeing all that?" He began to set up a new run.

She shrugged. "Lincoln remains an impressive figure. Even though he wasn't gay."

That jolted David. "What? Are you sure?"

She smiled. "Not even bi."

From the neighboring cubicle he could hear a faint sound of high-pitched screaming.

Heather smiled at him tiredly. "Mary. She's watching the Beatles again."

"The Beatles?"

Heather listened for a moment. "The Top Ten Club in Hamburg. April 1961, probably. Legendary performances, where the Beatles are thought to have played better than they ever did again. Never filmed, and so of course never seen again until now. Mary is working her way through the performances, night after night of them."

"Umm. How are things between you?"

She glanced at the partition, spoke in a subdued whisper. "I'm worried that our relationship is heading for a full-scale breakdown. David, I don't know what she does half the time, where she goes, who she meets. . . . All I get is her anger. It was only the bribe of using an OurWorld WormCam that brought her here today. Aside from the Beatles, I don't even know what she's using it for."

He hesitated. "I'm somewhat dubious about the ethics of what I'm offering. But—would you like me to find out?"

She frowned, and pushed greying hair out of her eyes. "Can you do that?"

"I'll talk to her."

The SoftScreen image stabilized.

The world will little note nor long remember what we say here, but it can never forget what they did here . . .

Lincoln's audience—in their stiff top hats and black coats, almost all of them male—looked unutterably alien, David thought. And Lincoln himself towered above them, so tall and spare he seemed almost grotesque, his voice an irritatingly high, nasal whine. And yet—

"And yet," he said, "his words still have the power to move."

"Yes," Heather said. "I think Lincoln will survive the TrueBio process. He was complex, ambiguous, never straightforward. He told audiences what they wanted to hear—sometimes pro-Abolition, sometimes not. He certainly wasn't the Abe of the legend. Old Abe, honest Abe, father Abe . . . But he was living in difficult times. He came through a hellish war by turning it into a crusade. If not for Abe, who knows if the nation could have survived?"

"And he wasn't gay."

"Nope."

"What about the Joshua Speed diary?"

"A clever forgery, put together after Lincoln's death by the ring of Confederate sympathizers who were behind his assassination. All designed to blacken his character, even after they'd taken his life. . . ."

Abraham Lincoln's sexuality had come under scrutiny following the discovery of a diary supposedly written by Joshua Speed, a merchant in Springfield, Illinois, with whom Lincoln, as a young, impoverished lawyer, had lodged for some years. Although both Speed and Lincoln had later married—and in fact both had reputations as womanizers—rumors had developed that they had lived as gay lovers.

In the difficult opening years of the twenty-first century, Lincoln had been reborn as a figure of toleration and broad appeal—"Pink Lincoln," a divided hero for a divided age. At Easter 2015, the 150th anniversary of Lincoln's assassination, this had climaxed in an open-air celebration around the Lincoln Memorial in Washington, D.C.; for a single night, the great stone figure had been bathed in gaudy pink spotlights.

". . . I have notarized WormCam records to prove it," Heather said now. "I've had expert systems fast-forward through Lincoln's every sexual encounter. There's not a single trace of gay or bi behavior in there."

"But Speed—"

"He and Lincoln shared a bed, those years in Illinois. But that wasn't uncommon back then—Lincoln couldn't afford a bed of his own!"

David scratched his head. "This," he said, "is going to annoy everybody."

She said, "You know, we're going to have to get used to this. No more heroes, no more fairy tales. Successful leaders are pragmatic. Almost every choice they make is between bad options; the wisest of them, like Lincoln, pick out the least worst, consistently. And that's about all you can ask of them."

David nodded. "Perhaps. But you Americans are lucky that you are already running out of history. We Europeans have thousands more years left to witness."

They fell silent, and gazed at the stiff images of Lincoln and his audience, the tinny voices, the rustle of applause from men long dead.

18

HINDSIGHT

After six months, Kate's case was still held up.

Bobby put in calls every few days to see FBI Special Agent Michael Mavens. Mavens steadfastly refused to see him.

Then, abruptly, to Bobby's surprise, Mavens invited Bobby to come out to FBI Headquarters in Washington, D.C. Bobby hastily arranged a flight.

He found Mavens in his office, a small anonymous box, windowless and stuffy. Mavens was sitting behind his littered desk—feet propped up on a pile of file boxes, jacket off, tie loose—watching a news show on a small SoftScreen. He waved Bobby silent.

The piece was about the extension of the scope of citizens' truth squad activities to the murkier corners of the past, now that—in response to a powerful and immediate clamor—past-viewing WormCam facilities had at last been made available for private use.

In the midst of poring over each other's grubby past, in between staring at their own younger selves in awe or amazement or shame, people had been turning the WormCam's unforgiving gaze on the rich and powerful. There had been a whole new spate of resignations from public office and prominent organizations and corporations, as various past crimes were disinterred. A whole series of old outrages were being turned over. The coals of the old scandal of the tobacco companies' knowledge of, indeed manipulation of, the addictive and toxic effects of their products, were being raked once more. The involvement and profit-making of the world's larger companies in Nazi Germany—many of them still operating, some of them American—had been even more extensive than imagined; the justification that de-Nazification had been left incomplete in order to assist economic recovery after the war looked, at this remove, dubious. Most computer manufacturers had indeed made inadequate provisions to shield their customers when microwave-frequency microchips had come on the market in the first decade of the century, leading to a rash of cancers. . . .

Bobby said, "So much for the scare predictions of how we ordinary folk wouldn't be mature enough to handle a technology as powerful as the past viewer. All this seems pretty responsible to me."

Mavens grunted. "Maybe. Although we're all using WormCams for the sleazy stuff too. At least these crusading citizen types aren't just beating up on the government. I always thought the big corporations were a bigger threat to freedom than anything *we* were likely to do. In fact we in government were the ones holding them in check."

Bobby smiled. "We—OurWorld—were caught by the microwave row. The compensation claims are still being assessed."

"Everybody's apologizing to everybody else. What a world. . . . Bobby, I got to tell you I still don't think we can achieve much progress on Ms. Manzoni's case. But we can talk about it, if you like." Mavens looked exhausted, his eyes black-rimmed, as if he hadn't been sleeping.

"If there's no progress, why am I here?"

Mavens looked unhappy, uncomfortable, somehow out of place. He had lost the brave youthful certainty Bobby remembered about him. "Because I have time on my hands, all of a sudden. I'm not suspended, in case you're thinking that. Call it a sabbatical. One of my old cases has been under review." He eyed Bobby. "And—"

"What?"

"I want you to see what your WormCam is really doing to us. Just one time, one example. You remember the Wilson murder?"

"Wilson?"

"New York City, a couple of years ago. A young teenager from Bangladesh—he'd been orphaned by the floods in '33."

"I remember."

"The UN placement agency found this particular relocate, called Mian Sharif, an adoptive home in New York. A middle-aged, childless couple who'd taken one adopted kid before—a girl, Barbara—and brought her up successfully. Apparently.

"The story looked simple. Mian is killed at home. Mutilated, before and after death, apparently raped. The father was the prime suspect." He grimaced. "Family members always are.

"I worked on the case. The forensics were ambiguous, and Wilson's mind maps showed no particular propensity to violence, sexual or otherwise. But we had enough to convict the man. Philip George Wilson was executed by lethal injection on November 27, 2034."

"But now . . ."

"Because of the demand on WormCam time for new and unresolved cases, the review of closed cases like Wilson has been a low priority. But now the public have gotten online to the WormCams, they are looking for themselves, and they are starting to agitate for some old cases to be reopened: friends, family, even the convicted themselves."

"And now the Wilson case."

"Yeah." Mavens smiled thinly. "Maybe you can understand how I'm feeling. You see, before the WormCam, I could never be sure what the truth is in any given case. No witness is a hundred percent reliable. The perps know how to lie through forensics. I couldn't *know* what happened, unless I was there.

"Wilson was the first convicted criminal to be executed because of my work. I knew I'd done the best I could to establish the truth. But now, years after the event, I've been able to see Wilson's alleged crime for the first time. And I found out the truth about the man I sent to the needle."

"Are you sure you ought to show me—"

"It will be in the public domain soon enough." Mavens twisted the SoftScreen around so Bobby could see, and began to dial up a recording.

The 'Screen cleared to show a bedroom. There was a wide bed, a wardrobe and cupboards, animated posters of rock and sports stars and movie icons on the wall. A boy lay facedown on the bed: slim, dressed in T-shirt and jeans, he was propped up on his elbows over books and a primary-color SoftScreen, sucking a pencil. He was dark, his hair a rich black mass.

Bobby said, "That's Mian?"

"Yeah. Bright kid, lived quietly, worked hard. He's doing his homework. Shakespeare, as it happens. Aged thirteen, though I guess he looks a little younger. Well, he won't get any older. . . . Tell me if you want to stop this."

Bobby nodded, curtly, resolved to see this through. This was a test, he thought. A test of his new humanity.

The door opened outward, admitting a burly middle-aged man. "Here comes the father. Philip George Wilson." Wilson was carrying a soda bottle; he opened it and set it down on a bedside table. The boy looked around and said a few words.

Mavens said, "We know what they said. What are you working on, what time does Mom get home, blah blah. Nothing consequential; just an ordinary exchange."

Wilson ruffled the boy's hair and left the room. Mian smoothed back his hair and went back to work.

Mavens froze the image; the boy turned to a statue, his image flickering slightly.

"Let me tell you what we thought happened next—as we reconstructed it back in '34.

"Wilson comes back into the room. He makes some kind of pass at the boy. The boy rebuffs him. So Wilson attacks him. Maybe the boy fights back; if so, he didn't do Wilson any damage. Wilson has a knife—which, incidentally, we don't find. He cuts and rips at the kid's clothes. He mutilates him. After he kills the boy, by cutting his throat, he may have performed sex on the body, or he may have masturbated; we find flecks of Wilson's semen on the body.

"And *then*, cradling the body, covered in blood, he yells 911 at the Search Engine."

"You're kidding."

Mavens shrugged. "People act in strange ways. The facts are that there was no way in or out of the apartment save for locked windows and doors, none of which were forced. The hallway security cams showed nothing.

"We had no suspects save for Wilson, and a lot of evidence against him. He never denied what he did. I think maybe he believed himself that he really had done it, even though he had no memory of it.

"Our experts were split. We have psychoanalysts who say Wilson's knowledge of his appalling act was too much for his ego to bear. So he repressed it, came out of the episode, returned to something like normal. Then we have cynics who say he's lying, that he knew exactly what he was doing; when he realized he couldn't get away with the crime, he feigned mental problems to secure a softer sentence. And we have neurologists who say he probably suffers from a form of epilepsy."

Bobby prompted, "But now we have the truth."

"Yes. Now, the truth." Mavens tapped the SoftScreen, and the recording resumed.

There was an air-conditioning grille in the corner of the bedroom. It popped open. The boy, Mian, got to his feet quickly, looking startled, and backed into a corner.

"He didn't call out at this point," Mavens said softly. "If he had . . ."

Now a figure crawled out through the open grille. It was a girl, dressed in a tight-fitting spandex ski suit. She looked sixteen, might have been older. She was holding a knife.

Mavens froze the image again.

Bobby frowned. "Who the hell is that?"

"The Wilsons' first adopted daughter. She's called Barbara—you remember I mentioned her. Here she was eighteen years old, and she'd been living away from home a couple of years."

"But she still had the security code to get into the building."

"Yeah. She came in disguise. Then she got into the air ducts, big fat ones in a building that age. And that's how she got into the apartment.

"We used the 'Cam to track her back a couple of years deeper into the past. Turns out her relationship with her father was a little more complex than anyone had known.

"They got on fine when she lived at home. After she left for college, she had a couple of bad experiences. She wanted to come home. The parents talked it over, but encouraged her to stay away, to become independent. Maybe they were wrong to do that, maybe they were right. But they meant well.

"She came home anyway, one night when the mother was away. She crawled in bed with her sleeping father, and performed oral sex on him. She was the initiator. But he didn't stop her. Afterward he was full of guilt. The boy, Mian, was asleep in the next room."

"So they had a row—"

"No. Wilson was distressed, ashamed, but tried to remain sensible. He sent her back to college, talking about putting this behind them, it's a one-off. Maybe he really thought time would heal the wounds. Well, he was wrong.

"What he didn't understand was Barbara's jealousy. She'd become convinced that Mian had displaced her in her parents' affections, and that was the reason she was shut out, kept away from home."

"Right. So she tries to seduce the father, to find another way back. . . ."

"Not exactly." Mavens hit the SoftScreen, and the little drama began to unfold once more.

Mian, recognizing his adoptive sister, got over his shock and stepped forward.

But with startling speed Barbara closed on him. She elbowed him in the throat, leaving him clutching his neck, gasping.

"Smart," said Mavens professionally. "Now he *can't* call out."

Barbara pushed the boy onto his back and straddled him. She grabbed his hands, held them over his head and began to slash at his clothes.

"She doesn't look strong enough to do that," Bobby said.

"It isn't strength that counts. It's determination. Mian couldn't believe, even now, this girl, a girl he thought of as his sister, was going to do him real harm. Would you?"

Now the boy's chest was bare. Barbara reached down with the knife—

Bobby snapped, "Enough."

Mavens hit a button, and the SoftScreen cleared, to Bobby's profound relief.

Mavens said, "The rest is detail. When Mian was dead she propped him against the door, and called for her father. Wilson came running. When he opened the door his son's warm body fell into his arms. And he called the Search Engine."

"But Wilson's semen—"

"She stored it, after that night she blew him, in a cute

little cryo-flask she liberated from a medical lab. She'd been planning this, even as far back as that." He shrugged. "It all worked out. Revenge, the destruction of the father who had spurned her, as she saw it. It all worked, at least until the WormCam came along. And so—"

"And so the wrong man was convicted."

"Executed."

Mavens tapped the 'Screen and brought up a fresh image. It was of a woman—fortyish, blond. She was sitting in some dingy office. Her face was crumpled with grief.

"This is Mae Wilson," Mavens said. "Philip's wife, mother to the two adopted children. She'd had to come to terms with the death of the boy, what she thought of as her husband's dreadful crime. She'd even reconciled with Barbara, found comfort with her. Now—at this moment—she had to face a much more dreadful truth."

Bobby felt uncomfortable, confronted by this horror, this naked grief. But Mavens froze the image.

"Right here," he murmured. "*That's* where we tore her heart in two. And it's my responsibility."

"You did your best."

"No. I could have done better. The girl, Barbara, had an alibi. But with hindsight it's an alibi I could have taken apart. There were other small things: discrepancies in the timing, the distribution of the blood. But I didn't *see* any of that." He looked at Bobby, his eyes bright. "I didn't see the truth. That's what your WormCam is. It's a truth machine."

Bobby shook his head. "No. It's a hindsight machine."

"It has to be right to bring the truth to light," Mavens said. "I still believe that. Of course I do. But sometimes the truth hurts, beyond belief. Like poor Mae Wilson, here. And you know what? The truth didn't help *her*. It didn't bring Mian back, or her husband. All it did was take her daughter away too."

"We're all going to go through this, one way or another, being forced to confront every mistake we ever made."

"Maybe," Mavens said softly. He smiled and ran his finger along the edge of his desk. "Here's what the WormCam has done for me. My job isn't an intellectual exercise anymore, Sherlock Holmes puzzles. Now I sit here every day and I get to watch the determination, the savagery, the—the calculation. We're animals, Bobby. Beasts, under these neat suits of clothing." He shook his head, still smiling, and he ran his finger along the desk, back and forth, back and forth.

19

TIME

As the availability and power of the WormCam extended relentlessly, so invisible eyes fell like snowflakes through human history, deeper and deeper into time. . . .

Princeton, New Jersey, USA. April 17, 1955 A.D.:

His good humor, in those last hours, struck his visitors. He talked with perfect calm, and joked about his doctors, and in general seemed to regard his approaching end as simply an expected natural phenomenon.

And, of course, even to the end, he issued gruff orders. He was concerned not to become an object of pilgrimage, and he instructed that his office at the Institute should not be preserved as he left it, and that his home should not become a shrine, and so on.

Doctor Dean looked in on him for the last time at eleven P.M., and found him sleeping peacefully.

But a little after midnight his nurse—Mrs. Alberta Roszel—noticed a change in his breathing. She called for help and, with the help of another nurse, cranked up the head of the bed.

He was muttering, and Mrs. Roszel came close to hear.

Even as the finest mind since Newton began, at last, to unravel, final thoughts floated to the surface of his consciousness. Perhaps he regretted the great physics unification project he had left unfinished. Perhaps he wondered if his pacifism had after all been the right course—if he had been correct to encourage Roosevelt to enter the nuclear age. Perhaps, simply, he regretted how he had always put science first, even over those who loved him.

But it was too late for all that. His life, so vivid and complex in youth and middle age, was now reducing, as all lives must, to a single thread of utter simplicity.

Mrs. Roszel bent close to hear his soft voice. But his words were in German, the language of his youth, and she did not understand.

. . . And she did not see, could not see, the swarm of spacetime flaws which, in these last moments, crowded around the trembling lips of Einstein to hear those final words: ". . . *Lieserl! Oh, Lieserl!*"

Extracted from testimony by Prof. Maurice Patefield, Massachusetts Institute of Technology, chair of the "Wormseed" campaign group, to the Congressional Committee for the Study of the American Electorate, 23 September, 2037:

As soon as it became apparent that the WormCam can reach, not just through walls, but into the past, a global obsession of the human species with its own history opened up.

At first we were treated to professionally-made "factual" WormCam movies showing such great events as wars, assassinations, political scandals. *Unsinkable,* the multi-viewpoint reconstruction of the *Titanic* disaster, for example, made harrowing, compelling viewing—even though it demolished many sea-story myths propagated by uncritical storytellers, and much of the event took place in pitch North Atlantic darkness.

But we soon grew impatient with the interpolation of the professionals. We wanted to see for ourselves.

The hasty inspection of many notorious moments of the recent past has revealed both banality and surprise. The depressing truths surrounding Elvis Presley, O. J. Simpson and even the deaths of the Kennedys surely surprised nobody. On the other hand, the revelations about the murders of so many prominent women—from Marilyn Monroe through Mother Teresa to Diana, Princess of Wales— caused a wave of shock, even in a society becoming accustomed to too much truth. The existence of a shadowy, relentless cabal of misogynistic men whose activities against (as they saw it) too-powerful women, actions carried across decades, caused much soul-searching among both sexes.

But many true-story versions of historic events— the Cuba missile crisis, Watergate, the fall of the Berlin Wall, the collapse of the euro—while of interest to aficionados, have turned out to be muddled, confusing and complex. It is dismaying to realize that even those supposedly at the centers of power generally know little and understand less of what is going on around them.

With all respect to the great traditions of this House, almost all the key incidents in human history are screwups, it seems, just as almost all the great passions are no more than crude and manipulative fumblings.

And, worse than that, the truth generally turns out to be *boring*.

The lack of pattern and logic in the overwhelming, almost unrecognizable true history that is now being revealed is proving so difficult and wearying for all but the most ardent scholar that fictionalized accounts are actually making a comeback: stories which provide a narrative structure simple enough to engage the viewer. We need story and meaning, not blunt fact. . . .

Toulouse, France. 14 January, 1636 A.D.:

In the dusty calm of his study, he took down his beloved copy of Diophantus' *Arithmetica*. With great excitement he turned to Book II, Problem 8, and hunted for a quill.

> *. . . On the other hand, it is impossible for a cube to be written as a sum of two cubes or a fourth power to be written as a sum of two fourth powers, or, in general, for any number which is a power greater than the second to be written as a sum of two like powers. I have a truly marvelous demonstration of this proposition which this margin is too narrow to contain . . .*

Bernadette Winstanley, a fourteen-year-old student from Harare, Zimbabwe, booked time on her high-school WormCam and devoted herself to tracking back from the moment of Fermat's brief scribbling in that margin.

. . . This was where it had started for him, and so it was appropriate that it was here that it should end. It was after all Diophantus' eighth problem which had so intrigued him, and sent him on his voyage of mathematical discovery: *Given a number which is a square, write it as a sum of two other squares.* This was the algebraic expression of Pythagoras' theorem, of course; and every schoolchild knew solutions: 3 squared plus 4 squared, for example, meaning 9 plus 16, summed to 25, which was 5 squared.

Ah, but what of an extension of the notion beyond this geometric triviality? Were there numbers which could be expressed as sums of *greater* powers? 3 cubed plus 4 cubed made 27 plus 64, summing to 91—not itself a cube. But did *any* such triplets exist? And what of the higher powers, the fourth, fifth, sixth . . . ?

It was clear the ancients had known of no such cases—nor had they known a proof of impossibility.

But now *he*—a lawyer and magistrate, not even a professional mathematician—had managed to prove that no triple of numbers existed for *any* index higher than two.

Bernadette imaged sheets of notes expressing the essence of the proof Fermat believed he had found, and, with some help from a teacher, deciphered their meaning.

. . . For now he was pressed by his duties, but when he had time he would assemble a formal expression of his proof from the scribbled notes and sketches he had accumulated. Then he would communicate it to Desargues, Descartes, Pascal, Bernoulli and the others—how they would marvel at its far-reaching elegance!

And then he could explore the numbers further: those pellucid yet stubbornly complex entities, which seemed at times so strange he fancied they must have an existence independent of the human mind which had conceived them. . . .

Pierre de Fermat never wrote out the proof of what would become known as his Last Theorem. But that brief marginalia, discovered after Fermat's death by his son, would tantalize and fascinate later generations of mathematicians. A proof *was* found—but not until the 1990s, and it was of such technical intricacy, involving abstract properties of elliptic curves and other unfamiliar mathematical entities, that scholars believed it was impossible Fermat could have found a proof in his day. Perhaps he had been mistaken—or had even perpetrated a huge hoax on later generations.

Then, in the year 2037, to general amazement, armed with no more than high-school math, fourteen-year-old Bernadette Winstanley was able to prove that Fermat had been right.

And when at last Fermat's proof was published a revolution in mathematics began.

Patefield Testimony: Of course, the kooky fringe immediately found a way to get online to history. As a scientist and a rationalist I regard it as a great fortune that the WormCam has proven the greatest debunker yet discovered.

And so it is now indisputable, for example, that there was no crashed UFO at Roswell, New Mexico, in 1947. Not a single alien-abduction incident yet inspected has turned out to be anything more than a misinterpretation of some innocent phenomenon—often complicated by disturbed neurological states. Similarly, not a shred of evidence has emerged for any paranormal or supernatural phenomenon, no matter how notorious.

Whole industries of psychics, mediums, astrologers, faith healers, homeopathists and others are being systematically demolished. We must look forward to the day when the WormCam's delvings reach as far as the building of the Pyramids, Stonehenge, the Nazca geoglyphs and other sources of "wisdom" or "mystery." And then will come Atlantis . . .

It may be a new day is dawning—it may be that in the not too distant future the mass of humanity will at last conclude that truth is more interesting than delusion.

Florence, Italy. 12 April, 1506 A.D.:
Bernice would readily admit she was no more than a junior researcher in the Louvre's curatorial office. And so it was a surprise—a welcome one!—when she was asked to perform the first provenance check on one of the museum's most famous paintings.

Even if the result was less welcome.

At first the search had been simple: in fact, confined to the walls of the Louvre itself. Before a blur of visitors, attended by generations of curators, the fine old lady sat in semidarkness behind her panes of protective glass, silently watching time unravel.

The years before the transfer to the Louvre were more complex.

Bernice glimpsed a series of fine houses, generations of elegance and power punctuated by intervals of war and social unrest and poverty. Much of this, back as deep as the seventeenth century, confirmed the painting's documented record.

Then—in the early years of that century, more than a hundred years after the painting's supposed composition—came the first surprise. Bernice watched, stunned, as a scrawny, hungry-looking young painter stood before two side-by-side copies of the famous image—and, time-reversed, with brushstroke after brushstroke, eliminated the copy that had passed down the centuries to the care of the Louvre.

Briefly she detoured to track forward in time, following the fate of the older "original" from which the Louvre's copy—just a copy, a replica!—had been made. That "original" was to last little more than two centuries, she saw, before being lost in a massive house fire in Revolutionary France.

WormCam studies had exposed many of the world's best-known works of art as forgeries and copies—more than *seventy percent* of pre-twentieth-century paintings (and a smaller proportion of sculptures, smaller presumably only because of the effort required to make copies). History was a dangerous, destructive corridor through which very little of value survived unscathed.

But still there had been no indication that *this* painting, of all of them, had been a fake. Although at least a dozen replicas had been known to circulate at various times and places, the Louvre had a continuous record of ownership since the artist had laid down his brush. And there was besides evidence of changes to the composition under the top layer of paint: an indication more of an original, assayed and reworked, than a copy.

But then, Bernice reflected, composition techniques and records could be faked too.

Bewildered, she returned down the decades to that dingy room, the ingenious, forging painter. And she began to follow the "original" he had copied deeper into the past.

More decades flickered by, more transfers of ownership, all of it an uninteresting blur around the changeless painting itself.

At last she approached the start of the sixteenth century, and was nearing *his* studio, in Florence. Even now copies were being made, by the master's own students. But all of the copies were of this, the lost "original" she had identified.

Perhaps there would be no more surprises.

She was to be proved wrong.

Oh, it was true that *he* was involved in the composition, preliminary sketches, and much of the painting's design. It was to be the ideal portrait, he declared grandly, the features and symbolic overtones of its subject synthesized into a perfect unity, and with a sweeping, flowing style to astound his contemporaries and fascinate later generations. The conception, indeed, was *his*, and the triumph.

But not the execution. The master—distracted by many commissions and his wider interests in science and technology—left *that* to others.

Bernice, awe and dismay swirling in her heart, watched as a young man from the provinces called Raphael Sanzio painstakingly applied the last touches to that gentle, puzzling smile. . . .

Patefield Testimony: It is a matter of regret that many cherished—and harmless—myths, now exposed to the cold light of this future day, are evaporating.

Betsy Ross is a notorious recent instance.

There really was a Betsy Ross. But she was never

visited by George Washington; she was not asked to make a flag for the new nation; she did not work on its design with Washington; she did not make up the flag in her back parlor. As far as can be determined, all this stuff was a concoction of her grandson's, almost a century later.

Davy Crockett's myth was self-manufactured, his coonskin legend developed fairly cynically to create popularity by the Whig party in Congress. There has been not one WormCam observation of him using the phrase "b'ar-hunting" on Capitol Hill.

Paul Revere, on the other hand, has had his reputation enhanced by the WormCam.

For many years Revere served as the principal rider for Boston's Committee of Safety. His most famous ride—to Lexington to warn revolutionary leaders that the British were on the march—was, ironically, more hazardous, Revere's achievement still more heroic, even than the legend of Longfellow's poem. But still, many modern Americans have been dismayed by the heavy French accent Revere had inherited from his father.

And so it goes on—not just in America, but around the world. There are even some famous figures—the commentators call them "snowmen"—who prove never to have existed at all! What is becoming more interesting than the myths themselves has been the study of how the myths were constructed from sparse or unpromising facts—indeed, sometimes from *no* facts—in a kind of mute conspiracy of longing, very rarely under anybody's conscious control.

We must wonder where this will lead us. Just as the human memory is not a passive recorder but a tool in the construction of the self, so history has never been a simple record of the past, but a means of shaping peoples.

But, just as each human will now have to learn

to construct a personality in the glare of pitiless WormCam inspection, so communities will have to come to terms with the stripped-bare truth of their own past—and find new ways to express their common values and history, if they are to survive the future.

And the sooner we get on with it, the better.

Similaun Glacier, Alps. April, 2321 B.C.:
It was an elemental world: black rock, blue sky, hard white ice. This was one of the highest passes in the Alps. The man, alone, moved through this lethal environment with utter confidence.

But Marcus knew the man he watched was already approaching the place where, slumped over a boulder and with his Neolithic tool kit stacked neatly at his side, he would meet his death.

At first—as he had explored the possibilities of the WormCam, here at the Institute of Alpine Studies at the University of Innsbruck—Marcus Pinch had feared that the WormCam would destroy archaeology and replace it with something more resembling butterfly hunting: the crude observation of "the truth," perhaps by untrained eyes. There would be no more Schliemanns, no more Troys, no more patient unraveling of the past from shards and traces.

But as it turned out there was still a role for the accumulated wisdom of archaeology, as the best intellectual reconstruction available of the true past. There was just too much to see—and the WormCam horizon expanded all the time. For the time being, the role of the WormCam was be to supplement conventional archaeological techniques: to provide key pieces of evidence to resolve disputes, to reinforce or overthrow hypotheses, as a more correct consensual narrative of the past slowly emerged.

And in this case, for Marcus, the truth that would be revealed—here now, by the blue-white-black images relayed through time and space to his SoftScreen—would provide answers to the most compelling questions in his own professional career.

This man, this hunter, had been dug out of the ice fifty-three centuries after he died. The smears of blood, tissue, starch, hair and fragments of feather on his tools and clothing had enabled the scientists, Marcus included, to reconstruct much of his life. Modern researchers had even, whimsically, given him a name: Ötzi, the Ice Man.

His two arrows were of particular interest to Marcus—in fact, they had served as the basis of Marcus's doctorate. Both the arrows were broken, and Marcus had been able to demonstrate that before he died, the hunter had been trying to dismantle the arrows, intent on making one good arrow out of the two broken ones, by fitting the better arrowhead into the good shaft.

It was such painstaking detective work as this that had drawn Marcus into archaeology. Marcus saw no limit to the reach of such techniques. Perhaps in some sense *every* event left some mark on the universe, a mark that could one day be decoded by sufficiently ingenious instruments. In a sense the WormCam was the crystallization of the unspoken intuition of every archaeologist: that the past is a country, real, out there somewhere, which can be explored, fingertip by fingertip.

But a new book of truth was opening. For the 'Cam could answer questions left untouched by traditional archaeology, no matter how powerful the techniques—even about this man, Ötzi, who had become the best-known human of all those who had lived throughout prehistory.

What had never been answered—what was impossible to answer from the fragments recovered—was *why* the Ice Man had died. Perhaps he was fleeing warfare, or pursuing a love affair. Perhaps he was a criminal, fleeing the rough justice of his time.

Marcus had intuited that all these explanations were parochial, projections of a modern world on a more austere past. But he longed, along with the rest of the world, to know the truth.

But now the world had forgotten Ötzi, with his skin clothes and tools of flint and copper, the mystery of his lonely death. Now, in a world where *any* figure from the past could be made to come to vibrant life, Ötzi was no longer a novelty, nor even particularly interesting. Nobody cared to learn how, after all, he had died.

Nobody save Marcus. So Marcus had sat in the chill gloom of this university facility, struggling through that Alpine pass at Ötzi's shoulder, until the truth had become apparent.

Ötzi was a high-status Alpine hunter. His copper axehead and bearskin hat were marks of hunting prowess and prestige. And his goal, on this fatal expedition, had been the most elusive quarry of all, the only Alpine animal which retires to high rocky areas at night: the ibex.

But Ötzi was old—at forty-six, he had already reached an advanced age for a man of his period. He was plagued by arthritis, and afflicted today by an intestinal infection which had given him chronic diarrhea. Perhaps he had grown weaker, slower than he knew—or cared to admit.

He had followed his quarry ever deeper into the cold heights of the mountains. He had made his simple camp in this pass, intending to repair the arrowheads he had broken, continue his pursuit the next day. He had taken a final meal, of salted goat flesh and dried plums.

But the night had turned crystal clear, and the wind had howled through the pass, drawing Ötzi's life heat with it.

It was a sad, lonely death, and Marcus, watching, thought there was a moment when Ötzi tried to rise, as if aware of his terrible mistake, as if he knew he was dying. But he could not rise; and Marcus could not reach through the WormCam to help him.

And so Ötzi would lie alone, entombed in his ice, for five thousand years.

Marcus shut down the WormCam, and once more Ötzi was at peace.

Patefield Testimony: Many nations—not just America—are facing grave internal dialogues about the new truths revealed about the past, truths in many cases barely reported, if at all, in conventional histories.

In France, for example, there has been much soul-searching about the unexpectedly wide nature of collaboration with the Nazi regime during the German occupation of the Second World War. Reassuring myths about the significance of the wartime Resistance have been severely damaged—not least by the new revelations about David Moulin, a revered Resistance leader. Barely anyone who knows the legend of Moulin was prepared to learn that he had begun his career as a Nazi mole—although he was later persuaded to his national cause, and was in fact tortured and executed by the SS in 1943.

Modern Belgians seem overwhelmed by their confrontation with the brutal reality of the "Congo Free State," a tightly centralized colony designed to strip the territory of its natural wealth—principally rubber—and maintained by atrocity, murder, starvation, exposure, disease and hunger, resulting in the uprooting of whole communities and the massacre, between 1885 and 1906, of eight million people.

In the lands of the old Soviet Union, people are fixated on the era of the Stalinist terror. The Germans are confronting the Holocaust once more. The Japanese, for the first time in generations, are having to come to terms with the truth of their wartime massacres and other brutalities in Szechwan and elsewhere. Israelis are uncomfortably aware of their own crimes against the Palestinians. The fragile Serbian democracy is threatening to collapse under the new exposure of the horrors in Bosnia and elsewhere after the breakup of the old Yugoslavia.

And so on.

Most of these past horrors were well known before the WormCam, of course, and many honest and conscientious histories were written. But still the endless dismal banality of it all, the human reality of so much cruelty and pain and waste, remains utterly dismaying.

And stronger emotions than dismay have been stirred.

Ethnic and religious disputes centuries old have been the trigger for many past conflicts. So it has been this time: we have seen interpersonal anger, riots, interethnic struggles, even coups and minor wars. And much of the anger is still directed at OurWorld, the messenger who has delivered so much dismal truth.

But it could have been worse.

As it turns out—while there has been much anger expressed at ancient wrongs, some never even exposed before—by and large each community has become too aware of its own crimes, against its own people and others, to seek atonement for those of others. No nation is without sin; none seems prepared to cast the first stone, and almost every surviving major institution—be it nation, corporation, church—finds itself forced to apologize for crimes committed in its name in the past.

But there is a deeper shock to be confronted.

The WormCam, after all, does not deliver its history lessons in the form of verbal summaries or neat animated maps. Nor does it have much to say of glory or honor. Rather, it simply shows us human beings, one at a time—very often starving or suffering or dying at the hands of others.

Greatness no longer matters. We see now that

each human being who dies is the center of a universe: a unique spark of hope and despair, hate and love, going alone into the greater darkness. It is as if the WormCam has brought a new democracy to the viewing of history. As Lincoln might have remarked, the history emerging from all this intent WormCam inspection will be a new story of mankind: a story of the people, by the people, for the people.

Now, what matters most is *my* story—or my lover's, or my parent's, or my ancestor's, who died the most mundane, meaningless of deaths in the mud of Stalingrad or Passchendaele or Gettysburg, or simply in some unforgiving field, broken by a life of drudgery. Empowered by the WormCam, assisted by such great genealogical record centers as the Mormons', we have all discovered our ancestors.

There are those who argue that this is dangerous and destabilizing. After all, the spate of divorces and suicides which followed the WormCam's first gift of openness has now been followed by a fresh wave as we have become able to spy on our partners, not just in the real time of the present, but in the past as far back as we care to look, and every past misdeed, open or hidden, is made available for scrutiny, every old wound reopened. But this is a process of adjustment, which the strongest relationships will survive. And anyhow, such comparatively trivial consequences of the WormCam are surely insignificant compared to the great gift of deeper historical truth which, for the first time, is being made available to us.

So I do not endorse the doomsayers. I say, trust the people. Give us the tools and we will finish the job.

There is a growing clamor—tragically impossible to satisfy—to find a way, some way, any way, to *change* the past: to help the suffering long-dead, even to redeem them. But the past is immutable; only the future is there to be shaped.

With all the difficulties and dangers, we are privileged to be alive at such a time. There will surely never again be a time when the light of truth and understanding spreads with such overwhelming rapidity into the darkness of the past, never again a time when the mass consciousness of mankind is transformed so dramatically. The new generations, born in the omnipresent shadow of the WormCam, will grow up with a very different view of their species and its past.

For better or worse.

Middle East. c. 1250 B.C.:

Miriam was a tutor of accounting expert systems: certainly no professional historian. But, like almost everybody else she knew, she had gotten hold of WormCam time as soon as it had become available, and started to research her own passions. And, in Miriam's case, that passion focused on a single man: a man whose story had been her lifelong inspiration.

But the closer the WormCam brought Miriam to her subject, the more, maddeningly, he seemed to dissolve. The very act of observing was destroying him, as if he was obeying some unwelcome form of historical uncertainty principle.

Yet she persisted.

At last, having spent long hours searching for him in the harsh, confusing sunlight of those ancient deserts, she began to consult the professional historians who had gone before her into these wastes of time. And, piece by piece, she confirmed for herself what they had deduced.

The career of the man himself—shorn of its supernatural elements—was a fairly crude conflation of the biographies of several leaders of that era, as the nation of Israel had coalesced from groups of Palestinian refugees fleeing the collapse of Canaanite city-states. The rest was invention or theft.

That business, for instance, of being concealed in a wicker basket and floated down the Nile, in order to save him from murder as a firstborn Israelite: that was no more than a conflation of older legends from Mesopotamia and Egypt—about the god Horus, for example—none of which was based on fact either. And he'd never been an Egyptian prince. That fragment seemed to come from the story of a Syrian called Bay who had served as Egypt's chief treasurer, and had made it to Pharaoh, as Ramosekhayemnetjeru.

But what is truth?

After all, as preserved by the myth, he had been a complex, human, inspiring man. He was marked by imperfection: he had stammered, and often fell out with the very people he led. He even argued with God. But his triumph over those imperfections had been an inspiration, over three thousand years, to many people, including Miriam herself—named for his beloved sister—who had had to overcome the obstacles set in her own life by her cerebral palsy.

He was irresistible, as vividly real as any personage from "true" history, and Miriam knew he would live on into the future. And given that, did it *matter* that Moses never truly existed?

It was a new obsession, Bobby saw, as millions of figures from history—renowned and otherwise—came briefly to life once more, under the gaze of this first generation of WormCam witnesses.

Absenteeism seemed to be reaching an all-time high, as people abandoned their work, their vocations, even their loved ones to devote themselves to the endless fascination of the WormCam. It was as if the human race had become suddenly old, content to hide away, feeding on its memories.

And perhaps that was how it was, Bobby thought. After all, if the Wormwood couldn't be turned away, there was no future to speak of. Maybe the WormCam, with its gift of the past, was precisely what the human race required right now: a bolt-hole.

And each of those witnesses was coming to understand that one day she too would be no more than a thing of light and shadow, embedded in time, perhaps scrutinized in her turn from some unknowable future.

But to Bobby, it was not the mass of mankind that concerned him, not the great currents of history and thought that were stirred, but the breaking heart of his brother.

20

CRISIS OF FAITH

David had turned into a recluse, it seemed to Bobby. He would come to the Wormworks unannounced, perform obscure experiments, and return to his apartment, where—according to OurWorld records—he continued to make extensive use of WormCam technology, pursuing his own obscure, undeclared projects.

After three weeks, Bobby sought him out. David met him at his door, seemed on the point of refusing to let him in. Then he stood aside.

The apartment was cluttered, books and SoftScreens everywhere. A place where a man was living alone, habits unmoderated by consideration of others.

"What the hell happened to you?"

David managed to smile. "The WormCam, Bobby. What else?"

"Heather said you assisted her with the Lincoln project."

"Yes. That was what gave me the bug, perhaps. But now I have seen too much history. . . . I am a bad host. Would you like a drink, some beer—"

"Come on, David. Talk to me."

David rubbed his blond scalp. "This is called a crisis of faith, Bobby. I don't expect you to understand."

In fact Bobby, irritated, did understand, and he was disappointed with the mundanity of his brother's condition. Every day, WormCam addicts, hooked on history, beat on OurWorld's corporate doors, demanding ever more 'Cam access. But then David had isolated himself; perhaps he didn't know how much a part of the human race he remained, how common his addiction had become.

But how to tell him?

Bobby said carefully, "You're suffering history shock. It's a—fashionable—condition right now. It will pass."

"Fashionable, is it?" David glowered at him.

"We're all feeling the same." He cast around for examples. "I watched the premiere of Beethoven's Ninth: the Karntnertor Theater, Vienna, 1824. Did you see that?" The symphony performance had been professionally recorded and rebroadcast by one of the media conglomerates. But the ratings had been poor. "It was a mess. The playing was lousy, the choir discordant. The Shakespeare was even worse."

"Shakespeare?"

"You really have been locked away, haven't you? It was the premiere of *Hamlet*, at the Globe in 1601. The playing was amateurish, the costumes ridiculous, the crowd a drunken rabble, the Theater not much more than a thatched cesspit. And the accents were so foreign the play had to be subtitled. The deeper into the past we look, the stranger it all seems.

"A lot of people are finding the new history hard to accept. OurWorld is a scapegoat for their anger, so I know that's true. Hiram has been hit by endless suits— libel, incitement to riot, incitement to provoke racial hatred—from national and patriotic groups, religious organizations, families of debunked heroes, even a few national governments. That's aside from the physical threats. Of course it isn't helping that he is trying to copyright history."

David couldn't help but guffaw. "You're joking."

"Nope. He's arguing that history is out there to be discovered, like the human genome; if you can patent pieces of *that*, why not history—or at any rate those stretches of it OurWorld 'Cams have been first to reach?

The fourteenth century is the current test case. If that fails, he has plans to copyright the snowmen. Like Robin Hood."

Like many semi-mythical heroes of the past, under the WormCam's pitiless glare Robin had simply melted away into legend and confabulation, leaving not a trace of historical truth. The legend had stemmed, in fact, from a series of fourteenth-century English ballads born out of a time of baronial rebellions and agrarian discontent, which had culminated in the Peasants' revolt of 1381.

David smiled. "I like that. Hiram always did like Robin Hood. I think he fancies himself as a modern equivalent—even if he's deluding himself; in fact he probably has more in common with King John. . . . How ironic if Hiram came to *own* Robin."

"Look, David—many people feel just as you do. History is full of horror, of forgotten people, of slaves, of people whose lives were stolen. But we can't change the past. All we can do is to move on, resolving not to make the same mistakes again."

"You think so?" David snapped bitterly. He stood, and with brisk movements he opaqued the windows of his cluttered apartment, shutting out the afternoon light. Then he sat beside Bobby and unrolled a SoftScreen. "Watch now, and see if you still believe it is so easy." With confident keystrokes he initiated a stored Worm-Cam recording.

Side by side, the brothers sat, bathed in the light of other days.

. . . The small, round, battered sailing ship approached the shore. Two more ships could be seen on the horizon. The sand was pure, the water still and blue, the sky huge.

People came out onto the beaches: men and women naked, dark, handsome. They seemed full of wonder. Some of the natives swam out to meet the approaching vessel.

"Columbus," Bobby breathed.

"Yes. These are the Arawaks. The natives of the Bahamas. They were friendly. They gave the Europeans gifts, parrots and balls of cotton and spears made of cane. But they also had gold, which they wore as ornaments in their ears.

"Columbus immediately took some of the Arawaks by force, so that he could extract information about the gold. And it developed from there. The Spaniards had armor and muskets and horses. The Arawaks had no iron, no means of defending themselves from the Europeans' weapons and discipline.

"The Arawaks were taken as slave labor. On Haiti, for example, mountains were stripped from top to bottom, in the search for gold. The Arawaks died by the thousands, roughly a third of the workers every six months. Soon mass suicides began, using cassava poison. Infants were killed to save them from the Spaniards. And so on. There seem to have been about a quarter of a million Arawaks on Haiti when Columbus arrived. Within a few years, half of them were dead of murder, mutilation or suicide. And by 1650, after decades of ferocious slave labor, none of the original Arawaks or their descendants were left on Haiti.

"It turned out there were no gold fields after all: only bits of dust the Arawaks garnered from streams for their pathetic, deadly jewelery.

"And that, Bobby, was how our invasion of the Americas began."

"David—"

"Watch." He tapped the 'Screen and brought up a new scene.

Bobby saw blurred images of a city: small, cluttered, crowded, of white stone that glowed in the flat sunlight.

"Jerusalem," David said now. "Fifteen July, 1099. Full of Jews and Muslims. The Crusaders, a military mission from Western Christendom, had laid siege to the city for a month. Now their attack is reaching its peak."

Bobby watched bulky figures clambering over walls, soldiers rushing to meet them. But the defenders fell back, and the knights advanced, wielding their swords. Bobby saw, incredibly, a man beheaded with a single blow.

The Crusaders fought their way to the Temple area. There the defending Turks held out for a day. At last— wading in blood up to their ankles—the Crusaders broke through and quickly slew the surviving defenders.

The knights and their followers swarmed through the city, taking horses and mules, gold and silver. Lamps and candelabras were stripped from the Dome of the Rock. Corpses were butchered, for sometimes the Crusaders found coins in the bellies of the dead.

And, as the long day of pillage and butchery went on, Bobby saw Christians tear strips of flesh from their fallen foe, smoke and eat them.

All this in violent, color-filled glimpses: the vermilion splash of bloody swords, the frightened cries of horses, the hard eyes of grimy, half-starved knights who sang psalms and hymns, eerily, even as they swung their great swords. But the fighting was oddly quiet: there were no guns here, no cannon, the only weapons wielded by human muscles.

David murmured, "This was an utter disaster for our civilization. It was an act of rape, and it caused a schism between East and West that has never truly healed. And it was all in the name of Christ.

"Bobby, thanks to the WormCam, I've been privileged to watch centuries of Christian terrorism, an orgy of cruelty and destruction that stretched from the Crusades to the sixteenth-century plundering of Mexico and beyond: all of it driven by the religion of the Popes— *my* religion—and the frenzy for money and property, the capitalism of which my own father is such a prominent champion."

With their mail and bright crosses the Crusaders were

like magnificent animals, rampaging in the sunlit dust. The barbarism was astonishing.

But still . . .

"David, we knew this. The Crusades were well chronicled. The historians have been able to pick out fact from propaganda, long before the WormCam."

"Perhaps. But we're human, Bobby. It is the cruel power of the WormCam to retrieve history from the dust of textbooks and make it live again, accessible to our poor human senses. And so we must experience it again, as the blood spilled centuries back flows once more.

"History is a river of blood, Bobby. That is what the WormCam forces us to see. History washes away lives like grains of sand, down to the sea of darkness—and every one of those lives is, was, as precious and vibrant as yours or mine. And none of it, not one drop of blood, can be changed." He eyed Bobby. "You ready for more?"

"David—"

David, you aren't the only one. All of us share the horror. You are sinking into self-indulgence, if you suppose that you alone are witnessing these scenes, feeling this way.

But he had no way to say this.

David brought up another image. Bobby longed to leave, to turn his head away. But he knew he must face this, if he was to help his brother.

Once again, life and blood fled across the 'Screen.

In the midst of this, his most difficult time, David kept his promise to Heather, and sought out Mary.

He had never regarded himself as particularly competent in affairs of the human heart. So, in his humility—and consumed by his own inner turmoil—he had spent a long time seeking a way to approach Heather's difficult, anguished daughter. And the way he found, in the end, was technical: through a piece of software, in fact.

He came to her workstation in the Wormworks. It was late, and most of the other researchers had gone. She sat in a pool of light, colored by the flickering glow of the workstation SoftScreen, surrounded by the greater, brooding darkness of this dusty place of engineering and electronics. When he arrived, she hastily cleared down the 'Screen. But he glimpsed a sunny day, a garden, children running with an adult, laughing, before the darkness returned. She glowered up at him sulkily; she wore a baggy, grubby T-shirt bearing a brazen message:

SANTA CLAUS IS COMING TO TOWN

David admitted to himself he didn't understand the significance, but he wasn't about to ask her about it.

She made it clear, by her silence and posture, that he wasn't welcome here. But he wasn't about to be put off so easily. He sat beside her.

"I've been hearing good things about the tracking software you've been developing."

She looked at him sharply. "Who's been telling *you* what I've been doing? My mother, I suppose."

"No. Not your mother."

"Then who . . . ? I don't suppose it matters. You think I'm paranoid, don't you? Too defensive. Too prickly."

He said evenly, "I haven't made up my mind yet."

She actually smiled at that. "At least that's a fair answer. Anyway, how did you know about my software?"

"You're a WormCam user," he said. "One of the conditions of use of the Wormworks is that any innovation you make to the equipment is the intellectual property of OurWorld. It's in the agreement I had to sign on behalf of your mother—and you."

"Typical Hiram Patterson."

"You mean, good business? It seems reasonable to me. We all know this technology has a long way to go—"

"You're telling me. The whole user interface sucks, David."

"—and who better to come up with ways of putting that right than the users themselves, the people who need to make it better now?"

"So you have spies? People watching the past-watchers?"

"We have a layer of metasoftware which monitors user customization, assessing its functionality and quality. If we see a good idea we may pick up on it and develop it; best of all, of course, is to find something which is a bright idea *and* well developed."

She showed a flicker of interest, even pride. "Like mine?"

"It has potential. You're a smart person, Mary, with a bright future ahead of you. But—how would you put it?—you know diddly-squat about developing quality software."

"It works, doesn't it?"

"Most of the time. But I doubt that anybody but you could make an enhancement without rebuilding the whole thing from the ground up." He sighed. "This isn't the 1990s, Mary. Software development is a craft now."

"I know, I know. We get all this at school. . . . You think my idea works, though."

"Why don't you show me?"

She reached for the SoftScreen; he could see she was about to clear the settings, set up a fresh WormCam run.

Deliberately he put his hand over hers. "No. Show me what you were looking at when I sat down."

She glared at him. "So that's it. My mother did send you, didn't she? And you're not interested in my tracking software at all."

"I believe in the truth, Mary."

"Then start telling it."

He picked off the points on his fingers. "Your mother's concerned about you. It was my idea to come to you, not hers. I do think you ought to show me what you're watching. Yes, it serves as a pretext to talk to you, but I am interested in your software innovation in its own right. Is there anything else?"

"If I refuse to go along with this, will you throw me out of the Wormworks?"

"I wouldn't do that."

"Compared to the equipment here, the stuff you can access via the net sucks—"

"I told you, I'm not threatening you with that."

The moment stretched.

Subtly, she subsided in her seat, and he knew he had won the round.

With a few keystrokes she restored the scene.

It was a small garden—a yard, really, strips of sun-baked grass separated by patches of gravel, a few poorly tended flower beds. The image was bright, the sky blue, the shadows long. There were toys everywhere, splashes of color, some of them autonomously toiling back and forth on their programmed tasks and routines.

Here came two children: a boy and a girl, aged maybe six and eight respectively. They were laughing, kicking a ball between them, and they were being chased by a man, also laughing. He grabbed the girl and whirled her high in the air, so that she flew through shadows and light—

Mary froze the scene.

"A cliché," she said. "Right? A childhood memory, a summer's afternoon, long and perfect."

"This is your father and your brother—and yourself."

Her face twisted into a sour smile. "The scene is barely eight years old, but two of the protagonists are dead already. What do you think of that?"

"Mary—"

"You wanted to see my software."

He nodded. "Show me."

She tapped at the 'Screen; the viewpoint panned from side to side, and stepped forward and back in time, through a few seconds. The girl was raised and lowered and raised again, her hair tumbling this way and that, as if this was a film being wound back and forth.

"Right now I'm using the standard workstation interface. The viewpoint is like a little camera floating in the air. I can control its location in space and move it through time, adjusting the position of the wormhole mouth. Which is fine for some applications. But if I want to scan more extended periods, it's a drag—as you know."

She let the scene run on. The father put down child-Mary. Mary focused the viewpoint on her father's face and, with taps of the SoftScreen, tracked it, jerkily, as the father ran after his daughter across that vanished lawn. "I can follow the subject," she said clinically, "but it's difficult and tedious. So I've been seeking a way to automate the tracking." She tapped more virtual buttons. "I used pattern-recognition routines to latch on to faces. Like this."

The WormCam viewpoint swung down, as if guided by some invisible cameraman, and focused on her father's face. The face stayed there, central to the image, as he moved his head this way and that, talking, laughing, shouting; the background swung around him disconcertingly.

"All automated," David said.

"Yes. I have subroutines to monitor my preferences, and make the whole thing a little more professional. . . ." More keystrokes, and now the viewpoint pulled back a little. The camera angles were more conventional, stabilized, no longer slaved to that face. The father was still the central protagonist, but his context became more clear.

David nodded. "This is valuable, Mary. This, tied to interpretative software, might even allow us to automate the compilation of historic-figure biographies, at first draft anyhow. You're to be commended."

She sighed. "Thanks. But you still think I'm a wacko

because I'm watching my father rather than John Lennon. Don't you?"

He shrugged. He said carefully, "Everybody else is watching John Lennon. His life, for better or worse, is common property. *Your* life—this golden afternoon—is your own."

"But I'm an obsessive. Like those nuts you find watching their own parents making love, watching their own conception—"

"I'm no psychoanalyst," he said gently. "Your life has been hard. Nobody denies that. You lost your brother, your father. But—"

"But what?"

"But you're surrounded by people who don't want you to be unhappy. You have to believe that."

She sighed heavily. "You know, when we were little—Tommy and I—my mother had a habit of using other adults against us. If I was bad, she'd point to something in the adult world—a car sounding its horn a kilometer away, even a jet airplane screaming overhead—and she'd say, 'That man heard what you said to your mother, and he's showing you what he thinks about it.' It was terrifying. I grew up with the impression that I was alone in a huge forest of adults, all of whom watched over me, judging me the whole time."

He smiled. "Full-time surveillance. Then you won't find it hard to get used to life with the WormCam."

"You mean, the damage has been done to me already? I'm not sure that's a consolation." And then she eyed him. "So, David—what do *you* watch when you have the WormCam to yourself?"

He went back to his apartment. He slaved his own workstation to Mary's back at the Wormworks, and ran through the recordings OurWorld routinely made of every user's utilization of its WormCams.

He'd done enough, he felt, not to feel guilty over what

he had to do next to fulfill his obligation to Heather. Which was to spy on Mary.

It didn't take him long to get to the heart of it. She did, after all, view the same incident, over and over.

It had been another bright afternoon of sun and play and family, not long after the one he'd watched with her. Here she was at age eight with her father and family, hiking—easily, at a six-year-old's pace—through the Rainier National Park. Sunlight, rock, trees.

And then he came to it: the crux of Mary's life. It lasted only seconds.

It wasn't as if they'd taken any risks; they hadn't strayed from the marked path, or attempted anything ambitious. It had just been an accident.

Tommy had been riding his father's neck, clinging to handfuls of thick black hair, with his legs draped over his shoulders, firmly grasped by his father's broad hands. Mary had gone running past, eager to chase what looked like the shadow of a deer. Tommy reached for her, unbalancing a little, and the father's grasp slipped—just a little, but enough.

The impact itself was unspectacular: a soft crack as that big skull hit a sharp volcanic rock, the strange limp crumpling of the body. Just unfortunate, even in the way he hit the ground so lethally. Nobody's fault.

That was all. Over in a heartbeat. Unfortunate, commonplace, nobody's fault—save, he thought with unwelcome anger, the Cosmic Designer who chose to lodge something as precious as the soul of a six-year-old in a container so fragile.

The first time Mary (and now David, like an unwelcome ghost) had watched this incident, she'd used a remarkable WormCam viewpoint: looking out through child-Mary's own eyes. It was as if the viewpoint was lodged right at the center of her soul, that mysterious place in her head where "she" resided, surrounded by the soft machinery of her body.

Mary saw the boy falling. She reacted, reached out

her arms, took a pace toward him. He seemed to fall slowly, as if in a dream. But she was too far away to reach him, could do nothing to change what unfolded.

. . . And now, tracking Mary's usage, David was forced to watch the same incident from the father's point of view. It was like looking down from a watchtower, with child-Mary a blur below him, the boy a thing of dark shadows around his head. But the same events unfolded with grisly inevitability: the unbalancing, the slip, the boy falling, his legs impeding him so that he fell upside down and descended headfirst toward the stony ground.

But what Mary watched over and over, obsessively, was not the death itself, but the moments before. Little Tommy, falling, was only a meter from Mary, but that was too far, and no more than centimeters from his father's grasp, a fraction of a second's reaction time. It might have been a kilometer, hours of delay; it would have made no difference.

And this, David suspected, was the real reason her father had committed his suicide. Not the publicity that suddenly surrounded him and his family—though that couldn't have helped. If he was anything like Mary, he must have seen immediately the implications of the WormCam for himself—just like millions of others, now exploring the capabilities of the WormCam, and the darkness in their own hearts.

How could that bereaved father not watch *this*? How could he not relive those terrible moments over and over? How could he turn away from this child, trapped within the machine, as vivid as life and yet unable to grow a second older or to do anything the slightest bit different, ever again?

And how could that father bear to live in a world in which the terrible clarity of the incident was available for him to replay any time he wished, from any angle he chose—and yet knowing he would never be able to change a single detail?

How indulgent *he* had been—David himself—to sit and watch gruesome episodes from the history of the Church, incidents centuries removed from his own reality. After all, Columbus' crimes hurt nobody now—save perhaps the man himself, David thought grimly. How much greater had been the courage of Mary, a lonely, flawed child, as, alone, she faced the moment that had shaped her life, for good or ill.

For *this*, he realized, is the core of the WormCam experience: not timid spying or voyeurism, not the viewing of some impossibly remote period of history, but the chance to review the glowing incidents that make up *my* life.

But my eyes have not evolved to see such sights. My heart has not evolved to cope with such repeated revelations. Once, time was called the great healer; now the healing balm of distance has been torn away.

We have been granted the eyes of God, he thought, eyes which can see the immutable, bloodstained past as if it were today. But we are not God, and the burning light of that history may destroy us.

Anger coalesced. *Immutability.* Why should he accept such unfairness? Maybe there was something he could do about *that*.

But first he would have to figure out what to say to Heather.

The next time he called, when more weeks had gone by, Bobby was shocked by David's deterioration.

David was wearing a baggy jumpsuit that looked as if it hadn't been changed for days. His hair was mussed, and he had shaved only carelessly. The apartment was even more of a mess now, the furniture littered with SoftScreens, opened-out books and journals, yellow pads, abandoned pens. On the floor, stacked around an overflowing garbage pail, there were soiled paper plates and pizza boxes and microwave junk-food cartons.

But David seemed defensive, perhaps apologetic. "It's not what you're thinking. WormCam addiction, yes? I may be an obsessive, Bobby, but I think I pulled myself back from *that*."

"Then what—"

"I have been working."

A whiteboard had been set up against one wall; it was covered with scarlet scrawl, equations, scraps of phrases in English and French, connected by swirling arrows and loops.

Bobby said carefully, "Heather told me you dropped out of the 12,000 Days project. The Christ TrueBio."

"Yes, I dropped out. Surely you understand why."

"Then what have you been doing here, David?"

David sighed. "I tried to touch the past, Bobby. I tried, and I failed."

". . . Whoa," said Bobby. "Did I understand that right? You tried to use a wormhole to affect the past? Is that what you're saying? But your theory says that's impossible. Doesn't it?"

"Yes. I tried anyway. I ran some tests in the Wormworks. I tried to send a signal back in time, through a small wormhole, to myself. Just across a few milliseconds, but enough to prove the principle."

"And?"

David smiled wryly. "Signals can travel *forward* in time through a wormhole. That's how we view the past. But when I tried to send a signal *back* in time, there was feedback. Imagine a photon leaving my wormhole mouth a few seconds in the past. It can fly to the future mouth, travel back in time, and emerge from the past mouth at the precise moment it started its trip. It overlies its earlier self—"

"—and doubles the energy."

"Actually more than that, because of Doppler effects. It's a positive feedback loop. The bit of radiation can travel through the wormhole over and over, piling up energy extracted from the wormhole itself. Eventually it becomes so strong it destroys the wormhole—a fraction of a second *before* it operates as a full time machine."

"And so your test wormhole went bang."

David said dryly, "With more vigor than I'd anticipated. It looks as if dear old Hawking was right about chronology protection. The laws of physics do *not* allow backwards-operating time machines. The past is a relativistic block universe, the future is quantum uncertainty, and the two are joined at the present—which, I suppose, is a quantum gravity interface. . . . I am sorry. The technicalities do not matter. The past, you see, is like an advancing ice sheet, encroaching on the fluid future; each event is frozen into its place in the crystal structure, fixed forever.

"What is important is that *I* know, better than anyone on the planet, that the past is immutable, unchangeable—open to us to observe, through the wormholes, but fixed. Do you understand how this *feels*?"

Bobby walked through the apartment, stepping over mounds of paper and books. "Fine. You're suffering. You use abstruse physics as therapy. What about your family? Do you ever spare a thought for us?"

David closed his eyes. "Tell me. Please."

Bobby took a breath. "Well, Hiram's gone into deeper hiding. But he's planning to make even more money from weather forecasting—vastly better predictions, based on precise data centuries deep, thanks to the WormCam. He thinks it may even be possible to develop climate control systems, given the new understanding we have of long-term climate shifts."

"Hiram is—" David sought the right word. "—a phenomenon. Is there no limit to his capitalistic imagination? And the news of Kate?"

"The jury's out."

"I thought the evidence was circumstantial."

"It is. But to actually *see* her at her terminal at the time the crime was committed, to see that she had the opportunity—I think that swayed a lot of the jurors."

"What will you do if she's convicted?"

"I haven't decided." That was true. The end of the trial was a black hole, waiting to consume Bobby's future, as unavoidable and as unwelcome as death. So he did his best not to think about it.

"I saw Heather," he said. "She's well, in spite of everything. She's published her Lincoln TrueBio."

"Good piece of work. And her pieces on the Aral Sea war were remarkable." David eyed Bobby. "You must be proud of her—of your mother."

Bobby thought that over. "I suppose I should be. But I'm not sure how I'm supposed to feel about her. You know, I watched her with Mary. For all their friction, there's a bond there. It's like a steel rope that connects them. I don't feel anything like that. It's probably my fault—"

"You said you *watched* them? Past tense?"

Bobby faced him. "I guess you haven't heard. Mary left home."

". . . Ah. How disappointing."

"They had one final fight about the way Mary was using the WormCam. Heather is frantic with worry."

"Why doesn't she trace Mary?"

"She's tried."

David snorted. "Ridiculous. How can any of us hide from the WormCam?"

"Evidently there are ways. . . . Look, David, isn't it time you rejoined the human race?"

David caged his hands, a big man, deeply distressed. "But it is so unbearable," he said. "This is surely why Mary fled. *I tried*, remember. I tried to find a way to fix things—to fix the broken past. And I found that none of us has a choice about history. Not even God. *I have experimental proof.* Don't you see? Watching all that blood, that rapine and plunder and murder. . . . If I could deflect one Crusader's sword, save the life of one Arawak child—"

"And so you're escaping into arid physics."

"What would you suggest I do?"

"You can't fix the past. But you can fix yourself. Sign up for the 12,000 Days."

"I've told you—"

"I'll help you. I'll be there. Do it, David. Go find Jesus." Bobby smiled. "I dare you."

After a long silence, David returned his smile.

21

BEHOLD THE MAN

Extracted from the Introduction by David Curzon to The 12,000 Days: A Preliminary Commentary, *eds. S. P. Kozlov and G. Risha, Rome 2040:*

The international scholarly project known popularly as the 12,000 Days has reached the conclusion of its first phase. I was one of a team of (actually a little more than) twelve thousand WormCam observers worldwide who were assigned to study the historical life and times of the man known to His contemporaries as Yesho Ben Pantera, and to later generations as Jesus Christ. It is an honor to be asked to pen this introduction. . . .

We have always known that when we meet Jesus in the Gospels, we see Him through the eyes of the evangelists. For example Matthew believed that the Messiah would be born in Bethlehem, as appeared to be predicted by the Old Testament prophet Micah; and so he reports Jesus as being born in Bethlehem (though Jesus, the Galilean, was in fact—naturally enough—born in Galilee).

We understand this; we compensate for it. But how many Christians over the centuries have longed to meet Jesus for themselves through the neutral medium of a camera—or better still, face-to-face? And how many would have believed that ours would be the first generation for which such a meeting would be possible?

But that is precisely what has happened.

Each of we Twelve Thousand was assigned a single Day of the short life of Jesus: a Day which we would observe with WormCam technology—in real time, from midnight to midnight. In this way a first-draft "true" biography of Jesus could rapidly be compiled.

This visual biography and attached reports are no more than a first draft: a simple observation, a laying-out of the events of Jesus' tragically brief life. There is much subsidiary research to be done. For example, even the identities of the fourteen Apostles (not twelve!) have yet to be determined, and the fate of His brothers, sisters, wife and child are known only sketchily. Then will come the mapping of the blunt events of the central human story against the various accounts, canonical and apocryphal, which survived to tell us of Jesus and His ministry.

And then, of course, the true debate will begin: a debate into the meaning of Jesus and His ministry—a debate which may last as long as the human race itself.

This first encounter has not been easy. But already the clear light of Galilee has burned away many falsehoods.

David lay in his couch and tested its systems: the VR apparatus itself, the nursing agents which would manage the intravenous feeds and catheters, turn his abandoned body to reduce the risk of bedsores—even clean him if he desired, as if he were a coma victim.

Bobby sat before him, in this quiet, darkened room, his face shining in complex SoftScreen light.

David felt absurd amid all this gear, like an astronaut preparing for launch. But that Day of long ago, embedded in time like an insect in amber, unchanging and brilliant, was waiting for his inspection; and he submitted.

David lifted the Mind'sEye headset and settled it over his head. He felt the familiar squirming texture as the headset wrapped itself tightly around his temples.

He fought panic. To think that people subjected themselves to this for mere entertainment!

. . . And light burst over him, hard and brilliant.

He was born in Nazareth, a small and prosperous Galilean hill town. The birth was routine—for the time. He was indeed born to a Mary, who had been a virgin—a Temple Virgin.

As his contemporaries knew Him, Jesus Christ was the illegitimate son of a Roman legionary, an Illyrian called Pantera.

It was a relationship based on love, not coercion—even though Mary had been betrothed at the time to Joseph, a prosperous master builder and widower. But Pantera was transferred from the district when Mary's pregnancy became known. It is to Joseph's credit that he took in Mary and raised the boy as his own.

Nevertheless Jesus was not ashamed of His origin, and would later style Himself Yesho Ben Pantera: that is, Jesus, son of Pantera.

That is the sum of the historical facts of Jesus' birth. Any deeper mystery lies beyond the reach of any WormCam.

There was no census, no trek to Bethlehem, no stable, no manger, no cattle, no wise men, no shepherds, no Star. All of that—devised by the evangelists to show how this boy-child was a fulfilment of prophecy—was no more than an invention.

The WormCam is stripping away many of our illusions about ourselves and our past. There are those who argue that the WormCam is a mass therapy tool which is enabling us to become more sane as a species. Perhaps. But it is a hard heart which does not mourn the debunking of the Christmas story! . . .

He was standing on a beach. He could feel the heat like a heavy moist blanket, and sweat prickled on his forehead.

To his left there were hills, folded in green, and to his right a blue sea lapped softly. On the horizon, mist-laden, he could make out fishing boats, brown-blue shadows as still and flat as cardboard cutouts. On the northern shore of the sea, perhaps five kilometers distant, he could make out a town: a clutter of brown-walled, flat-roofed buildings. That must be Capernaum. He knew he could use the Search Engine to be there in an instant. But it seemed more appropriate to walk.

He closed his eyes. He could feel the warmth of the sun on his face, hear the lapping of water, smell grass and the sourness of fish. The light here was so bright that it shone, pink, through his closed eyelids. But in the corner of his eye, within his eyelid, glowed a small gold OurWorld logo.

He set off, the sharp coolness of the Galilee water at his feet.

. . . He had several brothers and sisters, and also some half-siblings (from Joseph's previous marriage). One of His brothers, James, bore a remarkable similarity to Him, and would go on to lead the Church (at any rate a strand of it) after Jesus' death.

Jesus was apprenticed to His uncle Joseph of Arimathea—not as a carpenter, but a builder. He spent much of His late youth and early manhood in the city of Sepphoris, five kilometers north of Nazareth.

Sepphoris was a major city—the largest in Judaea, in fact, apart from Jerusalem and the capital of Galilee. There was a great deal of work for builders, masons and architects in the city at this time, for Sepphoris had been largely destroyed by a Ro-

man action against a Jewish uprising in the year 4
B.C.

His time in Sepphoris was significant for Jesus.
For here, Jesus became cosmopolitan.

He was exposed to Hellenic culture, for example
through Greek Theater, and—most significantly—
to the Pythagorean tradition of number and proportion. Jesus even attached Himself, for a time, to a
Jewish Pythagorean group called the Essenes. This
was in turn part of a much older tradition that
spanned Europe—it had, in fact, reached as far as
the Druids of Britain.

Jesus became, not a humble carpenter, but a
craftsman in a highly sophisticated and ancient tradition. Joseph's trade would lead the young Jesus
to travel extensively throughout the Roman world.

Jesus' life was full. He married. (The Bible story
of the marriage of Cana, with water turning into
wine, seems to have been embroidered from an incident at Jesus' own wedding.) His wife died in
childbirth; He did not remarry. But the child
survived, a daughter. She disappeared in the con-
fusion surrounding the end of her father's life. (The
search for this daughter of Jesus, and any descendants living today, is one of the most active areas
of WormCam research.)

But Jesus was restless. At a precociously early
age He began to formulate His own philosophy.

This could be regarded, simplistically, as based
on a peculiar synthesis of Mosaic with Pythagorean
lore: Christianity would grow out of this collision
between Eastern mysticism and Western logic. Jesus saw Himself, metaphorically, as a mean between God and mankind—and the concept of the
mean, particularly the Golden Mean, was of course
the subject of much contemplation in the Pythagorean tradition.

He was, and would always remain, a good Jew.

But He did develop strong ideas about how the practice of His religion could be bettered.

He began to cultivate friendships among those His family deemed definitely unsuitable for a man of His station: the poor, criminals. He even forged shadowy links with various groups of *lestai*, would-be insurrectionists.

He argued with His family, and He left for Capernaum, where He would live with friends.

And, during these years, He began to practice miracles.

Two men were walking toward him.

They were shorter than he was, but stockily well muscled, each with thick black hair tied back behind his head. Their clothing was functional, what looked like one-piece cotton shifts with deep, well-used pockets. They were walking at the edge of the sea, careless as small waves broke over their feet. They looked forty, but were probably younger. They were healthy, well fed, prosperous; they were probably merchants, he thought.

They were so immersed in their conversation they hadn't noticed him yet.

. . . No, he reminded himself. They could not see David—*for he hadn't been there*, on that long-gone day when this sun-drenched conversation had taken place. They were all unaware that a man of their remote future would one day marvel at them, a man with the ability to make this everyday moment come alive and run through, again and again, utterly changeless.

He flinched as the men collided softly with him. The light seemed to dim, and he no longer felt the stones' sharpness beneath his feet.

But then they were past, walking away from him, their conversation not disturbed by so much as a word by his ghostly encounter. And the vivid "reality" of the landscape was restored, as smoothly as if he had adjusted the controls on some invisible SoftScreen.

He walked on, toward Capernaum.

Jesus was able to "cure" mind-mediated and placebo diseases such as back pains, stuttering, ulcers, stress, hay fever, hysterical paralysis and blindness, even false pregnancies. Some of the "cures" are remarkable, and very moving to witness. But they were restricted to those whose belief in Jesus was stronger than their belief in their illness. And, like every other "healer" before or since, Jesus was unable to cure deeper organic illnesses. (To His credit, He never claimed He could.)

His healing miracles naturally attracted a great following. But what distinguished Jesus from the many other *hasidim* of His day was the message He preached with His healing.

Jesus believed that the Messianic Age promised by the prophets would come—not when the Jews were militarily victorious, but when they became pure of heart. He believed that this inner purity was to be achieved not just through a life of outer virtue, but through a submission to the terrible mercy of God. And He believed that this mercy extended to the whole of Israel: to the untouchables, the impure, the outcasts and the sinners. Through His healing and exorcisms He demonstrated the reality of that love.

Jesus was the Golden Mean between the divine and the human. No wonder His appeal was electric; He seemed able to make the most wretched sinner feel close to God.

But few in this occupied nation were sophisticated enough to understand His message. Jesus grew impatient at the clamoring demands for Him to reveal Himself as the Messiah. And the *lestai* who were attracted to His charismatic presence began to see in Him a convenient focal point for a rising against the hated Romans.

Trouble coalesced.

David wandered through the small, boxy rooms like a ghost, watching the people, women, servants and children, come and go.

The house was more impressive than he had expected. It was built on the pattern of a Roman villa, with a central open atrium and various rooms opening off it, in the manner of a cloister. The setting was very Mediterranean, the light dense and bright, the rooms open to the still air.

Already, so early in Jesus' ministry, there was a permanent encampment outside the house walls: the sick, the lame, would-be pilgrims, a miniature tent city.

Later, a house church would be built on this site, and then, in the fifth century, a Byzantine church that would survive to David's own day—together with the legend of those who had once lived here.

Now there was noise outside the house: the sound of running feet, people calling. He walked briskly outside.

Most of the inhabitants of the tent city—some of them showing surprising alacrity—were making their way toward the glimmering sea, which David glimpsed between the houses. He followed the gathering crowd, towering above the people around him, and he tried to ignore the stink of unwashed humanity, much of it extrapolated by the controlling software with unwelcome authenticity; the direct detection of scent through WormCams was still an unreliable business.

The crowd spread out as they reached the rudimentary harbor. David made his way through the crush to the water's edge, ignoring the temporary dimmings as Galileans brushed past or through him in their eagerness.

There was a single boat on the still water. It was perhaps six meters long, wooden, its construction crude. Four men were patiently rowing toward the shore; beside a stocky helmsman at the stern was a piled-up fishing net.

Another man was standing at the prow, facing the people on the shore.

David heard eager muttering. He had been preaching, from the boat, at other sites along the shore. He had a commanding voice which carried well across the water, this Yesho, this Jesus.

David struggled to see Him more clearly. But the light on the water was dazzling.

. . . And so we must turn, with reluctance, to the true story of the Passion.

Jerusalem—sophisticated, chaotic, built of the radiantly bright white local stone—was crowded this Passover with pilgrims come to eat the Paschal Lamb within the confines of the holy city, as tradition demanded. And the city also contained a heavy presence of Roman soldiers.

And, this Passover, it was a place of tension. There were many insurrectionist groups working here: for example the Zealots, fierce opponents of Rome, and *iscarii*, assassins who would customarily work the large festival crowds.

Into this historic crucible walked Jesus and His followers.

Jesus' group ate their Passover feast. (But there was no rehearsal of the Eucharist: no commandment by Jesus to take bread and wine in memory of Him, as if they were fragments of His own body. This rite is evidently an invention of the evangelists. That night, Jesus had much on His mind; but not the invention of a new religion.)

We know now that Jesus had links to many of the sects and groups which operated at the fringe of His society. But Jesus' intent was *not* insurrection.

Jesus made His way to the place called Gethsemane—where olive trees still grow today, some of them (we can verify now) survivors from Jesus' own day. Jesus had worked to cleanse Judaism of sectarianism. He thought He would meet the authorities and leaders of various rebel groups here, and seek a peaceful unity. As ever, Jesus sought to be the Golden Mean, a bridge between these groups in conflict.

But the humanity of Jesus' time was no more rational than that of any other era. He was met by a group of armed soldiers sent by the chief priests. And the events thereafter unfolded with a deadly, familiar logic.

The Trial was no grand theological event. All that mattered to the High Priest—a tired, conscientious, worn-down old man—was to maintain public order. He knew he had to protect his people from the Romans' savage reprisals by accepting the lesser evil of handing over this difficult, anarchistic faith healer.

That done, the High Priest returned to his bed, and an uncomfortable sleep.

Pilate, the Roman Procurator, had to come out to meet priests who would not enter his Praetorium for fear of being defiled. Pilate was a competent, cruel man, a representative of an occupying power centuries old. Yet he too hesitated, it seems for fear of inciting worse violence by executing a popular leader.

We have now witnessed the fears and loathing and dreadful calculations which motivated the men facing each other that dark night—and each of them, no doubt, believed he was doing the right thing.

Once his decision was made, Pilate acted with brutal efficiency. Of what followed, we know the dreadful details too well. It was not even a grand spectacle—but then the Passion of Christ is an event which has taken not two days, but two thousand years to unfold.

But there is still much we do not know. The moment of His death is oddly obscured; WormCam exploration there is limited. Some scientists have speculated that there is such a density of viewpoints in those key seconds that the fabric of spacetime itself is being damaged by wormhole intrusions. And these viewpoints are *presumably sent down by observers from our own future*—or perhaps from a multiplicity of possible futures, if what lies ahead of us is undetermined.

So we still have not heard His last words to His mother; we still do not know if—beaten, dying, bewildered—He cried out to His God. Even now, despite all our technology, we see Him through a glass darkly.

At the center of the town there was a market square, already crowded. Suppressing a shudder, David forced himself to push *through* the people.

At the center of the crowd a soldier, crudely uniformed, was holding a woman by one arm. She looked wretched, her robe torn, her hair matted and filthy, her plump, once-pretty face streaked by crying. Beside her were two men in fine, clean religious garb. Perhaps they were priests, or Pharisees. They were pointing to the woman, gesticulating angrily, and arguing with a figure before them, who—hidden by the crowd—was squatting in the dust.

David wondered if this incident had left any trace in the Gospels. Perhaps this was the woman who had been condemned for adultery, and the Pharisees were confronting Jesus with another of their trick questions, trying to expose His blasphemy.

The man in the dust had a phalanx of friends. They were sturdy-looking men, perhaps fishermen; gently but firmly they were keeping the crushing crowds away. But still—David could see as he approached, wraithlike— some of the people were coming near, reaching out a tentative hand to touch a robe, even stroke a lock of hair.

I do not think His death—humiliated, broken—need remain the center of our obsession with Jesus, as it has been for two thousand years. For me the zenith of His life as I have witnessed it is the moment when Pilate produces Him, already tortured and bloody, to be mocked by the soldiers, sacrificed by His own people.

With everything He had intended apparently in ruins, perhaps already feeling abandoned by God, Jesus should have been crushed. And yet He stood straight. A man immersed in His time, defeated and yet unbeaten, He is Gandhi, He is Saint Francis, He is Wilberforce, He is Elizabeth Fry, He is Father Damien among the lepers. He is His own people, and the dreadful suffering they would endure in the name of the religion founded in His name.

The major religions have all faced crises as their origins and tangled pasts had become open to scrutiny. None of them have emerged unscathed; some have collapsed altogether. But religion is not simply about morality, or the personalities of founders and practitioners. It is about the numinous, a higher dimension of our nature. And there are still those who hunger for the transcendent, the meaning of it all.

Already—cleansed, reformed, refounded—the Church is beginning to offer consolation to many people left bewildered by the demolition of privacy and historic certainty.

Perhaps we have lost Christ. But we have found Jesus. And His example can still lead us into an unknown future—even if that future holds only the Wormwood, and our religions' only remaining role is to comfort us.

And yet history still holds surprises for us: for one of the most peculiar yet stubborn legends about the life of Jesus has, against all expectation, been borne out. . . .

The man in the dust was thin, His hair severely pulled back, prematurely greying at the temples. His robe was stained with dust and trailed in the dirt. His nose was prominent, proud and Roman, His eyes black, fierce, intelligent. He seemed angry, and was drawing in the dust with one finger.

This silent, brooding man had the measure of the Pharisees, without even the need to speak.

David stepped forward. Beneath his feet he could feel the dust of this Capernaum marketplace. He reached forward to the hem of that robe.

. . . But, of course, his fingers slid through the cloth; and, though the sun dimmed, David felt nothing.

The man in the dust looked up and gazed directly into David's eyes.

David cried out. The Galilean light dissipated, and the concerned face of Bobby hovered before him.

As a young man, following a well-established trade route with His uncle, Joseph of Arimathea, Jesus visited the tin mine area of Cornwall.

With companions, He traveled further inland, as far as Glastonbury—at the time a significant port— where He studied with the Druids, and helped design and build a small house, on the future site of Glastonbury Abbey. This visit is remembered, after a fashion, in scraps of local folklore.

We have lost so much. The harsh glare of the WormCam has revealed so many of our fables to be things of shadows and whispers: Atlantis has evaporated like dew; King Arthur has stepped back into the shadows from which he never truly emerged. And yet it is after all true, as Blake sang, that those feet in ancient time did walk upon England's mountains green.

22

THE VERDICT

In Christmas week, 2037, Kate's trial concluded.

The courtroom was small, paneled in oak, and the Stars and Stripes hung limply at the back of the room. The judge, the attorneys and the court officers sat in grave splendor before rows of benches containing a few scattered spectators: Bobby, officials from OurWorld, reporters tapping notes into SoftScreens.

The jury was an array of random-looking citizenry, though some of them were sporting the highly colored masks and SmartShroud clothes that had become fashionable in the last few months. If Bobby didn't look too carefully he could lose sight of a juror until she moved— and then a face or lock of hair or fluttering hand would appear as if from nowhere, and the rest of the juror's body would become dimly visible, outlined by a patchy, imperfect distortion of the background.

It was a sweet irony, he thought, that SmartShrouds were another bright idea of Hiram's: one new OurWorld product sold at high profit to counteract the intrusive effects of another.

. . . And there, sitting alone in the dock, was Kate. She was dressed in simple black, her hair tied back, her mouth set, eyes empty.

Cameras had been banned from the courtroom itself, and there had been little of the usual media scrum at the courthouse entrance. But everybody knew that restraining orders meant nothing now. Bobby imagined the air around him speckled with hovering WormCam view-points, no doubt great swarms of them clustered on Kate's face and his own.

Bobby knew that Kate had conditioned herself never to forget the scrutiny of the WormCam, not for a second; she couldn't stop the invisible voyeurs gazing at her, she said, but she could deny them the satisfaction of seeing how she hurt. To Bobby, her frail, lone figure represented more strength than the mighty legal process to which she was subject, and the great, rich corporation which had prosecuted her.

But even Kate could not conceal her despair when her sentence was at last handed down.

"Dump her, Bobby," Hiram said. He was pacing around his big conference desk. Storm rain lashed against the picture window, filling the room with noise. "She's done you nothing but harm. And now she's a convicted felon. What more proof do you want? Come on, Bobby. Cut yourself loose. You don't need her."

"She believes you framed her."

"Well, I don't care about that. What do *you* believe? That's what counts for me. Do you really think I'm so devious that I'd frame the lover of my son—no matter what I thought about her?"

"I don't know, Dad," Bobby said evenly. He felt calm, controlled; Hiram's bluster, obviously manipulative, was unable to reach him. "I don't know what I believe anymore."

"Why discuss it? Why don't you use the WormCam to go check up on me?"

"I don't intend to spy on you."

Hiram stared at his son. "If you're trying to find my conscience, you're going to have to dig deeper than that. Anyhow it's only reprogramming. Hell, they should lock her up and wipe the key. Reprogramming is nothing."

Bobby shook his head. "Not to Kate. She's fought

against the methodology for years. She has a real dread of it, Dad."

"Oh, bull. *You* were reprogrammed. And it didn't hurt you."

"I don't know if it did or not." Bobby stood now, and faced his father. He felt his own anger rising. "I felt different when the implant was turned off. I was angry, terrified, confused. I didn't even know how I was *supposed* to feel."

"You sound like her," Hiram shouted. "She's reprogrammed you with her words and her pussy more than I ever could with a bit of silicon. Don't you see that? Ah, Christ. The one good thing the bloody implant did do to you was make you too dumb to see what's happening to you. . . ." He fell silent, and averted his eyes.

Bobby said coldly, "You'd better tell me what you meant by that."

Hiram turned, anger, impatience, even something like guilt appearing to struggle for dominance within him. "Think about it. Your brother is a brilliant physicist. I don't use the word lightly; he may be nominated for a Nobel Prize. And as for me—" He raised his hands. "I built up all this, from scratch. No dummy could have achieved that. But you—"

"Are you saying that's because of the implant?"

"I knew there was a risk. Creativity is linked to depression. Great achievement is often linked to an obsessive personality. Blah, blah. But you don't need bloody brains to become the President of the United States. Isn't that right? Isn't it?" And he reached for Bobby's cheek, as if to pinch it, like a child's.

Bobby flinched back. "I remember a hundred, a thousand times as a child when you said that to me. I never knew what you meant before."

"Come on, Bobby—"

"You did it, didn't you? You set Kate up. You know she's innocent. And you're prepared to let them screw around with her brain. Just as you screwed around with mine."

Hiram stood there for a moment, then dropped his arms. "Bugger it. Go back to her if you want, bury yourself in her quim. In the end you always come running back, you little shit. I've got work to do." And he sat at his desk, tapped the surface to open up his SoftScreens, and soon the glow of scrolling digits lit up his face, as if Bobby had ceased to exist.

After she was released, Bobby took her home.

As soon as they arrived she stalked around the apartment, closing curtains compulsively, shutting out the bright noon sunlight, trailing rooms of darkness.

She pulled off the clothes that she had worn since leaving the courtroom and consigned them to the garbage. He lay in bed listening to her shower, in pitch darkness, for long minutes. Then she slid beneath the duvet. She was cold, shivering in fact, her hair not quite dry. She had been showering in cold water. He didn't question that; he just held her until his warmth had permeated her.

At last she said, in a whisper, "You need to buy thicker curtains."

"Darkness can't hide you from a WormCam."

"I know that," she said. "And I know that even now they are listening to every word we say. But we don't have to make it easy for them. I can't bear it. Hiram beat me, Bobby. And now he's going to destroy me."

Just as, he thought, Hiram destroyed *me*.

He said, "At least your sentence isn't custodial; at least we have each other."

She balled her fist and punched his chest, hard enough to hurt. "That's the whole point. Don't you see? You won't have *me*. Because by the time they've finished, there won't be a *me* anymore. Whatever I will have become, I'll be—different."

He covered her fist with his hand until he felt her fingers uncurl. "It's just reprogramming—"

"They said I must suffer from Syndrome E. Spasms of overactivity in my orbito-frontal and medial prefrontal lobes. Excessive traffic from the cortex prevents emotions rising to my consciousness. And *that's* how I can commit a crime, directed at the father of my lover, without conscience or remorse or self-disgust."

"Kate—"

"And then I'm to be conditioned against the use of the WormCam. Convicted felons like me, you see, aren't to be allowed access to the technology. They will lay down false memory traces in my amygdala, the seat of my emotions. I'll have a phobia, unbeatable, about even considering the use of a WormCam, or viewing its results."

"There's nothing to be afraid of."

She propped herself up on her elbows. Her shadowed face loomed before him, her eye sockets smooth-rimmed wells of darkness. "How can you defend them? You, of all people."

"I'm not defending anybody. Anyhow, I don't believe there's a *them*. Everybody involved has just been doing her job: the FBI, the courts—"

"And Hiram?"

He didn't try to answer. He said, "All I want to do is hold you."

She sighed, and laid her head down on his chest; it felt heavy, her cheek warm against his flesh.

He hesitated. "Anyhow, I know what the real problem is."

He could feel her frowning.

"It's me. Isn't it? You don't want a switch in your head, because that's what *I* had when you found me. You have a dread of becoming like me, like I was. On some level—" He forced it out. "On some level, you despise me."

She pulled herself back from him. "All you're thinking about is yourself. But *I'm* the one who's about to have her brains removed by an ice-cream scoop." She got out of bed, walked out of the room, and shut the door with cold control, leaving him in darkness.

He slept awhile.

When he woke, he went to find her. The living room was still dark, the curtains closed and lights off. But he could tell she was here.

"Lights on."

Light, garish and bright, flooded the room.

Kate was sitting on a sofa, fully dressed. She was facing a table, on which sat a bottle of some clear fluid, and another bottle, smaller. Barbiturates and alcohol. Both bottles were unopened, their seals intact. The liquor was an expensive absinthe.

She said, "I always did have good taste."

"Kate—"

Her eyes were watering in the light, her pupils huge, making her seem childlike. "Funny, isn't it? I must have covered a dozen suicides, more attempted. I know there are quicker ways than this. I could slit my wrists, or even my neck. I could even blow out my brains, before they get screwed up. This will be slower. Probably more painful. But it's easy. You see? You sip and swallow, sip and swallow." She laughed, coldly. "You even get drunk in the process."

"You don't want to do this."

"No. You're right. I don't want to do it. Which is why I need you to help me."

For answer he picked up the liquor and hurled it across the room. It smashed against a wall, creating a spectacular, expensive splash stain on the plaster there.

Kate sighed. "That's not the only bottle in the world. I'll do it eventually. I'd rather die than let them screw with my brain."

"There must be another way. I'll go back to Hiram, and tell him—"

"Tell him what? That if he doesn't 'fess up I'm going to destroy myself? He'll laugh at you, Bobby. He wants me destroyed, one way or the other."

He paced the room, growing desperate. "Then let's get out of here."

She sighed. "They can watch us leave this room, follow us anywhere. We could go to the Moon and never be free—"

The voice seemed to come out of thin air. "If you believe that, you may as well give up now."

Kate gasped; Bobby jumped and whirled. It had been the voice of a woman, or a girl—a familiar voice. But the room seemed empty.

Bobby said slowly, "*Mary?*"

Bobby saw her face first, floating in the air, as she began to peel back a hood. Then, as she started to move against the background, the perfection of her Smart-Shroud concealment began to break down, and he could make out her outline: a shadowed limb here, a vague discolored blur where her torso must be, the whole overlaid by an odd, eye-deceiving fish-eye effect, like the earliest WormCam images. He noted, absently, that she seemed clean, healthy, even well fed.

"How did you get in here?"

She grinned. "If you come with me, Kate, I'll show you."

Kate said slowly, "Come with you? Where?"

"And why?" Bobby asked.

" 'Why' is obvious, Bobby," Mary said, an echo of her adolescent prickle returning. "Because, as Kate keeps saying, if she doesn't get out of here the man is going to stir her brains with a spoon."

Bobby said reasonably, "Wherever she goes she can be traced."

"Right," Mary said heavily. "The WormCam. But you haven't been able to trace *me* since I left home three months ago. You didn't see me coming. You didn't know I was in the apartment until I revealed myself. Look, the WormCam is a terrific tool. But it isn't a magic wand. People are paralyzed by it. They've stopped thinking. Even if Santa Claus can see you, what is he going to do? By the time he arrives you can be long gone."

Bobby frowned. "Santa Claus?"

Kate said slowly, "Santa can see you all the time. On Christmas Eve, he can look back over the whole year and see if you've been naughty or nice."

Mary grinned. "Santa must have had the first WormCam of all. Right? Merry Christmas."

"I always thought that was a sinister myth," Kate said. "But you can only keep away from Santa if you can see him coming."

Mary smiled. "That's easy." She raised her arm, pulled back her SmartShroud sleeve and revealed what looked like a fat wristwatch. It was compact, scuffed, and had the look of something out of a home workshop. The instrument's face was a miniature SoftScreen; it showed views of the corridor outside, the street, the elevators, what must be neighboring apartments. "All empty," murmured Mary. "Maybe some goon somewhere is listening to everything we say. Who cares? By the time he gets here, we'll be gone."

"That's a WormCam," Kate said. "On her wrist. Some kind of pirate design."

"I can't believe it," said Bobby. "Compared to the giant accelerators in the Wormworks—"

"And," said Mary, "Alexander Graham Bell probably never thought a telephone could be made without a cable, and so small it could be implanted in your wrist."

Kate's eyes narrowed. "A Casimir injector could never be miniaturized that far. This has to be squeezed-vacuum technology. The stuff David was working on, Bobby."

"If it is," Bobby said heavily, "how did the technology

development leak out of the Wormworks?" He eyed Mary. "Does your mother know where you are?"

"Typical," Mary snapped. "A couple of minutes ago Kate was about to kill herself, and now you're accusing me of industrial espionage and worrying about my relationship with my mother."

"My God," Kate said. "What kind of world is it going to be where every damn kid wears a WormCam on her wrist?"

"I'll tell you a secret," Mary said. "We already do. The details are on the Internet. There are home workshops churning them out, all over the planet." She grinned. "The djinn is out of the bottle. Look, I'm here to help you. There are no guarantees. Santa Claus isn't all powerful, but he has made it harder to hide. All I'm offering you is a chance." She stared at Kate. "That's better than what you're facing now, isn't it?"

Kate said, "Why do you want to help me?"

Mary looked embarrassed. "Because you're family. More or less."

Bobby said, "Your mother is family too."

Mary glared at him. "I'll cut you a deal, if it'll make you feel better. Let me get you out of here. Let me save Kate's head from being sliced open. In return I'll call my mother. Deal?"

Kate and Bobby exchanged a glance. "Deal."

Mary dug into her tunic and produced a swatch of cloth, which she shook out. "SmartShroud."

Bobby said, "Is there room for two in there?"

Mary was grinning. "I was hoping you'd say that. Come on, let's get out of here."

Hiram's security guards, alerted by a routine WormCam monitor, arrived ten minutes later. The apartment, brightly lit, was empty. The guards began to squabble over who would have to tell Hiram and take the blame—and then fell silent, as they realized he was, or would be, watching anyhow.

THREE

THE LIGHT OF OTHER DAYS

Oft, in the stilly night,
Ere Slumber's chain has bound me,
Fond Memory brings the light
Of other days around me.

—THOMAS MOORE (1779–1852)

23

THE FLOODLIT STAGE

Rome, A.D. 2041: Holding Heather's hand, David was walking through the dense, swarming heart of the city; the night sky above, layered with smog, looked as orange as the clouds of Titan.

Even this late Rome was crowded with sightseers. Many, like Heather, were walking around with Mind'sEye headbands or Glasses-and-Gloves.

Four years after the first mass-market release of the WormCam, it had become a fashionable and alluring pastime to become a time tourist at many of the world's ancient sites, wandering through deep layers of past: David had determined he must try the Scuba tour of sunken Venice before he left Italy. . . . Alluring, yes: and David understood why. The past had become a comfortable and familiar place, its exploration a safe, synthetic adventure, the perfect place to avert the eyes from the blank meteoric wall that terminated the future. How ironic, thought David, that a world denied its future was suddenly granted its past.

And escape was tempting, from a world where even the transformed present was a strange and disturbing place.

Almost everybody now wore a WormCam of some kind, generally the wristwatch-sized miniaturized version powered by squeezed-vacuum technology. The personal WormCam was a link to the rest of mankind, to the glories and horrors of the past—and, not least, a useful gadget for looking around the next corner.

And everybody was reshaped by the WormCam's relentless glare.

People didn't even dress the way they used to. Some of the older people, here in Rome's crowded streets, still wore clothing that would have been recognizable, even fashionable, a few years before. Some tourist types, in fact, walked around defiantly dressed in loud T-shirts and shorts, just as they had for decades. One woman was wearing a shirt with a gaudy, flashing message:

HEY, UP THERE IN THE FUTURE:
GET YOUR GRANDMOM OUT OF HERE!

But many more people had covered up, wearing seamless one-piece coveralls that buttoned high on the neck, and with long sleeves and trouser legs that terminated in sewn-on gloves and boots. There were even some examples of all-over-cover styles imported from the Islamic world: shapeless smocks and tunics that trailed along the ground, headpieces hiding all but the eyes, which were uniformly staring and wary.

Others had reacted quite differently. Here was a nudist couple, two men hand in hand wearing slack middle-aged bellies over shrunken genitalia with defiant pride.

But, cautious or defiant, the older folk—among whom David reluctantly counted himself—displayed a continual uncomfortable awareness of the WormCam's unblinking gaze.

The young, growing up with the WormCam, were different.

Many of the young went simply naked, save for practical items like purses and sandals. But they seemed to David to have none of the shyness or self-consciousness of their elders, as if they were making a choice about what to wear based simply on practicality or a desire to display personality, rather than any modesty or taboo.

One group of youngsters wore masks that showed projections of the broad face of a young man. Girls and boys alike wore the face, and it displayed a range of conditions and emotions—rain-lashed, sun-drenched, bearded and clean-shaven, laughing and crying, even sleeping—that seemed to have nothing to do with the activities of the wearers. It was disconcerting to watch, like seeing a group of clones wandering through the Rome night.

These were Romulus masks, the latest fashion accessory from OurWorld. Romulus, founder of the city, had become quite a character for the young Romans since the WormCam had proved he really existed—even if his brother and all that stuff about the wolf had proved mythical. Each mask was just a SoftScreen, molded to the face, with inbuilt WormCam feeds, and it showed the face of Romulus as he had been at the exact age, to the minute, of the wearer. OurWorld was targeting other parts of the world with regional variants of the same idea.

It was a terrific piece of marketing. But David knew it would take him a lifetime to get used to the sight of the face of a young Iron Age male above a pair of pert bare breasts.

They passed through a small square, a patch of unhealthy-looking greenery surrounded by tall, antique buildings. On a bench here David noticed a young couple, boy and girl, both naked. They were perhaps sixteen. The girl was on the boy's lap, and they were kissing ardently. The boy's hand was urgently squeezing the girl's small breast. And her hand, dug in between their bodies, was wrapped around his erection.

David knew that some (older) commentators dismissed all this as hedonism, a mad dancing of the young before the onset of the fire. It was a mindless, youthful reflection of the awful, despairing nihilist philosophies that had grown recently in response to the looming existence of the Wormwood: philosophies in which the universe was seen as little more than a giant fist intent on smashing flat all of life and beauty and thought, over and over. There never had been a way to survive the universe's slow decline, of course; now the Wormwood had made that cosmic terminus gruesomely real, and there was nothing to do but dance and rut and cry.

Such notions were dismally seductive. But the explanation for the ways of modern youth was surely simpler than that, David thought. It was surely another WormCam consequence: the relentless, disconcerting shedding of taboos, in a world where all the walls had come down.

A handful of people had stopped to watch the couple. One man—naked too, perhaps in his twenties—was slowly masturbating.

Technically *that* was still illegal. But nobody was trying to enforce such laws anymore. After all, that lonely man could go back to his hotel room and use his WormCam to zoom in on anybody he chose, any time of the day or night—which was what people had been using the WormCam for since it was released, and movies and magazines and such for a lot longer than that. At least, in this age of the WormCam, there was no more hypocrisy.

But such incidents were already becoming rare. New social norms were emerging.

The world seemed to David to be a little like a crowded restaurant. Yes, you could listen in to what the man on the next table was saying to his wife. But it was impolite; if you indulged, you would be ostracized. And, after all, many people actually relished crowded, public places; the buzz, the excitement, the sense of belonging could override any desire for privacy.

As David watched, the girl broke away, smiling at her lover, and she slid down his body, smooth as a seal, and took his erection in her mouth. And—

David turned away, face burning.

Their lovemaking had been clumsy, amateurish, perhaps overeager; their two bodies, though young, were not specially attractive specimens. But then, this was not art, or even pornography; this was human life, in all its clumsy animal beauty. David tried to imagine how it must be to be that boy, here and now, freed of taboos, reveling in the power of his body and his lover's.

Heather, however, saw none of this. Wandering beside him, eyes glinting, she was still immersed in the deep past—and perhaps it was time he joined her there. With a sense of relief—and a brief word to the Search Engine, requesting guidance—David donned his own Mind'sEye and slid into another time.

. . . He walked into daylight. But this crowded street, lined by great, boxy multistory apartment blocks, was dark. Hemmed in by the peculiar topography of the site—the famous seven hills—Romans, already a million strong, had built up.

In many ways, the city had a remarkably modern feel. But this was not the twenty-first century: he was glimpsing this swarming, vibrant capital on a bright Italian summer afternoon just five years after the cruel death of Christ Himself. There were no motor vehicles, of course, and few animal-drawn carts or carriages. The most common form of transport, other than by foot, was by hired litter or sedan chair. Even so, the streets were so crowded that even foot traffic could circulate at little more than a crawl.

There was a crush of humanity—citizens, soldiers, paupers and slaves—all around them. David and Heather towered over most of these people; and besides, walking on the modern ground surface, they were hovering above the cobbled floor of the ancient city. The poor and the slaves looked stunted, some visibly ravaged by malnourishment and disease, even ratlike, as they crowded around the public water fountains. But many of the citizens—some in brilliant-white gold-stitched togas, benefiting from generations of affluence funded by the expanding Empire—were as tall and well fed as David, and, in suitable clothes, would surely not have looked out of place in the streets of any city of the twenty-first century.

But David could not get used to the way the swarming crowds simply pushed *through* him. It was hard to accept that to these Romans, busily engaged with their own concerns, he was no more than an insubstantial ghost. He longed to be here, to play a part.

They came now to a more open place. This was the Forum Romanum: a finely paved rectangular court surrounded by grand, two-story public buildings, fronted by rows of narrow marble columns. A line of triumphal columns, each capped by gold-leafed statues, strode boldly down the center of the court, and farther ahead, beyond a clutter of characteristically Roman red-tiled, sloping roofs, he could see the curving bulk of the Colosseum.

In one corner he noticed a group of citizens, grandly dressed—Senators, perhaps—arguing vehemently, tapping at tablets, oblivious of the beauty and marvel around them. They were proof that this city was no museum, but very obviously the operational capital of a huge, complex and well-run empire—the Washington of its day—and its very mundanity was exhilarating, so different from the seamless, shining, depopulated reconstructions of the old, pre-WormCam museums, movies and books.

But this Imperial city, already ancient, had just a few centuries more to survive. The great aqueducts would fall, the public fountains fail; and for a thousand years afterward the Romans would be reduced to drawing their water by hand from the Tiber.

There was a tap on his shoulder.

David turned, startled. A man stood there, dressed in a drab, charcoal-gray suit and tie, utterly out of place here. He had short-cropped blond hair, and he was holding up a badge. And, like David and Heather, he was floating a few meters above the ground of Imperial Rome.

It was FBI Special Agent Michael Mavens.

"You," David said. "What do you want with us? Don't you think you've done enough damage to my family, Special Agent?"

"I never intended any damage, sir."

"And now—"

"And now I need your help."

Suppressing a sigh, David lifted his hands to his Mind'sEye headband. He could feel the indefinable tingle that came with the breaking of the equipment's transceiver link to his cortex.

Suddenly he was immersed in the hot Roman night.

And around him the Forum Romanum was reduced. Great chunks of marble rubble littered the floor, their surfaces brown, decaying in the foul air of the city. Of the great buildings, only a handful of columns and crosspieces survived, poking out of the ground like exposed bones, and sickly urban-poisoned grass grew through cracks in the flags.

Bizarrely, amid the gaudy twenty-first-century tourists, gray-suited Mavens looked even more out of place than in ancient Rome.

Michael Mavens turned and studied Heather. Her eyes, dilated widely, sparkled with the unmistakable pearly glint of viewpoints, cast by the miniature WormCam generators implanted in her retinas. David took her hand. She squeezed gently.

Mavens caught David's eye. He nodded, understanding. But he pressed: "We need to talk, sir. It's important."

"My brother?"

"Yes."

"Very well. Will you accompany us back to our hotel? It isn't far."

"I'd appreciate it."

So David walked from the ruined Forum Romanum,

gently guiding Heather around the fallen masonry. Heather turned her head like a camera stand, still immersed in the bright glories of a city long dead, and spacetime distortion shone in her eyes.

They reached the hotel.

Heather had barely spoken since the Forum Romanum. She allowed David to kiss her on the cheek before she went to her room. There she lay down in the dark, facing the ceiling, her wormhole eyes sparkling; David realized, uneasily, that he had absolutely no idea what she was looking at.

When he returned to his own room, Mavens was waiting. David prepared them drinks from the minibar: a single malt for himself, a bourbon for the agent.

Mavens made small talk. "You know, Hiram Patterson's reach is awesome. In your bathroom just now I used a WormCam mirror to pick the spinach out of my teeth. My wife has a wormhole NannyCam at home. My brother and his wife are using a WormCam monitor to keep track of their thirteen-year-old daughter, who's a little wild, in their opinion. . . . And so on. To think of it: the miracle technology of the age, and we use it in such trivial ways."

David said briskly, "As long as he continues to sell it, Hiram doesn't care what we do with it. Why don't you tell me why you've come so far to see me, Special Agent Mavens?"

Mavens dug into a pocket of his crumpled jacket, and pulled out a thumbnail-sized data disk; he turned it like a coin, and David saw hologram shimmers in its surface. Mavens placed the disk carefully on the small polished table beside his drink. "I'm looking for Kate Manzoni," he said. "And Bobby Patterson, and Mary Mays. I drove them into hiding. I want to bring them back. Help them rebuild their lives."

"What can I do?" David asked sourly. "After all, you

have the resources of the FBI behind you."

"Not for this. To tell the truth the Agency has given up on the three of them. I haven't."

"Why? You want to punish them some more?"

"Not at all," Mavens said uncomfortably. "Manzoni's was the first high-profile case which hinged on WormCam evidence. And we got it wrong." He smiled, looking tired. "I've been checking. That's the wonderful thing about the WormCam, isn't it? It's the world's greatest second-guess machine.

"You see, it's now possible to read many types of information through the WormCam: particularly, the contents of computer memories and storage devices. I checked through the equipment Kate Manzoni was using at the time of her alleged crime. And, eventually, I found that what Manzoni claimed had been true all along."

"Which is?"

"That Hiram Patterson was responsible for the crime—though it would be difficult to pin it on him, even using the WormCam. And he framed Manzoni." He shook his head. "I knew and admired Kate Manzoni's journalism long before the case came up. The way she exposed the Wormwood cover-up—"

"It wasn't your fault," David said levelly. "You were only doing your job."

Mavens said harshly, "It's a job I screwed up. Not the first. But those who were harmed—Bobby and Kate—have dropped out of sight. And they aren't the only ones."

"Hiding from the WormCam," David said.

"Of course. It's changing everybody. . . ."

It was true. In the new openness, businesses boomed. Crime seemed to have dropped to an irreducible minimum, a rump driven by mental disorder. Politicians had, cautiously, found ways to operate in the new glass-walled world, with their every move open to scrutiny by a concerned and online citizenry, now and in the future. Beyond the triviality of time tourism, a new true history, cleansed of myths and lies—and no less wonderful for that—was entering the consciousness of the species; nations and religions and corporations seemed almost to have worked through their round of apologies to each other and to the people. The surviving religions, refounded and cleansed, purged of corruption and greed, were reemerging into the light, and—it seemed to David—were beginning to address their true mission, which was humanity's search for the transcendent.

From the highest to the lowest. Even manners had changed. People seemed to be becoming a little more tolerant of one another, able to accept each other's differences and faults—because each person knew he or she was under scrutiny too.

Mavens was saying, "You know, it's as if we have all been standing in spotlights on a darkened stage. Now the theater lights are up, and we can see all the way to the wings—like it or not. I guess you've heard of MAS?—Mutually Assured Surveillance—a consequence of the fact that everybody carries a WormCam; everybody is watching everybody else. Suddenly our nation is full of courteous, wary, watchful citizens. But it can be harmful. Some people seem to be becoming surveillance obsessives, unwilling to do anything that will mark them out as different from the norm. It's like living in a village dominated by prying gossips. . . ."

"But surely the WormCam has been, on balance, a force for good. Open Skies, for instance."

Open Skies had been President Eisenhower's old dream of international transparency. Even before the WormCam there had been an implementation of something like that vision, with aerial reconnaissance, surveillance satellites, weapons inspectors. But it was always limited: inspectors could be thrown out, missile silos camouflaged by tarpaulins.

"But now," said Mavens, "in this wonderful WormCam world, we're watching them, and we know they are watching us. And nothing can be hidden. Arms-reduction treaties can be verified; a number of armed conflicts have been frozen into impasse, both sides knowing what the other is about to do. Not only that, the citizens are watching as well. All over the planet . . ."

Dictatorial and repressive regimes, exposed to the light, were crumbling. Though some totalitarian governments had sought to use the new technology as an instrument of oppression, the (deliberate) flooding of those countries by the democracies with WormCams had resulted in openness and accountability. This was an extension of past work done by groups like the Witness Program, who for decades had supplied video equipment to human-rights groups: *Let truth do the fighting.*

"Believe me," Mavens said, "the U.S. is getting off lightly. The worst scandal we suffered recently was the exposure of the Wormwood bunkers." A pathetic, half-hearted exercise, a handful of hollowed-out mountains and converted mines, meant as a refuge for the rich and powerful—or at least their children—on Wormwood Day. The existence of such facilities had long been suspected; when they were exposed, their futility as refuges was quickly demonstrated by the scientists, and their builders mocked into harmlessness. Mavens said, "If you think about it, there was usually a lot more scandal than *that* to be exposed, at any moment in the past. We're all getting cleaner. There are some who argue that we may be on the brink of a true consensual world government at last—even a utopia."

"Do you believe it?"

Mavens grinned sourly. "Not for a second. I have the feeling that wherever we're going, wherever the WormCam is taking us, it's somewhere much stranger."

"Perhaps," David said. "I suppose we've lived through one of those perspective-changing moments: the last generation was the first to see the Earth whole from space; ours has been the first to see all of true history—and the truth about ourselves. You know, *I* should be able to deal with all this." David forced a smile. "Take it from a Catholic, Special Agent Mavens. I grew up encouraged to believe I was already under the scrutiny of a kind of WormCam . . . but *that* 'Cam was the all-seeing eye of God. We must learn to live without subterfuge and shame. Yes, it's hard for us—hard for *me*. But thanks to the WormCam, it seems to me everyone is becoming a little more sane."

And it was remarkable that all of this had flowed from the introduction of a gadget which Hiram, its driving force, had thought was no more than a smarter TV camera. But now Hiram, in deep hiding, was, in the manner of such entrepreneurs all the way back to Frankenstein, in danger of being destroyed by his machine.

"Maybe in a generation or two this will leave us cleansed," Mavens said. "But not everybody can stand being exposed. The suicide rate remains high—you'd be surprised if you knew *how* high. And there are many people, like Bobby, disappearing off the registers—poll returns, censuses. Some even dig traceable implants out of their arms. We can see them, of course, but we can't give them a name." He eyed David. "This is the kind of group we believe Bobby and the others have joined. They call themselves Refugees. And those are the kind of people we have to trace if we want to pick up Bobby."

David frowned. "He has made his choice. He may be happy."

"He's on the run. He has *no* choices right now."

"If you find him, you'll find Kate too. And she will face her sentence."

Mavens shook his head. "I can guarantee that won't happen. I told you, I've evidence she's innocent. I'm already preparing material for a fresh appeal." He picked up the data disk and tapped it on the table. "So," he said. "You want to give your brother a lifeline?"

"What is it you want me to do?"

"We can track people with the WormCam simply by following them," Mavens said. "It isn't easy, and it's labor-intensive, but it's possible. But eyeball-tracking can be fooled. Nor can a WormCam trace reliably be keyed to any external indicator, even an implant. Implants can be dug out, transferred, reprogrammed, destroyed. So an FBI research lab has been working on a better method."

"Based on?"

"DNA. We believe it will be possible to begin from any analyzable organic fragment—a flake of skin or a nail clipping, enough to record the DNA fingerprint—and then track back the fragment until it, umm, rejoins the individual in question. And then, using the DNA key, we can track the subject back and forward in time as far as we like.

"This disk contains trace software. What we need from you is to tie it to an operational WormCam. You guys at OurWorld—you specifically, Dr. Curzon—are still ahead of the game with this stuff.

"We think it might be possible ultimately to establish a global DNA-sequence database—children would be sequenced and registered as they are born—and use it as the basis of a general search procedure, without relying on holding a physical fragment. . . ."

"And then," David said slowly, "you will be able to sit in FBI Headquarters, and your wormhole spies will scour the planet until they find anyone you seek—even in complete darkness. It will be the final death of privacy. Correct?"

"Oh, come on, Dr. Curzon," Mavens pressed. "What is privacy? Look around you. Already the kids are screwing in the street. In another ten years you'll have to explain what *privacy* used to mean. These kids are different. The sociologists say it. You can *see* it. They are growing up used to openness, in the light, and they talk to each other the whole time. Have you heard of the Arenas?—gigantic, ongoing discussions transmitted via WormCam links, unmoderated, international, sometimes involving thousands. And hardly anybody involved over the age of twenty-five. They're starting to figure things out for themselves, with hardly any reference to the world we built. By comparison, we're screwed up, right?"

David, reluctantly, found he agreed. And it wouldn't stop here. Perhaps it was going to be necessary for the damaged elder generations, including himself, to clear their way off the stage, taking with them their hangups and taboos, before the young could inherit this new world, which only they truly understood.

"Maybe," Mavens growled when David voiced that thought. "But I ain't ready to quit just yet. And in the meantime—"

"In the meantime, I might find my brother."

Mavens studied his glass. "Look, it's nothing to do with me. But—Heather is a wormhead, isn't she?"

A wormhead was the ultimate result of WormCam addiction. Since taking her retinal implants, Heather had spent her life in a virtual dream. Of course she was able to tune her WormCam eyes to view the present—or at least the very recent past—as if her eyes were still the organic original. But, David knew, she barely ever chose to.

Habitually she wandered through a world illuminated by the lost glow of the deep past. Sometimes she would walk with her own younger self, even looking out through her own eyes, reliving past events over and over. David was sure she was with Mary almost all the time— the infant in her arms, the little girl running to her— unable, and anyhow unwilling, to change a single detail.

If Heather's condition was nothing to do with Mavens, it was little enough to do with David. Perhaps his impulse for protecting her had been his own brush with the seduction of the past.

"There are some commentators," David said slowly, "who say this is the future for all of us. Wormholes in our eyes, our ears. We will learn a new perception, in which the layers of the past are as visible to us as the present. It will be a new way of thinking, of living in the universe. But for now—"

"For now," Mavens said gently, "Heather needs help."

"Yes. She took the loss of her daughter pretty hard."

"Then do something about it. Help me. Look—this DNA trace isn't just a bugging device." Mavens leaned forward. "Think what else you could do with it. Disease eradication, for instance. You could track a spreading plague back through time along its vectors, airborne or waterborne or whatever, replacing what can be months of painstaking and dangerous detective work with a moment's glance. . . . The Centers for Disease Control are already looking at that. And what about history? You could track an individual right back to the womb. It wouldn't take much of an extension to the software to transfer the trace to the DNA of either parent. And to their parents before them. You could follow family trees back into time. And you could work the other way, start with any historical character and trace all their living descendants. . . . You're a scientist, David. The WormCam has already turned science and history on their heads—right? Think where you could go with this."

He held the disk out before him, before David's face, holding it between thumb and forefinger, like, David thought, a Communion host.

24

WATCHING BOBBY

Her name was Mae Wilson.

Her intent was clear, like a piece of crystal.

That was true from the moment her adopted daughter, Barbara, was convicted of the murder of her adopted son, Mian, and sentenced to follow her father—Mae's husband, Phil—to a room where she would be delivered a lethal injection.

The fact of it was that she'd gotten used to the idea that her husband had been a monster who had abused and killed the boy in their care. Over the years she'd learned to blame Phil, even learned to hate his shade—and, clinging to that, found a little peace.

And she still had Barbara, out there somewhere, a fragment left over from the wreck of her life, proof that some good had come of it all.

But now, because of the WormCam, that wasn't an option anymore. It hadn't been Phil after all—but *Barbara*. It just wasn't acceptable. The monster hadn't been the one who had lied to her all these years, but one she had nurtured, grown, *made*.

And she, Mae, wasn't a victim of deception, but, somehow, an agent of the whole disaster.

Of course to expose Barbara had been *just*. Of course it was *true*. Of course it was a great wrong that had been done to Phil, to all of them, in his wrongful conviction, a wrong now put right, at least partially, thanks to the WormCam.

But it wasn't justice or truth or rightness that Mae wanted. Nobody did. Why couldn't these people who so loved the WormCam see that? All Mae wanted was consolation.

Her intent was clear from the start, then. It was to find somebody new to hate.

She could never hate Barbara, of course, despite what she'd done. She was still Barbara, bound to Mae as if by a steel cable.

So Mae's focus shifted, as she deepened and developed her thinking.

At first she had fixed her attention on FBI Agent Mavens, the man who might have found the truth in the first place, in the old pre-WormCam days. But that wasn't appropriate, of course; he had been, literally, an agent, dumbly pursuing his job with whatever technology had been available to him.

The technology itself, then—the ubiquitous WormCam? But to hate a mere piece of machinery was shallow, unsatisfying.

She couldn't hate *things*. She had to hate people.

Hiram Patterson, of course.

He had blighted the human race with his monstrous truth machine, for no purpose she could detect other than profit.

As if incidentally, the machine had even destroyed the religion that had once brought her comfort.

Hiram Patterson.

It took David three days' intensive work at the Wormworks to link the federal lab's trace software to an operational wormhole.

Then he went to Bobby's apartment. He searched it until he found, clinging to a cushion, a single hair from Bobby's head. He had its DNA sequenced at another of Hiram's facilities.

The first image, bright and clear in his SoftScreen,

was of the hair itself, lying unremarked on its cushion.

David began to track back in time. He had devised a way to make the viewpoint effectively fast-rewind into the past—in reality a succession of fresh wormholes was being established, back along the world-line of DNA molecules from the hair.

He accelerated, days and nights passing in a blur of gray. Still the hair and the cushion sat unchanging at the center of the image.

There was a flurry of motion.

He backed up, reestablished the image, and allowed it to run forward at normal pace.

The date was more than three years in the past. He saw Bobby, Kate, Mary. They were standing, talking earnestly. Mary was half-concealed by a SmartShroud. They were preparing their disappearance, he realized swiftly; already, by this point, they had all three left the lives of David and Heather.

The test was over. The trace worked. He could track forward, approaching the present, until he located Bobby and the others. . . . But perhaps that was best left to Special Agent Mavens.

His test concluded, he prepared to shut down the WormCam—then, on a whim, David arranged the WormCam image so that it centered on Bobby's face, as if an invisible camera had hovered there, just before his eyes, through the entirety of his young life.

And David began to scan back.

He kept the speed high as the crucial moments of Bobby's recent life unraveled: at the court with Kate, in the Wormworks with David himself, arguing with his father, crying in Kate's arms, braving the virtual citadel of Billybob Meeks.

David increased the pace of the rewind further, still fixing on the face of his brother. He saw Bobby eat, laugh, sleep, play, make love. The background, the flickering light of night and day, became a blur, an irrelevant frame to that face; and expressions passed so rapidly across the face that they too became smoothed out, so that Bobby's face looked permanently in repose, his eyes half-closed, as if he was sleeping. Summer light came and went like tides, and every so often, with a suddenness that startled David, Bobby's hairstyle would change: from short to long, natural dark to blond, even, at one point, to a shaven-head crewcut.

And, as the years unwound, Bobby's skin lost the lines he had acquired around his mouth and eyes, and a youthful smoothness lapped over his bones. Imperceptibly at first and then more rapidly, his de-aging face softened and shrank, as if simplifying, those flickering half-open eyes growing rounder and more innocent, the shadows beyond—of adults and huge, unidentifiable places—more formidable.

David froze the image a few days after Bobby's birth. The round, formless face of a baby stared out at him, blue eyes wide and empty as windows.

But behind him David did not see the maternity-hospital scene he had expected. Bobby was in a place of harsh fluorescents, gleaming walls, elaborate equipment, expensive testing gear and green-coated technicians.

It looked like a laboratory of some kind.

Tentatively, David ran the image forward.

Somebody was holding the infant Bobby in the air, gloved hands under the child's armpits. With practiced ease David swiveled the viewpoint, expecting to see a younger Heather, or even Hiram.

He saw neither. The smiling face before him, looming like the Moon, was of a middle-aged man, greying, skin wrinkled and brown, distinctively Japanese.

It was a face David knew. And suddenly he understood the circumstances of Bobby's birth, and many other things beside.

He stared at the image a long while, considering what to do.

*   *   *

Mae knew, better maybe than anybody alive, that it wasn't necessary to injure somebody physically to hurt him.

She hadn't been directly involved in the horrific crime which had destroyed her family; she hadn't even been in the city at the time, hadn't seen so much as a bloodstain. But now everybody else was dead and *she* was the one who must carry all the hurt, on her own, for the rest of her life.

So to get to Hiram, to make him suffer as she did, she had to hurt the one Hiram loved the most.

It didn't take much study of Hiram, the most public man on the planet, to figure out who that was. Bobby Patterson, his golden son.

And of course it must be done in such a way that Hiram would know *he* was responsible, ultimately—just as Mae had been. That was the way to make the hurt deepest of all.

Slowly, in the dark hollows of her mind, she drew up her plans.

She was careful. She had no intention of following her husband and daughter to the cell with the needle. She knew that as soon as the crime was committed the authorities would use the WormCam to scan back through her life, looking for evidence that she'd planned the crime, and for intent.

She must never forget that fact. It was as if she was on an open stage, her every action being monitored and recorded and analyzed by expert observers from the future, taking notes all around her, just out of the light.

She couldn't conceal her actions. So she had to make it look like a crime of passion.

She knew she even had to pretend she was unaware of the future scrutiny itself. If it looked like an act, it wouldn't convince anybody. So she kept doing all the private natural things everybody did, farting and picking her nose and masturbating, trying to show no more awareness of scrutiny than anybody else in this glass-walled age.

She had to gather information, of course. But it was possible to conceal even that in the open too. Hiram and Bobby were, after all, two of the most famous people on the planet. She could appear, not an obsessive stalker, but a lonely widow, comforted by TV shows about famous people's lives.

After a time she thought she found a way to reach them.

It meant a new career. But again, it was nothing unusual. This was an age of paranoia, of watchfulness; personal security had become common, a booming industry, an attractive career for valid reasons for many people. She began to exercise, to strengthen her body, to train her mind. She took jobs elsewhere, guarding people and their property, unconnected with Hiram and his empire.

She wrote nothing down, said nothing aloud. As she slowly changed the trajectory of her life, she tried to make each incremental step seem natural, driven by a logic of its own. As if she was almost by accident drifting toward Hiram and Bobby.

And meanwhile she watched Bobby over and over, through his gilded boyhood, to his growth into a man. He was Hiram's monster, but he was a beautiful creature, and she came to feel she knew him.

She was going to destroy him. But as she spent her waking hours with Bobby, against her will, he was lodging in her heart, in the hollow places there.

25

REFUGEES

Bobby and Kate, seeking Mary, made their cautious way along Oxford Street.

Three years ago, soon after delivering the pair of them to a Refugee cell, Mary had disappeared out of their lives. That wasn't so unusual. The loose network of Refugees, spread worldwide, worked on the cell-organization basis of the old terrorist groups.

But recently, concerned he'd had no news of his half-sister for many months, Bobby had tracked her down to London. And today, he had been assured, he would meet her.

The London sky overhead was a gray, smoggy lid, threatening rain. It was a summer's day, but neither hot nor cold, an irritating urban nothingness. Bobby felt annoyingly hot inside his SmartShroud—which, of course, had to be kept sealed up at all times.

Bobby and Kate slid with smooth, unremarkable steps from group to group. With practiced skill they would join a transient crowd, worm their way to the center; then, as it broke up, they would set off again, always in a different direction from the way they had come. If there was no other choice they would even go backward, retracing their steps. Their progress was slow. But it was all but impossible for any WormCam observer to trace them for more than a few paces—a strategy so effective, in fact, that Bobby wondered how many other Refugees there were here today, moving through the crowds like ghosts.

It was obvious that, despite climate collapse and general poverty, London still attracted tourists. People still came here, presumably to visit the art galleries and see the ancient sites and palaces, now vacated by England's Royals, decanted to a sunnier throne in monarchist Australia.

But it was also sadly clear that this was a city that had seen better days. Most of the shops were unfronted bargain bazaars, and there were several empty lots, gaps like teeth missing from an old man's smile. Still, the sidewalks of this thoroughfare, an east-west artery that had long been one of the city's main shopping areas, were crowded with dense, sluggish rivers of humanity. And that made them a good place to hide.

But Bobby did not enjoy the press of flesh around him. Four years after Kate had turned off his implant he knew he was still too easily startled—and too easily repulsed by unwelcome brushes with his fellow humans. He was particularly offended by unwitting contact with the bellies and flabby buttocks of the many middle-aged Japanese here, a nation who seemed to have responded to the WormCam with a mass conversion to nudity.

Now, above the hubbub of conversation around them, he made out a shout: "Oi! Move it!" Ahead of them people parted, scattering as if some angry animal were forcing its way through. Bobby pulled Kate into a shop doorway.

Through the corridor of annoyed humanity came a rickshaw. It was hauled by a fat Londoner, stripped to the waist, with big slicks of sweat under his pillowy breasts. The woman in the rickshaw, talking into a wrist implant, might have been American.

When the rickshaw had passed Bobby and Kate joined the flow which was forming anew. Bobby shifted his hand so that his fingers were brushing Kate's palm, and began to handspell. *Charming guy.*

Not his fault, Kate replied. *Look around. Probably rickshaw guy once Chancellor of Exchequer . . .*

They pressed on further, making their way east toward Oxford Street's junction with Tottenham Court Road. The crowds thinned a little as they left Oxford Circus behind, and Kate and Bobby moved more cautiously and quickly, aware of their exposure; Bobby made sure he was aware of escape routes, several avenues available at any moment.

Kate wore her 'Shroud hood a little open, but beneath it her heat mask was smooth and anonymous. When she stood still, the 'Shroud's hologram projectors, throwing images of the background around her, would stabilize and make her reasonably invisible from any angle around her—a good illusion, at least, until she began to move again, and processing lag caused her fake image to fragment and blur. But, despite its limitations, a SmartShroud might throw off a careless or distracted WormCam operator, and so it was worth wearing.

In the same spirit, Bobby and Kate were today both wearing their heat masks, molded to seamless anonymity. The masks gave off false infrared signatures, and were profoundly uncomfortable, with their built-in heating elements warm against Bobby's skin. It was possible to wear all-over body masks working on the same principle—some of which were capable of masking a man's characteristic IR signature as a woman's, and vice versa. But Bobby, having tried the requisite jockstrap laced with heating wires, had drawn back before reaching that particular plateau of discomfort.

They passed one smart-looking town house, presumably converted from a shop, which had had its walls replaced by clear glass panes. Looking into the brightly lit rooms, Bobby could see that even the floors and ceilings were transparent, as was much of the furniture—even the bathroom suite. People moved through the rooms, naked, apparently oblivious of the stares of people outside. This minimal home was yet another response to WormCam scrutiny, an in-your-face statement that the occupants really didn't care who was looking at them—as well as a constant reminder to the occupants themselves that any apparent privacy was now and forever illusory.

At the junction with Tottenham Court Road, they approached the Center Point ruin: a tower block, never fully occupied, then wrecked during the worst of the Scottish-separatist terrorism problem.

And it was here that Bobby and Kate were met, as they had been promised.

A shimmering outline blocked Bobby's path. He glimpsed a heat mask within an open 'Shroud hood, and a hand stretched out toward his. It took him a few seconds to tune into the other's fast, confident handspelling.

. . . 25. 4712425. I am 4712425. I am—

Bobby flipped his hand over and replied. *Got you. 4712425. 5650982 me 8736540 other.*

Good whew good at last, the reply came, brisk and sure. *Come now.*

The stranger led them off the main street and into a maze of alleys. Bobby and Kate, still holding hands, kept to the sides of the street, sticking to the shadows wherever they could. But they avoided the doorways, most of which—before doors heavily bolted—were occupied by panhandlers.

Bobby slipped his hand into the stranger's. *Think I know you.*

The other's hand, with an iconic form, registered alarm. *So much for 'Shrouds and numbers bloody useless.* She meant the anonymous ID number each member of the worldwide informal network of Refugee tribes was encouraged to adopt each day. The numbers were provided on demand from a central source, accessible by WormCam, rumored to be a random number generator buried in a disused mine in Montana, based on uncrackable quantum-mechanical principles.

Not that, he signed back.

What then. Shape of big fat arse can't conceal even with 'Shroud.

Bobby suppressed a laugh. That was confirmation enough that "4712425" was who he thought: a woman, southern English, somewhere in her sixties, barrel-shaped, good-humored, confident.

Recognize style. Handspell style.

She made an acknowledgment sign. *Yes yes yes. Heard that before. Must change.*

Can't change everything.

No but can try.

The handspelling alphabets, with the fingertips brushing the palms and fingers of the recipient's hands, had originally been developed for people afflicted with both deafness and blindness. They had been adopted and adapted eagerly by WormCam Refugees; handspelling communication, taking place inside cupped hands, was almost impossible to decipher by an observer.

. . . Almost, but not quite. Nothing was foolproof. And Bobby was always aware that WormCam observers had the luxury of looking back into the past and rerunning anything they missed, as often as they liked, from whatever angle and in as tight a close-up as they chose.

But there was no need for the Refugees to make the lives of the snoops any easier than they had to.

Bobby knew, from scraps of gossip and acquaintance, that "4712425" was a grandmother. She had retired from her profession a few years earlier, and had no criminal record, or experience of unwelcome surveillance activity, or any other obvious reason to go underground—like, in fact, many of the Refugees he had met during his years on the run. She just didn't want people looking at her.

At last "4712425" brought them to a door. With a silent gesture their guide had Bobby and Kate stop here and adjust their 'Shrouds and heat masks to ensure nothing of themselves was showing.

The door opened, revealing only darkness.

... And then, in a final misdirection, "4712425" touched them both lightly and led them farther down the street. Bobby looked back, and saw the door closing silently.

A hundred meters further on, they came to a second door, which opened to admit them into a well of darkness.

Take it easy. Step step step, two more ... In pitch-darkness, "4712425" was guiding Bobby and Kate down a short staircase.

He could sense the room before him, from echoes and scent: it was large, the walls hard—plaster, painted over perhaps—with a sound-deadening carpet on the floor. There was a scent of food and hot drinks. And there were people here: he could smell their mixed scent, hear the soft rustle of their bodies as they moved around.

I'm getting better at this, he thought. Another couple of years I won't need to use my eyes at all.

They reached the base of the stairs. *Single room maybe fifteen meters square*, "4712425" handspelled now. *Two doors off at the back. Toilets. People here, eleven twelve thirteen fourteen, all adults. Windows opaqueable.* That was a common ruse: rooms which were kept dark continually were liable to become renowned as nests of Refugees.

Think okay, Kate spelled out now. *Food here and beds. Come on.* She began to tug at her 'Shroud, and then at the jumpsuit she was wearing beneath.

With a sigh, Bobby began to follow suit. He handed his clothes one by one to "4712425," who added them to a rack he couldn't see. Then, naked save for their heat masks, they joined hands once more and entered the group, all of them anonymous in their nudity. Bobby expected that he would even exchange his heat mask before the meeting was over, the further to confuse those who might choose to watch them.

They were greeted. Hands—male and female, notice-ably different in texture—fluttered at Bobby's face. At last somebody picked him out—he had the holistic impression of a woman, fiftyish, shorter than he was—and her hands, small and clumsy, stroked his face, hands and wrists.

Thus, touching in the darkness, the Refugees tentatively explored each other. Recognition—sought with difficulty, confirmed with caution, even reluctance—was based not on names, or faces, or visual or audible labels, but on more intangible, subtler signs: the shape of a person in the dark before him, her scent—ineradicable and characteristic despite layers of dirt or the most vigorous washing—her firmness or weakness of touch, her modes of communication, her warmth or coolness, her style.

At his first such encounter Bobby had cowered, shrinking in the dark from every touch. But it was a far from unpleasant way to greet people. Presumably—Kate had diagnosed for him—all this nonverbal stuff, the touching and stroking, appealed to some deep animal level of the human personality.

He began to relax, to feel safe.

Of course the anonymity of the Refugee communities was sought out by cranks and criminals—and the communities were relatively easy to infiltrate by those seeking others who hid, for good or ill. But in Bobby's experience the Refugees were remarkably effective at self-policing. Though there was no central coordination, it was in everyone's interest to maintain the integrity of the local group and of the movement as a whole. So bad guys were quickly identified and thrown out, as were federal agents and other outsiders.

Bobby wondered if this might be a model for how human communities might organize themselves in the wired-up, WormCammed, interconnected future: as loose, self-governing networks, chaotic and even inefficient perhaps, but resilient and flexible. As such, he supposed, the Refugees were no more than an extension of groupings like the MAS networks and Bombwatch and the truth squads, and even earlier groupings like the amateur sky watchers who had turned up the Wormwood.

And, with their taboos and privacy being stripped away by the WormCam, perhaps humans were reverting to an earlier form of behavior. The Refugees spoke by grooming, like chimpanzees. Suffused by the warmth and scent and touch and even the taste of other people, these gatherings were extremely sensual, and even at times erotic—Bobby had known more than one such gathering descend to a frank orgy, though he and Kate had made their (nonverbal) apologies before getting too involved.

Being a Refugee, then, wasn't such a bad thing. And it was certainly better than the alternatives on offer for Kate.

But it was a shadow life.

It was impossible to stay in one place for very long, impossible to own significant possessions, impossible even to grow too close to anyone else, for fear of betrayal. Bobby knew the names of only a handful of the Refugees he'd met in his three years underground. Many had become comrades, offering invaluable help and advice, especially at the beginning, to the two helpless neophytes Mary had rescued. Comrades, yes, but without a minimum of human contact, it seemed, they could never be true friends.

The WormCam couldn't necessarily deprive him of his liberty or his privacy, but, it seemed, it could wall off his humanity.

Suddenly Kate was tugging at his arm, ramming her fingers into his palm. *Found her. Mary. Mary is here. Over here. Come come come.*

Startled, Bobby let himself be led forward.

She was sitting alone in a corner of the room.

Bobby explored the setup, lightly, with his fingers.

She was clothed, wearing a jumpsuit. There was a plate of food, cooling and untouched, at her side. She wasn't wearing a heat mask.

Her eyes were closed. She didn't respond to their touches, but he sensed she wasn't asleep.

Kate poked grumpily at Bobby's palm. . . . *Might as well wear neon sign here I am come get me . . .*

Is she okay?

Don't know can't tell.

Bobby picked up his sister's limp hand, massaged it, and handspelled her name, over and over. *Mary Mary Mary, Mary Mays, Bobby here, Bobby Patterson, Mary Mary—*

Abruptly, she seemed to come awake. "Bobby?"

He could sense the shocked, deepened silence around the room. It was the first word anybody had spoken aloud since they had arrived here. Kate, beside him, reached forward and clamped her hand over Mary's mouth.

Bobby found Mary's hand and let her spell to him.

Sorry sorry. Distracted. She lifted his hand to her mouth, and he felt her lips pull up into a smile. Distracted and happy, then. But that wasn't necessarily a good thing. Happy meant careless.

What happened to you?

Her smile broadened. *Not supposed to be happy, big brother?*

Know what I mean.

Implant, she replied simply.

Implant what implant?

Cortical.

Oh, he thought, dismayed. Rapidly he relayed the information to Kate.

Shit bad shit, Kate signed. *Illegal.*

Know that.

. . . Jamaica, Mary signed to him now.

What?

Cell friend in Jamaica. See through his eyes, hear

through his ears. Better than London. Mary's touch in his hand was delicate, an analogue of a whisper.

The new cortical implants, adapted from neural-implant VR apparatus, were the final expression of WormCam technology: a small squeezed-vacuum wormhole generator, together with neural sensor apparatus, buried deep in the cortex of the recipient. The generator was laced with neurotropic chemicals so that, over several months, the recipient's neurons would grow pathways into the generator. And the neural sensor was a highly sensitive neuron activity pattern analyzer, capable of pinpointing individual neuronal synapses.

Such an implant could read and write to a brain, and link it to others. By a conscious effort of will, an implant recipient could establish a WormCam connection from the center of her own mind to any other recipient's.

Armed with the implants, a new linked community was emerging from the Arenas and the truth squads and other swirling maelstroms of thought and discussion that had come to characterize the new, young, worldwide polity. Brains joined to brains. Minds linked.

They called themselves the Joined.

It was, Bobby supposed, a bright new future. What it amounted to here and now, however, was an eighteen-year-old girl, his sister, with a wormhole in her head.

You scared, signed Mary now. *Horror stories. Group mind. Lose soul. Blah blah.*

Hell yes.

Fear unknown. Maybe—

But suddenly Mary pulled back from him and got to her feet. Bobby reached out blindly, found her head, but she pulled away, was gone.

All over the room, at exactly the same moment, others had moved. It was like a flock of birds rising as one from a tree.

There were slivers of light as the front door was opened.

Come on, Bobby signed. He grabbed Kate's hand and

they made their way with the rest toward the door.

Scared, Kate signed as they walked, hurriedly. *You scared. Cold palm. Pulse. Can tell.*

He was scared, he conceded. But not of the abrupt detection; they had been through situations like this before, and a group in a safe house like this always had an elaborate system of WormCam-equipped sentries. No, it wasn't detection or even capture he was scared of.

It was the way Mary and the others had acted as one. A single organism. *Joined.*

He slid into his 'Shroud.

26

THE GRANDMOTHERS

In the Wormworks, David sat before a large wall-mounted SoftScreen.

Hiram's face peered out at him: a younger Hiram, a softer face—but indubitably Hiram. The face was framed by a dimly lit urban landscape, decaying housing blocks and immense road systems, a place that seemed to have been designed to exclude human beings. This was the outskirts of Birmingham, a great city at the heart of England, just before the end of the twentieth century—some years before Hiram had abandoned this old, decaying country in hope of a better opportunity in America.

David had succeeded in combining Michael Mavens' DNA-trace facility with a WormCam guidance system, and he had extended it to cross the generations. So, just as he had managed to scan back along the line of Bobby's life, now he had traced back to Bobby's father, the originator of Bobby's DNA.

And now, driven by curiosity, he intended to go further back yet, tracing his own roots—which was, in the end, the only history that mattered.

In the darkness of the cavernous lab, a shadow drifted across the wall, sourceless. He caught it in his peripheral vision, ignored it.

He knew it was Bobby, his brother. David didn't know why Bobby was here. He would join David when he was ready.

David wrapped his fingers around a small joystick control, and pressed it forward.

Hiram's face smoothed out, growing younger. The background became a blur around him, a blizzard of days and nights, dimly visible buildings—suddenly replaced by gray-green plains, the fen country where Hiram grew up. Soon Hiram's face shrank on itself, became innocent, boyish, and shriveled in a moment to an infant.

And it was replaced suddenly by a woman's face.

The woman was smiling at David—or rather, at somebody behind the invisible wormhole viewpoint which hovered before her eyes. He had chosen from this point to follow the line of mitochondrial DNA, passed unchanged from mother to daughter—and so this was, of course, his grandmother. She was young, mid-twenties—of course she was young; the DNA trace would have switched to her from Hiram at the instant of his conception. Mercifully, he would not see these grandmothers grow old. She was beautiful, in a quiet way, with a look that he thought of as classically English: high cheekbones, blue eyes, strawberry blond hair tied up into a tight bun.

Hiram's Asian ancestry had come from his father's line. David wondered what difficulty that love affair had caused this pretty young woman in such a time and place.

And behind him, in the Wormworks, he sensed that shadow drifting closer.

He pressed at the joystick, and the rattle of days and nights resumed. The face grew girlish, its changing hairstyle fluttering at the edge of visibility. Then the face seemed to lose its form, becoming blurred—bursts of adolescent puppy fat?—before shrinking into the formlessness of infancy.

Another abrupt transition. His great-grandmother, then. This young woman was in an office, frowning, concentrating, her hair a ridiculously elaborate sculpture of tightly coiled plaits. In the background David glimpsed more women, mostly young, toiling in rows at clumsy mechanical calculators, laboriously turning keys and levers and handles. This must be the 1930s, decades before the birth of the silicon computer; this was perhaps as complex an information processing center as anywhere on the planet. Already this past, so close to his own time, was a foreign country, he thought.

He released the girl from her time trap, and she imploded into infancy.

Soon another young woman stared out at him. She was dressed in a long skirt and ill-fitting, badly made blouse. She was waving a British Union Flag, and she was being embraced by a soldier in a flat tin helmet. The street behind her was crowded, men in suits and caps and overalls, the women in long coats. It was raining, a dismal autumnal day, but nobody seemed to mind.

"November 1918," David said aloud. "The Armistice. The end of four years of bloody slaughter in Europe. Not a bad night to be conceived." He turned. "Don't you think, Bobby?"

The shadow, motionless against the wall, seemed to hesitate. Then it separated, moved freely, took on the outline of a human form. Hands and face appeared, hovering disembodied.

"Hello, David."

"Sit with me," David said.

His brother sat with a rustle of SmartShroud smart cloth. He seemed awkward, as if unused to being so close to anybody in the open. It didn't matter; David demanded nothing of him.

The Armistice Day girl's face smoothed, diminished, shrank to an infant, and there was another transition: a girl with some of the looks of her descendants, the blue eyes and strawberry hair, but thinner, paler, her cheeks hollow. Shedding her years, she moved through a blur of dark urban scenes—factories and terraced houses—

and then a flash of childhood, another generation, another girl, the same dismal landscape.

"They seem so young," Bobby murmured; his voice was scratchy, as if long unused.

"I think we're going to have to get used to that," David said grimly. "We're already deep in the nineteenth century. The great medical advances are being lost, and hygiene awareness is rudimentary. People are dying of simple, curable diseases. And of course we're following a line of women who at least lived long enough to reach childbearing age. We aren't glimpsing their sisters who died in infancy, leaving no descendants."

The generations fell away, faces deflating like balloons, one after the other, subtly changing from generation to generation, slow genetic drift working.

Here was a girl whose scarred face was marked by tears at the moment she gave birth. Her baby had been taken from her, David saw—or rather, in this time-reversed view, *given* to her—moments after the birth. Her pregnancy unraveled in misery and shame, until they reached the moment that defined her life: a brutal rape committed, it seemed, by a family member, a brother or uncle. Cleansed of that darkness, the girl grew younger, pretty, smiling, her face filling with hope despite the squalor of her life, as she found beauty in simplicity: a flower's brief bloom, the shape of a cloud.

The world must be full of such anguished biographies, David thought, unraveling as they sank into the past, effects preceding cause, pain and despair falling away as the blankness of childhood approached.

Suddenly the background changed again. Now, around this new grandmother's face, some ten generations remote, there was countryside: small fields, pigs and cows scratching at the ground, a multitude of grimy children. The woman was careworn, gap-toothed, her face lined, appearing old—but David knew she could be no more than thirty-five or forty.

"Our ancestors were farmers," Bobby said.

"Most everybody was, before the great migrations to the cities. But the Industrial Revolution is unwinding. They probably can't even make steel."

The seasons pulsed, summer and winter, light and dark; and the generations of women, daughter to mother, followed their slower cycle from careworn parent to bright maiden to wide-eyed child. Some of the women erupted onto the 'Screen with faces twisted in pain: they were those unfortunates, increasingly more common, who had died in childbirth.

History withdrew. The centuries were receding, the world emptying of people. Elsewhere the Europeans were drawing back from the Americas, soon to forget those great continents even existed, and the Golden Horde—great armies of Mongols and Tartars, their corpses leaping from the ground—was re-forming and drawing back into central Asia.

None of that touched these toiling English peasants, without education or books, working the same piece of ground for generation on generation: people to whom, David reflected, the local collector of tithes would be a far more formidable figure than Tamerlaine or Kublai Khan. If the WormCam had shown nothing else, he thought, it was this, with pitiless clarity: that the lives of most humans had been miserable and short, deprived of freedom and joy and comfort, their brief moments in the light reduced to sentences to be endured.

At last, around the framed face of one girl—hair matted and dark, skin sallow, expression ratlike, wary—there was an abrupt blur of scenery. They glimpsed dismal countryside, a ragged family of refugees walking endlessly—and, here and there, heaps of corpses, burning.

"A plague," Bobby said.

"Yes. They are forced to flee. But there is nowhere to go."

Soon the image stabilized on another anonymous scrap of land set in a huge, flat landscape; and once more the generations of toil, so calamitously interrupted, resumed.

On the horizon there was a Norman cathedral, an immense, brooding, sandstone box. If this was the fens, the great plain to the east of England, then that could be Ely. Already centuries old, the great construction looked like a giant sandstone spaceship which had descended from the sky, and it must utterly have dominated the mental landscapes of these toiling people—which was, of course, its purpose.

But even the great cathedral began to shrink, collapsing with startling swiftness into smaller, simpler forms, at last disappearing from view altogether.

And the numbers of people were still falling, the great tide of humanity drawing back all over the planet. The Norman invaders must already have dismantled their great keeps and castles and withdrawn to France. Soon the waves of invaders from Scandinavia and Europe would return home from Britain. Farther afield, as the death and birth of Muhammad approached, the Muslims were withdrawing from northern Africa. By the time Christ was brought down from the Cross, there would be only around a hundred million people left in all the world, less than half the population of the United States of David's day.

As the faces of their ancestors pulsed by, there was another change of scene, a brief migration. Now these remote families scratched at a land of ruins—low walls, exposed cellars, the ground littered with blocks of marble and other building stone.

Then buildings grew like time-lapsed flowers, the scattered stones coalescing.

David paused. He fixed on the face of a woman, his own remote ancestor some eighty generations removed. She was perhaps forty, handsome, her strawberry hair tinged with gray, her eyes blue. Her nose was proudly prominent, Romanesque.

Behind her the dismal fields had vanished, to be replaced by an orderly townscape: a square surrounded by colonnades and statues and tall buildings, their roofs tiled red. The square was crowded with stalls, vendors frozen in the act of hawking their wares. The vendors seemed comical, so intent were they on their slivers of meaningless profit, all unaware of the desolate ages that lay in their own near future, their own imminent deaths.

"A Roman settlement," Bobby said.

"Yes." David pointed at the 'Screen. "I think this is the forum. *That* is probably the basilica, the town hall and law courts. These rows of colonnades lead to shops and offices. And the building over *there* might be a temple. . . ."

"It looks so orderly," Bobby murmured. "Even modern. Streets and buildings, offices and shops. You can see it's all set out on a rectangular grid, like Manhattan. I feel as if I could walk into the 'Screen and go look for a bar."

The contrast of this little island of civilization with the centuries-wide sea of ignorance and toil that surrounded it was so striking that David felt a reluctance to leave it.

"You're taking a risk to come here," he said.

Bobby's face, hovering above the 'Shroud, was like an eerie mask, illuminated by the frozen smile of his distant grandmother. "I know that. And I know you've been helping the FBI. The DNA trace—"

David sighed. "If not me, somebody else would have developed it. At least this way I know what they're up to." He tapped his SoftScreen. A border of smaller images lit up around the image of the grandmother. "Here. WormCam views of all the neighboring rooms and the corridors. This aerial view shows the parking lot. I've mixed in infrared recognition. If anybody approaches—"

"Thanks."

"It's been too long, brother. I haven't forgotten the way you helped me through my own crisis, my brush with addiction."

"We all have crises. It was nothing."

"On the contrary . . . You haven't told me why you've come here."

Bobby shrugged, the movement inside his 'Shroud a shadowy blur. "I know you've been looking for us. I'm alive and well. And so is Kate."

"And happy?"

Bobby smiled. "If I wanted happy, I could just turn on the chip in my head. There's more to life than happiness, David. I want you to take a message to Heather."

David frowned. "Is it about Mary? Is she hurt?"

"No. No, not exactly." Bobby rubbed his face, hot in his SmartShroud. "She's become one of the Joined. We're going to try to get her to come home. I want you to help me set it up."

It was disturbing news. "Of course. You can trust me."

Bobby grinned. "I know it. Otherwise I wouldn't have come."

And I, David thought uneasily, have, since we last met, discovered something momentous about *you*.

He looked into Bobby's open, curious face, lit up by a day two millennia gone. Was this the time to hit Bobby with another revelation about Hiram's endless tinkering with his life—perhaps, indeed, the greatest crime Hiram had committed against his son?

Later, he thought. Later. There will be a moment.

And besides, the WormCam image still glowed on the 'Screen, enticing, alien, utterly irresistible. The Worm-Cam in all its manifestations had changed the world. But none of that mattered, he thought, compared to *this*: the power of the technology to reveal what had been thought lost forever.

There would be time enough for life, for their complex affairs, to deal with the unshaped future. For now, history beckoned. He took the joystick, pushing it forward; and the Roman buildings evaporated like snowflakes in the sun.

*   *   *

Another brief blur of migrations, and now here was a new breed of ancestor: still with the characteristic strawberry hair and blue eyes, but with no trace of the Romanesque nose.

Around the flickering faces David glimpsed fields, small and rectangular, worked by ploughs drawn by oxen, or even, in poorer times, by humans. There were timber granaries, sheep and pigs, cattle and goats. Beyond the grouped fields he saw earthwork banks, making the area into a fort—but abruptly, as they sank deeper into the past, the earthworks were replaced by a cruder wooden palisade.

Bobby said, "The world's getting simpler."

"Yes. How did Francis Bacon put it? . . . 'The good effects wrought by founders of cities, law-givers, fathers of the people, extirpers of tyrants, and heroes of that class, extend but for short times: whereas the work of the Inventor, though a thing of less pomp and show, is felt everywhere and lasts forever.' Right about now the Trojan War is being fought with bronze weapons. But bronze breaks easily, which is why that war lasted twenty years with comparatively few casualties. We forgot how to make iron, so we can't kill each other as efficiently as we used to. . . ."

The earnest toil in the fields continued, largely unchanging from generation to generation. The sheep and cattle, though domesticated, looked like much wilder breeds.

A hundred and fifty generations deep, and the bronze tools gave way, at last, to stone. But the stone-worked fields were little changed. As the pace of historical change slowed, David let them fall faster. Two hundred, three hundred generations passed, the fleeing faces blurring one into the other, slowly molded by time and toil and the mixing of genes.

But soon it will mean nothing, David thought bleakly—nothing, after Wormwood Day. On that dark morning all of this patient struggle, the toil of billions of small lives, will be obliterated; all we have learned and built will be lost, and there may not even be minds to remember, to mourn. And time's wall was close, much closer even than the Roman spring they had glimpsed; so little history might be left to play itself out.

Suddenly it was an unbearable thought, as if he had imaginatively absorbed the reality of the Wormwood for the first time. We *must* find a way to push it aside, he thought. For the sake of these others, the old ones who stare out at us through the WormCam. We must not lose the meaning of their vanished lives.

And then, suddenly, the background was a blur once more.

Bobby said, "We've become nomads. Where are we?"

David tapped a reference panel. "Northern Europe. We forgot how to do agriculture. The towns and settlements have dispersed. No more empires, no cities. Humans are pretty rare beasts, and we live in nomadic groups and clans, settlements that last a season or two at best."

Twelve thousand years deep, he paused the scan.

She might have been fifteen years old, and there was a round sigil of some kind crudely tattooed onto her left cheek. She looked in rude health. She carried a baby, swaddled in animal hide—my remote great-uncle, David thought absently—and she was stroking its round cheek. She wore shoes, leggings, a heavy cloak of plaited grasses. Her other garments seemed to have been stitched together from strips of skin. There was grass stuffed into her shoes and under her hat, presumably for insulation.

Cradling her baby, she was walking after a group of others: men, women with infants, children. They were making their way up a shallow, sloping ridge of rock. They were walking casually, easily, a pace that seemed destined to carry them many kilometers. But some of the adults had flint-tipped spears at the ready: presumably as a guard against animal attack rather than any human threat.

She topped the ridge. David and Bobby, riding at their grandmother's shoulder, looked with her over the land beyond.

". . . Oh, my," David said. "Oh, my."

They were looking down over a broad, sweeping plain. In the far distance, perhaps the north, there were mountains, dark and brooding, striped with the glaring white of glaciers. The sky was crystal blue, the sun high.

There was no smoke, no tracery of fields, no fencing. All the marks made by humans had been erased from this chill world.

But the valley was not empty.

. . . It was like a carpet, thought David: a moving carpet of boulder-like bodies, each coated in long red-brown fur that dangled to the ground, like the fur of a musk ox. They moved slowly, feeding all the while, the greater herd made up of scattered groups. At the near fringe of the herd, one of the young broke away from its parent, incautiously, and began to paw at the ground. A wolf, gaunt, white-furred, crept forward. The calf's mother broke from the pack, curved tusks flashing. The wolf fled.

"Mammoth," David said.

"There must be tens of thousands of them. And what are *they*, some kind of deer? Are *those* camels? And— oh, my God—I think it's a saber-toothed cat."

" 'Lions and tigers and bears,' " David said. "Do you want to go on?"

"Yes. Yes, let's go on."

The Ice Age valley disappeared, as if into mist, and only the human faces remained, falling away like the leaves of a calendar.

Still David felt he could recognize the faces of his ancestors: round, almost always devastatingly young when giving birth, and still retaining that signature of blue eyes and strawberry-blond hair.

But the world had changed dramatically.

Great storms battered the sky, some lasting years. The ancestors struggled across landscapes of ice or drought, even desert, starving, thirsty, never healthy.

"*We've* been lucky," David said. "We've had millennia of comparative climate stability. Time enough to figure out agriculture and build our cities and conquer the world. Before that, *this.*"

"So very fragile," Bobby said, wondering.

More than a thousand generations deep, the faces began to grow darker.

"We're migrating south," Bobby said. "Losing our adaptation to the colder climates. Are we going back to Africa?"

"Yes." David smiled. "We're going home."

And in a dozen more generations, as this first great migration was undone, the images began to stabilize.

This was the southern tip of Africa, east of the Cape of Good Hope. The ancestral group had reached a cave, close to a beach from which thick, tan sedimentary rocks protruded.

It seemed a generous place. Grassland and forest, dominated by bushes and trees with huge, colorful, thistly flowers, lapped right down to the sea's edge. The ocean was calm, and seabirds wheeled overhead. The intertidal shoreline was rich with kelp, jellyfish and stranded cuttlefish.

There was game in the forest. At first they glimpsed familiar creatures like eland, springbok, elephant and wild pig, but deeper in time there were more unfamiliar species: long-horned buffalo, giant hartebeest, a kind of giant horse, striped like a zebra.

And here, in these unremarkable caves, the ancestors stayed, generation on generation.

The pace of change was now terribly slow. At first the ancestors wore clothes, but—as hundreds of generations withered away—the clothing was of decreasing quality, reducing at last to simple skin bags tied around naked waists, and at length not even that. They would hunt with stone-tipped spears and hand axes, no longer with arrows. But the stone tools too were of increasing coarseness, the hunting less ambitious, often no more than a patchy attempt to finish off a wounded eland.

In the caves—whose floors gradually sank deeper over the millennia, as successive layers of human detritus were removed—at first there was something like the sophistication of a human society. There was even art, images of animals and people, laboriously layered on the walls with dye-stained fingers.

But at last, more than twelve hundred generations deep, the walls became blank, the last crude images scraped away.

David shivered. He had reached a world without art: there were no pictures, no novels, no sculptures, perhaps not even songs or poetry. The world was draining of mind.

Deeper and deeper they fell, through three, four thousand generations: an immense desert of time, crossed by a chain of ancestors who bred and squabbled in this unadorned cave. The succession of grandmothers showed little meaningful change—but David thought he detected an increasing vagueness, a bewilderment, even a state of habitual, uncomprehending fear in those dark faces.

At last there was a sudden, jarring discontinuity. And this time it was not the landscape that changed but the ancestral face itself.

David slowed the fall, and the brothers stared at this most remote grandmother, peering from the mouth of the African cave her descendants would inhabit for thousands of generations.

Her face was outsized, with her eyes too far apart, nose flattened, and features spread too wide, as if the whole face had been pulled wide. Her jaw was thick, but her chin was shallow and sliced back. And bulging out of her forehead was an immense brow, a bony swelling like a tumor, pushing down the face beneath it and making the eyes sunken in their huge hard-boned sockets. A swelling at the back of her head offset the weight of that huge brow, but it tilted her head downward, so that her chin almost rested on her chest, her massive neck snaking forward.

But her eyes were clear and knowing.

She was more human than any ape, and yet she was not human. And it was that degree of closeness yet difference which disturbed him.

She was, unmistakably, Neandertal.

"She's beautiful," Bobby said.

"Yes," David breathed. "*This* is going to send the paleontologists back to the drawing board." He smiled, relishing the idea.

And, he wondered suddenly, how many watchers from his own far future would be studying him and his brother, even now, as they became the first humans to confront their own deep ancestors? He supposed he could never begin to imagine their forms, the tools they used, their thoughts—even as this Neandertal grandmother could surely never have envisaged this lab, his half-invisible brother, the gleaming gadgets here.

And beyond *those* watchers, still further into the future, there must be others watching them in turn— and on, off into the still more unimaginable future, as long as humanity—or those who followed humans— persisted. It was a chilling, crushing thought.

All of it supposing the Wormwood spared anybody at all.

". . . Oh," Bobby whispered. He sounded disappointed.

"What is it?"

"It's not your fault. I knew the risk." There was a rustle of cloth, a blurred shadow.

David turned. Bobby had gone.

But here was Hiram, storming into the lab, clattering

doors and yelling. "I got them. Bugger me, I got them." He slapped David on the back. "That DNA trace worked like a charm. Manzoni and Mary, the pair of them." He raised his head. "You hear me, Bobby? I know you're here. *I got them.* And if you want to see either of them again, you have to come to me. You got that?"

David stared into the deep eyes of his lost ancestor—a member of a different species, five thousand generations removed from himself—and cleared down the Soft-Screen.

27

FAMILY HISTORY

When she was forcibly restored to open human society, Kate was relieved to find she'd been cleared of the criminal conviction brought against her. But she was stunned to find she was taken away from Mary, her friends, and immediately incarcerated—by Hiram Patterson.

The door to the suite opened, as it did twice a day.

There stood her guard: a woman, tall, willowy, dressed in a sober businesslike trouser suit. She was even beautiful—but with a deadness of expression and in her dark eyes that Kate found chilling.

Her name, Kate had learned, was Mae Wilson.

Wilson pushed a small trolley through the door, hauled out yesterday's, cast a fast, professional glance around the room, then shut the door. And that was that, over without a word.

Kate had been sitting on the room's sole piece of furniture, a bed. Now she got up and crossed to the trolley, pulled back its white paper cover. There was cold meat, salad, bread, fruit, and drinks, a flask of coffee, bottled water, orange juice. On a lower deck there was laundry, fresh underwear, jumpsuits, sheets for Kate's bed. The usual stuff.

Kate had long exhausted the possibilities of the twice-daily trolley. The paper plates and plastic cutlery were useless for anything but their primary purpose, and nearly useless for that. Even the wheels of the trolley were of soft plastic.

She went back to her bed and sat desultorily munching on a peach.

The rest of the room was just as unpromising. The walls were seamless, coated with a clear plastic she couldn't dig her nails through. There wasn't even a light fitting; the gray glow that flooded the room—twenty-four hours a day—came from fluorescents behind ceiling panels, sealed off behind plastic, and anyhow out of her reach. The bed was a plastic box seamlessly attached to the floor. She'd tried ripping the sheets, but the fabric was too tough. (And anyhow she wasn't yet ready to visualize herself garrotting anybody, even Wilson.)

The plumbing, a john and a shower fixture, was likewise of no value to her greater purpose. The toilet was chemical, and it seemed to lead to a sealed tank, so she couldn't even smuggle out a message in her bodily waste—even supposing she could figure out how.

. . . But despite all that, she had come close to escape, once. It was enjoyable to replay her near-triumph in her mind.

She'd concocted the scheme in her head, where even the WormCam couldn't yet peer. She'd worked on her preparations for over a week. Every twelve hours she had left the food trolley in a slightly different place—just that fraction further inside the room. She choreographed each setup in her head: three paces from bed to door, cut the second pace by that fraction more . . .

And each time she'd come to the door to collect the trolley, Wilson had been forced to reach a little further.

Until at last there came a time when Wilson, to reach the trolley, had to take a single pace into the room. Just a pace, that was all—but Kate hoped it would be enough.

Two running steps took her to the doorway. A shoulder charge knocked Wilson forward into the room, and

Kate made it as far as two paces out the door.

Her room turned out to be just a box, standing alone in a giant, hangar-sized chamber, the walls high and remote and dimly lit. There were other guards all around her, men and women, getting up from desks, drawing weapons. Kate looked around frantically, seeking a place to run—

The hand that had closed on hers was like a vise. Her little finger was twisted back, and her arm bent sideways. Kate fell to her knees, unable to keep from screaming, and she felt bones in her finger break in an explosion of grinding pain.

It was, of course, Wilson.

When she'd come to, she was on the floor of her prison, bound there with what felt like duct tape, while a medic treated her hand. Wilson was being held back by another of the guards, with a murderous look on that steely face.

When it was done, Kate had a finger that throbbed for weeks. And Wilson, when she next came to the door on her twice-daily routine, fixed Kate with a glare full of hate. I wounded her pride, Kate realized. Next time, she will kill me without hesitation.

But it was clear to Kate that, even after her attempted escape, all that hate wasn't directed at *her*. She wondered who was Wilson's real target—and if Hiram knew.

In the same way, she knew, she had never been Hiram's real target. She was just bait, bait in a trap.

She was just in the way of these crazy people with their unguessable agendas.

It did no good to brood on such things. She lay back on her bed. Later, in the routine she'd used to structure her empty days, she'd take some exercise. For now, suspended in light that was never quenched, she tried to blank her mind.

A hand touched hers.

*   *   *

Amid the chaos and recrimination and anger that followed the retrieval of Mary and Kate, David asked to see Mary in the cool calm of the Wormworks.

He was immediately jolted by the familiarity of Mary's blue eyes, so like the eyes he had followed deep into time, all the way back to Africa.

He shivered with a sense of the evanescence of human life. Was Mary really no more than the transient manifestation of genes which had been passed to her through thousands of generations, even from the long-gone Neandertal days, genes which she in turn would pass on into an unknown future? But the WormCam had destroyed that dismal perspective. Mary's life was transient, but no less meaningful for that; and now that the past was opened up, she would surely be remembered, cherished by those who would follow.

And her life, shaped in a fast-changing world, might yet take her to places he couldn't even imagine.

She said, "You look worried."

"That's because I'm not sure who I'm speaking to."

She snorted, and for an instant he saw the old, rebellious, discontented Mary.

"Forgive my ignorance," David said. "I'm just trying to understand. We all are. This is something new to us."

She nodded. "And therefore something to fear? . . . Yes," she said eventually. "Yes, then. *We're* here. The wormhole in my head never shuts down, David. Everything I do, everything I see and hear and feel, everything I think, is—"

"Shared?"

"Yes." She studied him. "But I know what you imply by that. *Diluted.* Right? But it isn't like that. I'm no less me. But I am enhanced. It's just another layer of mind. Or of information processing, if you like: layered over my central nervous system, the way the CNS is layered over older networks, like the biochemical. My memories are still mine. Does it matter if they are stored in somebody else's head?"

"But this isn't just some kind of neat mobile phone network, is it? You Joined make higher claims than that. Is there a new person in all this, a new, combined *you*? A group mind, linked by wormholes, emergent from the network?"

"You think that would be a monstrosity, don't you?"

"I don't know what to think about it."

He studied her, trying to grasp Mary within the shell of Joinedness.

It didn't help that the Joined had quickly become renowned as consummate actors—or liars, to be more blunt. Thanks to their detached layers of consciousness, each of them had a mastery over their body language, the muscles of their faces—a power over communication channels that had evolved to transmit information reliably and honestly—that could beat out the most expert thespian. He had no reason to suppose Mary was lying to him, today; it was just that he couldn't see how he could tell if she was or not.

She said now, "Why don't you ask me what you really want to know?"

Disturbed, he said, "Very well. Mary—how does it *feel*?"

She said slowly: "The same. Just—*more*. It's like coming fully awake—a feeling of clarity, of full consciousness. *You* must know. I've never been a scientist. But I've solved puzzles. I play chess, for instance. Science is something like that, isn't it? You figure something out—suddenly see how the game fits together— it's as if the clouds clear, just for a moment, and you can see far, much farther than before."

"Yes," he said. "I've had a few moments like that in my life. I've been fortunate."

She squeezed his hand. "But for me, that's how it feels *all the time*. Isn't that wonderful?"

"Do you understand why people fear you?"

"They do more than fear us," she said calmly. "They hunt us down. They attack us. But they can't damage us. We can see them coming, David."

That chilled him.

"And even if one of us is killed—even if *I* am killed—then we, the greater being, will go on."

"What does *that* mean?"

"The information network that defines the Joined is large, and growing all the time. It's probably indestructible, like an Internet of minds."

He frowned, obscurely irritated. "Have you heard of attachment theory? It describes our need, psychologically, to form close relationships, to reach out to intimates. We need such relationships to conceal the awful truth, which we confront as we grow up, that each of us is alone. The greatest battle of human existence is to come to terms with that fact. And *that* is why to be Joined is so appealing.

"But the chip in your head will not help you," he said brutally. "Not in the end. For you must die alone, just as I must."

She smiled, coldly forgiving, and he felt ashamed.

"But that may not be true," she said. "Perhaps I will be able to live on, survive the death of my body—of Mary's body. But *I*, my consciousness and memories, will not be resident in one member's body or another, but—distributed. Shared amongst them all. Wouldn't that be wonderful?"

He whispered, "And would it be you? Could you truly avoid death that way? Or would this distributed self be a copy?"

She sighed. "I don't know. And besides the technology is some way away from realizing that. Until it does, we will still suffer illness, accident, death. And we will always grieve."

"The wiser you are, the more it hurts."

"Yes. The human condition is tragic, David. The

greater the Joined becomes, the more clearly I can see that. And the more I feel it." Her face, still young, seemed overlaid by a ghostly mask of much greater age.

"Come with me," he said. "There's something I want to show you."

Kate couldn't help but jump, snatch her hand away.

She finessed her involuntary gasp into a cough, extended the motion of her hand to cover her mouth. Then, delicately, she returned her hand to where it had been, resting on the top sheet of her bed.

And that gentle touch came again, the fingers warm, strong, unmistakable despite the SmartShroud glove which must cover them. She felt the fingers squirm into her palm, and she tried to stay still, eating the peach.

Sorry shocked you. No way warn.

She leaned back a little, seeking to conceal her own handspelling behind her back. *Bobby?*

Who else??? Nice prison.

In Wormworks right?

Yes. DNA trace. David helped. Refugee methods. Mary helped. All family together.

Shouldn't have come, she signed quickly. *What Hiram wants. Get you. Bait in trap.*

Not abandon you. Need you. Be ready.

Tried once. Guards smart, sharp . . .

She risked a glimpse to her side. She could see no sign of his presence, not so much as a false shadow, an indentation in the bedcover, a hint of distortion. Evidently SmartShroud technology was improving as rapidly as the WormCam itself.

I might not get another chance, she thought. I must tell him.

Bobby. I saw David. Had news. About you.

His signing now was slower, hesitant. *Me what me?*

Your family . . . I can't do it, she thought. *Ask Hiram*, she signed back, feeling bitter.

Asking you.
Birth. Your birth.
Asking you. Asking you.
Kate took a deep breath.
Not what you believe. Think it through. Hiram wanted dynasty. David big disappointment, out of control. Mother a big inconvenience. So, have boy without mother.
Don't understand. I have mother. Heather mother.
She hesitated. *No she isn't. Bobby, you're a clone.*

David settled back and fixed the cold metal Mind'sEye hoop over his head. As he sank into virtual reality the world turned dark and silent, and for a brief moment he had no sense of his own body, couldn't even feel Mary's soft, warm hand wrapped around his own.

Then, all around them, the stars came out. Mary gasped and grabbed at his arm.

He was suspended in a three-dimensional diorama of stars, stars spread over a velvet black sky, stars more crowded than the darkest desert night—and yet there was structure, he saw slowly. A great river of light—stars crammed so close they merged into glowing, pale clouds—ran around the equator of the sky. It was the Milky Way, of course: the great disc of stars in which he was still embedded.

He glanced down. Here was his body, familiar and comfortable, clearly visible in the complex, multiply sourced light that fell on him. But he was floating in the starlight without enclosure or support.

Mary drifted beside him, still holding on to his arm. Her touch was comforting. Odd, he thought. We can cast our minds more than two thousand light years from Earth, and yet we must still grasp at each other, our primate heritage never far from the doors of our souls.

This alien sky was populated.

There was a sun, planet and moon here, suspended

around him, like the trinity of bodies that had always dominated the human environment. But it was a strange enough sun—in fact, not a single star like Earth's sun, but a binary.

The principal was an orange giant, dim and cool. Centered on a glowing yellow core, it was a mass of orange gas, growing steadily more tenuous. There was much detail in that sullen disc: a tracery of yellow-white light that danced at the poles, the ugly scars of gray-black spots around the equator.

But the giant star was visibly flattened. It had a companion star, small and bluish, little more than a point of light, orbiting so close to its parent it was almost within the giant's scattered outer atmosphere. In fact, David saw, a thin streamer of gas, torn from the parent and still glowing, had wrapped itself around the companion and was falling to its surface, a thin, hellish rain of fusing hydrogen.

David looked down to the planet that hovered beneath his feet. It was a sphere the apparent size of a beachball, half-illuminated by the complex red and white light of its parent stars. But it was obviously airless, its surface a complex mesh of impact craters and mountain chains. Perhaps it had once had an atmosphere, even oceans; or it might have been the rocky or metallic core of a gas giant, an erstwhile Neptune or Uranus. It was even possible, he supposed, that it had harbored life. If so, that life was now destroyed or fled, every trace of its passing scorched from the surface by the dying sun.

But this dead, blasted world still had a moon. Though much smaller than its parent, the moon glowed more brightly, reflecting more of the complex mixed light of the twin stars. And its surface appeared, at first glance, utterly smooth, so that the little worldlet looked like a cue ball, machined in some great lathe. When David looked more closely, however, he could see there was a network of fine cracks and ridges, some of them evidently hundreds of kilometers long, all across the surface. The moon looked rather like a hard-boiled egg, he thought, whose shell had been assiduously if gently cracked with a spoon.

This moon was a ball of water ice. Its smoothed surface was a sign of recent global melting, presumably caused by the grotesque expansion of the parent star, and the ridges were seams between plates of ice. And perhaps, like Jupiter's moon Europa, there was still a layer of liquid water somewhere beneath this deep-frozen surface, an ancient ocean that might serve as a harbor, even now, for retreating life. . . .

He sighed. Nobody knew. And right now, nobody had the time or resources to find out. There was simply too much to do, too many places to go.

But it wasn't the rocky world, or its ice moon—not even the strange double star itself—but something much grander, beyond this little stellar system, which had drawn him here.

He turned now, and looked beyond the stars.

The nebula spanned half the sky.

It was a wash of colors, ranging from bright blue-white at its center, through green and orange, to somber purples and reds at its periphery. It was like a giant watercolor painting, he thought, the colors smoothly flowing, one into another. He could see layers in the cloud—the texture, the strata of shadows made it look surprisingly three-dimensional—with finer structure deeper in its heart.

The most striking aspect of the larger structure was a pattern of dark clouds, rich with dust, set out in a startlingly clear V-shape before the glowing mass, like an immense bird raising black wings before a flame. And before the bird shape, like a sprinkling of sparks from that bonfire behind, there was a thin veil of stars, separating him from the cloud. The great river of light that was the Galaxy flowed around the nebula, passing behind it as if encircling it.

Even as he turned his head from side to side, it was impossible to grasp the full scale of the structure. At times it seemed close enough to touch, like a giant dynamic wall-sculpture he might reach into and explore. And then it would recede, apparently to infinity. He knew his imagination, evolved to the thousand-kilometer scale of Earth, was inadequate to the task of grasping the immense distances involved here.

For if the sun was moved to the center of the nebula, humans could build an interstellar empire without reaching the edge of the cloud.

Wonder surged in him, sudden, unexpected. I am privileged, he thought anew, to live in such a time. One day, he supposed, some WormCam explorer would sail beneath the icy crust of the moon and seek out whatever lay at its core; and perhaps teams of investigators would scour the surface of the planet below, seeking out relics of the past.

He envied those future explorers the depth of their knowledge. And yet, he knew, they would surely envy his generation most of all. For, as he sailed outward with the expanding front of WormCam exploration, David was here *first*, and nobody else in all of history would be able to say that.

Long story. Japanese lab. The place he used to clone tigers for witch doctors. Heather just a surrogate. David WormCammed it all. Then all that mind control. Hiram didn't want more mistakes . . .

Heather. I felt no bond. Know why now. How sad.

She thought she could feel his pulse in the invisible touch at her palm. *Yes sad sad.*

And then, without warning, the door crashed open.

Mae Wilson walked in holding a pistol. Without hesitation she fired once, twice, to either side of Kate. The gun was silenced, the shots mere pops.

There was a cry, a patch of blood hovering in the air, another like a small explosion where the bullet exited Bobby's body.

Kate tried to stand. But the nozzle of Wilson's gun was at the back of her head. "Don't even think about it."

Bobby's 'Shroud was failing, in great concentric circles of distortion and shadow that spread around his wounds. Kate could see he was trying to get to the door. But there were more of Hiram's goons there; he would have no way through.

Now Hiram himself arrived at the door. His face twisted with unrecognizable emotion as he looked at Kate, at Bobby's body. "I knew you couldn't resist it. Gotcha, you little shit."

Kate hadn't been out of her boxy cell for—how long? Thirty, forty days? Now, out in the cavernous, dimly lit spaces of the Wormworks, she felt exposed, ill at ease.

The shot turned out to have passed straight through Bobby's upper shoulder, ripping muscle and shattering bone, but—through pure chance—his life was not in danger. Hiram's medics had wanted to give Bobby a general anaesthetic as they treated him, but, staring at Hiram, he refused, and suffered the pain of the treatment in full awareness.

Hiram led the way across a floor empty of people, past quiescent, hulking machinery. Wilson and the other goons circled Bobby and Kate, some of them walking backward so they could watch their captives, making it obvious there was no way to escape.

Hiram, immersed in whatever project he was progressing now, looked hunted, ratlike. His mannerisms were strange, repetitive, obsessive: he was a man who had spent too much time alone. He's the subject of an experiment himself, Kate thought sourly: a human being deprived of companionship, afraid of the darkness, subject to constant, more or less hostile glares from the rest of the planet's population, their invisible eyes surrounding him. He was being steadily destroyed by a machine he had never imagined, never intended, whose implications he probably didn't understand even now. With a pang of pity, she realized there was no human in history who had more right to feel paranoid.

But she could never forgive him for what he had done to her—and to Bobby. And, she realized, she had absolutely no idea what Hiram intended for them, now that he had trapped his son.

Bobby held Kate's hand tight, making sure her body was never out of contact with his, that they were inseparable. And even as he protected her he was able subtly to lean on her without allowing the others to see, drawing strength she was glad to give him.

They reached a part of the Wormworks Kate had not seen before. A kind of bunker had been constructed, a massive cube half-set into the floor. Its interior was brightly lit. A door was set in its side, operated by a heavy wheel as if this was a submarine bulkhead.

Bobby stepped forward cautiously, still clutching Kate. "What is this, Hiram? Why have you brought us here?"

"Quite a place, isn't it?" Hiram grinned, and slapped the wall confidently. "We borrowed some engineering from the old NORAD base they dug into the Colorado mountains. This whole damn bunker is mounted on huge shock-absorbent springs."

"Is that what this is for? To ride out a nuclear attack?"

"No. These walls aren't to keep out an explosion. They're supposed to contain one."

Bobby frowned. "What are you talking about?"

"The future. The future of OurWorld. *Our* future, son."

Bobby said, "There are others who knew I was coming here. David, Mary. Special Agent Mavens of the FBI. They will be here soon. And then I'll be walking out of here. With her."

Kate watched Hiram's eyes, glancing from one to the other of them, scheming. He said, "You're right, of course. I can't keep you here. Although I could have fun trying. Just give me five minutes. Let me make my case, Bobby." He forced a smile.

Bobby struggled to speak. "That's all you want? To—convince me of something? That's what this is all about?"

"Let me show you." And he nodded his head to the goons, indicating that Bobby and Kate should be brought into the bunker.

The walls were of thick steel. The bunker was cramped, with room only for Hiram, Kate, Bobby and Wilson.

Kate looked around, tense, alert, overloaded. This was obviously a live experimental lab: there were whiteboards, pin boards, SoftScreens, flip charts, fold-up chairs and desks fixed to the walls. At the center of the room was the equipment which, presumably, was the focus of interest here: what looked like a heat exchanger and a small turbine, and other pieces of equipment, white, anonymous boxes. On one of the desks there was a coffee, half-drunk and still steaming.

Hiram walked to the middle of the bunker. "We lost the monopoly on the WormCam quicker than I wanted. But we made a pile of money. And we're making more; the Wormworks is still far ahead of any similar facility around the world. But we're heading for a plateau, Bobby. In another few years the WormCams are going to be able to reach across the universe. And already, now that every punk kid has her own private WormCam, the market for generators is becoming saturated. We'll be in the business of replacement and upgrade, where the profit margins are low and the competition ferocious."

"But you," said Kate, "have a better idea. Right?"

Hiram glared. "Not that it will concern you." He walked to the machinery and stroked it. "We've gotten bloody good at plucking wormholes out of the quantum foam and expanding them. Up to now we've been using them to transmit information. Right? But your smart brother David will tell you that it takes a finite piece of energy to record even a single bit of information. So if we're transmitting *data* we must be transmitting *energy* as well. Right now it's just a trickle—not enough to make a lightbulb glow."

Bobby nodded, stiffly, obviously in pain. "But you're going to change all that."

Hiram pointed to the pieces of equipment. "That's a wormhole generator. It's squeezed-vacuum technology, but far in advance of anything you'll find on the market. I want to make wormholes bigger and more stable— *much* more, more than anything anybody's achieved so far. Wide enough to act as conduits for significant amounts of energy.

"And the energy we mine will be passed through this equipment, the heat exchanger and the turbine, to extract usable electrical energy. Simple, nineteenth-century technology—but that's all I need as long as I have the energy flow. This is just a test rig, but enough to prove the point of principle, and to solve the problems— mainly the stability of the wormholes—"

"And where," Bobby said slowly, "will you mine the energy from?"

Hiram grinned and pointed to his feet. "From down there. The core of the Earth, son. A ball of solid nickel-iron the size of the Moon, glowing as hot as the surface of the sun. All that energy trapped in there since the Earth formed, the engine that powers the volcanoes and earthquakes and the circulation of the crust plates. . . . *That's* what I'm planning to tap.

"You see the beauty of it? The energy we humans burn up, here on the surface, is a candle compared to that furnace. As soon as the technical guys solve the wormhole stability problem, every extant power-generating business will be obsolete overnight. Nuclear fusion, my hairy arse! And it won't stop there. Maybe some day we'll learn how to tap the stars themselves. Don't you see, Bobby? Even the WormCam was nothing compared to this. We'll change the world. We'll become rich—"

"Beyond the dreams of avarice," Bobby murmured.

"Here's the dream, boy. This is what I want us to work on together. You and me. Building a future, building OurWorld."

"Dad—" Bobby spread his free hand. "I admire you. I admire what you're building. I'm not going to stop you. But I don't want this. None of this is real—your money and your power—all that's real is me. Kate and me. I have your genes, Hiram. But I'm not you. And I never will be, no matter how you try to make it so. . . ."

And as Bobby said that, links began to form in Kate's mind, as they used to as she neared the kernel of truth that lay at the heart of the most complex story.

I'm not you, Bobby had said.

But, she saw now, that was the whole point.

As she drifted in space, Mary's mouth was open wide. Smiling, David reached out, touched her chin and closed her jaw.

"I can't believe it," she said.

"It's a nebula," he said. "It's called the Trifid Nebula, in fact."

"It's visible from Earth?"

"Oh, yes. But we are so far from home that the light that set off from the nebula around the time of Alexander the Great is only now washing over Earth." He pointed. "Can you see those dark spots?" They were small, fine globules, like drops of ink in colored water. "They are called Bok globules. Even the smallest of those spots could enclose the whole of our Solar System. We think they are the birthplaces of stars: clouds of dust and gas which will condense to form new suns. It takes a long time to form a star, of course. But the final stages—when fusion kicks in, and the star blows away its surrounding shell of dust and begins to shine—can happen quite suddenly." He glanced at her. "Think about it. If you lived here—maybe on that ice ball below us—you would be able to see, during your lifetime, the birth of dozens, perhaps hundreds of stars."

"I wonder what religion we would have invented," she said.

It was a good question. "Perhaps something softer. A religion dominated more by images of birth than death."

"Why did you bring me here?"

He sighed. "Everybody should see this before they die."

"And now we have," Mary said, a little formally. "Thank you."

He shook his head, irritated. "Not them. Not the Joined. *You*, Mary. I hope you'll forgive me for that."

"What is it you want to say to me, David?"

He hesitated. He pointed at the nebula. "Somewhere over there, beyond the nebula, is the center of the Galaxy. There is a great black hole there, a million times the mass of the sun. And it's still growing. Clouds of dust and gas and smashed-up stars flow into the hole from all directions."

"I've seen pictures of it," Mary said.

"Yes. There's a whole cluster of stapledons out there already. They are having some difficulty approaching the hole itself; the massive gravitational distortion plays hell with wormhole stability—"

"Stapledons?"

"WormCam viewpoints. Disembodied observers, wandering through space and time." He smiled, and indicated his floating body. "When you get used to this virtual-reality WormCam exploration, you'll find you don't need to carry along as much baggage as this.

"My point is, Mary, that we're sending human minds like a thistledown cloud out through a block of spacetime two hundred thousand light years wide and a hundred millennia deep: across a hundred billion star systems, all the way back to the birth of humanity. Already there's more than we can study even if we had a thousand times as many trained observers—and the boundaries are being pushed back all the time.

"Some of our theories are being confirmed; others are unsentimentally debunked. And that's good; that's how science is supposed to be. But I think there's a deeper, more profound lesson we're already learning."

"And that is—"

"That mind—that life itself—is precious," he said slowly. "Unimaginably so. We've only just begun our search. But already we know that there is no significant biosphere within a thousand light years, nor as deep in the past as we can see. Oh, perhaps there are microorganisms clinging to life in some warm, slime-filled pond, or deep in the crevices of some volcanic cleft somewhere. *But there is no other Earth.*

"Mary, the WormCam has pushed my perception out from my own concerns, inexorably, step by step. I've seen the evil and the good in my neighbor's heart, the lies in my own past, the banal horror of my people's history.

"But we've reached beyond that now, beyond the clamor of our brief human centuries, the noisy island to which we cling. Now we've seen the emptiness of the wider universe, the mindless churning of the past. We are done with blaming ourselves for our family history, and we are beginning to see the greater truth: that we are surrounded by abysses, by great silences, by the blind working-out of huge mindless forces. The WormCam is, ultimately, a perspective machine. And we are appalled by that perspective."

"Why are you telling me this?"

He faced her. "If I must speak to you—to all of you— then I want you to know what a responsibility you may hold.

"There was a Jesuit called Teilhard de Chardin. He believed that just as life had covered the Earth to form the biosphere, so mankind—thinking life—would eventually encompass life to form a higher layer, a cogitative layer he called the noosphere. He argued that the rough organization of the noosphere would grow, until it cohered into a single supersapient being he called the Omega Point."

"Yes," she said, and she closed her eyes. " 'The end of the world: the wholesale internal introversion upon itself of the noosphere, which has simultaneously reached the uttermost limit of its complexity and centrality—' "

"You've read de Chardin?"

"*We* have."

"It's the Wormwood, you see," he said hoarsely. "That's my problem. I can take no comfort from the new nihilist thinkers. The notion that this tiny scrap of life and mind should be smashed—at this moment of transcendent understanding—by a random piece of rock is simply unacceptable."

She touched his face with her small young hands. "I understand. Trust me. We're working on it."

And, looking into her young-old eyes, he believed it.

The light was changing now, subtly, growing significantly darker.

The blue-white companion star was passing behind the denser bulk of the parent. David could see the companion's light streaming through the complex layers of gas at the periphery of the giant—and, as the companion touched the giant's blurred horizon, he actually saw shadows cast by thicker knots of gas in those outer layers against the more diffuse atmosphere, immense lines that streamed toward him, millions of kilometers long and utterly straight. It was a sunset on a star, he realized with awe, an exercise in celestial geometry and perspective.

And yet the spectacle reminded him of nothing so much as the ocean sunsets he used to enjoy as a boy, as he played with his mother on the long Atlantic beaches of France, moments when shafts of light cast by the thick ocean clouds had made him wonder if he was seeing the light of God Himself.

Were the Joined truly the embryo of a new order of humanity—of mind? Was he making a sort of first contact here, with a being whose intellect and understanding might surpass his own as much as he might surpass his Neandertal great-grandmother?

But perhaps it was necessary for a new form of mind to grow, new mental powers, to apprehend the wider perspective offered by the WormCam.

He thought, You are feared and despised, and now you are weak. *I* fear you; *I* despise you. But so was Christ feared and despised. And the future belonged to Him. As perhaps it does to you.

And so you may be the sole repository of my hopes, as I have tried to express to you.

But whatever the future, I can't help but miss the feisty girl who used to live behind those ancient blue eyes.

And it disturbs me that not once have you mentioned your mother, who dreams away what is left of her life in darkened rooms. Do we who preceded you mean so little?

Mary pulled herself closer to him, wrapped her arms around his waist and hugged him. Despite his troubled thoughts, her simple human warmth was a great comfort.

"Let's go home," she said. "I think your brother needs you."

Kate knew she had to tell him. "Bobby—"

"Shut up, Manzoni," Hiram snarled. He was raging now, throwing his arms in the air, stalking around the room. "What about me? *I made you,* you little shit. I made you so I wouldn't have to die, knowing—"

"Knowing that you'd lose it all," Kate said.

"Manzoni—"

Wilson took a step forward, standing between Hiram and Bobby, watching them all.

Kate ignored her. "You want a dynasty. You want your offspring to rule the fucking planet. It didn't work with David, so you tried again, without even the inconvenience of sharing him with a mother. Yes, you *made* Bobby, and you tried to control him. But even so he doesn't want to play your games."

Hiram faced her, fists bunching. "What he wants doesn't matter. I won't be blocked."

"No," Kate said, wondering. "No, you won't, will you? My God, Hiram."

Bobby said urgently, "Kate, I think you'd better tell me what you're talking about."

"Oh, I don't say this was his plan from the beginning. But it was always a fallback, in case you didn't— cooperate. And of course he had to wait until the technology was ready. But it's there now. Isn't it, Hiram? . . ." And another piece of the puzzle fell into place. "*You're funding the Joined.* Aren't you? Covertly, of course. But it's your resources that are behind the brain-link technology. You had your own purpose for it."

She could see in Bobby's eyes—black-ringed, marked by pain—that he understood at last.

"Bobby, you're his clone. Your body and nervous structures are as close to Hiram's as is humanly possible to manufacture. Hiram wants OurWorld to live on after his death. He doesn't want to see it dispersed—or, worse, fall into the hands of somebody from outside the family. You're his one hope. But if you won't cooperate . . ."

Bobby turned to his clone-parent. "If I won't be your heir, then you'll kill me. You'll take my body and you'll upload your own foul mind into me."

"But it won't be like that," Hiram said rapidly. "Don't you see? We'll be together, Bobby. I'll have beaten death, by God. And when you grow old, we can do it again. And again, and again."

Bobby shook off Kate's arm, and strode toward Hiram.

Wilson stepped between Hiram and Bobby, pushing Hiram behind her, and raised her pistol.

Kate tried to move forward, to intervene, but it felt as if she were embedded in treacle.

Wilson was hesitating. She seemed to be coming to a decision of her own. The gun muzzle wavered.

Then, in a single lightning-fast movement, she turned and slapped Hiram over the ear, hard enough to send him sprawling, and she grabbed Bobby. He tried to land a blow on her, but she took his injured arm and pressed a determined thumb into his wounded shoulder. He cried out, eyes rolling, and he fell to his knees.

Kate felt overwhelmed, baffled. What now? How much more complicated can this get? Who was this Wilson? What did she *want*?

With brisk movements Wilson laid Bobby and his clone-parent side by side, and began to throw switches on the equipment console at the center of the room. There was a hum of fans, a crackle of ozone; Kate sensed great forces gathering in the room.

Hiram tried to sit up, but Wilson knocked him back with a kick in the chest.

Hiram croaked, "What the hell are you doing?"

"Initiating a wormhole," Wilson murmured, concentrating. "A bridge to the center of the Earth."

Kate said, "But you can't. The wormholes are still unstable."

"I know that," Wilson snapped. "That's the point. Don't you understand yet?"

"My God," Hiram said. "You've intended this all along."

"To kill you. Quite right. I waited for the opportunity. And I took it."

"*Why*, for Christ's sake?"

"For Barbara Wilson. My daughter."

"Who? . . ."

"You destroyed her. You and your WormCam. Without you—"

Hiram laughed, an ugly, strained sound. "Don't tell me. It doesn't matter. Everyone has a grudge. I always knew one of you bitter arseholes would get through in the end. But I trusted you, Wilson."

"If not for you I would be happy." Her voice was pellucid, calm.

"What are you talking about? . . . But who gives a fuck? Look—you've got me," Hiram said desperately. "Let Bobby go. And the girl. They don't matter."

"Oh, but they do." Wilson seemed on the verge of crying. "Don't you see? *He* is the point." The hum of the equipment rose to a crescendo, and digits scrolled over the SoftScreen monitor outputs on the wall. "Just a couple of seconds," Wilson said. "That isn't long to wait, is it? And then it will all be over." She turned to Bobby. "Don't be afraid."

Bobby, barely conscious, struggled to speak. "What?"

"You won't feel a thing."

"What do you care?"

"But I do care." She stroked his cheek. "I spent so long watching you. I knew you were cloned. It doesn't matter. I saw you take your first step. I love you."

Hiram growled. "A bloody WormCam stalker. Is that all you are? How—*small*. I've been hunted by priests and pimps and politicians, criminals, nationalists, the sane and the insane. Everybody with a grudge about the inventor of the WormCam. I evaded them all. And now it comes down to *this*." He began to struggle. "No. Not this way. Not this way—"

And, with a single, snake-like movement, he lunged at Wilson's leg and sank his teeth into her hamstring.

She cried out and staggered back. Hiram clung on with his teeth, like a dog, the woman's blood trickling from his mouth. Wilson rolled on top of him and raised her fist. Hiram released Wilson's leg and yelled at Kate. "Get him out of here! Get him out . . ." But then Wilson drove her fist into his bloodied throat, and Kate heard the crunch of cartilage and bone, and his voice turned to a gurgle.

Kate grabbed Bobby by his good arm and hauled him, by main force, over the threshold of the bunker. He cried out as his head rattled on the door's thick metal sill, but she ignored him.

As soon as his dangling feet were clear she slammed the door, masking the rising noise of the wormhole, and began to dog it shut.

Hiram's security goons were approaching, bewildered. Kate, hauling on the wheel, screamed at them. "Help him up and get out of here!—"

But then the wall bulged out at her, and she glimpsed light, as bright as the sun. Deafened, blinded, she seemed to be falling.

Falling into darkness.

28

THE AGES OF SISYPHUS

As two apledons, disembodied WormCam viewpoints, Bobby and David soared over southern Africa.

It was the year 2082. Four decades had elapsed since the death of Hiram Patterson. And Kate, Bobby's wife of thirty-five years, was dead.

A year after he had accepted that brutal truth, it was never far from Bobby's thoughts, no matter what wonderful scenery the WormCam brought him. But *he* was still alive, and he must live on; he forced himself to look outward, to study Africa.

Today the plains of this most ancient of continents were covered with a rectangular gridwork of fields. Here and there buildings were clustered, neat plastic huts, and machines toiled, autonomous cultivators looking like overgrown beetles, their solar-cell carapaces glinting. People moved slowly through the fields. They all wore loose white clothes, broad-brimmed hats and gaudy layers of sunblock.

In one farmyard, neatly swept, a group of children played. They looked clean, well dressed and well fed, running noisily, bright pebbles on this immense tabletop landscape. But Bobby had seen few children today, and this rare handful seemed precious, cherished.

And, as he watched more closely, he saw how their movements were complex and tightly coordinated, as if they could tell without delay or ambiguity what the oth-

ers were thinking. As, perhaps, they could. For—he was
told—there were children being born now with wormholes in their heads, linked into the spreading group
minds of the Joined even before they left the womb.

It made Bobby shudder. He knew his body was responding to the eerie thought, abandoned in the facility
that was still called the Wormworks—though, forty
years after the death of Hiram, the facility was now
owned by a trust representing a consortium of museums
and universities.

So much time had elapsed since that climactic day,
the day of Hiram's death at the Wormworks—and yet it
was all vivid in Bobby's mind, as if his memory were
itself a WormCam, his mind locked to the past. And it
was now a past that contained all that was left of Kate,
dead a year ago of cancer, her every action embedded
in unchangeable history, like all the nameless billions
who had preceded her to the grave.

Poor Hiram, he thought. All he ever wanted to do was
make money. Now, with Hiram long dead, his company
was gone, his fortune impounded. And yet, by accident,
he changed the world. . . .

David, an invisible presence here with him, had been
silent for a long time. Bobby cut in empathy subroutines
to glimpse David's viewpoint.

. . . The glowing fields evaporated, to be replaced by
a desolate, arid landscape in which a few stunted trees
struggled to survive.

Under the flat, garish sunlight a line of women worked
their way slowly across the land. Each bore an immense
plastic container on her head, containing a great weight
of brackish water. They were stick-thin, dressed in rags,
their backs rigid.

One woman led a child by the hand. It seemed obvious that the wretched child—naked, a thing of bones and
papery skin—was in the grip of advanced malnutrition,
or perhaps even AIDS: what they used to call here,
Bobby remembered with grim humor, the slims disease.

He said gently, "Why look into the past, David? Things are better now."

"But this was the world *we* made," David said bitterly. His voice sounded as if he were just a few meters away from Bobby in some warm, comfortable room, rather than floating in this disregarded emptiness. "No wonder the kids think we old folk are a bunch of savages. It was an Africa of AIDS and malnutrition and drought and malaria and staph infections and dengue fever and endless futile wars, an Africa drenched in savagery . . . But," he said, "it was an Africa with elephants."

"There are still elephants," Bobby said. And that was true: a handful of animals in the zoos, their seed and eggs flown back and forth in a bid to maintain viable populations. There were even zygotes, of elephants and many other endangered or otherwise lost species, frozen in their liquid nitrogen tanks in the unchanging shadows of a lunar south pole crater—perhaps the last refuge of life from Earth if it proved, after all, impossible to deflect the Wormwood.

So there were still elephants. But none in Africa: no trace of them save the bones occasionally unearthed by the robot farmers, bones sometimes showing teeth marks left by desperate humans. In Bobby's lifetime, they had all gone to extinction: the elephant, the lion, the bear— even man's closest relatives, the chimps and gorillas and apes. Now, outside the homes and zoos and collections and labs, there was no large mammal on the planet, none save man.

But what was done was done.

With an effort of will Bobby grasped his brother's viewpoint and rose straight upward.

As they ascended in space and time the shining fields were restored. The children dwindled to invisibility and the farmland shrank to a patchwork of detail, obscured by mist and cloud.

And then, as Earth receded, the bulbous shape of Africa itself, schoolbook-familiar, swam into Bobby's view.

Farther to the west, over the Atlantic, a solid layer of clouds lay across the ocean's curving skin, corrugated in neat gray-white rows. As the turning planet bore Africa toward the shadow of night, Bobby could see equatorial thunderheads spreading hundreds of kilometers toward the land, probing purple fingers of darkness.

But even from this vantage Bobby could make out the handiwork of man.

There was a depression far out in the ocean, a great cappuccino swirl of white clouds over blue ocean. But this was no natural system; it had a regularity and stability that belied its scale. The new weather management functions were, slowly, reducing the severity of the storm systems that still raged across the planet, especially around the battered Pacific Rim.

To the south of the old continent Bobby could clearly see the great curtain-ships working their way through the atmosphere, the conducting sheets they bore shimmering like dragonfly wings as they cleansed the air and restored its long-depleted ozone. And off the western coast pale masses followed the line of the shore for hundreds of kilometers: reefs built up rapidly by the new breed of engineered coral, laboring to fix excess carbon—and to provide a new sanctuary for the endangered communities of plants and animals which had once inhabited the world's natural reefs, long destroyed by pollution, over-fishing and storms.

Everywhere, people were working, repairing, building.

The land, too, had changed. The continent was almost cloud free, its broad land gray-brown, the green of life suppressed by mist. The great northern mass which had been the Sahara was broken by a fine tracery of blue-white. Already, along the banks of the new canals, the glow of green was starting to spread. Here and there he could see the glittering jewel-like forms of PowerPipe plants, the realization of Hiram's last dream, drawing heat from the core of Earth itself—the energy bounty, free and clean, which had largely enabled the planet's stabilizing and transformation. It was a remarkable view, its scale and regularity stunning; David said it reminded him of nothing so much as the old dreams of Mars, the dying desert world restored by intelligence.

The human race, it seemed, had gotten smart just in time to save itself. But it had been a difficult adolescence.

Even as the human population had continued to swell, climatic changes had devastated much of the world's food and water supply, with the desertification of the great grain regions of the U.S. and Asia, the drowning of many productive lowland farming areas by rising sea levels, and the pollution of aquifers and the acidification or drying of freshwater lakes. Soon the problem of excess population went into reverse as drought, disease and starvation culled communities across the planet. It was a crash only in relative terms; most of Earth's population had survived. But as usual the most vulnerable—the very old and the very young—had paid the price.

Overnight, the world had become middle-aged.

New generations had emerged into a world that was, recovering, still crowded with aging survivors. And the young—scattered, cherished, WormCam-linked—regarded their elders with increasing intolerance, indifference and mistrust.

In the schools, the children of the WormCam made academic studies of the era in which their parents and grandparents had grown up: an incomprehensible, taboo-ridden pre-WormCam age only a few decades in the past in which liars and cheats had prospered, and crime was out of control, and people killed each other over lies and myths, and in which the world had been systematically trashed through willful carelessness, greed, and an utter lack of sympathy for others or foresight regarding the future.

And meanwhile, to the old, the young were a bunch of incomprehensible savages with a private language and about as much modesty as a tribe of chimpanzees. . . .

But the generational conflict was not the full story. It seemed to Bobby that a more significant rift was opening up.

The mass minds were still, Bobby supposed, in their infancy, and they were far outnumbered by the Unjoined older generations—but already their insights, folded down into the human world, were having a dramatic effect.

The new superminds were beginning to rise to the greatest of challenges: challenges which demanded at once the best of human intellect and the suppression of humanity's worst divisiveness and selfishness. The modification and control of the world's climate, for example, was, because of the intrinsically chaotic nature of the global weather systems, a problem that had once seemed intractable. But it was a problem that was now being solved.

The new generations of maturing Joined were already shaping the future. It would be a future in which, many feared, democracy would seem irrelevant, and in which even the consolation of religion would not seem important; for the Joined believed—with some justification— that they could even banish death.

Perhaps it would not even be a human future at all.

It was wonderful, awe-inspiring, terrifying. Bobby knew that he was privileged to be alive at such a moment, for surely such a great explosion of mind would not come again.

But it was also true that he—and David and the rest of their generation, the last of the Unjoined—had come to feel more and more isolated on the planet that had borne them.

He knew this shining future was not for him. And— a year after Kate's death, the illness that had suddenly taken her from him—the present held no interest. What remained for him, as for David, was the past.

And the past was what he and David had decided to explore, as far and as fast as they could, two old fools who didn't matter to anybody else anyhow.

He felt a pressure—diffuse, almost intangible, yet summoning. It was as if his hand were being squeezed. "David?"

"Are you ready?"

Bobby let a corner of his mind linger in his remote body, just for a second; shadowy limbs formed around him, and he took a deep breath, squeezed his hands into fists, relaxed again. "Let's do it."

Now Bobby's viewpoint began to fall from the African sky, down toward the southern coast. And as he fell, day and night began to flap across the patient face of the continent, centuries falling away like leaves from an autumn tree.

A hundred thousand years deep, they paused. Bobby and David hovered like two fireflies before a face: heavy-browed, flat-nosed, clear-eyed, female.

Not quite human.

Behind her, a small family group—powerfully built adults, children like baby gorillas—were working at a fire they had built on this ancient beach. Beyond them was a low cliff, and the sky above was a crisp, deep blue; perhaps this was a winter's day.

The brothers sank deeper.

The details, the family group, the powder-blue sky, winked out of existence. The Neandertal grandmother herself blurred, becoming expressionless, as one generation was laid over another, too fast for the eye to follow. The landscape became a grayish outline, centuries of weather and seasonal growth passing with each second.

The multiple-ancestor face flowed and changed. Half a million years deep her forehead lowered, her eye socket ridges growing more prominent, her chin receding, her teeth and jaws pronounced. Perhaps this face was now apelike, Bobby thought. But those eyes remained curious, intelligent.

Now her skin tone changed in great slow washes, dark to light to dark.

"*Homo Erectus*," David said. "A toolmaker. Migrated around the planet. We're still falling. A hundred thousand years every few seconds, good God. But so little changes! . . ."

The next transition came suddenly. The brow sank lower, the face grew longer—though the brain of this remote grandmother, much smaller than a modern human's, was nevertheless larger than a chimpanzee's.

"*Homo Habilis*," said David. "Or perhaps this is *Australopithecus*. The evolutionary lines are tangled. We're already two million years deep."

The anthropological labels scarcely mattered. It was profoundly disturbing, Bobby found, to gaze at this flickering multigeneration face, the face of a chimpanzee-like creature he might not have looked at twice in some zoo . . . and to know that *this was his ancestor*, the mother of his grandmothers, in an unbroken line of descent. Maybe this was how the Victorians felt when Darwin got back from the Galápagos, he thought.

Now the last vestiges of humanity were being shed, the brain pan shrinking further, those eyes growing cloudy, puzzled.

The background, blurred by the passage of the years, became greener. Perhaps there were forests covering Africa, this deep in time. And still the ancestor diminished, her face, fixed in the glare of the WormCam viewpoint, becoming more elemental, those eyes larger, more timid. Now she reminded Bobby more of a tarsier, or a lemur.

But yet those forward-facing eyes, set in a flat face, still held a poignant memory, or promise.

David impulsively slowed their descent, and brought them fleetingly to a halt some forty million years deep.

The shrewlike face of the ancestor peered out at Bobby, eyes wide and nervous. Behind her was a background of leaves, branches. On a plain beyond, dimly glimpsed through green light, there was a herd of what looked like rhinoceros—but with huge, misshapen heads, each fitted with six horns. The herd moved slowly, massive, tails flicking, browsing on low bushes, and reaching up to the dangling branches of trees. Herbivores, then. A young straggler was being stalked by a group of what looked like horses—but these "horses," with prominent teeth and tense, watchful motions, appeared to be predators.

David said, "The first great heyday of the mammals. Forests all over the planet; the grasslands have all but disappeared. And so have the modern fauna: there are no fully-evolved horses, rhinos, pigs, cattle, cats, dogs . . ."

The grandmother's head flicked from side to side, nervously, every few seconds, even as she chewed on fruit and leaves. Bobby wondered what predators might loom out of this strange sky to target an unwary primate.

With Bobby's unspoken consent, David released the moment, and they fell away once more. The background blurred into a blue-green wash, and the ancestor's face flowed, growing smaller, her eyes wider and habitually black. Perhaps she had become nocturnal.

Bobby glimpsed vegetation, thick and green, much of it unfamiliar. And yet now the land seemed strangely empty: no giant herbivores, no pursuing carnivores crossed the empty stage beyond his ancestor's thin-cheeked, shadowed, huge-eyed face. The world was like a city deserted by humans, he thought, with the tiny creatures, the rats and mice and voles burrowing among the huge ruins.

But now the forests began to shrink back, melting away like summer mist. Soon the land became skeletal, a plain marked by broken stumps of trees that must once have risen tall.

Ice gathered suddenly, to lie in thick swaths across the land. Bobby sensed life drawing out of this world like a slow tide.

And then clouds came, immersing the world in darkness. Rain, dimly glimpsed, began to leap from the darkened ground. Great heaps of bones assembled from the mud, and flesh gathered over them in gray lumps.

"Acid rain," murmured David.

Light flared, dazzling, overwhelming.

It was not the light of day, but of a fire that seemed to span the landscape. The fire's violence was huge, startling, terrifying.

But it drew back.

Under a leaden sky, the fires began to collapse into isolated blazes that dwindled further, each licking flame restoring the greenery of another leafy branch. The fire drew at last into tight, glowing pellets that leapt into the sky, and the fleeing sparks merged into a cloud of shooting stars under a black sky.

Now the thick black clouds drew back like a curtain. A great wind passed, restoring smashed branches to the trees, gently ushering flocks of flying creatures to the branches. And on the horizon a fan of light was gathering, growing pink and white, at last turning into a beacon beam of brilliance pointing directly up into the sky.

It was a column of molten rock.

The column collapsed into an orange glow. And, like a second dawn, a glowing, diffuse mass rose above the horizon, a long, glowing tail spreading across half the sky in a great flamboyant curve. Masked by the daylight, brilliant in the night, the comet receded, day by day, drawing its cargo of destruction back into the depths of the Solar System.

The brothers paused in a suddenly restored world, a world of richness and peace.

The ancestor was a wide-eyed, frightened creature that lingered above ground, perhaps incautiously trapped there.

Beyond her, Bobby glimpsed what appeared to be the shore of an inland sea. Lush jungles lapped the swampy lowlands along the coast, and a broad river decanted from distant blue mountains. The broad ridged backs of what must be crocodiles sliced through the river's sluggish, muddy waters. This was a land thick with life—unfamiliar in detail, and yet not so unlike the forests of his own youth.

But the sky was not a true blue—more a subtle violet, he thought; even the shapes of the clouds, scattered overhead, seemed wrong. Perhaps the very air was different here, so deep in time.

A herd of horned creatures moved along the swampy coast, looking something like rhinos. But their movements were strange, almost birdlike, as, lumbering, they mingled, browsed, nested, fought, preened. And there was a herd of what looked at first glance like ostriches—walking upright, with bobbing heads, nervous movements and startled, suspicious glances.

In the trees Bobby glimpsed a huge shadow, moving slowly, as if tracking the giant plant-eaters. Perhaps this was a carnivore—even, he thought with a thrill, a raptor.

All around the dinosaur herds, clouds of insects hovered.

"We're privileged," David said. "We've a relatively good view of the wildlife. The dinosaur age has been a disappointment for the time tourists. Like Africa, it turns out to be huge and baffling and dusty and mostly empty. It stretches, after all, over hundreds of millions of years."

"But," Bobby said dryly, "it was kind of disappointing to discover that *T. rex* was after all just a scavenger. . . . All this beauty, David, and no mind to appreciate it. Was it waiting for *us* all this time?"

"Ah, yes, the unseen beauty. 'Were the beautiful volute and cone shells of the Eocene epoch and the gracefully sculpted ammonites of the Secondary period created that man might ages afterward admire them in his cabinet?' Darwin, in the *Origin of Species*."

"So he didn't know either."

"I suppose not. This is an ancient place, Bobby. You can see it: an antique community that has evolved together, across hundreds of millions of years. And yet—"

"And yet it would all disappear, when the Cretaceous Wormwood did its damage."

"The Earth is nothing but a vast graveyard, Bobby. And, as we dive deeper into the past, those bones are rising again to confront us. . . ."

"Not quite. We have the birds."

"The birds, yes. Rather a beautiful end to this particular evolutionary subplot, don't you think? Let's hope *we* turn out so well. Let's go on."

"Yes."

So they plunged once more, dropping safely through the dinosaurs' Mesozoic summer, two hundred million years deep.

Ancient jungles swept in a meaningless green wash across Bobby's view, framing the timid, mindless eyes of millions of generations of ancestors, breeding, hoping, dying.

The greenery abruptly cleared, revealing a flat dusty plain, an empty sky.

The denuded land was a desert, baked hard and flat beneath a high, harsh sun, the sands uniformly reddish in color. Even the hills had shifted and flowed, so deep was time.

The ancestor here was a small reptile-like creature who nibbled busily on what looked like the remains of a baby rat. She was on the fringe of a scrubby forest, of stunted ferns and conifers, that bordered a straggling river.

Something like an iguana scampered nearby, flashing rows of sharp teeth. Perhaps that was the mother of all the dinosaurs, Bobby mused. And, beyond the trees,

Bobby made out what looked like warthogs, grubbing in the mud close to the sluggish water.

David grunted. "*Lystrosaurs*," he said. "Luckiest creatures who ever lived. The only large animal to survive the extinction event—"

Bobby was confused. "You mean the dinosaur-killer comet?"

"No," David said grimly. "I mean another, the one we must soon pass through, two hundred and fifty million years deep. The worst of them all . . ."

So that was why the great lush jungle panorama of the dinosaurs had drawn back. Once again, the Earth was emptying itself of life. Bobby felt a profound sense of dread.

They descended once more.

At last the final, stunted trees shuddered back into their buried seeds, and the last greenery—struggling weeds and shrubs—shriveled and died. A scorched land began to reconstitute itself, a place of burned-out stumps and fallen branches and, here and there, heaped-up bones. The rocks, increasingly exposed by the receding tide of life, became powerfully red.

"It's like Mars."

"And for the same reason," David said grimly. "Mars has no life to speak of; and, in life's absence, its sediments have rusted: slowly burning, subject to erosion and wind, killing heat and cold. And so Earth, as we approach this greatest of the deaths, was the same: all but lifeless, the rocks eroding away."

And all through this, a chain of tiny ancestors clung to life, subsisting in muddy hollows at the fringes of inland seas that had almost—but not quite—dried to bowls of lethal Martian dust.

Earth in this era was very different, David said. Tectonic drift had brought all of the continents into a single giant assemblage, the largest landmass in the history of the planet. The tropical areas were dominated by immense deserts, while the high latitudes were scoured by glaciation. In the continental interior the climate swung wildly between killing heat and dry freezing.

And this already fragile world was hit by a further calamity: a great excess of carbon dioxide, which choked animals and added greenhouse heating to an already near-lethal climate.

"Animal life in particular suffered: almost knocked back to the level of pond life. But for us it's nearly over, Bobby; the excess CO_2 is drawing back into where it came from: deep sea traps and a great outpouring of flood basalts in Siberia, gases brought up from Earth's interior to poison its surface. And soon that monstrous world continent will break up.

"Just remember this: *life survived*. In fact, our ancestors survived. Fix on that. If not, we wouldn't be here."

As Bobby studied the flickering mix of reptile and rodent features that centered in his vision, he found that idea cold comfort.

They moved beyond the extinction pulse into the deeper past.

The recovering Earth seemed a very different place. There was no sign of mountains, and the ancestors clung to life at the margins of enormous, shallow inland seas that washed back and forth with the ages. And, slowly, after millions of years, as the choking gases drew back into the ground, green returned to planet Earth.

The ancestor had become a low-slung, waddling creature, covered with short dun fur. But as the generations fluttered past, her jaw lengthened, her skull morphing back, and at last she seemed to lose her teeth, leaving a mouth covered with a hard, beaklike material. Now the fur shrank away and the snout lengthened further, and the ancestor became a creature indistinguishable, to Bobby's untrained eye, from a lizard.

He realized, in fact, that he was approaching so great a depth in time that the great families of land animals—the turtles, the mammals and the lizards, crocodiles and birds—were merging back into the mother group, the reptiles.

Then, more than three hundred and fifty million years deep, the ancestor morphed again. Her head became blunter, her limbs shorter and stubbier, her body more streamlined. Perhaps she was amphibian now. At last those stubby limbs became mere lobed fins that melted into her body.

"Life is retreating from the land," David said. "The last of the invertebrates, probably a scorpion, is crawling back into the sea. On land, the plants will soon lose their leaves, and will no longer be upright. And after that the *only* form of life left on land will be simple encrusting forms. . . ."

Suddenly Bobby was immersed, carried by his retreating grandmother into a shallow sea.

The water was crowded. There was a coral reef below, stretching into the milky blue distance. It was littered with what looked like giant long-stemmed flowers, through which a bewildering variety of shelled creatures cruised, looking for food. He recognized nautiloids, what looked like a giant ammonite.

The ancestor was a small, knifelike, unremarkable fish, one of a school which darted to and fro, their movements as complex and nervous as those of any modern species.

In the distance a shark cruised, its silhouette unmistakable, even over this length of time. The fish school, wary of the shark, darted away, and Bobby felt a pulse of empathy for his ancestors.

They accelerated once more: four hundred million years deep, four hundred and fifty.

There was a flurry of evolutionary experimentation, as varieties of bony armor fluttered over the ancestors' sleek bodies, some of them appearing to last little more than a few generations, as if these primitive fish had lost the knack of a successful body plan. It was clear to Bobby that life was a gathering of information and complexity, information stored in the very structures of living things—information won painfully, over millions of generations, at the cost of pain and death, and now, in this reversed view, being shed almost carelessly.

. . . And then, in an instant, the ugly primeval fish disappeared. David slowed the descent again.

There were no fish in *this* antique sea. The ancestor was no more than a pale wormlike animal, cowering in a seabed of rippled sand.

David said, "From now on it gets simpler. There are only a few seaweeds—and at last, a billion years deep, only single-celled life, all the way back to the beginning."

"How much further?"

He said gently, "Bobby, we've barely begun. We must travel *three times* as deep as to this point."

The descent resumed.

The ancestor was a crude worm whose form shifted and flickered—and now, suddenly, she shriveled to a mere speck of protoplasm, embedded in a mat of algae.

And when they fell a little further, there was only the algae.

Abruptly they were plunged into darkness.

"Shit," Bobby said. "What happened?"

"I don't know."

David let them fall deeper, one million years, two. Still the universal darkness persisted.

At last David broke the link with the ancestor of this period—a microbe or a simple seaweed—and brought the viewpoint out of the ocean, to hover a thousand kilometers above the belly of the Earth.

The ocean was white: covered in ice from pole to equator, great sheets of it scarred by folds and creases hundreds of kilometers long. Beyond the icy limb of the planet a crescent Moon was rising, that battered face unchanged from Bobby's time, its features already unimaginably ancient even at this deep epoch. But the cradled new Moon shone almost as brightly, in Earth's reflected light, as the crescent in direct sunlight.

Earth had become dazzling bright, perhaps brighter than Venus—if there had been eyes to see.

"Look at that," David breathed. Somewhere close to Earth's equator there was a circular ice structure, the walls much softened, a low eroded mound at its heart. "That's an impact crater. An old one. That ice covering has been there a *long* time."

They resumed their descent. The shifting details of the ice sheets—the cracks and crumpled ridges and lines of dunelike mounds of snow—were blurred to a pearly smoothness. But still the global freeze persisted.

Abruptly, after a fall of a further fifty million years, the ice cleared, like frost evaporating from a heated window. But, just as Bobby felt a surge of relief, the ice clamped down again, covering the planet from pole to pole.

There were three more breaks in the glaciation, before at last it cleared permanently.

The ice revealed a world that was Earthlike, and yet not. There were blue oceans and continents. But the continents were uniformly barren, dominated by harsh ice-tipped mountains or by rust-red deserts, and their shapes were utterly unfamiliar to Bobby.

He watched the slow waltz of the continents as they assembled themselves, under the blind prompting of tectonics, into a single giant landmass.

"There's the answer," David said grimly. "The supercontinent, alternately coalescing and breaking up, is the cause of the glaciation. When that big mother breaks up, it creates a lot more shoreline. That stimulates the production of a lot more life—which right now is restricted to microbes and algae, living in inland seas and shallow coastal waters—and the life draws down an excess of carbon dioxide from the atmosphere. The greenhouse effect collapses, and the sun is a little dimmer than in our times—"

"And so, glaciation."

"Yes. On and off, for two hundred million years. There can have been virtually no photosynthesis down there for millions of years at a time. It's astonishing life survived at all."

The two of them descended once more into the belly of the ocean, and allowed the DNA trace to focus their attention on an undistinguished mat of green algae. Somewhere here was embedded the unremarkable cell which was the ancestor of all the humans who ever lived.

And above, a small shoal of creatures like simple jellyfish sailed through the cold blue water. Farther away, Bobby could make out more complex creatures: fronds, bulbs, quilted mats attached to the seafloor or free-floating.

Bobby said, "*They* don't look like seaweed to me."

"My God," David said, startled. "They look like ediacarans. Multicelled life-forms. But the ediacarans aren't scheduled to evolve for a couple of hundred million years. Something's wrong."

They resumed their descent. The hints of multicelled life were soon lost, as life shed what it had painfully learned.

A billion years deep and again darkness fell, like a hammer blow.

"More ice?" Bobby asked.

"I think I understand," David said grimly. "It was a pulse of evolution—an early event, something we haven't recognized from the fossils—an attempt by life to grow past the single-celled stage. But it's doomed to be wiped out by the snowball glaciation, and two hundred million years of progress will be lost. . . . Damn, damn."

When the ice cleared, a further hundred million years deep, again there were hints of more complex, multicelled life forms grazing among the algae mats: another false start, to be eliminated by the savage glaciation, and again the brothers were forced to watch as life was crushed back to its most primitive forms.

As they fell through the long, featureless aeons, five more times the dead hand of global glaciation fell on the planet, killing the oceans, squeezing out of existence all but the most primitive life-forms in the most marginal environments. It was a savage feedback cycle initiated every time life gained a significant foothold in the shallow waters at the fringe of the continents.

David said, "It is the tragedy of Sisyphus. In the myth, Sisyphus had to roll the rock to the top of the mountain, only to watch it roll back again and again. Thus, life struggles to achieve complexity and significance, and is again and again crushed down to its most primitive level. It is a series of icy Wormwoods, over and over. Maybe those nihilist philosophers are right; maybe *this* is all we can expect of the universe, a relentless crushing of life and spirit, because the equilibrium state of the cosmos is death. . . ."

Bobby said grimly, "Tsiolkovski once called Earth the cradle of mankind. And so it is, in fact the cradle of life. But—"

"But," said David, "it's one hell of a cradle which crushes its occupants. At least *this* couldn't happen now. Not quite this way, anyhow. Life has developed complex feedback cycles, controlling the flow of mass and energy through Earth's systems. We always thought the living Earth was a thing of beauty. It isn't. Life has had to learn to defend itself against the planet's random geological savagery."

At last they reached a time deeper than any of the hammer-blow glaciations.

This young Earth had little in common with the world it would become. The air was visibly thick—unbreathable, crushing. There were no hills or shores, cliffs or forests. Much of the planet appeared to be covered by a shallow ocean, unbroken by continents. The seabed was a thin crust, cracked and broken by rivers of lava that scalded the seas. Frequently, thick gases clouded the planet for years at a time—until volcanoes thrust above the surface and sucked the gases back into the interior.

When it could be seen through the thick rolling smog, the sun was a fierce, blazing ball. The Moon was huge, the size of a dinner plate, though many of its familiar features were already etched into place.

But both Moon and sun seemed to race across the sky. This young Earth spun rapidly on its axis, frequently plunging its surface and its fragile cargo of life into night, and towering tides swept around the bruised planet.

The ancestors, in this hostile place, were unambitious: generation after generation of unremarkable cells living in huge communities close to the surface of shallow seas. Each community began as a spongelike mass of matter, which would shrivel back layer on layer until a single patch of green remained, floating on the surface, drifting across the ocean to merge with some older community.

The sky was busy, alive with the flashes of giant meteors returning to deep space. Frequently—terribly frequently—walls of water, kilometers high, would race around the globe and converge on a burning impact scar, from which a great shining body, an asteroid or comet, would leap into space, briefly illuminating the bruised sky before dwindling into the dark.

And the savagery and frequency of these backward impacts seemed to increase.

Now, abruptly, the green life of the algal mats began to migrate across the surface of the young, turbulent oceans, dragging the ancestor chain—and Bobby's viewpoint—with it. The algal colonies merged, shrank again, merged, as if shriveling back toward a common core.

At last they found themselves in an isolated pond, cupped in the basin of a wide, deep impact crater, as if on a flooded Moon: Bobby saw jagged rim mountains, a stubby central peak. The pond was a livid, virulent green, and, somewhere within, the ancestor chains continued their blind toil back toward inanimacy.

But now, suddenly, the green stain shriveled, reducing to isolated specks, and the surface of the crater lake was covered by a new kind of scum, a thick brownish mat.

". . . Oh," David breathed, as if shocked. "We just lost chlorophyll. The ability to manufacture energy from sunlight. Do you see what's happened? This community of organisms was isolated from the rest by some impact or geological accident—the event that formed this crater, perhaps. It ran out of food here. The organisms were forced to mutate or die."

"And mutate they did," Bobby said. "If not—"

"If not, then not *us*."

Now there was a burst of violence, a blur of motion, overwhelming and unresolved—perhaps this was the violent, isolating event David had hypothesized.

When it was over, Bobby found himself beneath the sea once more, gazing at a mat of thick brown scum that clung to a smoking vent, dimly lit by Earth's own internal glow.

"Then it has come to this," said David. "Our deepest ancestors were rock-eaters: thermophiles, or perhaps even hyperthermophiles. That is, they relished high temperature. They consumed the minerals injected into the water by the vents: iron, sulphur, hydrogen . . . Crude, inefficient, but robust. They did not require light or oxygen, or even organic material."

Now Bobby sank into darkness. He passed through tunnels and cracks, diminished, squeezed, in utter darkness broken only by occasional dull red flashes.

"David? Are you still there?"

"I'm here."

"What's happening to us?"

"We're passing beneath the seabed. We're migrating through the porous basalt rock there. All the life on the planet is coalescing, Bobby, shrinking back along the ocean ridges and seafloor basalt beds, merging to a single point."

"Where? *Where* are we migrating to?"

"To the deep rock, Bobby. A point a kilometer down. It will be the last retreat of life. All life on Earth has come from this cache, deep in the rock, this shelter."

"And what," Bobby asked with foreboding, "did life have to shelter *from*?"

"We are about to find out, I fear."

David lifted them up, and they hovered in the foul air of this lifeless Earth.

There was light here, but it was dim and orange, like twilight in a smoggy city. The sun must be above the horizon, but Bobby could not locate it precisely, or the giant Moon. The atmosphere was palpably thick and crushing. The ocean churned below, black, in some places boiling, and the fractured seabed was laced with fire.

The graveyard is truly empty now, Bobby thought. Save for that one small deep-buried cache—containing my most remote ancestors—these young rocks have given up all their layered dead.

And now a blanket of black cloud gathered, as if hurled across the sky by some impetuous god. An inverted rain began, rods of water that leapt from the dappled ocean surface to the swelling clouds.

A century wore by, and still the rain roared upward out of the ocean, its ferocity undiminished—indeed, so voluminous was the rain that soon ocean levels were dropping perceptibly. The clouds thickened further and the oceans dwindled, forming isolated brine pools in the lowest hollows of Earth's battered, cracked surface.

It took two thousand years. The rain did not stop until the oceans had returned to the clouds, and the land was dry.

And the land began to fragment further.

Soon bright glowing cracks in the exposed land were widening, brightening, lava pulsing and flowing. At last there were only isolated islands left, shards of rock which shriveled and melted, and a new ocean blanketed the Earth: an ocean of molten rock, hundreds of meters deep.

Now a new reversed rain began: a hideous storm of bright molten rock, leaping up from the land. The rock droplets joined the water clouds, so that the atmosphere became a hellish layer of glowing rock droplets and steam.

"Incredible," David shouted. "The Earth is collecting an atmosphere of rock vapor, forty or fifty kilometers thick, exerting hundreds of times the pressure of our air. The heat energy contained in it is stupendous. . . . The planet's cloud tops must be glowing. Earth is shining, a star of rock vapor."

But the rock rain was drawing heat away from the battered land and—rapidly, within a few months—the land had cooled to solidity. Beneath a glowing sky, liquid water was beginning to form again, new oceans coalescing out of the cooling clouds. But the oceans were formed boiling, their surfaces in contact with rock vapor. And between the oceans, mountains formed, unmelting from puddles of slag.

And now a wall of light swept past Bobby, dragging after it a front of boiling clouds and steam in a burst of unimaginable violence. Bobby screamed—

David slowed their descent into time.

Earth was restored once again.

The blue-black oceans were calm. The sky, empty of cloud, was a greenish dome. The battered Moon was disturbingly huge, the Man's face familiar to Bobby— save for a missing right eye . . . And there was a second sun, a glowing ball that outshone the Moon, with a tail that stretched across the sky.

"*A green sky,*" murmured David. "Strange. Methane, perhaps? But how . . ."

"What," Bobby said, "the hell is *that*?"

"Oh, the comet? A real monster. The size of modern-day asteroids like Vesta or Pallas, perhaps five hundred kilometers across. A hundred thousand times the mass of the dinosaur killer."

"The size of the Wormwood."

"Yes. Remember that the Earth itself was formed from impacts, coalescing from a hail of planetesimals that orbited the young sun. The greatest impact of all was probably the collision with another young world that nearly cracked us open."

"The impact that formed the Moon."

"After that the surface became relatively stable—but still, the Earth was subject to immense impacts, tens or hundreds of them within a few hundred million years, a bombardment whose violence we can't begin to imagine. The impact rate tailed off as the remnant planetesimals were soaked up by the planets, and there was a halcyon period of relative quiescence, lasting a few hundred million years . . . and then, *this*. Earth was unlucky to meet such a giant so late in the bombardment. An impact hot enough to boil the oceans, even melt the mountains."

"But we survived," Bobby said grimly.

"Yes. In our deep, hot niche."

They fell down into the Earth once more, and Bobby was immersed in rock with his most distant ancestors, a scraping of thermophilic microbes.

He waited in darkness, as countless generations peeled back.

Then, in a blur, he saw light once more.

He was rising up some kind of shaft—like a well—toward a circle of green light, the sky of this alien, pre-bombardment Earth. The circle expanded until he was lifted into the light.

He had some trouble interpreting what he saw next.

He seemed to be inside a box of some glassy material. The ancestor must be here with him, one crude cell among millions subsisting in this container. The box was

set on some form of stand, and from here, he could look
out over—

"Oh, dear God," said David.

It was a city.

Bobby glimpsed an archipelago of small volcanic islands, rising from the blue sea. But the islands had been
linked by wide, flat bridges. On the land, low walls
marked out geometrical forms—they looked like fields—
but this was not a human landscape; the shapes of these
fields seemed to be variants of hexagons. There were
even buildings, low and rectangular, like airplane han-
gars. He glimpsed movement between the buildings,
some kind of traffic, too distant to resolve.

And now something was moving toward him.

It looked like a trilobite, perhaps. A low segmented
body that glittered under the green sky. Sets of legs—
six or eight?—that flickered with movement. Something
like a head at the front.

A head with a mouth that held a tool of gleaming
metal.

The head was raised toward him. He tried to make
out the eyes of this impossible creature. He felt as if he
could reach out and touch that chitinous face, and—

—and the world imploded into darkness.

They were two old men who had spent too long in virtual reality, and the Search Engine had thrown them out.
Bobby, lying there stunned, thought it was probably a
blessing.

He stood, stretched, rubbed his eyes.

He blundered through the Wormworks, its solidity and
grime seeming unreal after the four-billion-year spectacle he had endured. He found a coffee drone, ordered
two cups, gulped down a hot mouthful. Then, feeling
somewhat restored to humanity, he returned to his
brother. He held out the coffee until David—mouth
open, eyes glazed—sat up to take it.

"The Sisyphans," David murmured, his voice dry.

"What?"

"That's what we must call them. They evolved on early Earth, in the interval of stability between the early and late bombardments. They were *different* from us. . . . That methane sky. What could *that* have meant? Perhaps even their biochemistry was novel, based on sulphur compounds, or with ammonia as a solvent, or . . ." He grabbed Bobby's arm. "And of course you understand that they need have had little in common with the creatures they selected for the cache. The cache of our ancestors. No more than we have with the exotic flora and fauna which still cling to the deep-sea vents in our world. But *they*—the thermophiles, our ancestors—were the best hope for survival. . . ."

"David, slow down. What are you talking about?"

David looked at him, baffled. "Don't you understand yet? *They were intelligent.* The Sisyphans. But they were doomed. They saw it coming, you see."

"The great comet."

"Yes. Just as we can see our own Wormwood. And they knew what it would do to their world: boil the oceans, even melt the rock for hundreds of meters down. You saw them. Their technology was primitive. They were a young species. They had no way to escape the planet, or outlive the impact themselves, or deflect the impactor. They were doomed, without recourse. And yet they did not succumb to despair."

"They buried the cache—deep enough so the heat pulse couldn't reach it."

"Yes. You see? They labored to preserve life—*us*, Bobby—even in the midst of the greatest catastrophe the planet has suffered.

"And that is our destiny, Bobby. Just as the Sisyphans preserved their handful of thermophilic microbes to outlive the impact—just as those algal mats and seaweed struggled to outlast the savage glaciation episodes, just as complex life, evolving and adapting, survived the later catastrophes of volcanism and impact and geological accident—*so must we*. Even the Joined, the new evolution of mind, are part of a single thread which reaches back to the dawn of life itself."

Bobby smiled. "Remember what Hiram used to say? 'There's no limit to what we can achieve, if we work together.' "

"Yes. That's it exactly. Hiram was no fool."

Fondly, Bobby touched his brother's shoulder. "I think—"

—and, once again, without warning, the world imploded into darkness.

Epilogue

" $\mathbf{B}$obby. Please wake up. Bobby. Can you hear
... me? ..."

The voice came to him, as if from afar. A woman's
voice. He heard the voice, understood the words, even
before a sense of his body returned.

His eyes were closed.

He was lying flat on his back on what felt like a deep,
soft bed. He could feel his limbs, the slow pulse of his
heart, the swell of his breath. Everything seemed normal.

And yet he knew it was not: something was wrong,
as subtly askew as the violet sky of the Cretaceous.

He felt unaccountably afraid.

He opened his eyes.

A woman's face hovered before him: fine-boned,
blue-eyed, blond hair, some lines at the eyes. She might
have been forty, even fifty. Yet he recognized her.

". . . *Mary?*"

Was it his voice?

He raised his hand. A bony wrist protruded from a
sleeve of some silvery fabric. The hand was fine-boned,
the fingers narrow and long, like a pianist's.

Was it his hand?

Mary—if it was Mary—leaned forward and cupped
his face. "You're awake. Thank Hiram for that. Can you
understand me?"

"Yes. Yes, I—"

"What do you remember?"

"David. The Wormworks. We were—"

"Traveling. Yes. Good; you remember. On his Anastasis David told us what you had seen."

Anastasis, he thought. Resurrection. His fear deepened.

He tried to sit up. She helped him. He felt weak, light.

He was in a smooth-walled chamber. It was dark. A doorway led to a corridor, flooded with light. There was a single small window, circular. It revealed a slab of blue and black.

Blue Earth. Black sky.

The air of Earth was clear as glass. There was a silver tracery over the blue oceans, some kind of structure, hundreds of kilometers above the surface. Was he in orbit? No; the Earth was not turning. He was in some kind of orbital tower, then.

My God, he thought.

"Am I dead? Have I been resurrected, Mary?"

She growled, and ran her hand through loose hair. "David said you'd be like this. Questions, questions." Her intonation was clumsy, her voice dry, as if she wasn't used to speaking aloud.

"Why have I been brought back? . . . Oh. The Wormwood. Is that it?"

Mary frowned, and briefly seemed to be listening to remote voices. "The Wormwood? You mean the comet. We pushed *that* away long ago." She said it casually, as if a moth had been brushed aside.

Bemused, he asked, "Then what?"

"I can tell you *how* you got here," she said gently. "As to *why*, you'll have to figure that out for yourself. . . ."

Sixty more years had worn away, he learned.

It was the WormCam, of course. It was possible now to look back into time and read off a complete DNA sequence from any moment in an individual's life. And it was possible to download a copy of that person's mind—making her briefly Joined, across years, even decades—and, by putting the two together, regenerated body and downloaded mind, to restore her.

To bring her back from the dead.

"You were dying," said Mary. "At the instant we copied you. Though you didn't know it yet."

"My cloning."

"Yes. The procedure was still experimental in Hiram's time. There were problems with your telomeres." Genetic structures that controlled the aging of cells. "Your decline was rapid after—"

"After my last memory, in the Wormworks."

"Yes."

How strange to think that even as he handed that last cup of coffee to David his life had already been effectively over, the remnant, evidently, not worth living.

She took his hand. When he stood, he felt light, dreamlike, spindly. For the first time he noticed she was naked, but wearing a pattern of implants in the flesh of her arms and belly. Her breasts seemed to move oddly: languidly, as if the gravity wasn't quite right here.

She said, "There is so much you must learn. We have room now. The Earth's population is stable. We live on Mars, the moons of the outer planets, and we're heading for the stars. There have even been experiments in downloading human minds into the quantum foam."

". . . Room for what?"

"For the Anastasis. We intend to restore *all* human souls, back to the beginning of the species. Every refugee, every aborted child. We intend to put right the past, to defeat the awful tragedy of death in a universe that may last tens of billions of years."

How wonderful, he thought. A hundred billion souls, restored like the leaves of an autumnal tree. What will it be *like*?

"But," he said slowly, "are they the same people? Am I *me*?"

"Some philosophers argue that it's possible. Leibniz's

Identity of the Indiscernibles tells us that you are *you*. But—"

"But you don't think so."

"No. I'm sorry."

He thought that over.

"When we're all revived, what will we do next?"

She seemed puzzled by the question. "Why—anything we want, of course." She took his hand. "Come. Kate is waiting for you."

Hand in hand they walked into the light.

AFTERWORD

The concept of a "time viewer," though venerable, has been explored only sparingly in science fiction—perhaps because it is so much less dramatic than time travel. But there have been a number of remarkable works on the theme, ranging from Gardner Hunting's *The Vicarion* (1926) to Orson Scott Card's *Pastwatch: The Redemption of Christopher Columbus* (1996). One of us has briefly sketched its implications in previous works (*Childhood's End*, 1953, "The Parasite," 1953). Perhaps the best-known—and best—example is Bob Shaw's "slow glass" classic which shares our title (*Analog*, August 1966).

Today the notion has the first glimmers of scientific plausibility, offered by modern physics—and a resonance with our own times, surrounded as we are increasingly by the apparatus of surveillance.

The concept of spacetime wormholes is well described in Kip Thorne's *Black Holes and Time Warps: Einstein's Outrageous Legacy* (W. W. Norton, 1994). The proposal that wormholes might be generated by "squeezing the vacuum" was set out by David Hochberg and Thomas Kephart (*Physics Letters B*, vol. 268, pp. 377-383, 1991).

The very speculative and, we hope, respectful reconstruction of the historical life of Jesus Christ is largely drawn from A. N. Wilson's fine biography *Jesus* (Sinclair-Stevenson, 1992). For assistance with the passages on Abraham Lincoln the authors are indebted to Warren Allen

Smith, New York correspondent of *Gay and Lesbian Humanist* (UK).

The idea that primitive Earth was afflicted by savage glacial episodes has been proposed by Paul Hoffman of Harvard University and his coworkers (see *Science,* vol. 281, p. 1342, 28 August 1998). And the notion that primitive life might have survived Earth's early bombardment by sheltering deep underground is explored, for example, in Paul Davies' *The Fifth Miracle* (Penguin, 1998).

Thanks are due to Andy Sawyer of the Science Fiction Foundation Collection, Sydney Jones Library, Liverpool University, for his assistance with research, and to Edward James of Reading University and to Eric Brown for reading drafts of the manuscript. Any errors or omissions are, of course, our responsibility.

This book, of its nature, contains a great deal of speculation on historical figures and events. Some of this is reasonably well founded on current historical sources, some of it is at the remoter fringe of respectable theorizing, and some of it is little more than the authors' own wild imaginings. We leave it as an exercise to the reader to sort out which is which, in the anticipation that we are not likely to be proven wrong until the invention of the WormCam itself.